Escape to...

a glamorous world of sun-drenched passion, rising temperatures and romantic destinations...

Revel in those long, lazy summer days...

*Feel the rhythm of the tropics, see the sway of the palm trees...
Indulge yourself with
Escape to Caribbean Kisses,
two exotic, exciting bestselling
romances in one volume*

Available in the

Escape to

Collection...

19th May 2006

16th June 2006

21st July 2006

18th August 2006

Escape to...
CARIBBEAN KISSES

Containing

Groom by Arrangement
by Susanne McCarthy
&
The Children's Doctor
by Joanna Neil

M&B™ and M&B™ with the Rose Device
are trademarks of the publisher.
Harlequin Mills & Boon Limited, Eton House,
18-24 Paradise Road,
Richmond, Surrey TW9 1SR

ESCAPE TO CARIBBEAN KISSES
© by Harlequin Books S.A. 2006

The Children's Doctor and Groom by Arrangement were
first published in Great Britain by Harlequin Mills & Boon
Limited in separate, single volumes.

Groom by Arrangement © Susanne McCarthy 1999
The Children's Doctor © Joanna Neil 2001

ISBN 10: 0 263 85075 7
ISBN 13: 978 0 263 85075 8

108-0606

Printed and bound in Spain
by Litografia Rosés S.A., Barcelona

GROOM BY ARRANGEMENT

by

Susanne McCarthy

Susanne McCarthy grew up in South London, but she always wanted to live in the country, and shortly after her marriage she moved to Shropshire with her husband. They live in a house on a hill with lots of dogs and cats. She loves to travel – but she loves to come home. As well as her writing, she still enjoys her career as a teacher in adult education, though she only works part-time now.

CHAPTER ONE

'SEVEN. Bank pays nineteen.' Natasha's voice was soft and cool as she turned over the card. Deftly she paid out the winning bets, raked in the remaining chips and sorted them into the rack without even having to look at what she was doing.

Lord Neville had won a modest amount, and grinned as he put down his stake for the next hand. 'See—I told you this was my lucky table!'

Natasha glanced towards the man sitting next to him, an unspoken question in her fine blue eyes enquiring if he wished to continue play—he had been losing fairly consistently for the past hour, and now had only a handful of chips left. He shook his head, returning her a wry smile.

'No, thank you—you've just about cleaned me out.' He rose easily to his feet, pocketing his last few remaining chips. 'I think I'll adjourn to the bar and drown my sorrows.'

She conceded merely a nod, but from beneath her lashes she slanted him a searching glance. This was the second successive night he had visited the Spaniard's Cove Casino, and he had lost heavily both times. He didn't seem particularly bothered about it, accepting the setbacks with the casual unconcern of a seasoned—and habitually unlucky—gambler.

There was really no reason why she should be surprised at that, of course. The life-blood of the casino business was moderately wealthy young men like this, men whose drug of choice was money—whether they were winning it or losing it. Some of them were crazy boys, with large trust funds and a low boredom threshold, others were businessmen whose own money was made in ways that perhaps wouldn't stand too close a scrutiny.

And yet… Somehow this one didn't look like a loser. There was a casual arrogance in the set of those wide shoulders, a firmness in the line of his jaw in spite of the lazy smile, that hinted that behind the air of laid-back amiability he was not quite what he seemed.

Her assessing survey told her that his white dinner-jacket might well have come from the same expensive tailor as his friend Lord Neville's. But those impressive shoulders owed nothing to padding, and the immaculate cut did little to disguise a lithe, muscular physique that hinted at considerable reserves of strength. And his hands weren't pampered and soft like the English aristocrat's, either.

His hair was mid-brown, cut brush-short and pushed casually to one side, tipped with golden flecks which suggested that he was more at home out of doors than in these smoke-filled rooms—an impression heightened by the all-weather tan that certainly hadn't come from a sun-bed. And his eyes…they were the real giveaway. They were a dark, smoky grey, but something dangerous lurked in their secret depths. Predator's eyes—shark's eyes.

And they were regarding her now with a glint of sardonic amusement. 'Perhaps by way of consolation you'll have a dance with me later?' he suggested, an inflection of lazy self-mockery in his voice.

Natasha shook her head. 'I'm sorry—I don't dance,' she returned, distantly polite.

One dark eyebrow arched in mild surprise. 'Never?'

'Never.' She hadn't intended that slightly sharp note. But he unsettled her, and she didn't like that.

'That's right, old chap.' Lord Neville slapped his friend cheerfully on the shoulder. 'Should have warned you. Don't dance, and don't accept drinks off the punters—famous for it.'

'Is that so? What a pity.' That slow, lazy smile was deliberately provocative, and Natasha bristled at the casual insolence with which he let his gaze drift down over her slender shape, subtly defined by the silver-grey silk jersey of her elegant evening dress. 'But I shan't give up hope of persuading you. I can be very persuasive when I put my mind to it.'

Natasha's blue eyes flashed him a frost warning, but that aggravating smile lingered as he turned and strolled away across the room. Resolutely she turned her attention back to the blackjack table, refusing to let her gaze be drawn to follow that tall, well-made figure as he paused to watch the spin of a roulette wheel, slipping easily into a flirtation with a slinky brunette in a scarlet dress that was cut low enough to start a riot.

Her table was popular, and someone else had already slipped into his place as she flashed her professional smile and deftly shuffled the cards.

Her table was always popular, no matter what game she was dealing—and she was perfectly well aware that it wasn't just her skill with a pack of cards that was the attraction. Gentlemen preferred blondes—wasn't that what they said? And she was the classic blue-eyed blonde; one moonstruck young admirer had poetically likened the colour of her hair to a new-minted silver dollar.

But looks could be deceptive, and anyone who thought Natasha Cole was simply a pretty doll to decorate the tables and comfort a losing gambler when his wallet was empty soon learned their mistake. That cool smile, and those ice-blue eyes, could freeze a man at twenty paces.

As she dealt with the next hand, she cast a swift glance around the gaming room. It was busy tonight, all the roulette tables open, thousands of pounds worth of chips being traded for a few minutes of tense excitement. Another profitable night for Spaniard's Cove, she reflected with a twist of ironic humour. Surely she ought to be pleased? After all, she owned the place.

Spaniard's Cove had been a sugar plantation once, in her family for generations. But when the bottom had dropped out of the sugar-cane market her grandparents hadn't been able to sell the land even at giveaway prices. Struggling for survival, they had hit on the idea of starting up a small casino in the empty shell of the old sugar warehouse.

It had proved an amazing success, quickly building a reputation among the wealthy yachting set as a friendly little place, nothing like the glittering money-palaces of Monte Carlo and Las Vegas. And her grandmother had been its queen—a real *grande dame*, who'd smoked too much and laughed like a horse.

A familiar little twinge of pain tugged at her heart-strings as she remembered her grandmother. Though it was nearly eight years now since she had succumbed to the heart condition which the doctor had frequently warned her would kill her if she refused to give up those dreadful cigarettes, sometimes she still found it hard to believe that the doughty old lady was no longer around.

It had been her grandmother who had more or less brought her up. She barely remembered either her father or her grandfather—she had been little more than a baby when they had been killed in a boating accident. And her mother had been a wistful, pale creature, always preferring to stay in the background. It had been her grandmother who had encouraged her to go to university. She would have been so proud of the degree in Business Studies that she had achieved last year. She had come home with so many plans. None of which had involved dealing blackjack.

Lester. The problem she had inherited along with Spaniard's Cove. Her eyes penetrated across the smoky room to where her stepfather was holding court around the craps table with half a dozen of his high-rolling cronies.

Her grandmother had never really liked him, but as her health had started to fail she had been forced to hire a manager for the casino. Oh, Natasha couldn't deny that he was good at his job—under his control, the profits had increased year on year. It was his methods she didn't like, and what he had done to the place.

But, for the time being at least, she could do nothing about it. Three months after the old lady had died, he had married Natasha's mother. It had been quite a surprise—everyone had always believed that Belinda Cole's heart lay deep beneath the blue waters of the Mexican Gulf, where her first husband had drowned.

Somehow Lester had managed to convince her that his was the strong shoulder she'd needed to lean on. Had she ever loved him? Natasha had always doubted it. But in the end it hadn't really mattered—never robust, within a year of her second marriage she had fallen victim to a serious viral infection and died. And in her will she had passed on to Lester her responsibility as one of the trustees of the estate Natasha would inherit from her grandmother on her twenty-fifth birthday.

Time had been kind to Lester Jackson. Though he was in his middle fifties, only a slight thickening of his waistline marred his elegant figure, and he still had most of his hair, now a distinguished shade of silver. And many women found the crinkles around his eyes extremely attractive.

Oh, yes, he was still a good-looking man, affable and charming—everybody liked him. Everybody, it seemed, except Natasha.

Was she the only one who saw the lies, the unnecessary exaggerations, the empty boasts? Who knew how often the famous names he dropped so liberally into any conversation were of people he had never even met, how often the sharp business deals he claimed to have pulled off had never in fact taken place?

Every time she'd tried to discuss her plans for Spaniard's Cove, he had cut her off point-blank. 'Close down the casino? Don't talk rubbish,' had been his blunt response.

And her other trustee, Uncle Timothy, although sympathetic, hadn't been a lot of help. 'Well, strictly speaking, his duty is to ensure that the trust is secure, and achieving the best possible return,' he had explained in his dry, pedantic way. 'I'm afraid any changes—though I do think your ideas have excellent potential—could only be regarded as speculative at this point in time.'

So she had no choice but to wait until she was twenty-five. The only other way to have the trust wound up would be if she got married. But since she didn't have a boyfriend—or even much chance of meeting someone suitable, given her present circumstances—that really wasn't an option.

It had been her intention to go back to the States for a couple of years, or even to Europe—maybe get a job somewhere in the tourist industry, to gain some valuable experience for when she was able to have a free hand. But something had warned her to stay here, where she could keep an eye on her own interests.

Not that she had uncovered any evidence that Lester was cheating her—and she was quite sure that if she had missed anything Uncle Timothy would have noted it. He might be reluctant to argue with Lester over letting her develop Spaniard's Cove the way she wanted to, but he was most conscientious about checking the accounts. It was just…some vague instinct that warned her that something wasn't quite right.

So she kept her suspicions hidden—but those cool blue eyes were watchful. Two years. It wasn't that long to wait…

It was an exciting prospect. Since the airport had opened, on the northern tip of the island, the tourists had been pouring in. And Spaniard's Cove, with its smooth turquoise lagoon and white sandy beaches, sheltered within its spectacular surrounding hills, was a perfect spot for a luxury resort. There would be water-sports, of course—windsurfing, scuba-diving—and a golf-course, horse-riding, tennis. And the old sugar warehouse would be converted into an up-market health spa, complete with gymnasium, hydro-pool, aromatherapy…

And there would be no more smoke-filled rooms curtained from the outside world—and no more hot-eyed, sweaty-palmed gamblers.

Drifting back across the room, her gaze was drawn again to the tall figure of Lord Neville's enigmatic friend. He was watching at one of the roulette tables as that slinky brunette tossed her chips and fluttered her outrageous lashes at him. Trust Darlene, Natasha mused with a touch of wry humour—her antennae always managed to lock onto the most attractive man in the place, no matter how crowded it was.

Attractive? Yes, she would give him that, she conceded with a certain dry detachment. She would put him in his early thirties, perhaps—which made it odd that she had never seen him before, if he was a regular gambler. Perhaps he had recently inherited a fortune, and was intent on losing it as quickly as possible? He would have little trouble doing that if he was a friend of Lord Neville, she reflected wryly—his crowd elevated pointless bravura to an artform.

Not that she cared in the least, she reminded herself with a small shrug of her slim shoulders. He was just another fool—even if he did look as if he possessed a little more intelligence than he had so far displayed at the tables. And if he was anxious to fritter away his money on wasteful pursuits, Darlene was certainly the one to help him.

A little before midnight Natasha handed over the black-jack table to one of the other croupiers, and slipped outside for a few minutes' break in the fresh air.

She loved Spaniard's Cove—though she had grown up here, she never ceased to be enchanted by its beauty. Encircled by tall volcanic outcrops, their weird outlines softened by the blue-green rainforest trees that clothed their steep sides, its beach was a perfect crescent of pink-white coral sand, lapped by the warm blue Caribbean sea. And at night the sky was like black velvet, spangled with a million stars so bright that when she was a little girl she had always imagined the angels must spend all day polishing them.

Strolling through the casino's lush tropical gardens, breathing in the soft night breeze with its fragrance of jasmine and frangipani, she reminded herself for about the millionth time that it would be worth the wait, worth putting up with Lester, even for another two years...

A sudden shout, and the sound of running feet, startled

her out of her pleasant reverie. Hurrying towards the source of the commotion, she came to the old stable block behind the casino, now used as a general workshop and garages. Three figures were in the corner, behind Lester's prized Mercedes, their shadows thrown in sharp relief against the wall by the orange glow from a flickering storm lamp.

'Lester—no, stop it!' Debbie, her stepfather's most regular girlfriend, was sobbing and tugging at his arm.

Lester shook her off impatiently, and Debbie stumbled back. Now Natasha could see the third cowering figure— Jamie, the young son of the cook, a lad of about thirteen or fourteen. He had grown up here at Spaniard's Cove, and earned a little extra money by helping the gardener before and after school.

'You stinking little brat!' Lester was shouting, his voice harsh with fury. 'I'll flay the hide from your body, you damned little—'

'Lester!' Natasha's sharp word stilled him in the act of raising his hand—and she saw that in it he held an old horse-whip that he must have snatched down from the wall. The boy seized the opportunity to escape, darting away into the night before Lester could catch him.

He turned on her in fury. 'Damn you! What did you have to stop me for? I was going to giving him the hiding of his life!'

Natasha returned him a look of icy contempt. 'Why?' she queried, her voice deliberately calm in the face of his anger. 'What has he done?'

'Done? He's scratched my car, that's what he's done. Look! Just look at that!' He pointed dramatically to a small scrape along the front wing.

She glanced at it, one finely drawn eyebrow arched in

doubt. 'It looks as if you scraped it against the doorpost driving it in,' she pointed out.

'I did nothing of the sort!' he exploded. 'You think I can't manage to drive my own car into my own garage?'

'Not if you've had a few drinks,' she retorted coolly. 'Like yesterday.'

His face had taken on an alarming tomato hue, and he raised his hand—for one tense moment Natasha thought he was going to strike her with the whip. But she faced him down, refusing to let him intimidate her. And at last he threw the whip to the ground and, muttering a vicious curse, turned on his heel and stalked out of the garage.

She let go her breath in a long sigh, realising that she was more shaken than she had been aware. She had known that Lester had a temper, but not that he could be violent. Stooping, she picked up the whip and hung it back on its hook. Behind her, Debbie was sobbing quietly.

'Oh, Natasha... Thank you for stopping him,' she breathed, dabbing at her eyes with a sodden handkerchief. 'I was so frightened. He could have got into terrible trouble if he'd hurt that poor little boy.'

Natasha laughed dryly. She had always rather liked the older woman, though she could never quite understand what she saw in Lester—she could certainly have done a great deal better for herself. In her middle thirties, she was still extremely pretty, with soft golden hair and a dainty figure, and wide blue eyes which conveyed an air of gentle innocence—though she ran a very successful chain of beauty salons with concessions in all the best hotels on the island.

Suddenly an unpleasant thought struck her. 'He's never hit you, has he, Debbie?' she asked bluntly.

The blonde gazed up at her in open surprise. 'Oh, no,' she assured her, shaking her head. 'He'd never do a thing

like that. He was just...rather upset when he saw the
scratch on his car. He really loves that car, you know.'

Natasha nodded in wry agreement. It seemed a little
absurd to her to have a car with a top speed of over a
hundred and fifty miles an hour when the island was small
enough to walk around in one afternoon and the roads
would challenge the strongest automotive suspension. But
Lester had always had extravagant tastes.

Debbie stroked her slim hand over the leather hood.
'Sometimes I think he loves it more than he loves me,'
she mused sadly. 'I just wish he'd say for definite if we're
going to get married. I'll be forty before I know it.'

Natasha smiled crookedly. 'I really don't know why
you put up with him,' she remarked. 'It's not as if he
treats you the way he should. Why don't you finish with
him, and find yourself the sort of decent man you deserve?'

Debbie shrugged her slim shoulders. 'I love him,' was
her only explanation.

Natasha sighed, watching as the petite blonde quickly
checked her make-up in a tiny mirror, to make sure that
her tears hadn't done too much damage, and then hurried
away after Lester.

Natasha's thoughts were troubled. Two years was still
a long time—two years of living in Lester's shadow,
watching him, trying to make sure that he wasn't somehow cheating her. Two years...

Wryly she shook her head. There really wasn't a solution to her problem. Even if she found someone to
marry she could easily find herself jumping out of the
frying pan into the fire. Maybe working in the casino business had made her cynical, but the kind of marriages she
saw there wouldn't inspire anyone with much confidence
in the institution.

Men with large wallets and larger egos, parading their trophy wives—wives who would be traded in for a younger, fresher model every couple of years. Unless, of course, it was the wife's money they were splashing around the tables, while indulging in a little discreet dalliance with women like Darlene, happy to accept an arrangement of that nature in return for a few baubles.

No, marriage wasn't the answer, she reflected as she snuffed out the storm-lamp and closed the garage doors. But she would have to think of something.

There was no sign of young Jamie—the lad had very wisely made himself scarce. The memory of the scene she had just witnessed made her feel slightly sick. Lester really would have beaten the boy if she hadn't chanced upon the incident in time. What a nasty piece of work he was!

She was no longer in the mood for a pleasant stroll in the gardens, so instead she headed back around the building to the front entrance.

The casino bore little trace of its original function now. A solid construction of pink-tinged coral stone, with tall, narrow windows and a flat roof, it had been built to withstand the fierce hurricanes which occasionally swept in from the Atlantic to devastate the island. A large, square porch had been built over the main entrance, emblazoned with neon writing in pink and green that spelled out the words, 'Spaniard's Cove Casino' on three sides. A wide step led up to the bronzed glass doors—the original heavy strapped-wood ones were permanently pinned back against the walls, only closed when there was a hurricane warning.

As she stepped inside, Natasha was greeted by the doorman, a great bear of a man who never really looked quite comfortable in his elegant dinner jacket and bow tie. He flashed her a beaming smile. 'Evening, Miss Natasha.'

'Good evening, Jem. How are you keeping?'

'I've got no problems,' he responded with a shrug of his huge shoulders, beaming even wider. 'I never have any problems.'

She smiled, glad that someone at least was content with life, and moved on to pause briefly at the reception desk and cast her eye over the guest register.

The main foyer was filled with the noisy clatter of slot machines, all gaudy spinning lights and synthesised chimes. They were an innovation of Lester's—in her grandmother's day there had been just four, the old-fashioned one-arm-bandit type, discreetly ranged down one wall. Natasha hated them—though she couldn't deny that they made a tidy profit.

Beyond the foyer, the main gaming room was a glittering cavern, all polished wood and sparkling chandeliers, reflected into infinity by the gilded mirrors that lined the walls along both sides. A dark green carpet absorbed all the abuse of countless stiletto heels and casually discarded cigarette stubs, and slow fans on the ceiling redistributed the drifts of blue-grey cigarette smoke without having any noticeable impact on the heat.

Had it really been any different in her grandmother's day, she mused, gazing around, or was it just that she had been seeing it then through the eyes of a child? But it had always seemed to her that the place had been much… friendlier, somehow. Oh, there had still been the glamour, the occasional film stars, the high-rollers, but her grandmother had been more interested in seeing people having a good time than in trying to take as much money as possible out of their pockets.

There had only been six roulette tables then, where now there were ten, crammed into the same amount of space, as well as more blackjack and craps. And in those days you'd never see any of those narrow-eyed men from Miami that Lester seemed so friendly with, who never took their jackets off, no matter how hot it got.

To her left was the supper room, where there was often a cabaret or dancing. One of the mirrors cast her a fleeting glimpse of her own reflection as she cut across the corner of the dance floor towards the bar to have a brief word with Ricardo, the bar manager, before he left for his holidays.

With her tall, slender figure and delicately carved features, her fine silver-blonde hair swept up into a neat coil at the back of her head, her elegant dress skimming her curves without too much cling, she knew that she looked every inch the ice Maiden.

That was what they called her, all the handsome young men who were so eager for her attention. She treated them all with the same blend of friendliness and reserve, keeping them safely at arm's length with that cool, professional smile. She had no intention of getting involved with any of them. Her grandmother had warned her long ago that if she was ever going to let any man reach her heart, to make sure that he wasn't a gambler.

She was close to the far side of the dance floor when she suddenly found herself confronted by Lord Neville's enigmatic friend.

'Ah, Miss Cole,' he greeted her, completely blocking her way and smiling down at her with a glint of mocking humour. 'So you've changed your mind about dancing?'

'No, I haven't,' she protested indignantly—but those strong arms were already around her as he drew her smoothly into the middle of the dance floor. 'Please let me go.'

His hold tightened almost imperceptibly, warning her that she wouldn't escape unless she was willing to cause a scene. 'Ah, but it's such a romantic song,' he urged, his foolish pleading markedly at odds with the raw masculine power that was holding her prisoner. 'And I lost so much money at your table, too. Won't you spare me just one dance to cheer me up?'

'Somehow you don't seem particularly downcast,' she rapped back with a touch of asperity.

'I've learned to hide it.'

'Oh, really?' She returned him a glance of glittering suspicion. 'You've had plenty of experience, I suppose?'

'I'm afraid so.' He sighed, over-acting so ludicrously that she was almost forced to laugh. 'You'd think I'd have learned to play a little better by now.'

'If you're a regular card-player, I'm surprised I've never seen you here before,' she remarked, sure now that she was right—he had been losing deliberately. But why?

'I don't know how I can have missed it,' he countered blandly, giving nothing away. 'Have you worked here long?'

'I don't work here,' she responded coolly. She really didn't need this—the incident with Lester had left her already on edge. 'I own Spaniard's Cove.'

'Oh?' One brown eyebrow arched in interested question. 'I thought Lester Jackson owned it?'

She shook her head. 'He's my stepfather, and one of my trustees; he manages it for me until I come of age under the terms of my grandmother's will.'

'I see...' He seemed to be storing the information away in some kind of mental filing cabinet. 'What is this place?' He glanced up at the high ceiling, beamed with dark local mahogany. 'It looks like it was some kind of warehouse.'

'It was,' she confirmed. 'Spaniard's Cove used to be a sugar plantation.'

'Oh? What happened to it?'

'Market forces happened to it,' she explained, with a quirk of wry humour. 'Sugar-beet largely took over from cane, and most of the big plantations went bankrupt. My grandparents tried turning the old plantation house into a hotel, but it was never really very successful—most of the visitors to the island preferred to stay on their own yachts in those days. Then they hit on the idea of converting this place into a casino, to lure in the customers, and...well, that was it.'

He nodded with what seemed like genuine interest. 'What happened to the house?'

'It was blown down by a hurricane before I was born. They never bothered to rebuild it—they used up the wood instead to build the cottages along the beach.'

'And the land?' he enquired. 'I suppose it's all been sold off?'

'No.' She couldn't help wondering why he was asking so many questions. 'Some of it's used to grow bananas, and some of it's rented off as smallholdings, but the rest is just lying fallow at the moment. I have some plans for the future, but they will have to wait until I'm twenty-five.'

He smiled, a smile that seemed to have a very odd effect on her pulse-rate. 'So in the meantime you content yourself with dealing blackjack?'

'Yes.' For some reason it was difficult to keep her voice steady. Being held so close to him, she could breathe the subtle musky scent of his skin, like some kind of drug. 'And sometimes I work one of the roulette tables.'

'Ah, roulette.' He sighed, once again the amiable loser. 'I'm no luckier at that than I am at blackjack, I'm afraid.'

'So why keep playing?' she demanded, stung into irritation by the conviction that he was somehow mocking her.

He shrugged those wide shoulders in a gesture of casual dismissal. 'Oh, just for a little excitement,' he responded. 'Will you be on the roulette tables tonight?'

'No. I shall be dealing blackjack again when I've had my break.'

'And what time do you finish?'

'Not until we close.'

'And then?'

'I shall be checking the takings,' she returned crisply.

Again that questioning arched eyebrow. 'Oh? But I thought Lester managed the casino? Doesn't he take care of all that?'

Natasha slanted him a searching glance from beneath her lashes, a little surprised at the question. Beneath that casual mien, he seemed to be trying to find out an awful lot about the way the casino was run. 'We…take it in turns,' she responded stiffly.

He laughed, seeming to know somehow that she was lying—though how could he know, after being here only two days, that she generally checked the takings herself? 'You mean you don't trust him to count your money?' he queried, those disturbing shark-grey eyes glinting in sardonic amusement.

'Of course I do,' she insisted, injecting her voice with several degrees of frost. 'I trust him totally.' The lie came out easily—there was no way she was going to discuss her private affairs with this disturbing stranger. She twisted her wrist to glance pointedly at her watch. 'Well, I'm afraid my break is nearly over,' she announced coolly. 'If you'll excuse me, Mr…?'

'The name's Hugh.' There was a note of mocking reproof in his voice. 'I've told you twice already.'

'I'm sorry. The casino has a great many customers— I'm afraid I really can't remember every single name.'

She was lying—she *had* remembered his name. Hugh Garratt. Though why it had fixed itself in her mind, she wasn't quite sure.

'I thought it was a croupier's job, to remember names?' he taunted.

'No—to remember the cards,' she corrected him with a hint of lofty disdain.

'And you can do that?'

'Extremely well.'

'Ah!' He grinned, playing the big, amiable fool again. 'No wonder I kept losing.'

She didn't want to laugh, but she couldn't help it. 'So, will you be staying another night?' she asked, struggling to maintain her usual air of untouchability.

He smiled, that dangerous smile that made her heart kick against her ribs again. 'Do you want me to?' he countered, his voice a little huskier, his breath warm against her cheek.

She drew back, her eyes flashing him an instant frost warning. 'I was merely being polite,' she snapped.

That smile lingered, taunting her. 'Maybe I will,' he mused softly. 'I haven't made up my mind yet. It depends.'

'On what?'

'On whether I think it may be worth my while.'

She stiffened, her hackles rising. He appeared to have mistaken her for Darlene. 'If you mean what I think you mean, you might as well leave right now,' she retorted in a voice that would strip paint.

He merely laughed, feigning an innocence that would have fooled no one. 'Now, what could you possibly think I mean?' he taunted.

For one tense moment she felt an uncharacteristic urge to slap that arrogant face. She knew he had been deliberately needling her, but she was almost too angry to care if she made a scene. Instead she swept down and outwards with her elbows, to break his hold on her, and without another word turned him an aloof shoulder and stalked away.

CHAPTER TWO

'Who was that you were dancing with last night?'

'No one,' Natasha responded coolly, reaching for a second croissant. It was rare for Lester to appear at the breakfast table—he didn't usually get up until the afternoon—and it didn't augur a good start to the day. After the scene last night in the garage, she would have preferred to have had as little contact with him as possible.

Lester laughed unpleasantly. 'It wasn't "no one",' he insisted. 'You never dance with the customers—what makes that one so special?'

'He caught me as I was walking back to the bar,' she conceded stiffly. 'I couldn't very well avoid him.'

'It was the guy that's been losing heavily on the blackjack tables.' Lester's pale eyes glinted with greed. 'That's the sort of punter I like. You be nice to him, girl. Schmooze him a little. Play him along. The guy's a sucker—if he thinks he's in with a chance of making it with you he'll stick around until his pockets are empty.'

Natasha returned him a look of cold dislike, spreading her croissant with apricot jam and biting into it delicately. The table was their usual one, set in the sunny bay window of the empty supper room. None of the other tables was laid—the casino wouldn't be open for another couple of hours.

Only the cleaners were in—she could hear one of them singing tunelessly as she worked, the quiet hum of a vacuum cleaner replacing the usual clamour of the slot machines in the foyer. In the gaming room the curtains at

24

the long windows had been drawn back and the windows opened to air the room, letting the bright, unfamiliar sunshine stream in.

'You're suggesting I should let him think I might go to bed with him so that he'll stay and go on losing money at the tables?' she clarified with icy disdain.

'So what's wrong with that?' Lester demanded, sneering. 'You don't have to deliver. Come on—you know how the game works.'

'I might *know* how it works, but that doesn't mean I have to *like* how it works,' she countered. 'Not the way you play it, anyway.'

Her stepfather slammed down his coffee cup, his face as red as a tomato. 'Damned toffee-nosed bitch!' he snarled. 'This place'd be losing money hand over fist if it wasn't for me. And what thanks do I get? You can't even bring yourself to be civil to my friends.'

'If by "friends" you mean that creep you brought over here last month, and if by "civil" you mean not objecting to his hands wandering all over me when I was talking to him, then forget it,' she returned crisply. 'His sort don't warrant civility—in fact he's damned lucky he didn't get my knee in his groin. And you can warn him that if he tries that sort of thing on with me again, that's exactly what he will get.'

Lester leaned forward, prodding a finger at her across the table. 'You'd better watch your tongue, my girl. Nobody speaks to Tony de Santo like that,' he warned menacingly. 'He's got connections.'

Natasha merely laughed. Her stepfather was always boasting of his friends and their 'connections', but she wasn't impressed. 'I'll speak to him how I like,' she retorted. 'The man's a snake—and that's probably being unfair to snakes.' Her appetite gone, she drained her coffee and got up from the table without bothering to finish her breakfast.

The family's private apartment was on the upper floor of the casino, in the old warehouse manager's quarters. Natasha still shared it with Lester—somehow neither of them had got around to moving out. But, since neither of them spent very much time there, even taking their meals downstairs in the supper room, sharing it had never really been a problem.

But now, as she climbed the narrow staircase, she pulled a wry face. Maybe it was time to start talking about one of them living elsewhere.

What she needed was a swim to burn the edge off her tension, she decided briskly. She changed into a swimsuit and pulled her T-shirt and shorts back on over the top, and then, pausing only to pick up some sunscreen and a towel, a broad-brimmed hat and a good book, she slipped down the back stairs, past the kitchens and out into the clear morning sunshine.

The beach would be crowded, but she knew of another one, hidden away, just ten minutes' walk through the trees. It was quite small, so few people ever found it, and she could usually be guaranteed almost total privacy. Swinging her straw bag across her shoulder, she set off along the path which led past the beach cottages and up over a spur of dark volcanic rock, and then down to the tree-sheltered cove, with its deserted patch of white sand lapped by the turquoise-blue Caribbean Sea.

At this time of the morning the water had already been pleasantly warmed by the sun. She swam for a while with a smooth, powerful stroke, diving down beneath the sparkling surface to visit the rock pools and pockets of coral where shoals of tiny bright fish darted about, until she felt the coiled springs inside her begin to unwind and a pleasant ache of tiredness in her muscles.

The tiny beach was still empty as she climbed up out of the water. Scrubbing her hair roughly dry with the towel, she tucked it beneath her sunhat and then spread the towel out beneath a convenient rock, smoothed a generous dollop of suncream into her skin, perched her sunglasses on her nose and sat down with her back against the rock to enjoy the sheer bliss of solitude and a good book.

For about a minute. She had barely read half a page when the peace of the morning was abruptly shattered by a banging and thumping, and she glanced up to see a tall, familiar figure emerging from beneath the trees, a windsurf board clutched clumsily under his arm. Uttering a most unladylike expletive under her breath, she bent her head over her book, shielding her face with the brim of her hat.

Dammit! Any intrusion on her quiet retreat would have been unwelcome—but if it *had* to be invaded, why on earth did it have to be by Hugh Garratt…?

'Hello, there,' he greeted her with amiable good humour. 'What a pleasant surprise.'

'Indeed.' Her tone would have dampened most men's attempts to engage her attention.

'I hope I'm not disturbing you?' he queried politely—though the unmistakable lilt of amusement in his voice confirmed that he actually knew perfectly well that he was disturbing her. In fact, she wouldn't be at all surprised if he had come down here with that deliberate intention.

'Not in the least,' she rapped in answer, not bothering to look up from her book.

'I came down to try out this windsurfing lark,' he confided disarmingly. 'Only I didn't want anyone to see me making a fool of myself until I can get the hang of it.'

She tilted up her head, slanting him a suspicious glance from behind her sunglasses. 'You've never tried it before?'

He shook his head. 'I'm afraid not. I've often promised myself I'd have a go, though, so I thought I might as well take this chance, while I'm here.'

'Well, don't let me stop you.' She returned her attention to her book, doing her best to ignore him as he stripped off his faded T-shirt to reveal a remarkably well-made torso, all smooth, hard muscle beneath lightly bronzed skin, with a smattering of rough dark hair across the width of his chest, arrowing down to...

Swiftly she snatched her eyes back to the jumbled words on the page, angry at her own awareness of him. He was just another punter—and one who couldn't tell the difference between a brush-off and a come-on, apparently. Hadn't she known more than enough of those? Her mouth compressed in irritation, she turned the page of her book—and then realised that she hadn't read any of the previous three paragraphs.

'Excuse me...?'

His shadow fell across her, a few grains of sand sprinkling onto her feet. She drew in a long, slow breath to indicate her annoyance, and then looked up at him. 'Yes?'

'I'm sorry to bother you, but I wondered if I could borrow a little of your suncream?' he queried with a hint of diffidence, as if afraid she would bite his head off. 'I forgot to bring any, and I don't want to get burned.'

She was tempted to remark that he already seemed to have a pretty good tan, but she knew that wasn't necessarily enough protection from the damaging rays of the hot Caribbean sun. 'Of course.' She nodded curtly, dipping her hand into her bag and pulling it out. 'Here.'

'Thank you.'

Even without looking up, she was still aware of him standing so close to her—and to judge from the sounds of the gloops and slurps he was using up half the tube of cream. Then there was another moment of hesitation.

'I don't like to bother you again...' His voice was all innocent apology, his smile one of ingratiating charm. 'But would you mind putting some on my back for me? I can't reach.'

With a sigh of weary exasperation, she laid down her hat and her book, and, rising to her feet, almost snatched the tube from him. 'Turn around, then,' she ordered grudgingly, squeezing out a pool of cream into the palm of her hand.

She began at the nape of his neck, working out along his wide shoulders, smoothing the cream briskly into his warm skin. Beneath her hand, those well-defined muscles were firm and resilient over the steel hardness of bone. She had been right about how fit he was, she mused absently—this was all prime male, not a trace of softness in him.

Slicking the cream across his back, she continued to rub it in, circling slowly, over and over, all her attention focused on her task as she worked her way over the smooth ridges of muscle and down the long cleft of his spine. Last night, even with the three-inch heels of her evening sandals, she had been aware of how tall he was, but now, barefoot in the sand, his six-foot plus seemed to tower over her.

Her mouth felt suddenly dry, and the sun seemed to have grown hotter, making her feel a little light-headed. And some kind of strange magnetic force was drawing her closer, closer, until she could have slid her arms around his waist, leaned herself against him, felt the raw power in that hard male body next to hers...

Abruptly she drew back, startled. She had been within an inch of actually doing it, of making a complete fool of herself.

'There you are.' Her voice was stiff from the effort of suppressing the slight tremor in her throat. 'That's enough.'

'Thank you.' He turned, smiling slowly—and she was quite sure that he knew exactly what effect he was having on her. At least she still had her sunglasses on—he couldn't see her eyes. But he must be aware of how ragged her breathing was, the way her hand was trembling as she tried to put the lid back on the cream. He was much too close—and that wide chest, hard-muscled and hair-roughened, was much too male. She just had to touch...

'There's a bit there you haven't rubbed in properly,' she excused herself awkwardly, putting up her fingertips to a melting streak of white just above his heart, where that fascinating smattering of rough hair curled over the sculpted curve of a well-defined pectoral muscle.

'Thank you.' His voice had taken on a huskier timbre, and with an odd little frisson of excitement she realised that he too was aware of that strange sizzle of electricity between them...

But he had deliberately engineered this, the warming voice inside her brain reminded her sharply—it hadn't happened by chance. He was sly, devious, manipulative—in short, a man. She drew back, retreating behind her usual façade of icy disdain. 'There. You shouldn't get sunburned now, so long as you don't stay out too long.'

He laughed that lazily mocking laugh. 'I'm very obliged to you. You can go back to your book now.'

'Thank you!' she retorted snappily, sitting down again and slapping her hat on her head, snatching up her book and focusing all her attention on the page.

But she could no more forget his presence than fly to the moon. A few minutes later, she glanced up to see him floundering around on the sailboard, lurching from one side to the other. She watched with growing impatience, until finally she sighed, and shook her head. 'Don't over-compensate,' she called to him. 'You're gripping the bar too tight.'

He glanced over his shoulder, wobbled, but by some miracle didn't fall in.

'Stand up straight. Hold your head up,' she instructed. 'You don't need to watch your feet.'

He wobbled again, righted it, and wobbled the other way. 'The darned thing just seems to go all over the place!' he protested wryly.

'Don't think about it too hard. Bend your knees a little, and let the board ride.' She put the book down and walked to the water's edge. 'Don't watch the front of the board— keep your eyes on where you're going.'

He sped along nicely for a moment, but then seemed to hit a lump in the water and lost it again. 'Damn—I just can't get the hang of it,' he complained. 'I seem to have rotten balance.'

Her eyes narrowed suspiciously—he didn't look the sort who would be poor at sports. He turned clumsily, letting the board run in towards the shore.

'It might be better if you showed me,' he suggested hopefully.

The look she slanted him warned him that she was pretty sure he was playing games, but she received only the most innocent smile in response. With nothing else to say, she took the board from him. 'The first thing is to balance the board and up-haul the sail,' she explained. 'Don't bother about sinking—snap it up and sheet it in as quickly as you can.'

She felt the familiar tug as the wind caught in the sail, felt the bounce of the waves beneath her feet, and instinctively turned the rig to gybe around and skim out across the water. 'See? You keep your shoulders forward, lift onto your toes…'

'What…?' he called from the shore. 'I can't hear you.'

'Lift onto your toes…' Impatiently she realised that it was no good—the wind was carrying her words away. Reluctantly she swung the board around again, and headed back to the beach. 'Get up behind me, and I'll show you.'

He accepted the invitation with an alacrity which confirmed her suspicion that he had planned for just such an outcome, stepping up behind her and reaching around to grasp the bar, listening attentively as she instructed him how to hold it. With two of them on it the board was a little less stable, but as soon as the breeze caught the sail it began to scud out across the water, as graceful as a bird.

Natasha had always thought that this swimsuit was perfectly respectable—soft shades of blue and green, with a satiny sheen, and not cut particularly low. But now, with Hugh Garratt's bare chest against her bare back, his bare thighs brushing against hers, she was rather too conscious that all he had to do was glance down over her shoulder and he would have an unhindered view into the soft shadow between her breasts. And she was heatedly aware of their ripe swell, and the way the tender peaks had puckered into taut buds, their contours clearly visible beneath the damp, clinging Lycra.

As she stiffened in tension, the board snatched and started to topple. Instantly Hugh righted it, the small movement not the sort of instinctive reaction she would have expected of a beginner.

'You suddenly seem to be getting very good at this,' she remarked, a sardonic inflection in her voice.

'I am, aren't I?' he responded with simple pride, his breath warm against her hair. 'You must be a good teacher.'

'It's got nothing to do with me,' she retorted. 'You've been on a sail board before.'

'A few times,' he conceded, his laughter soft and husky. 'But with you sitting there so frosty, frowning at me over your sunglasses, I couldn't think of any other way of getting close to you.'

And close he was, much closer than was necessary to keep the sail board afloat—folded around her, every inch of his body seeming to touch hers somewhere. 'You're...nothing but a fraud!' she protested, the tremor in her voice betraying the confusing responses she didn't know how to control.

He chuckled, a low, sensuous sound that she could feel as well as hear. 'Oh, no—I assure you I'm a lot more besides that, when you get to know me.'

'I don't want to get to know you,' she insisted. 'You probably cheat at cards.'

'I can't be a very good cheat, then,' he countered promptly. 'I lost all that money.'

In spite of herself, she was forced to laugh. 'Are you never lost for words?' she demanded, exasperated.

He didn't answer at once, and she glanced briefly up at him over her shoulder—to find him gazing down into her eyes, holding them in a strangely hypnotic spell. 'I am now,' he murmured smokily. 'Do you know, you're even more beautiful when you laugh?'

She felt something inside her beginning to melt…but then the folly of flirting while balanced on a sail board was brought home to her forcefully as it started to tilt.

'Whoops…' She corrected it with small movement, but the weight of the two of them was upsetting the balance. It swayed the other way, jolting as it hit a wave, and Natasha knew it was going to dump them both in the water.

Hugh's arm slipped around her waist as they tipped backwards, holding her close against him. They went under with a splash, both shrieking with laughter. The water was warm and clear, sunlight turning the spray to a sparkling cascade of diamonds. Her hair streamed around her as he turned her in his arms, and they surfaced together, body on body, legs entwined, their mouths so close…

When had she ever said he could kiss her? But as his lips brushed over hers she made no effort to push him away. Maybe she had been hoping that he would, wondering what it would be like…

But the compelling heat of his mouth was far more than she could have dreamed, dizzying her senses, driving any last shreds of rational thought from her mind. Slowly, languorously, his tongue lapped along the full curve of her lower lip, arousing a sensuous response from somewhere deep inside her, turning all her bones to jelly.

All her defences were designed to keep men at arm's length—they were of no use at such close quarters. His wicked tongue slid again across the silky membranes just inside her lips, and then sought to plunder deeper, swirling into all the most sensitive corners of her mouth in a flagrantly erotic invasion.

Her whole body was curved against his, her aching

breasts crushed by the hard wall of his chest, their tender peaks sensitive to the friction of every tiny movement between them. Her arms had somehow tangled themselves around his neck, and his hand had slipped slowly down over her bare back, holding her close enough to warn her of the tension of male arousal in him.

But the rational part of her brain had been stunned into silence by the unexpected impact of that kiss. She was kissing him back, a fierce hunger awakening inside her like nothing she had ever known before, a temptation so sweet that she didn't know how to resist it.

Her head tipped back as she gasped raggedly for breath, and his kisses trailed a hot path down the long, slender column of her throat, into the sensitive hollows at its base, as his hand stroked up over her slim midriff to cup and mould the ripe, aching curve of her breast, crushing it beneath his palm, the taut bud of her nipple sizzling beneath that delicious abrasion.

She was floating in a world of pure sensation, the soft, warm waters of the Caribbean lapping around her part of the magic of his caresses. But suddenly her foot touched the sandy bottom, her toes grazing against a jagged edge of broken coral, and the sharp sting brought her abruptly to her senses.

Shocked by her own wantonness, she pulled back out of his arms, suddenly aware that he had eased the strap of her swimsuit down over her shoulder, almost exposing the naked curve of her breast. 'Wh... What do you think you're doing?' she demanded fiercely, fumbling to pull the awkward wet Lycra back up again.

'You don't know?' His sardonic laughter taunted her as he shook his head in mocking disbelief. 'I'd heard you were a mite frostbitten, but I'm sure you must have been kissed at least a couple of times before.'

She had struck out at him before she had formed the conscious thought in her brain, but he was much too quick for her, catching her wrists as she fought against him, simply amused by her fury.

'Temper…!' he chided, holding her off with ease. 'You're really blowing your image this morning.'

Natasha snatched her hands away from him, splashing back into the water. It was impossible to retreat with any semblance of dignity, half-wading half-swimming up to the beach, but she just wanted to get away as quickly as possible—away from those mocking, mesmerising eyes, away from that taunting smile. As soon as she reached the shallows she stood up, striding across the soft sand towards the tree-shaded path, snatching up her book and her towel as she passed.

'No more bets now, please, ladies and gentlemen.' Natasha cast a cool glance along the table to check that all the players were ready, and then set the roulette wheel spinning, dropping in the silver ball with a deft hand so that it whirled and danced in the bowl, clattering in and out of the dish until at last it settled. 'Fifteen, black,' she announced, swinging out her rake to pull in the losing chips and deftly counting out to the winners.

'Trying a change of scenery tonight?' a familiar, faintly mocking voice murmured close behind her.

A hot little prickle of awareness ran down her spine, but she disdainfully refused to even turn her head. 'I frequently run a roulette table,' she countered in voice of icy dignity.

'Ah, well—perhaps I'll have better luck if I change my game,' Hugh responded with that air of amiable good humour that was beginning to seriously annoy her, strolling round to take a stool that had just been vacated right opposite her position.

Natasha kept her professional smile pinned firmly in place—she wasn't going to let Hugh Garratt see that she was the slightest bit bothered whether or not he joined her table. But she couldn't quite prevent her eyes from slanting in his direction—snatching them swiftly away again as his glance caught hers. And he smiled that idiotic smile that would fool absolutely no one that he was as stupid as he was trying to make people believe he was.

'No more bets now, please.' She was glad of the familiar routines of the game to anchor her concentration. 'Thank you, ladies and gentlemen—no more bets now.'

Hugh had put his chips on red—and it came up black. Natasha refused to allow herself to glance across the table as she raked in his chips. He was up to something—she was quite sure of it. Only a sucker would play even-money bets on a table with a double zero. But quite *what* he was up to she hadn't yet worked out.

He stayed at the table for about half an hour, and lost maybe a couple of thousand dollars, betting with a reckless good humour that had all the table laughing with him. That drew others to see what all the jollification was about, making the table the centre of attraction of the whole room.

'This time it's got to be the red!' he insisted, taking another large swig from the whisky tumbler he was waving around ostentatiously—though Natasha had noticed that, for all he appeared to be drinking from it, the level seemed to be remaining pretty much the same. 'It can't come up black five times in a row!'

Darlene was back, anchoring herself firmly to his side and fluttering her false eyelashes up at him. 'Well, if you're betting on the red, my money's on the black,' she giggled. 'Don't you *mind* losing all that money?'

'Ah, you have to hold on and wait for your luck to change,' he asserted cheerfully. 'It's got to happen—any minute now.'

'Well, I won't hold my breath.'

'Heartless wench.' He slipped his arm around her waist, smiling that wicked smile. 'Stick around and watch for the fireworks.'

'Last bets now, please,' Natasha rapped out, startled by the cutting edge in her own voice. 'Thank you, ladies and gentlemen,' she added more smoothly, flashing her cool smile. 'Last bets, please.'

Lester had wandered over to see what was causing all the excitement, and watched approvingly as Hugh carelessly tossed a pile of chips onto the red diamond.

It wasn't even a truly evens bet since along with the American wheel Lester had introduced the American rule—if the spin came up on the zero of double zero, the player lost the whole stake—instead of the English system of returning half. Natasha had argued vociferously against its introduction—it had seemed to her that the house advantage on the roulette table was already quite sufficient. But, as Lester had pointedly reminded her, most of the time the punters didn't even seem to notice.

Hugh certainly didn't seem to care. Apparently half drunk, he was laughing rather too loudly, his arm draped casually around Darlene's shoulders as if he needed her to prop him up. 'Come on, Lady Luck,' he pleaded, playing out the role of the reckless gambler from some cheap B movie. 'Spare me just one of your sweet smiles tonight.'

Natasha did her very best to ignore him. If he was the

sort who was attracted to Darlene's amply displayed charms, she wasn't remotely interested in him.

Not that she would have been interested anyway. So far as she was concerned, any man who came in through the doors of the casino carried a warning sign that spelled TROUBLE in giant red letters. No sensible woman would want to get involved with a gambler—even one that was winning.

But then across the table those wicked shark-grey eyes caught hers—and the glitter in them owed absolutely nothing to alcohol. Her heart gave a sudden thud. She was right—he was faking.

Was she the only person around the table who was aware of the charade? It seemed so—everyone else was laughing, enjoying the foolery. But why was he doing it? Last night she had wondered if he was working with a partner, drawing all the attention to himself while someone else worked a scam at one of the other tables. But her careful checking of all the surveillance videos had revealed nothing. So what was his game...?

He had held her gaze for much longer than she had intended, and she felt herself growing strangely warm, the memory of the way he had kissed her creeping into her mind, the way that strong, sensitive hand had caressed her breast... She drew in a long, deep breath, struggling to steady the beating of her own heart, and returned him the sort of cool, level look which would put most men very firmly in their place.

'Last bets now, please, ladies and gentlemen.' Damn—she had already said that.

Hugh lost yet again, and to Natasha's relief Lord Neville came over and demanded his attention, dragging him off to one of the blackjack tables, Darlene clinging to his arm like an leech.

With him gone from her table, she was able to feel a little more relaxed. She knew it was crazy to let him affect her like that. It was just because...she was still annoyed with herself about that encounter on the beach this morning. She wasn't even sure why she had let it happen. OK, so he had a good body, and a certain attractive way of smiling... And, yes, all right—she was intrigued. Why was he acting like some drunken, weak-minded fool, when she was pretty sure he was anything but? What was he up to?

Anyway, for the moment at least he was out of her hair. She refused to let herself think about him, and when she took her break she was careful to check that he was nowhere near the dance floor before crossing to the door that led to the back stairs and slipping up to the family apartment on the top floor.

She was surprised to find Lester there, kneeling on the floor beside the private safe in the little-used sitting room. He closed it quickly when she walked in, swinging back the section of bookshelves that concealed it. 'Well, we should be in for a pretty good night tonight,' he declared gleefully.

Natasha arched one finely drawn eyebrow in cool question.

'It seems our Mr Hugh Garratt thinks he can play poker,' Lester explained, riffling a thick wad of banknotes. 'I've let him persuade me to cut him in on our game.'

'Poker?' With a sudden kick of certainty Natasha saw the whole puzzle fall into place. 'I don't think you should play poker with him, Lester,' she warned tautly.

Her stepfather laughed, cocksure. 'Why not? If he's sucker enough to sit down with me, why shouldn't I fleece him? Teach the sap a lesson.'

She shook her head, wondering why she should bother

to waste her breath. She really couldn't care less if Lester lost his money—or, come to that, if Hugh did. 'I think you'll find you've underestimated him,' she persisted. 'You might find it isn't you doing the fleecing.'

Lester sneered. 'You think I'm stupid? I've marked him these past few days. He's a friend of that chinless aristocrat Neville—what does that tell you?'

'Not a lot,' she responded dryly. 'He may be a friend of his, but that doesn't mean he's one of his crowd.'

'Fancy him, do you?' he queried, his voice edged with sarcasm. 'Well, there's a first—I always thought you had ice in your britches. It's a pity you couldn't have a bit more sense than to fall for some bonehead like that. You'd better say goodbye to him—I doubt if he'll stick around very long after I've finished with him. He'll be lucky if he can find a banana boat to work his passage home!'

'Well, don't say I didn't warn you,' she threw back at him. 'At least it'll be your own money you're losing.'

'Of course it is!' Was it her imagination, or had he been just a little too quick to respond, a little too indignant? 'I have no need to touch the casino's money.'

Natasha had no real reason to doubt him—although she didn't really know where his wealth had come from. Of course, as her trustee and manager of the casino he received a share of the profits, but she wasn't sure that that was sufficient to finance his extravagant lifestyle—the expensive Italian suits and hand-made silk shirts that stuffed his wardrobe, the prime Havana cigars he liked to smoke, the private jet he hired on a regular basis whenever he wanted to pop across to Miami.

He had hinted from time to time that it was down to his shrewd business dealings, but she was inclined to doubt that—from what she had heard, chatting to old friends of her grandmother's, he was something of a joke among the business community of the island. She had more or less assumed that it must be his poker winnings that supported his income—he was a reasonably good player, she had to admit that, and his weekly game was quite a feature, drawing in the high-rollers as well as plenty of ordinary punters attracted by the glamour.

And so it had drawn in Hugh Garratt. The amiable fool, losing his money with a cheerful shrug, inevitably attracting Lester's eye when he was looking for a couple of greenhorns to provide the stake-fodder to sweeten the kitty at the poker table. Except that tonight Natasha suspected he had made a very big mistake.

'You can come and watch if you like,' Lester added, tucking the wad of notes into his jacket pocket. 'Only don't be too long, or you'll miss the action.' Again he chuckled, confidently anticipating a rewarding evening's play, and with a swagger of his well-set shoulders went off downstairs.

CHAPTER THREE

IT WAS a little past midnight, and the casino was at its busiest, the atmosphere hot and stuffy, blue with the haze of cigarette smoke. There were crowds around the roulette tables, the blackjack tables were full, and every slot machine in the hall was flashing its coloured lights and chiming its bells like some kind of alien spacecraft that had overdosed on magic mushrooms.

Natasha was dealing blackjack again, but from time to time she heard reports on the progress of the poker game being conducted in the principal card room at the back of the casino. Eight players had sat down at ten o'clock, but already two had been dealt out, and unless Señor Santos had a significant run of luck he'd be out before long, too.

'Lester's having a good night tonight,' someone remarked.

'Maybe. But I reckon the Englishman's got his measure. They're still psyching each other out, but he's got the advantage—no one knows his game.'

'Yeah, but he don't know theirs, neither. Could get interesting.'

Natasha listened, but said nothing. The essence of poker was to control the table, to be able to out-guess your opponent, to read his tactics without giving away your own. She still wasn't sure if she had read Hugh Garratt's tactics correctly. Was he just a fool, about to lose his shirt, as Lester so confidently believed? Or was he very, very clever?

But those thoughts were well concealed behind her

cool, professional smile as she dealt out the cards and raked in the chips. And the hours slipped past, uncounted.

At last the crowd began to thin a little. Natasha glanced at her watch and signalled the pit boss that she was going to close down the table, then racked up the chips and returned them to the cage, where the cashiers were busy with cheques and banknotes, quiet and serious as they counted with swift fingers, rarely, if ever, making a mistake.

A glance around the gaming room confirmed that everything was in order, nothing needed her attention. Finally, a curiosity she couldn't resist drew her to the card rooms.

A low half-gallery ran along the length of the card rooms, so that spectators could watch without distracting the players or being able to interfere with play. Behind it, three curtained archways gave access to the main gaming room. Quite an audience had gathered tonight, hushed and intent as they watched the action at the table.

Hugh appeared to be quite relaxed—his jacket was on the back of his chair, his tie was loose and his shirt-collar unfastened, his cuffs rolled back over strong wrists that had been bronzed by the sun. His watch, she noticed for the first time, was a slim gold Cartier—nothing flashy, just very expensive. And he had a tumbler of whisky at his elbow, though she noticed that he was no longer bothering to even pretend to drink from it.

He seemed to sense her gaze, and glanced up, those grey shark-eyes glinting with a shared secret. He knew that she knew what no one else had yet guessed. They believed they had a pigeon for the plucking, one of those enthusiastic amateurs who was essential fodder for a good poker game, providing lots of money for everyone else to win. They were in for a surprise.

It was past two-thirty in the morning, but in here, as in the rest of the casino, time had no significance—day and night alike were excluded by the heavy dark green damask drapes which covered all the windows. But as Señor Santos tossed in his cards with an impatient gesture and rose to his feet Lord Neville glanced at his watch.

'Well, I don't know about you chaps, but I could do with stretching my legs,' he remarked. 'How about a break?'

Sheikh al-Khalid stubbed out his black cigarillo and glanced at the diamond-crusted Rolex on his wrist. 'I, too, am in need of a little fresh air. Shall we say twenty minutes?'

There was general agreement, and, at a nod from Lester, the card room manager ceremoniously opened the case of the elaborate ormolu clock on the wall. 'Play resumes at three,' he announced solemnly.

Within a couple of minutes the exodus of players and spectators had left only Lester, Natasha and Hugh in the room. Lester began neatly stacking his plaques into rows—he had more than anyone else at the table. 'You're playing pretty well, son,' he said to Hugh. 'But a word of advice. If you're showing a good pair, don't be too eager to raise the first couple of rounds. Play 'em a bit. That way you won't scare 'em off too soon, and you'll get a decent pot instead of a paltry couple of big ones.'

Hugh returned him a long, level look from across the table, smiling slowly. 'Thank you,' he responded, polite, but with just the faintest thread of amusement in his voice. 'A free lesson from a poker player? That's a little unusual.'

Lester laughed, slightly unsure whether he was being mocked. But his usual arrogant self-confidence quickly reasserted itself. 'Oh, I can afford to be generous, son,' he expanded, grinning. 'At the end of the day, I'm more interested in a good game of poker than the size of my winnings. Well, I think I'll take me a breath of fresh air, too. See you later.'

The card room manager was moving discreetly around the table, emptying ashtrays and dusting down the smooth green baize. Still Hugh hadn't moved. Natasha watched him, frowning slightly. He seemed impervious—to the smoky, airless atmosphere, to the time of night, to any bodily discomforts like hunger or the need to stretch his legs.

'Aren't you going to take a break?' she queried, stiffly aloof. 'It's hot in here.'

He glanced up at her, that lazy smile taunting her. 'I suppose it is.'

'There are only another fifteen minutes before play starts again,' she reminded him crisply. 'If you're late, you'll be deemed to have been dealt out.'

He conceded a nod, that smile undisturbed, but remained in his seat.

Turning impatiently, she stalked from the room. Maybe she had been wrong about him—maybe he had realised that he really was out of his depth in this game after all, but didn't have the guts to admit it and leave the table as Señor Santos had done. Maybe he was planning to be late back, and be dealt out by a default.

The casino was much quieter now. Three of the roulette tables had closed down, and only the more serious gamblers remained at the blackjack tables. In another couple of hours they, too, would have drifted away.

Gamblers.

Probably even her grandmother wouldn't have understood how she felt. Of course, on a purely intellectual level she could accept that it was simply a form of adult entertainment—if people wished to spend their time and their money in that way, it was their own choice. But she hated having to have anything to do with it.

Only another two years, she reminded herself grimly. It wasn't too long to wait.

With a brisk step she crossed to the bar to check that the staff were coping while the bar manager was on holiday, and whether they needed any more wine brought up from the cellar. Satisfied that all was well at the bar, she let herself through the discreet door concealed in the wood panelling, into the surveillance room.

A bank of video screens showed the gaming rooms from all angles. Concealed cameras could zoom in, watching for any signs of cheating. A woman sat before them, her eyes flicking from screen to screen, missing nothing as her knitting needles clicked swiftly in her fingers.

'Everything OK?' Natasha enquired quietly.

The woman nodded. 'No problem, Miss Natasha. A nice, well-behaved crowd we have in tonight. Interesting game up in the back room, eh?'

She tilted her head towards two of the screens in the top row, which showed the principal card room. The table was now empty—Hugh had gone. Only the card room manager and the security guard remained, the faces that had been so impassive earlier now relaxed as they chatted between themselves. 'Yes, Mabel,' she confirmed pensively. 'A very interesting game.'

There was just enough time to slip upstairs to make sure her hair and make-up were still perfect before she returned to the card room to relieve the manager. The spectators had all returned to the gallery in plenty of time to ensure themselves the best vantage point, and then the players strolled in—first the Sheikh, followed by the red-faced Texan oil billionaire who was a regular at the tables.

Lord Neville took his place, grinning benignly around the room and flexing his fingers until the joints snapped. Then Lester, paused to glance at the empty chair, and then pointedly up at the clock on the wall. The second hand was starting its last sweep before the twenty minutes would be up.

'So,' he remarked complacently, hooking out his chair and sitting down, 'looks like our friend has decided to opt out?'

Lord Neville regarded him in some surprise, and then looked up at the clock. 'I shouldn't have thought so,' he responded with confidence.

There was a tense pause—ten seconds, fifteen—as everyone watched that slowly sweeping hand. It was incredible how long those few seconds could seem when you were counting them. It swept past the Roman six at the bottom of the dial, and began to climb... He was cutting it very fine...

The curtain behind the gallery fell, and Hugh walked calmly down the steps and crossed to his chair, sitting down easily and then glancing around the table in some surprise, as if only just realising that everyone was staring at him. His eyes slanted up towards the clock as the second hand touched the top numeral.

'So—shall we play cards?' he enquired blandly.

Natasha closed the clock, and then watched as the players selected two fresh packs of the high-quality plastic cards that the best casinos always used for poker. It was Lord Neville's deal, and with deft expertise he slit open the Cellophane packs, stripped out the jokers, and then flipped each pack over, fanning them out in front of him so that they could all see that the suits were perfect. He shuffled, offered the pack for al-Khalid to cut, and began to deal.

The atmosphere was rather more intense now, the play more aggressive, the stakes running higher. Lester was still ahead, the stacks of high-value chips piling up in front of him. But Lord Neville was having a good night, and Hugh had also had several good wins. Nothing big yet, but Natasha had a sense that he was holding a good deal in reserve, giving little away, biding his time.

Several times she was sure she could feel him watching her, and kept her eyes carefully averted. But when she did risk a glance across the table, his gaze would be elsewhere. And then in one unguarded moment, as she was letting herself study that hard-boned face, with its high forehead and strong, angular cheekbones, he glanced up— and she found herself captured, those fathomless grey eyes weaving some kind of spell around her that she couldn't escape.

Suddenly her pulse was racing, making her feel a little dizzy. Unconsciously her lips parted as she drew in a ragged breath, remembering much too vividly the taste of his kiss, the way his mouth had scalded a path down the long, sensitive column of her throat... Quickly she looked away, struggling to keep her attention on the game.

Lord Neville appeared to be more than a little drunk— although Natasha knew of old that that rarely interfered with his acuity at cards. Lester looked edgy—perhaps no one else would notice, but Natasha knew that infinitesimal tightening around the corner of his mouth. He was betting deep, trying to intimidate the less confident players, but that didn't necessarily mean that he was holding the strongest cards.

As for Hugh, if he was giving away any clues, even Natasha's experienced eye couldn't spot them. He was sitting quite relaxed, one arm resting loosely on the arm of his chair. The role that he had been playing for the past

few days had slipped away in the past couple of hours—
now those shark-eyes were cool and calculating, and his
whole manner spoke of a bone-deep self-assurance that
had nothing to do with arrogance.

And he was a damned good poker player.

Of course, there was nothing illegal in what he had
done, deliberately losing money and acting the fool to lure
Lester into making a false judgement, the better to fleece
him. And she certainly didn't feel the least bit sorry for
Lester. He deserved everything that was coming to him.

But if Lester was being forced to recognize that his
earlier opinion of his opponent had been somewhat wide
of the mark, he wasn't yet ready to concede the table to
him.

There were several more hands—Lord Neville had a
reasonable win, and Hugh another, and then Lester
scooped the largest pot of the night so far.

'You should've known I wouldn't bet like that on anything less than a straight, sonny,' he advised Hugh, who
had plunged a little too recklessly on two pairs.

Hugh simply shrugged those wide shoulders in a gesture of casual unconcern. 'I like to play poker, not tiddly-
winks,' he responded, eyeing the substantial pile of chips
in front of Lester with mild contempt.

Lester's temper sparked. 'So do I, sonny,' he snarled
back. 'So do I.'

'Then why are we playing table limit?' Hugh returned
coolly. 'Let's take the gloves off, if we really want a
game.'

Natasha heard several sharp intakes of breath—one of
them her own. The knot of spectators on the half-gallery
seemed to press in a little closer, the tension notched up
by several degrees. Lord Neville laughed. 'I'm in,' he
agreed genially. 'How about you boys?'

He slanted a questioning glance at the other two players. Sheikh al-Khalid glanced around the circle of faces
and then nodded slowly. 'I will play.'

The big Texan leaned back in his chair and took his
cigar out of his mouth. 'Aw, dammit—count me in,'
he declared expansively. 'Maybe changing the limit'll
change my luck.' He had lost heavily on the last six
hands.

That left the final word to Lester. He reached out and
picked up one of his chips, tapping it on the table, that
faint hint of whiteness at the corner of his mouth the only
clue that he was feeling any strain. Across the table,
Natasha saw the two men's eyes meet, hard and challenging. And then Lester nodded slowly.

'No limit it is, then,' he conceded. 'What shall we set
for the ante? A thousand dollars?'

'Why not ten thousand?' Hugh suggested evenly. 'If
we're *really* going to play.'

'That's fine by me,' Lester agreed, his voice taut.

Natasha felt a small chill flicker down her spine. This
time it would be a fight to the death.

A tense hush reigned as the cards were dealt and the
play began. Every eye in the room was on the swirling
design on the backs of the two hole cards in front of each
player—anonymous, unrevealing. What secrets did they
hide? In the middle of the table, the kitty mounted steadily, and Natasha moved discreetly around the table as several of the players needed to buy in more chips.

Al-Khalid scrawled his signature on a marker and she
counted out his chips, aware as she bent over the table
that those shark-grey eyes were watching her. Conjuring
her cool, professional smile, she turned to him. 'Do you
wish to buy, Mr Garratt?'

He nodded assent, slanting a slow smile up at her, his
eyes glinting with a hint of intimate reminiscence that

made her heart kick sharply against her ribs. Quite deliberately he allowed that mocking gaze to drift down over
her body, lingering over every slender curve, evoking a
memory that was almost physical of that moment on the
beach when he had held her in his strong arms, his hand
caressing the aching swell of her breast through the damp
Lycra of her swimsuit, teasing the tender peak into a taut,
hardened bud.

And she could feel herself responding as if he was
touching her—could feel her lips grow warm and soft, her
breathing ragged—and knew that beneath the soft, clinging fabric of her dress her breasts were ripening, the delicate nipples puckering until their pert contours were
clearly shadowed against the lilac-silver silk.

His smile of mocking satisfaction told her that he had
noted that betraying evidence of the effect he had on her.
She struggled to tear her gaze away, but she was a prisoner of his will, bound by the spells he was weaving
around her. The card game, the casino, had melted away,
and he was stripping her naked, demanding her total surrender...

'Well? Are you playing this hand or what?' Lester demanded, betraying his agitation.

Which was exactly what Hugh had intended, Natasha
realised, struggling to regain the scattered threads of her
composure. He was controlling the table, making them all
wait on his timing—she had just been part of his game.
Had he been genuinely attracted to her at all? Or had it
been nothing but another charade?

And then he laughed softly, reaching out a smooth hand
to flick one of his hole cards across the table. 'I draw,'
he said.

The dealer pushed a replacement card towards him, and
he tipped up the corner to glance at it. For a fleeting mo-

ment Natasha thought she saw something flicker in those hard shark-eyes. A smile? But if he had good cards, why was he giving himself away? Or was he bluffing? She glanced at Lester, and realised that he too had noticed it. And he was quite sure that it was bluff.

A quick glance at her watch told her that it was a little after five-thirty. Outside, the birds would soon be starting their morning song, a fresh, salt-tanged breeze would rustle the leaves of the coconut palms and casuarinas along the shoreline, and the dark velvet sky would begin to pale to a mother-of-pearl sheen as the sun's first rays touched the tops of the steep volcanic hills.

But here in the card room the outside world was kept at bay by those heavy green damask drapes; the air was hot and heavy, blue with the haze of the night's cigarette smoke. She had lost count of the amount in the pot. The coloured blocks of plastic were heaped up and spilling over, looking like some child's cheap toys—it seemed incredible to think of the amount of money they represented.

The Sheikh and the Texan had dropped out, but Lord Neville seemed to have a good hand. Maybe he would win—in fact it would be a good thing if he did, Natasha mused fiercely. She would be spared from having to decide whether she was pleased or sorry if Hugh Garratt won.

And then Lester raised again, smiling in mocking arrogance. 'There. Let's see how much faith you have in that one little king of yours. Raise another hundred.'

Natasha felt her heartbeat pounding as if she was playing herself. One hundred thousand dollars—it was a ridiculous amount of money to stake on the turn of a card. Behind and all around her, Natasha could hear the murmur of interest. Hugh's hand looked weak—a king and an eight. The chances that those two mismatched cards would amount to any kind of winning hand were less than ten per cent. Even lower, in fact, because Lester already had another of the kings. But what were those hidden hole cards?

Hugh was still sitting quite relaxed—he didn't have the look of a man who was about to risk more money than most people saw in a lifetime on a single hand of poker. Not that it really mattered to her if he lost she reminded herself fiercely. He was just another punter—he meant nothing to her. If she *did* want him to win, it was only because she wanted Lester to be proved well and truly wrong. It had absolutely nothing to do with the jumbled emotions warring in her own heart.

Every eye in the room was on Hugh—but that cool façade didn't falter. He was looking across the table at Lester, still with that small smile curving his hard mouth. 'You don't think I've got any confidence in my cards? Very well—I'll double your raise.'

Lester drew in a hissing breath like a snake. 'You have a great deal of faith in your own luck,' he remarked, letting his upper lip curl into something close to a sneer.

Hugh merely arched one dark eyebrow, smiling slowly. 'Luck?' He repeated the word as if it was unfamiliar, and shook his head. 'I don't need luck to beat you.'

The contempt was as finely distilled as the malt whisky in his glass, and Lester's face turned puce. For one fraught moment it seemed as if he was going to shove back his chair and challenge the young usurper to a fist fight—if he thought better of it, it was only to signal that he would let the cards do the talking.

'So—let's play,' he grated tersely.

Natasha smiled wryly to herself. That little piece of gamesmanship had been perfectly calculated. Now Lester was angry, and an angry poker player was a careless poker player. Warily she flickered a glance across at Hugh, a puzzled suspicion starting to crystallise in her brain. This wasn't just a poker game—this was personal. And yet she knew that the two men had never met until just a couple of days ago. What was going on?

Lord Neville laughed a little wildly, and took a deep swallow of his whisky, the ice cubes chinking against the glass as his hand shook. 'This is crazy—just plain crazy.' He stacked his cards and tossed them face-down on the table. 'That's enough for me—I'm out.'

There was a murmur of sympathy around the room. Lord Neville was a popular figure—as even-tempered drunk or sober, accepting a bad beat as equably as a winning streak, and always the perfect gentleman. He came over to the island about three or four times a year, usually with a crowd of equally well-heeled cronies, and they would stay for a couple of weeks, visiting the casino most nights and losing a great deal of money between them.

This time, though, was a little different. It was less than a month since his last visit—that in itself was an odd occurrence. And he was with none of his usual crowd— only Hugh Garratt.

Yet again her eyes slid covertly towards the Englishman, studying him from beneath her lashes. He wasn't much like Lord Neville's other friends—he was a little older, for a start, and there was something about him that was...harder.

It was Lester's play, and for the first time he was looking a little uncertain. A small bead of sweat had broken from above his temple and tracked its way slowly down past his ear as he stared at the cards face-down on the table in front of his opponent. Natasha could almost hear his mind working; was Garratt bluffing? He had to be bluffing. That hint of reaction to his draw card had been clever, but not quite clever enough.

'OK—let's go for it,' Lester summoned Natasha to his side, his hand not quite steady as he opened the briefcase at his feet and handed her the last four packs of banknotes it contained. 'Double it again.'

The tension in the room seemed ready to crack—there was more than half a million dollars in the pot. Still the only person who seemed unaffected by it was Hugh. He was simply watching Lester, that faintly mocking smile curving his hard mouth. And then with a slow deliberation he began to count out his chips, laying them down in front of him before sliding them into the middle of the table. 'I call you.'

Lester drew in a long, deep, breath, and his mouth widened into a broad grin which broke into a gloating laugh. 'Full house!' he announced, turning over his hole cards to reveal three kings and two fives. 'Kings and fives. Can you beat that?'

He clearly expected it to be a rhetorical question, but Hugh was still smiling. His king and his eight lay face-up on the table, and one by one he turned over his remaining cards. The eight of spades, the eight of diamonds, and the eight of clubs. 'Four of a kind,' he stated softly. 'My pot, I think.'

No one seemed to care that it was almost six o'clock in the morning—everyone wanted to party. Lord Neville had extracted a pile of chips from his friend's winnings and given them to the head barman, with the generous instruction that the drinks were on Hugh; Natasha had gone behind the bar to help with the rush; Lester had disappeared.

The only person who didn't seem to be celebrating his win was Hugh Garratt himself. He had remained alone in the card room, sitting quietly at the table, accepting with a brief nod the congratulations of the few who from time to time remembered what the party was about.

It was some time before the bar quietened down sufficiently for Natasha to leave it to the staff. She hesitated for a moment, and then walked quickly back through the gaming room, drawing aside the heavy curtain that separated it from the more private card rooms.

Hugh glanced up as she appeared, and smiled at her, one dark eyebrow arched in quizzical enquiry. She stayed at the top of the short flight of steps that led down from the half-gallery, one hand resting lightly on the newel post. The height seemed to give her an added advantage, helping her project an image of unruffled composure—she didn't want him to look at her again the way he had earlier.

'Congratulations,' she said coolly. 'It was a good game.'

A glint of mocking amusement sparked in those shark-grey eyes. 'You don't mind that I won all that money from your stepfather?'

She shrugged her slender shoulders in a dismissive gesture. 'Why should I? It's Lester's money—it's his problem if he's stupid enough to gamble more than he can afford to lose.' She didn't trouble to conceal the edge of contempt in her voice. However unsettling the past few days had been, it had been worth it to see Lester so thoroughly worsted.

He slanted her a look of quizzical enquiry. 'I gather you're not a particularly close-knit family?'

'You could say that,' she conceded tersely. 'So—I suppose you'll want to see about cashing that little lot,' she added with a hint of a smile, gesturing with a graceful hand towards the heap of chips on the table. 'I'll send for the senior cashier to count them for you. Would you like to have an independent witness? Lord Neville, perhaps?'

He laughed dryly, and shook his head. 'I think I trust you. Besides, if Nev's sober enough to count his own fingers it'll be a miracle.'

She acknowledged the truth of that with a small smile as José, the senior cashier, anticipating her request, came bustling through the curtain. He held out his hand to Hugh, smiling broadly. 'Congratulations, sir. Best game of poker I've seen on these islands for a long time.'

'Thank you,' Hugh responded easily.

José sat himself down at the table, regarding the mountain of chips with some respect. 'If you would care to check the count as I go?' he suggested to Hugh. 'If there is any discrepancy, we will count again. Then, when we reach a total on which we both agree, we will be pleased to present you with a banker's draft for that amount.'

Hugh accepted the arrangements with a brief nod. Natasha moved over to sit down at the table, watching as José began to stack the chips into their separate denominations. She was beginning to realise just how subtly Lester had been played; that hint of a smile when Hugh had seen his draw card had been calculated to convince him that he was bluffing. And, confident of his own cleverness, he had fallen into the trap, certain that his was the better hand. But it had been the fourth eight, a virtually unbeatable hand—a perfect double bluff.

So now the night was over, and he had got what he had come for. From beneath her lashes she slanted him a covert gaze, refusing to acknowledge the small ache that had lodged itself in some deep corner of her heart. Soon now he would be leaving—leaving Spaniard's Cove, going back home to England, to whatever life he usually led there. Probably to a regular girlfriend—perhaps even a wife. It was unlikely that he would ever be back...

It took some time to complete the count, but at last they came to an agreed figure and the senior cashier filled in the draft, which had already been signed by Uncle Timothy, as co-trustee and director of the casino. Then he handed it to Natasha to countersign.

'So...' She dashed off her signature with a flourish and held it out to Hugh between her fingers, a sardonic glint in her cool blue eyes. His play-acting had achieved its goal. He had lured Lester into his trap, playing on his greed and arrogance, and Lester had fallen for it perfectly. 'Your winnings, Mr Garratt.'

'Thank you.' His smile was one of mocking amusement as he took the draft from her, glancing at it only fleetingly as he tucked it into his wallet. Then he rose easily to his feet, extending his hand to shake the cashier's in farewell. 'Goodnight, then—or rather, good morning,' he said with a genial smile.

'Good morning to you, sir.' The cashier's voice conveyed the marked respect of everyone in the casino business for someone who had the skill and nerve to win a really big coup—with perhaps an added note of pleasure because most of it had been Lester's money. Natasha was aware that her stepfather wasn't liked by the casino's staff. Had there been other incidents like the one she had witnessed in the garage, which she hadn't known about?

The casino was almost deserted as Natasha walked with Hugh to the front door—at this late hour, the revellers had tired quickly. The tables were closed, and only a few last guests lingered on the slot machines. The smell of stale cigar smoke and human sweat lingered in the air, and Natasha wrinkled her nose in distaste.

Hugh noticed the gesture—those shrewd grey eyes noticed everything, she suspected. 'The morning after,' he remarked on a sardonic inflection. 'You don't much care for it, do you?'

'It is a bit of a fug,' she acknowledged with dignity. 'It'll be better when the cleaners have been in.'

He smiled. 'I wasn't talking about the fug.'

She hesitated, slanting him a searching glance from beneath her lashes. It would probably be impossible to explain how she felt to a man who had just pocketed a cheque for more than half a million dollars. After all, what would he know—why should he care?—about the darker side of the business? The addicted gamblers who would stake their grandmother's pension on the roll of the dice, the desperate ones who broke down and wept when they couldn't cover their losses—and the constant, nagging anxiety that the hard men who dominated the gambling industry on the mainland would decide that her small operation was worth their attention.

'Tell me, if you don't like the gambling business, why do you choose to run a casino?'' Hugh enquired, softly mocking.

'It isn't my choice.' Her voice was gritty with the frustration of all her endless arguments with Lester about it. 'Unfortunately, under the terms of my trust, I have to have both trustees' agreement to make any major changes to the estate.'

He arched one quizzical eyebrow. 'I take it they won't agree?'

'Oh, Uncle Timothy would.'

'So—it's Lester that's the problem,' he surmised dryly.

There seemed little point in denying it. 'But in two years' time the trust will come to an end, and I can be rid of him,' she averred, her mouth tight. 'I can wait.'

'Two years?' Again she had the impression that he was

taking more than a passing interest in the affairs of the casino. 'So the trust will end when you're…what? Twenty-five? Or, presumably, if you should marry before that date?'

For no accountable reason his words made her heart thump against her ribs like the kick of a mule. 'Yes. But I doubt if that…I mean, that isn't very likely to happen,' she choked out.

They had reached the wide front doors, and she paused for a moment, looking out over the curving sweep of the bay. A soft mother-of-pearl mist lay over the sea, drifting across the steep tree-clad slopes of the volcanic hills that sheltered the pink coral beach, and the morning dew lent a sweet moistness to the air.

'It's such a beautiful place…' she sighed, half to herself, drawing in a long, deep breath, clearing her lungs of the heavy, smoke-laden air of the night.

At least it had been once. But Lester was making it ugly, with his greed for more and more profit. She glanced back over her shoulder as one of the slot machines inside began piping out its synthetic chimes as someone pumped money into it, clashing with the sweet early-morning song of the bananaquits.

'You want to get rid of Lester?' Hugh queried, his voice low and quiet, seeming to speak right into her thoughts. 'There could be a way.'

She glanced up at him in startled question.

'Get married.'

She laughed a little uncertainly, not sure if it was a joke. 'What, you mean…put an advert in the paper? *"Husband Required"*. I could turn up every psycho on the island.'

He shook his head, smiling that slow, lazy smile. 'I wasn't thinking of an ad in the paper. I was thinking of you marrying me.'

CHAPTER FOUR

NATASHA stared up at him, stunned her first words of protest choked in her throat. The most she could manage was an inelegant, *'What?'*

Those shark-grey eyes glinted with sardonic humour. 'It's quite simple. We get married, you break the trust— and the casino is yours to do whatever you want with. You can get rid of Lester, and there won't be a thing he can do about it.'

'But...I can't possibly marry you,' she protested, her heart thudding so hard she felt faint. 'I mean...I barely even know you.'

'True,' he conceded, utterly reasonable. 'Perhaps there's someone else you could ask to stand in as a sufficiently plausible bridegroom...?'

'No...there isn't. But...' She shook her head, struggling for control of her thoughts—the long night in the smoke-thick air, the excitement of the game, seemed to have numbed her brain. 'Really, this whole discussion is quite ridiculous.' Forcing her usual cool smile into place, she held out her hand to him in a gesture of formal farewell. 'Thank you for the suggestion, but I have no intention of getting married—to you or anyone. Goodnight, Mr Garratt. Or perhaps, as you said before, it should be good morning.'

He regarded her for a moment, and a glint of enigmatic amusement lit those shark-grey eyes. And then he took her hand—but instead of shaking it he lifted it to his lips and laid a light, warm kiss on the backs of her fingers.

'Think it over,' he murmured—and when he smiled like that it was impossible to tell if he was mocking her or if he was serious. 'Goodbye, Miss Cole. It has been...a delight to make your acquaintance.'

And, turning, he walked away down the terrace steps and along the sweeping gravel path that curved beneath the shade of the tall coconut palms.

Natasha stood for a moment on the top step, watching him go. There were a score of unanswered questions buzzing in her brain. He hadn't come here just to play poker; he had been settling some kind of personal score against Lester—she was quite sure of it. But what had it been about? And had he ever really been attracted to her—or had that merely been part of the game?

And why had he suggested that she marry him...?

'Damn...!' She couldn't let him go without at least getting some of the answers. Picking up her long skirt, she skipped swiftly down the terrace steps and ran after him down the path. 'Hugh—wait!'

He turned, surprised—or maybe not—as she caught up with him.

'Who are you?' she demanded bluntly. 'Why did you come here? You're not a professional gambler, are you?'

He conceded a slightly crooked smile. 'How did you figure that out?'

'If you were I'd have heard of you,' she asserted, sure of her ground. 'The world circuit's not that big—good poker players are well known. So why *did* you come here? It was something to do with Lester, wasn't it?'

He hesitated, seeming to take a moment to decide whether to answer her, and then conceded a reluctant nod.

'But why?' Her puzzled gaze sought to find the truth in those changeable grey eyes. 'You've never met him before—at least, he certainly didn't know you. What did he do to make you go to so much trouble to get back at him?'

'I had my reasons,' he responded cagily. 'But I don't want you to get dragged into it.'

'I've already been dragged into it,' she pointed out with a touch of acerbic humour. 'I own the casino, in case you'd forgotten.'

He shook his head. 'I hadn't forgotten.' His silk bow tie was loosened, the collar of his shirt unfastened, his elegantly cut dinner jacket swinging loosely from his finger as it hung over his shoulder. He seemed to be studying the gravel at his feet, a deep frown creased between his dark, level brows. 'In a way...I suppose you are involved—pretty deeply involved. Maybe you have a right to know the whole story.'

Natasha drew in a breath. So she had been right all along. And at last the truth was within her grasp...

'Only right now I'm in need of some sleep,' Hugh appended, with that air of bland innocence she had learned to mistrust. The hint of sardonic humour in his smile confirmed that he was deliberately tormenting her. 'Have dinner with me tonight, and I'll tell you then.'

She stepped back, instinctively on the defensive. 'Have dinner with you?' she was shaking her head. 'I don't...'

He laughed in mocking challenge. 'You don't accept dates with punters? But if you want to know why I came here you'll have to have dinner with me,' he insisted.

She hesitated, the warning voices inside her head arguing fiercely with the ones urging her to take a chance— just this once. The warning voices lost. 'All right,' she conceded, feeling her heartbeat begin to race a little unsteadily. 'I'll...have dinner with you.' After all, she reminded her more cautious self, she really did want to find out what this was all about.

He nodded, acknowledging her acceptance, those smoky grey eyes unreadable. And as he put up his hand and stroked it across her cheek, smiling that slow, lazy, beguiling smile, she found herself captured, trapped by that spellbinding gaze, her breath stilling on her lips.

His hand slid through her hair, drawing her slowly towards him. What had happened to all her cool composure? The icy glance that kept every other man at arm's length? None of it seemed to have an impact on Hugh Garratt—he simply ignored it, taking what he wanted, arrogantly certain of winning every time.

But as his head bent over hers, his mouth moving closer, closer, she felt as if her will had been taken over by a force stronger than gravity itself. His breath was warm against her cheek as those strong arms folded around her, moulding every inch of her supple body against the hard length of his, and she closed her eyes, trembling inside as he dusted kisses, light as a butterfly's wing, across each delicate eyelid, over the fevered pulse that fluttered beneath her temple, around the delicate shell of her ear.

And then at last his mouth claimed hers, tender and tantalising, his sensuous tongue swirling languorously over the soft fullness of her lips, igniting her responses, tempting her beyond reason, and she could only surrender as he sought all the sweet, secret corners within in a flagrantly sensual exploration which ravaged her senses and melted her bones.

Her breathing was ragged and impeded as the heat flared between them. They were beneath the shelter of an old lime tree, leaning back against its gnarled trunk—the tree bark was rough against her bare shoulders, but she didn't even notice. Her breasts, aching and tender, were crushed, and she felt her defences crumbling, helpless in the grip of a hunger that she didn't know how to control.

His mouth broke from hers to trace a path of scalding kisses down the long, slender arch of her throat as her head tipped dizzily back, and she felt his hand slide upwards slowly, but with deliberate intent, until his fingers brushed against the firm, ripe curve of her breast.

The shriek of a parrot in the branches above them jolted through her senses. She opened dazed eyes, startled by the glittering brightness of the sun, now climbing high into the hot sky and burning off the last shreds of early-morning mist, shimmering on the brilliant blue waters of the Caribbean. And she was shocked at the realisation of how willingly she had been letting Hugh Garratt kiss her.

Her cheeks flamed scarlet as she pushed herself out of his arms. 'Don't... Stop it—I...' Her hair was falling loose from its neat coil, and one strap of her dress had slipped down over the curve of her shoulder—hastily she pulled it back, darting an anxious glance around in fear that someone might have seen them.

But Hugh merely laughed, mocking her confusion. 'It's all right—I don't think there was anyone around to be watching us at this time of the morning,' he assured her lazily. And then, taking her hand again, he lifted it to his lips, those shark's eyes taunting her as he brushed a kiss over her fingertips. 'I'll pick you up at eight,' he said.

And before she could recover sufficiently to speak, he had walked away.

She stood staring after him, her mind in turmoil. Why on earth had she let him inveigle her into agreeing to have dinner with him? She must be going soft in the head! Well, she wasn't going to go, she vowed grimly—no way was she going to risk spending a whole evening in his company. Never mind all her questions—she could live without the answers to them.

Besides, it would do him good to be stood up. He was a great deal too arrogant.

Just after lunch, there was a tap on the office door. Natasha looked up from the papers in front of her and called, 'Come in.'

The door opened a few inches, and Debbie's tearstained face appeared. 'I'm so sorry to bother you, Nat. But Lester's in a terrible state.'

'I'm not surprised,' she responded dryly.

'Yes, but…I'm afraid he might do something silly.'

Sillier than losing the best part of half a million dollars on a card game? Natasha mused. But Debbie's tearful face made her keep that thought to herself. 'Like what?' she asked patiently.

'I don't know.' Debbie came into the office and perched on the edge of the desk, her sapphire-blue eyes misty and troubled. 'He's not making any sense. He's locked himself in the apartment—he's going through the papers in the safe. He's got a gun, and he won't let me in.'

Natasha frowned. 'Want me to try?'

'Would you?' The older girl's expression was one of such relief that Natasha felt uncomfortable. She couldn't imagine that talking to her would make her stepfather feel any better—probably quite the reverse. But Debbie clearly had faith in her—however misplaced.

'Of course,' she agreed with a small sigh, which she turned quickly into a reassuring smile. Anything to get away from the tedium of lease renewal contracts on those damned slot machines that she hadn't wanted in the first place. 'I'll be up in a minute.'

She put the contracts to one side. Her concentration was

broken now—she would finish them later. So Lester was panicking about the money? That was hardly surprising—a loss like that must have made a very large dent in his bank account. And she would be the first to say that it served him right.

He had been a fool to let himself be lured into gambling more than he could afford to lose. But it was a taste of his own medicine. He had done it often enough, targeting some unfortunate young sucker—they were nearly always young—playing him along with a mixture of flattery and mocking taunts, goading him into trying to match the high-rollers, not giving a damn for the misery he caused.

And just where had he got that sort of money from anyway? Not from his poker winnings—he was good, but not that good. And not from his business dealings—from what she had heard, they were a disaster. Of course, as manager of the casino, he was entitled to a share of the profits, as well as a bonus related to the year-on-year increase in profits. It was a good income—but it was small beer to the amount he had lost last night.

Which brought her back inevitably to the question of Hugh Garratt. Why had he gone to so much trouble to set the thing up, taken the risk that it might have been him who had lost half a million dollars when by his own admission he wasn't even a professional gambler? He had said that she was somehow involved...but what could she possibly have to do with it?

And why had he made that ludicrous proposal of marriage?

At least... *Had* it been a proposal? A small frown shadowed her smooth brow. It hadn't seemed much like a proposal, not a genuine one... Perhaps it had just been a joke. Though it was a pretty odd sort of joke.

'Think about it,' he had said. She had thought of little

else, though she had tried as hard as she knew to put it out of her mind. The way he had looked at her, those shark-grey eyes glinting with some kind of message she didn't understand... It had troubled her sleep, and distracted her all through the day as she had tried to work.

A marriage of convenience—was that what he had meant? Of course it would be the perfect way to outflank Lester, she acknowledged. But could she trust Hugh Garratt any more than she could trust her stepfather? He had already proved himself more than capable of spinning a web of deceit, playing drunk and stupid, deliberately losing at the tables to lure Lester into his trap.

And playing stupid down on the beach, she reminded herself, feeling suddenly a little warm as she recalled the way he had pretended he had never been on a sail board before, teasing her into giving him an impromptu lesson. A marriage of convenience... But somehow she couldn't see Hugh Garratt sticking to the rules...

Abruptly she rose to her feet, tossing the bent piece of wire that had once been a perfectly serviceable paperclip into the wastepaper bin. She wasn't going to marry Hugh Garratt, or anyone else—she had already thought that one through and decided it wasn't an option. She wasn't going to waste another minute of her time on the idea.

Her mouth was a thin line as she climbed the narrow staircase to the upstairs apartment. She really didn't much care how much financial trouble Lester had dumped himself in—that was his problem. But Debbie had said that he had a gun in there. Surely he wasn't planning to shoot himself...?

She tried her key in the lock, but the door was bolted from the inside. She tapped on it, but there was no reply, so she tapped again more loudly. 'Lester?'

'Go away. I'm busy.'

His voice was rough and impatient, but Natasha wasn't
as easily intimidated as Debbie. 'You might as well let
me in,' she responded, flatly obstinate. 'Otherwise I shall
just keep knocking.'

She heard him swear, but after a moment he opened
the door. 'What do you want?' he demanded, already returning to what he had been doing without waiting for an
answer.

She strolled into the room, her cool blue eyes taking in
a scene of minor chaos. The false bookshelf which concealed the private safe stood ajar and the safe was wide
open, papers scattered in a wide arc on the floor around
it. 'What's going on?' she enquired with a studied lack
of interest.

'I'm taking care of some business,' he responded
grudgingly, kneeling amid the papers and shuffling some
aimlessly from one pile to another.

'So I see. It wouldn't be anything to do with last night,
would it?'

He returned her a seething glare—what Debbie had neglected to mention was that he was also drunk.

She sat down on the edge of the desk, the dislike and
contempt she had always felt for him crystallising as she
watched him, red-faced, ill-tempered, floundering in a mo-
rass of his own making. 'You can't say I didn't warn you
not to underestimate him,' she remarked, not without
some satisfaction.

'Damn you,' he growled. 'If I'd known he was a
damned grifter...'

'He's not a grifter!' she protested sharply. 'All he did
was gull you a little into believing he was a ripe one—
you did the rest yourself.'

'I'd just like to know who he is, and what he was doing
here,' Lester persisted, his brow dark. 'Has he gone yet?

Checked out of the beach cottage? Gone back to England?'

'I don't think so,' Natasha responded with caution.

'Who is he?' Lester's jaw was clenched, his eyes darting from side to side, as if trying to look over his own shoulders. 'What's he hanging around for? What does he want?'

It occurred to Natasha suddenly that her stepfather was actually afraid of Hugh Garratt. But why? So far as she knew, they hadn't even met until a few days ago. What was going on between the pair of them? She was determined to find out, particularly if it involved Spaniard's Cove.

'By the way, I came up to tell you that I won't be in tonight,' she announced with just a shade of hesitation. She heard herself saying it, though she wasn't quite sure when she had changed her mind and decided to accept Hugh's invitation after all.

Lester grunted, stacking the papers and beginning to put them back in the safe.

'I'm having dinner with him.'

The papers Lester was holding spilled out of his hands and scattered on the floor. He swore violently, scrabbling to pick them up while glowering up at her from beneath his lowered brows. 'Is that supposed to be some kind of a joke?'

'Not at all. He asked me out, and I said yes. It's as simple as that.'

'Damn you!' Lester blustered, his face going even redder. 'After what he did last night?'

'It was a fair game,' she pointed out, her voice cool with disdain. 'You lost.'

For a moment she thought she had pushed him too far, and he was going to explode. But then, with an effort that appeared to cost him some strain, he reined himself in, casting her a sly, searching look. 'So, you're having dinner with him, eh? Why did he ask you?'

She shrugged her slim shoulders, feigning indifference. 'Presumably for the pleasure of my company.'

'Huh! Not a guy like that.' He shook his head, his tension betrayed by the way he was grinding his fist into the palm of his other hand. 'He wasn't just here for a game of cards. It's something deeper than that.' Suddenly his manner changed, his smile warm, cozening, his eyes crinkling up in the way he always used when he was trying to turn on the charm. 'You could find out tonight,' he pleaded. 'You're a very pretty girl, you know—I could tell he was attracted to you. You could get it out of him— if you use a little persuasion.'

'Oh?' Natasha felt as if something slimy was crawling down her spine—somehow Lester being nice was a whole lot more unpleasant than Lester being nasty. 'What sort of persuasion, exactly? Sleep with him, perhaps?'

'Of course not!' The look of affronted dignity was very nearly perfect—if she hadn't known so well the way his nasty little mind worked, she might have been deceived. 'As if I'd suggest a thing like that!'

'Oh, no, Lester—of course you wouldn't,' she countered, her voice laced with sarcasm. 'You're the very soul of probity, aren't you?'

With a jerky movement he shoved the last of the papers back in the safe and slammed it shut, spinning the combination lock and swinging the bookshelf back into place in front of it. 'It's time you learned to keep a civil tongue in your head, my girl,' he warned, poking a menacing finger towards her. 'One of these days I might just decide to teach you a lesson.'

'Oh? Like you were going to teach Hugh Garratt a lesson?' she countered with fine disdain. Pushing herself up from the desk, she strolled across to the door. 'Anyway, I have work to do. The only reason I came up to see you was because Debbie was fretting herself about you—though why any decent woman should waste two seconds of her time on a sleazeball like you I really don't know.'

Natasha regarded her reflection in the mirror with a critical eye. The rational half of her brain had given up warning her that it wasn't a wise move to have dinner with Hugh Garratt, and had settled for persuading her that her usual cool, 'touch-me-not' image was called for tonight. Unfortunately the other half—the idiot half—wanted to make a serious impact, to have him drooling with desire for her. It was an uneasy compromise.

She had swept her pale blonde hair up into a sleek pleat on the back of her head, a style that was quite severe but emphasised her fine bone structure. The dress was new—she had had it in her wardrobe for some time, but had never been quite sure about wearing it. A silver satin slip-dress with shoestring straps, its slippery fabric shimmered over her willowy body all the way to her ankles—it wasn't the sort of dress you could wear very much underneath. Around her throat she wore a collar made of dozens of strands of tiny seed-pearls, and her feet were slipped into a pair of spike-heeled silver sandals that added several more inches to her height.

She was conscious of a strange, fluttering excitement in the pit of her stomach, and the blue eyes that gazed back at her from the mirror glittered with an electric sparkle that she had seen before—in the eyes of a gambler who had staked all his chips on a single spin of the roulette wheel. It took a few deep breaths to make her feel calm enough to walk out of the apartment and down the stairs to the casino.

The assistant manager was on duty tonight—Lester hadn't been seen since this afternoon. Natasha frowned a little as she remembered their discussion. What reason could he possibly have for being afraid of Hugh? She was half inclined to think he was just being paranoid. And yet…there *was* something. Hugh had promised to tell her tonight.

It was difficult to imagine Hugh Garratt ever having had anything to do with her stepfather, however indirectly. But then what did she really know about him—apart from the fact that he was a damned good poker player? And a pretty good actor too, come to that. But then the two things often went together. Those attributes weren't any kind of reason for her to trust him—quite the reverse, in fact.

She was going to have to be very careful tonight, she warned herself grimly. Particularly if he tried on that expert seduction technique of his. She wasn't sure that she was going to be able to handle it. A little experience would have come in useful there, she mused with a touch of wry humour.

An unfortunate side-effect of conforming to the stereotype of the blonde, blue-eyed babe image was that boys had tended to come on way too strong to her, putting her off 'that sort of thing', as she had called it once in discussion with friends at university, who had laughed themselves stupid at the idea that she had turned twenty without managing to lose her virginity. Twenty-three now, and rising…

The really worrying thing, she was forced to admit, was that with Hugh Garratt she wasn't put off 'that sort of thing' at all. In fact she was really rather tempted to investigate the possibilities. It was just that she was pretty sure that if she let herself get too carried away, her first experience of sex would be followed very rapidly by her first broken heart.

A swift glance at her watch told her that it was nearly eight o'clock as she strolled across the supper lounge, exchanging pleasant greetings with a few of the regular customers. She had been planning to be casually engaged in the gaming room when Hugh arrived, maybe talking to one of the pit bosses, whose job it was to supervise the tables. But as she crossed the foyer the receptionist gestured to her urgently. She glanced around for the assistant manager, but he was busy at the cashier's cage, so she went to see for herself what the problem was.

It proved to be simple enough—one of the guests with a party from one of the big hotels had forgotten to bring his passport, as required by the Gambling Commission's regulations. She stepped into the office to make a phone call to the manager of the hotel, whom she knew well, asking him to fax over a copy of the photocopy they would have taken of the relevant page on the guest's arrival.

She had just put the phone down when she heard Lord Neville's voice approaching the desk. '…got the money,' he was saying seriously. 'It could be dangerous to hang around.'

Her heart gave a sharp thud. Stepping back swiftly, she peeped through the crack in the door to confirm that it was indeed Hugh he was speaking to. Eavesdropping shamelessly, she heard Hugh's quiet response. 'I don't think so. And I don't want to leave the business half finished.'

'And Natasha?'

She heard him laugh softly. 'Ah, yes—the alluring Miss Cole…'

The babble of other guests arriving prevented her from hearing anything else he might have to say. Her mind was racing as she watched the two men sign in, and then move on through the foyer. *What* was this all about? Why did Lord Neville think it could be dangerous? And what 'business' was it that Hugh didn't want to leave half finished?

She wanted some answers—and if Hugh Garratt thought he could schmooze her out of getting them, he had another think coming!

Slipping from her hiding place, she circled round behind the banks of slot machines to appear as if she was coming from the gaming room. Fortunately long practice had given her the ability to conceal her thoughts—and her air of cool composure was perfect as she strolled into the bar a few moments later, giving no clue to the questions that were buzzing in her brain.

Several heads turned as she walked gracefully across the room, and she was gratified by the arrested look in Hugh Garratt's eyes when he saw her. He rose at once to his feet and came towards her, letting his smoky gaze drift down over every inch of her slender body, his slow smile registering an intimate approval that sent a hot little shiver down her spine.

'I'm sorry—am I late?' she queried, please to find that her voice was quite steady.

'Only by a couple of minutes,' he responded easily. 'Would you like a drink here, or shall we just go?'

'Oh, I think I'd prefer to go now—if you'll excuse us, Lord Neville?' she added with a light touch of apology. 'If I hang around, someone's bound to come and drag me into the kitchen to settle an argument with chef, or want me to sign something in the cashier's office.'

'I was hoping you'd say that.' His smile ought to carry a Government Health Warning. 'See you later, Nev.' Hugh nodded briefly to his friend, and, putting a possessive hand on Natasha's arm, he steered her towards the door.

Desmond's was the best restaurant on the island—it was often difficult to get a table, but Natasha had known Desmond since he was slim and had hair, and as soon as he saw her he came bouncing over to welcome them, kissing her on both cheeks. 'Nattie, sweetheart! Long time—ages!—no see! How's business? Hey, I heard all about last night. I bet old Lester's fit to bust!' He roared with delight at the idea. 'He always was a sore loser.'

'He isn't exactly over the moon about it,' Natasha confirmed dryly. 'As a matter of fact, this is the man who beat him. Hugh Garratt—Desmond.' She introduced the two men with polite formality.

Desmond's wide smile beamed even wider. 'Well! Let me shake your hand!' he enthused warmly. 'A man who can take half a million bucks off Lester Jackson is pretty OK in my book. Hey, come on—this calls for the best table. And champagne! It's on the house. Not that you need free champagne,' he added, laughing again at his own joke. 'Half a million bucks! That's some kind of poker game.'

He led them to a table in the corner of the terrace, quite secluded, with a stunning view over the wide bay of St Paul's. The sun had dipped below the horizon, and the sea was darkening to a misty indigo, dotted with the grey-green shadows of a dozen islands, silhouetted against the cobalt-blue sky. A steel band was playing, the soft silver rhythms mingling with the whispering of the evening breeze as it gently stirred the leaves of the palm trees arching gracefully overhead.

'Here we are.' One of the waiters had brought the champagne, and Desmond opened it himself, spilling the foaming liquid into two flute glasses. Then he left them with the menu, and went away to share his ebullient charm among the other diners—a little to Natasha's relief. She had been afraid he would stay chatting all evening. Although maybe that would have been better than being left alone with Hugh Garratt, she reflected, conscious again of that odd little flutter in the pit of her stomach. She wasn't sure that she was going to be able to eat very much.

In the event, Desmond's excellent Creole chef made sure that was no problem. They started with iced crab soup, followed by chicken in mangoes and ginger— cooked so tender that it almost seemed to melt on her tongue. And the dessert of bananas baked in rum, smothered with coconut sorbet, was irresistible.

The light, sparkling champagne was an excellent complement to the rich food, but Natasha sipped it cautiously—she had seen too often the effect of alcohol on people's judgement, and she knew she was going to need all her wits tonight.

'You seem to be quite famous,' she remarked, noting with a touch of amusement the attention their table seemed to be attracting. 'News of your win has got around.'

Hugh laughed, not at all bothered by the open stares.

'So, if you're not a professional gambler, what *do* you do for a living?' she asked him curiously.

'I'm in the building trade.'

'And where did you learn to play poker?'

'I had a crash course from some of the guys on the

building site,' he responded with wry amusement. 'Playing for matchsticks. I tell you, those guys and a packet of
Swan Vesta can make your high-rollers look like a party
of Sunday school teachers.'

Natasha had to laugh too. The conversation flowed easily—sparked by a casual remark of Hugh's, and prompted
by the occasional interested question, she found herself
telling him about the history of the island, particularly the
tales of the cut-throat pirates who had ravaged the Spanish
Main from the shelter of St Paul's Bay below them, about
the birds which lived among the trees that clothed the
steep hillsides around the bay, about the campaign to save
the fragile coral reefs around its shores.

But she knew she couldn't allow herself to relax too
much, in spite of the way the soft, haunting rhythms of
the steel band were drifting out across the calm, quiet
Caribbean waters, dark now beneath a canopy of stars.
She had a purpose in accepting his invitation, and it
wasn't just for the pleasure of watching how the flickering
glow of the candle on the table between them softened
the hard lines of his face, or seeing him smile at her with
those smoky, spellbinding eyes.

But she waited until the waiter had brought their coffee
before raising the subject.

'So…' She stirred a swirl of cream into the rich, dark,
aromatic brew, trying for an air of casual amusement.
'I've had dinner with you—now it's time for you to keep
your part of bargain. What brought you to Spaniard's
Cove?'

He laughed, that lazy, mocking laugh that she had come
to realise hid the machinations of a very sharp mind.
'Let's dance first,' he countered, rising to his feet and
holding out his hand.

She hesitated, struggling to resist the temptation to let

herself be held once again in those strong arms. 'Well…just for a little while,' she conceded cautiously. 'Then we talk.'

'Then we talk.'

CHAPTER FIVE

HUGH was a good dancer. She had known that he would be, Natasha reflected, letting him move her to the easy, lilting rhythms of the steel band. He held her close, but not too close, his hand resting on the curve of her spine, just below the small of her back—low, but not quite low enough for her to object.

They danced for a while, and then a singer came out to join the band, and the beat hotted up. The tiny dance floor was crowded now, bodies swaying sexily to the music. Hugh took her hands, the wicked glint in eyes challenging her to join in. She hesitated, glancing around for a way of escape, but it would have been difficult to get back to their table through that writhing, jiving mass of revellers.

Besides, she didn't want him to think that she *couldn't* dance like that. It was one thing to cultivate the image of a cool, poised Ice Maiden—it was quite another to be thought stiff and awkward.

So she let her spine loosen, let her hips sway, conscious of the way the cool satin of her dress slithered shimmeringly over her supple curves as she moved. She smiled back at him in bold amusement, delighted at the flicker of surprise that crossed his face, the unmistakable appreciation.

Was it just the crush that brought him closer, his thigh brushing briefly, tantalisingly against hers? Her head tipped back as she held his gaze in a bold challenge, her body curving into his, feeling the driving beat of the music pulsing in her blood, echoing rhythms as old as time. An electric excitement was sizzling through her veins. She knew that it was dangerous to stir up the sort of fire she was kindling, but she felt herself safe among the crowd of dancers.

Safe for now, at least, the sensible, rational part of her brain tried to warn her. But later…?

The band kept the energy high until a few people were beginning to wilt, and then, as the moon rose in the dark velvet of the sky, they switched the pace to a slow, tender love song. When Hugh drew her into his arms, she didn't even think of resisting.

They were dancing close, so close that she could feel the strong, steady beating of his heart against hers. His breath was warm against her hair, and she could feel the smooth power of hard muscle in his wide shoulder beneath her hand. It would be so easy to let herself slip into a dreamworld, where fantasies could become reality. All she had to do was close her eyes… And when he tilted up her face to kiss her, her lips parted in helpless invitation.

His mouth was warm and enticing, his sensuous tongue swirling languorously over the delicate inner membranes of her lips, exploring with unhurried ease all the deep, sweet corners within. His hand had slid down the length of her spine, curving her intimately against him as their bodies swayed to the evocative rhythms of the music.

And she was kissing him back, her tongue swirling around his, her body melting into his arms as if she was part of him, cast in one mould, finally complete. She was drifting in a world of dreams, where nothing had any meaning but the magic of this moment. The restaurant, the waiters, all the other dancers around them were forgotten—it could have been just the two of them, moving as if they were making love...

They danced as the moon traced its path slowly across the sky, reflecting a cascade of silver in the shimmering dark waters of the bay. Natasha had no sense of how long they had been dancing—it could have been forever. But at last he let her go. A small sound of protest escaped her lips as she felt the chill of the night air against her bare shoulders without his arms to warm her.

She stared up at him, slightly dazed... And then slowly she began to notice that the music had stopped. The band were packing up their instruments, and the waiters were clearing the last few tables. As she pulled back out of his arms, struggling to call her scattered defences to order, the band's singer gave them a slow and sardonic round of applause.

She felt her cheeks blush a deep, hot scarlet, aware that some of the pins had slipped from her hair and several long strands were falling from the neat twist. With fumbling fingers she tried to tuck them back up, but Hugh stopped her.

'No—leave it loose,' he urged softly. 'It'll be simpler anyway.'

She was forced to concede the point, knowing that whatever she did it was going to end up looking a mess. Pulling out the remaining pins, she let it tumble around her shoulders, raking it through with her fingers in a vain attempt to make it look a little tidier.

Hugh smiled slowly, and nodded. 'Yes—that's much better,' he confirmed, a husky note of appreciation in his voice. 'You look amazingly sexy like that.'

Her blue eyes flashed him a frost warning, but not with much conviction. After dancing with him like that, letting him kiss her like that, she had little chance of regaining the aloof Ice Maiden image she usually cultivated for her defence.

'I think we'd better be leaving,' she remarked tautly. 'They're waiting to close.'

He slanted her a faintly mocking smile, but nodded agreement. 'It's a beautiful night,' he added, glancing up at the stars. 'Shall we walk back to the casino, instead of taking a jitney?'

'All right,' she agreed, struggling to keep her voice steady. 'It'll give us a chance to talk.' Though to herself she was forced to admit that it would also give her a chance to be with him for just a little longer.

It was easy to see the way in the bright moonlight—which was fortunate. The road was Tarmac in places, while in others it was just compacted stones, but both surfaces were inclined to fissures and pot-holes, some of them deep enough to break an ankle. It wound beneath the trees, climbing up over a shoulder of the mountain that sloped lazily down to the sea, separating St Paul's Bay from Spaniard's Cove. The fragrance of frangipani and the shrill chirrup of tree frogs and cicadas filled the warm night air.

They walked for a while in silence, but Natasha was becoming impatient. Slanting an enquiring glance up at him, she prompted, 'So…?'

He smiled down at her a little crookedly. 'OK—I'll tell you.' For a moment he was quiet, and she thought she was going to have to ask him again, but before she could speak he began. 'Last summer, my nephew—my sister's son—decided to spend his long vacation from university with a friend in America. Peter had always been a sensible lad, so Margaret was happy to let him go.'

Natasha nodded, listening intently.

'They spent a while with his friend's parents in New

York, then decided to travel and see something of the country before they went back to England. They ended up in Miami.'

'Oh…' Natasha had a feeling she could guess what was coming.

'They were just a couple of lads—both twenty years old,' Hugh continued bitterly. 'One night they strolled into a club, just for a drink and a game of pool. They got talking to a guy at the bar. I expect he seemed pretty cool to them, talking big, dropping a few names. They were flattered. They had a few drinks with him, played a little pool—won a few dollars, lost a few. Then he suggested they go on somewhere else. They went to another club, where there were cards. They played blackjack, and won a couple of hundred dollars each.'

'So the next night they went back,' Natasha surmised. 'And won again.'

'Exactly. They had a remarkable run of luck.' There was no trace of humour in his voice. 'Four nights in a row they came out winners. So they decided—with a bit of encouragement from their new friend—to try poker. And guess what? They won again.'

'And then…?'

'Then Peter's friend decided to take his winnings and go home. But Peter stayed. Unfortunately his luck changed, and he lost pretty heavily, but this guy persuaded him to stick it out. And, sure enough, for the next couple of nights he was winning again.'

'Convincing him that all he had to do if he hit a losing streak was hold on and his luck would change,' Natasha put in. It was a standard ploy.

Hugh nodded. 'Then finally the guy offered to cut him in on a really big game—persuaded him that he was a natural-born poker player.'

'So how much did he lose?' she enquired, in the jaded tone of one who knew the inevitable outcome.

'Close to a hundred thousand dollars. Which, of course, he didn't have. So they roughed him up a little bit to force him to ring home and ask his family to wire him the money. Naturally I was pretty annoyed with him, but I sent him the money. Unfortunately Peter was too ashamed to come home.' His voice took on a heavier note. 'We had no idea where he was for more than four months. Then we got a phone call. He'd been arrested in New Mexico, trying to hold up a filling station.'

'Oh…'

'He hadn't eaten for three days. He had a piece of piping in his pocket which he tried to pretend was a gun, and he was trying to steal two bars of chocolate and a can of beer.'

'The poor kid,' Natasha sighed, genuinely sympathetic. 'And it was Lester, I suppose, the man they met in Miami?'

He slanted her a questioning glance. 'You don't seem surprised.'

'I'm not,' she admitted, a thread of contempt in her voice. 'It's just the sort of thing I'd expect of him. But you said I was involved,' she added, frowning up at him.

'Not you directly—the casino,' he explained smiling grimly. 'That was something I discovered when I went to Miami to investigate. I met a detective in the local police department who was very helpful. He told me he believes someone—and between us we worked out that it could be Lester—is laundering money for some people who are engaged in some not very nice business activities.'

'Tony,' Natasha breathed. 'Tony de Santo.'

Hugh glanced down at her sharply. 'That name was mentioned.'

'He's a friend of Lester's.' She shuddered, remembering those pawing hands. 'But how does that connect with your friend's son?' she added, puzzled.

'I'm not entirely sure. But I'd guess that if Lester really is laundering money for these guys, he may have occasionally been tempted into taking a little more than his percentage. And he'd have been pretty desperate to find the money to pay them back. Of course, most of the time he'd have been able to make it up out of his poker winnings…'

Natasha shook her head decisively. 'He's not that good. He loses almost as often as he wins.'

'Hence the little sideline in ripping off kids not old enough to know better—so that he can pay Tony back the money he owes him,' Hugh concluded, his voice laced with angry contempt.

Natasha nodded. It certainly seemed a likely explanation, fitting well with what she knew of Lester. And it accounted for a lot of his odd behaviour, too—the bouts of wild extravagance, interspersed with periods of moody anxiety, the lies about his business dealings, his embarrassing sycophancy around Tony de Santo and his cronies.

But that didn't necessarily mean that she could trust Hugh Garratt, she reminded herself cautiously. There were still a lot more things she wanted to ask, but she had to frame her questions with care—she didn't want him to know that she had been listening in on his conversation with Lord Neville.

'You must be very fond of your nephew,' she remarked in what she hoped was a tone of mere natural curiosity.

He nodded. 'His father died when he was just six, so I've had quite a lot to do with him as he's been growing up. He's a good kid—he was going to be an architect before all this happened.'

'Even so,' she persisted, probing cautiously to find any holes in his story, 'it could just as easily have been you who lost half a million dollars. Or was Lord Neville helping you?'

He returned her a look of mock indignation. 'Of course not. Nev's only role was to help me get into the game. But he'd told me about Lester's style of play, so I was able to work out how to beat him. Of course, it helped that I drew such lucky cards on that last game,' he added on light touch of humor. 'It meant I could finish the business in one hand.'

Did she believe him? Natasha mused to herself. It all seemed very plausible. And she was conscious that she *wanted* to believe him—wanted tonight, dancing in his arms, to have been real, not just a part of some elaborate charade.

'So, what happens now?' she enquired, schooling her voice into a tone of casual unconcern. 'You've won back your nephew's money, so I suppose that's it? You'll be going back to England?'

'Not quite.' He was frowning, his hands loosely in the pockets of his elegantly cut trousers. He kicked a stone before replying, sending it bouncing and scudding down the road. 'I promised the guy in Miami I'd try to get him some kind of information to help him nail this de Santo and his associates. And I'd really like to tie Lester into that as well.'

'What sort of information?' she asked, her eyes studying his strong profile, faintly etched in shadow by the moonlight.

'Evidence of any fraudulent money transactions. Papers—letters, perhaps. Bank records. Do you have any idea where he might keep stuff like that? Could it be in the safe at the casino?'

She shook her head, frowning. 'No—at least, I've never seen anything like that in there. But there's another safe upstairs, in our apartment—he uses that quite a lot. But I don't know the combination—Lester keeps that to himself.'

They had reached the last bend in the road and Spaniard's Cove was below them, the casino, amid its lush gardens, floodlit against the dark sweep of the sea. Hugh paused, staring down at it, his face grim. 'I need to get into that safe,' he grated abruptly. He turned to her, brushing his hand back through his hair. 'I really shouldn't be asking you to help me...'

Natasha searched his eyes, trying hard to weigh up the truth of what he had been telling her. It certainly made a grim kind of sense... But all she could think about was how easy it would be to drown in those sea-grey depths... *Careful*, she warned herself sharply. He had already proved himself more than capable of a weaving complex web of deception. Could she really trust him any more than she could trust Lester?

It was probably safest not to trust either of them. But that begged the question of whether she should help him find the information he claimed he was looking for. She frowned, turning it over in her mind, trying to weigh up all the information she had, trying not to let herself be influenced by that powerful tug of physical attraction—though it was extremely difficult to ignore.

'All right,' she conceded at last. 'I could let you into the apartment. But how will you get the safe open?'

He smiled crookedly, reaching for her and slipping his arms around her waist, drawing her close against him. 'Leave that to me.' He bent his head, resting his forehead against hers. 'But be careful,' he warned seriously. 'It

could be…difficult for you if Lester found out you were
involved.'

She laughed his reservations aside. 'Don't worry—I can
deal with Lester,' she assured him, airily dismissive. 'I'm
the goose that lays his golden eggs.'

He laughed with her, genuine amusement warming the
hard lines of his face. 'A goose? Oh, no—a swan,' he
insisted, his mouth coming down to claim hers once more.
'A beautiful, beautiful swan.'

The brush of his lips sent an electric charge sizzling
right through her veins, heating her blood. His hand slid
down the length of her spine, curving her intimately
against him. She knew that she only had to pull away and
he would let her go at once. But somehow her will seemed
to have been taken over by a stronger force, a force as
old as time itself.

As he sensed her surrender his kiss became deeper and
more demanding, probing ruthlessly into all the sweetest
corners of her mouth, exploring with a sensuality that ignited all her responses. Her grandmother had warned her
never to let a gambler reach her heart—but Hugh Garratt
wasn't a gambler…

But that didn't mean she could trust him, she reminded
herself sharply. There was far too much at stake—she
couldn't afford to let her judgement be swayed by a few
expert kisses.

Struggling against the weakness inside her, she turned
her head aside and eased herself out of his arms, glad of
the darkness to hide the betraying flush in her cheeks.
'I…think we'd better just concentrate on the task in hand,'
she managed, her voice only a little unsteady. 'You'd better come round to the back door—someone might see you
if you come through the casino.'

He nodded. 'It might be better to wait until after

Lester's gone to bed. We don't want to take the risk of him walking in on us.'

'That won't be for another couple of hours yet,' she warned him. 'And we'd better give him another hour to fall asleep.'

'OK. I'll be waiting.' He half let her go, but held onto her hand, squeezing it meaningfully. 'And be careful.'

'Don't worry,' she reiterated lightly. 'I'm not afraid of Lester.'

Will the real Hugh Garratt please stand up? Natasha regarded her own reflection in the mirror, her soft mouth quirked into a crooked smile. Who was he? So far she had seen him play the amiable fool, the hard-eyed gambler, the concerned uncle... And, of course, the expert seducer. But which of those roles was real, and which a lie?

With a flick of her foot she kicked off her sandals, perching them neatly side by side on the shoe-rack in the bottom of her wardrobe, and then slithered out of her dress. All she was wearing beneath it was a tiny lace G-string, shimmering white against her honey tanned skin.

For a moment she paused, studying the image reflected back to her. She had always looked after her body, in the sense of keeping it healthy with a sensible diet and lots of swimming. But she had never really given much thought to the way a man would look at it. Now her eyes skimmed over the firm, ripe swell of her breasts, slightly creamier in colour than the gold of the rest of her skin and delicately tipped with rosebud-pink, over the smooth curve of her midriff, her slender hips, her long, slim thighs...

Impatiently she shook her head. Thoughts like that could lead her into dangerous territory. Hugh hadn't repeated his proposal this evening, but it had been haunting her mind. To marry him would be crazy, even if it *was* only a convenient ploy to help her gain control of her inheritance.

'''With my body... And with all my worldly goods...''' she reminded herself sharply. Was that it? There had to be a good deal more than a sizzle of sexual attraction to induce a man like that to suddenly propose marriage to a woman he had only just met. And it didn't take much to work out what it was. All those questions about Spaniard's Cove... It might not have been worth a lot of money twenty—or even ten—years ago, but with the opening of the airport and the influx of tourists it could be a very valuable property indeed.

A small chill feathered down her spine. If she was right, he could be even more dangerous than Lester. At least she knew how to handle her stepfather most of the time. But with Hugh her defences were all too fragile.

So, by far the most sensible thing to do would be to take no more risks. Break her promise to let him into the apartment, leave him standing outside—all night, possibly. That would teach him that a few kisses, a little sweet talk, weren't going to lead her into making a complete fool of herself.

Except... That would make it look as if she was afraid of him, afraid that she couldn't resist his practised seduction. Oh, no, she wasn't going to let him think that. Besides, she reasoned to herself, it just so happened that their interests coincided where Lester was concerned. If he could find out enough to get her stepfather charged with a criminal offence, she could have him removed as her trustee without having to wait another two years.

Her mouth curved into a grim smile. Now that she was wise to him, why not use him? Go ahead with the agreement that they had made—but make it very clear to him that it was purely part of her strategy for dealing with Lester. No more than that. There would be no more kisses—no way.

Carefully she folded the silver dress and laid it across the back of a chair—she wasn't sure if she was ever going to feel like wearing it again. A loose black T-shirt and a pair of jeans came out of her wardrobe, and she brushed her hair back, tying it into a loose tail at the nape of her neck.

And then she sat down to wait, killing the time by reading a book, refusing to let her mind drift into the kind of foolish romantic fantasies in which, if she was honest, she had been letting herself indulge far too often over the past few days.

It was a couple of hours before she heard Lester come to bed—his footsteps were slightly unsteady, and she heard him bump into something, muttering a slurred curse. Good—he was drunk. That meant he would sleep heavily. And he hadn't brought Debbie back with him, either. That had been her greater worry. She knew that the older girl would promise to keep a secret if Natasha asked her to, but she wasn't a very good liar—she would be quite likely to let something slip by mistake.

She gave Lester half an hour, then crept down the passage to listen at his door. He was snoring loudly—it sounded as if a rhinoceros with sinus trouble was sleeping in there. But even so she was careful to make little sound as she tiptoed from the apartment and down the back stairs.

The kitchens were empty, the stainless steel units gleaming coldly beneath rows of damp teatowels drying on the wooden racks hung from the ceiling. Just a few plates of sandwiches and kebabs had been left on a side-table, in case any late gamblers felt in need of a snack. She took the key from the chef's office and opened the back door, peering out into the darkness and calling softly, 'Hugh?'

A shadow detached itself from the deeper shadows beneath the trees and slipped through the open door. 'No trouble?' he whispered.

'No.' A small frisson of excitement shivered down her spine as he brushed past her—but she refused to acknowledge that it was due to anything more than the clandestine nature of their activities. 'He's drunk, fast asleep and snoring loud enough for them to hear him in Miami.'

He laughed, and slid an arm around her waist to draw her close against him, sure of her response. But as he bent his head towards her she turned her face away.

'We have to be quick,' she reminded him stiffly, pulling back from him. 'This way.'

She was aware of the questioning lift of his eyebrow, but ignored it, locking the door behind them and slipping the key into her pocket, and then, with her head held very erect, she led the way through the empty kitchens. Reaching the far door, she opened it just a crack to check the hall—and drew back quickly at the sound of someone approaching. With a swift movement of her hand she gestured to Hugh to step behind the door, and pulled it wide open just as one of the bar staff reached for the handle from other side.

'Oh…!' he gasped, startled. 'Miss Natasha. I'm sorry— I didn't know you were there.'

'Good evening, John. I just popped down to get a drink.' She smiled, perhaps a little too brightly. 'Some of the customers are asking for late snacks?'

'Yes.' He moved over to pick them up—giving her an

excellent excuse to hold the door wide open for him, neatly concealing Hugh behind it. 'Thank you.'

'OK.' She followed him out into the hall, and dallied until he had disappeared around the corner. Then she stepped back and pushed the kitchen door open again. 'All clear,' she whispered tautly. 'Quick, up the stairs.'

He followed her up the two steep flights, surprisingly swift and silent on his feet for such a big man. A professional cat-burglar couldn't have made less sound, she reflected with a touch of dry humour. Reaching the top landing, she paused, her hand on the door of the apartment.

'There's just one thing I want to get clear,' she insisted firmly. 'You're not planning to actually remove anything from the safe, right?'

He shook his head. 'No. For one thing I don't want to alert him until I've got something like proof—and for another I don't want to remove any of the evidence. If there's anything that could be interesting, I'll just take a note of it.' He smiled down at her, that dangerous smile that had come so close to undermining all her defences. 'Not having second thoughts, are you?' he taunted softly.

'Of course not,' she insisted, ice-cool. 'This happens to be very convenient for me. If there's a chance you can remove Lester, I'm happy to assist you in any way I can.'

He laughed, low and husky, mocking her formality, and caught her against him to brush his lips fleetingly over hers before she had time to turn away. 'Then just trust me,' he murmured, a spark kindling in his eyes that reminded her how dangerous it could be to let herself gaze too long into their smoky grey depths, how quickly he could spin those beguiling spells that could make her forget all the reasons why she had to keep this strictly impersonal.

Swiftly lowering her lashes, she turned to open the door. 'I'll…go and make sure Lester's still asleep.'

The snoring seemed undisturbed. Natasha stood for a moment outside his door, listening—in truth, she'd needed a brief respite to re-gather the tattered threads of her composure. It wasn't enough to tell herself that Hugh Garratt was a deceitful, conniving rat—when she was close to him, all sorts of strange things happened to her senses.

But once this business was over with tonight, he would be gone—far, far away, back to England. She would never see him again… Which was exactly what she wanted. Drawing in a long, deep breath, and gathering up her customary air of cool composure, she returned to the door, her face an unsmiling mask in the darkness as she let Hugh in.

'OK—this way,' she whispered, beckoning in the darkness to lead him into the sitting room and across to the bookshelf which concealed the safe. 'Here it is.' She freed the hidden catch of the bookshelf and swung it aside. 'How will you open it?'

'The same way I beat him at poker.' He took a thin pencil-torch from his pocket and shone it at the safe—she noticed that he had pulled out a pair of thin latex gloves, the kind that surgeons wore. 'By out-guessing him.' He crouched down beside the safe, carefully examining the locking mechanism. 'What's Lester's date of birth?'

She looked at him in blank surprise. 'The tenth of June.'

He nodded, flexing his fingers again, and began turning the combination wheel. 'One, zero, six…'

Intrigued, she crouched beside him to watch.

'What year?' he asked.

She told him, guessing at once what he was trying to

do, and held her breath as he turned the handle. Nothing happened.

'OK, let's try the telephone number,' he suggested patiently. He tried the first five numbers, then the last five, but neither of those worked. 'What about the date he married your mother?' he asked.

Her soft mouth twisted into a crooked smile. 'I very much doubt if he'd remember that. It was the twenty-first of September.'

'It's worth a try. Two, one, nine…' He frowned, shaking his head. 'No, that's not it. Let's think…'

In the grip of the moment, Natasha had forgotten everything else, offering suggestions and watching eagerly, waiting for the magical combination that would turn the handle. They tried about a dozen different series of numbers that might have sufficient significance for Lester for him to have chosen them, but none of them were the right ones.

'Damn,' Hugh muttered quietly to himself. He sat back on his haunches, regarding the safe with a pensive expression. 'Of course, the theory's not going to work every time,' he conceded. 'But I would have had Lester down as the predictable sort.'

Natasha was inclined to agree. There must be something they had overlooked, something glaringly simple… 'Wait!' A sudden idea struck her. 'Try six, one, zero.'

'What's that?

'His birthday with the day and the month swapped round, the way the Americans write it,' she explained eagerly. 'Go on, try it.'

His eyes flicked her a glance of amused appreciation, and he began to spin the wheels. 'Ah…! I think…'

He tried the handle, and she watched in delighted amazement as the door swung easily open. 'My goodness,' she breathed. 'How could he be so stupid as to use such an obvious number?'

'Just be thankful that he is,' Hugh responded with a touch of dry humour. 'Now, let's see whether it was worth the effort.'

Her reservations forgotten, she knelt beside him, peering into the safe. To her disappointment, apart from the papers she had seen earlier when Lester had been going through them, it was almost empty. Hugh took the papers out carefully and laid them on the floor, and began to look at each one in turn.

'Bills, receipts, tax returns... It all looks like pretty routine stuff. That's about it—apart from this.' Lester's large leather briefcase was on the upper shelf. Hugh lifted it out carefully, and opened it—it was empty, and not even locked. 'Nothing. Although—it does seem a little odd to keep a briefcase in a safe,' he mused, frowning.

'It's the one he always takes when he goes to Miami,' Natasha supplied.

'Hmm...' Hugh's attention was intent on the briefcase. He picked it up and looked at it sideways on, and then put it down again, feeling carefully around the inside base. 'Is there anything about it that looks a little odd to you?' he queried.

'Well, not really, but...'

'Ah...!' He moved his hand—and lifted the base of the briefcase. 'Now, why would he be taking a briefcase with a false bottom to Miami?' he pondered aloud.

'Smuggling?' Natasha suggested, frowning.

'Could be... But what? Not drugs—far too risky.' He reached into the back of the safe, and pulled out a small square of dark blue velvet.

'It looks like the sort of stuff they wrap loose diamonds in,' she mused, taking it from him and turning it over in her fingers. 'You think that's how he's laundering the money for Tony? Buying diamonds?'

'Could be,' Hugh responded grimly. 'They're the ideal investment for anyone who doesn't want too many questions asked. Highly negotiable, highly transportable, and virtually untraceable. Unfortunately, interesting though it is, it doesn't constitute evidence.' He sat back on his haunches, regarding their haul with a frown of frustration. 'What we need is something that would tie him in directly to these guys in Miami. Records of financial transactions, a notebook...'

'There doesn't seem to be anything like that in here,' she mused, peering into the empty safe. 'That's the lot.'

Hugh nodded. 'I think we've found everything we're going to find. We might as well put this stuff back. Careful,' he added urgently as she scooped up a handful of papers. 'Make sure you put it all back exactly as it was before. We don't want him to know that it's been disturbed.'

'I doubt he'll even notice,' she assured him with a trace of acid humour.

Hugh shook his head, those smoky grey eyes serious. 'Don't underestimate him,' he warned. 'He could be dangerous.'

Natasha could almost have laughed. 'Dangerous? Lester? Don't be silly. He roars loud enough, but he's about as dangerous as the lion in *The Wizard of Oz*. But, if it'll make you feel better, I'll just go and check on him again.'

He nodded. 'Do that.'

She rose to her feet and moved quietly along the passage to Lester's door. The volume had subsided a little, but the snoring was still deep and regular.

Lester, dangerous? Just who was talking? she reminded

herself grimly. Lester might be foolish and greedy, but she knew how to deal with him. It was Hugh Garratt who was the dangerous one. And she couldn't afford to let herself forget that. Not for a second.

CHAPTER SIX

THE sitting room was in total darkness when Natasha crept back to it and opened the door. 'Hugh?' she whispered tensely.

'Here.'

The voice came from very close beside her, and she stepped back quickly, drawing in a ragged breath. 'Right, I…we'd better get out of here. I'll show you the way, and lock the door behind you.'

'OK.'

She couldn't see him, but she was very aware of him—she could hear him breathing, could detect the evocatively male, musky scent of his skin. He was close behind her as she moved cautiously along the short passage, her hand brushing against the wall as a guide until she found the front door and opened it, relieved to escape from the suddenly claustrophobic darkness of the apartment.

'This way,' she whispered, able now to see at least outlines in the glimmer of light seeping up from the far end of the downstairs corridor.

He was behind her on those silent feet as she hurried back down the stairs and through the deserted kitchen. They reached the back door without any alarms, but there she had to pause, fumbling in her pocket for the key. At last she found the lock, pushing open the door and drawing in a deep gulp of the cool, fresh night air.

'So…' She turned to him, her manner formal and businesslike. 'What happens now?'

'I really don't know.' He shrugged those wide shoulders, a wry smile quirking that intriguing mouth. 'I suppose it was pretty much a long shot that I would be able to find out anything that might incriminate Lester. There doesn't seem to be much else I can do.'

Which meant that he would be leaving.

Of course, so far as she was concerned, the sooner the better. And, even more, it pleased her to know that he would have to accept that he had failed to get her into bed.

'Well, then.' She held out her hand, distantly polite. 'I'd appreciate it, of course, if you would let me know if you do manage to turn up anything more.'

He glanced down at her hand, a glint of mocking amusement in his eyes, but he made no attempt to shake it. Instead she suddenly found herself trapped, with his two hands against the wall on each side of her shoulders, his face inches from her own. 'Tell me,' he murmured, his voice beguilingly husky, his breath warm against her cheek. 'Why have you frozen up on me all of a sudden?'

It took a conscious effort to relax her jaw sufficiently to speak. 'Frozen up?'

'You know what I mean.' One finger coiled idly into a loose strand of hair that had escaped from the band that held it in place. 'Are you the same woman I danced with just a couple of hours ago? Or do you have a twin, a *doppelgänger*?'

Natasha felt a surge of anger. He really did believe that no woman could resist him! Struggling to ignore the sizzling charge of electricity that seemed to be arcing across the few centimetres that still lay between them, she forced herself to lift her eyes to meet his. 'You seem to have the wrong impression.' Her voice was laced with cool disdain. 'The only reason I had dinner with you tonight was to find out what purpose you had in coming here.'

'Oh?' He laughed softly. 'And those kisses?'

She shrugged her slim shoulders in a gesture of casual unconcern. 'Oh, please... I was hoping you might turn out to be of some use to me in getting rid of Lester. I won't deny that it was a pleasant evening...'

'Thank you,' he returned with a heavy touch of irony.

'But our business is now at an end.' She injected a note of cool finality into her voice. 'So...good luck with your investigations, and goodnight, Mr Garratt.'

It was her very best performance, but he only laughed, soft and sensual, mocking her bluff. 'You know, I really don't like your hair like that,' he murmured. 'It suits you so much better all tumbled around your shoulders.' He was weaving his spells around her again—she could feel the quivering beat of her own heart, racing much too fast... 'Why don't you let it loose?'

What a damned nerve he had! She had absolutely no intention of taking the band from her hair, no intention of letting him kiss her. As if she would be such a fool... But as she gazed up into those smoky grey eyes some strange, mesmeric force seemed to be taking control of her will. She struggled against it, reminding herself of all the reasons why...

Her hands seemed to lift of their own volition, fumbling with clumsy fingers to disentangle her hair from the band at the nape of her neck—which had the additional effect, she realised with a stab of acute awareness, of lifting her breasts beneath the loose black T-shirt. And when she had changed out of her dress she hadn't bothered to put a bra on...

And he knew. A small shiver of heat ran through her as she felt the brush of her tender nipples against the soft cotton fabric, felt them ripening to hardened peaks, their contours outlined in betraying detail. Her heartbeat was racing so fast she felt too dizzy to stand—she had to lean back against the wall, watching his gaze drift down over the curves of her body, helpless as a chained slave as she waited for him to touch her, to caress her as he had before, to demand her total surrender.

He wanted her. Amid all the game-playing and charades, she was certain of that one thing. He really wanted her—even if it was just to satisfy a fleeting sexual impulse. The simmering anticipation made her mouth feel dry, and she swallowed hard, moistening her lips with the pink tip of her tongue.

He smiled that slow, lazy sensuous smile, hot embers kindling in the depths of his eyes. 'There—that's better,' he approved softly. 'You might be able to fool other people with that Ice Queen act, but you don't fool me. You're all woman.'

She dragged in a ragged breath, which had the effect of drawing even more attention to the inviting swell of her breasts, tipped by those pert, provocative nubs. The light abrasion of her T-shirt was enough to sensitise them, and she knew that her eyes were conveying the message of need that was gnawing inside her.

With the backs of his fingers he stroked one wayward strand of hair from her cheek, circling around the delicate shell of her ear—and then slowly, lazily, let it stray down the slender column of her throat, those grey predatory eyes holding her prisoner as his finger trailed on…down, with unmistakable intent…

Some part of her mind was watching this in angry denial, begging her to knock his hand away, reassert her dignity—but instead, as those long, clever fingers curved around the ripe, aching, swell of her breast, brushing his palm across the taut, tender peak, she let her head tip back against the wall behind her, a soft moan escaping her lips, her lashes fluttering down to shadow her cheeks.

'*All* woman…'

He bent towards her, his teeth grazing down the long, arched column of her throat, his hot, sinuous tongue swirling lazy circles into the sensitive hollow of her collarbone. Some kind of fever was burning in her blood, melting her bones, and as he drew her into his strong arms, his mouth claiming hers in a kiss of sweet intensity, she curved her body against his, quivering with the awareness of his raw male power.

His lips were demanding, parting hers with a masterful ease, kissing her hard and deep, his caressing hand still moulding her breast, crushing it deliciously beneath his palm, the taut peak rawly sensitive.

All rational thought had been driven from her mind— she could only cling to him, with a fierce, aching hunger gnawing at her, a hunger that she knew would only be assuaged when she gave her body up to his hard male possession. She was falling in love with him and there wasn't a thing she could do about it.

His hand had slipped beneath her T-shirt, sliding up to find the warm nakedness of her breast, his thumb brushing across the puckered bud of her nipple, teasing it between his fingers, igniting her responses, and she heard her own breathing, ragged and impeded, as her head tipped back, curving her body invitingly against his. His hard thigh had thrust between hers, moving with a slow, sensual rhythm against her, fuelling the aching hunger that was gnawing at the pit of her stomach.

'God, I want you,' he grated, his voice husky velvet. 'I want to make love to you in every way there is. I want to hold you naked in my arms, to taste every inch of your soft, warm skin, to feel your body moving beneath me…'

She gasped, the image he was painting so vivid that it was as if she could already feel the weight of his body on hers, feel her naked breasts crushed against the hard wall of his chest, feel her thighs part to invite his driving possession...

'But this is not exactly the place I had envisaged making love to you for the first time,' he added on a lilt of wry humour. 'Come with me. We can go back to my beach cottage—the bed there is very wide and very comfortable—and we can enjoy a long, long night of pure, uninterrupted pleasure.'

A night... One night. And then...

Reality sliced like a sword through the warm, dark cloak of sensuality that he had wrapped around her. Dear heaven, what was she *doing*? She had warned herself that he could be unscrupulous enough to use this sizzling sexual attraction between them to twist her judgement, lure her into accepting his crazy proposal of marriage so that he could sting her for a sizeable share of her inheritance. And she was walking right into his trap!

Conjuring all her strength, she pushed herself away from him, a cold lash of scorn in her laughter, springing from the depths of her own bitter humiliation. 'Oh, come on—you don't seriously expect me to go to bed with you?' she taunted. 'A few kisses are one thing, but that's all you get for taking me out to dinner.'

'I see.' Those grey eyes hardened with anger. 'So tell me, Miss Cole, what does it take to persuade you to deliver on those promises you hand out so liberally? Or is that why they call you the Ice Maiden? Don't you ever deliver?'

Her eyes flashed cold fury, and she turned him an aloof shoulder, ready to stalk away. But he grabbed her arm in a vice-like grip, turning her back to face him.

'But you nearly forgot yourself, didn't you?' he challenged mockingly. 'Oh, don't try telling me I was misreading the situation—the way your body responded every time I touched you was spelling out the message loud and clear. If I hadn't stopped just then, you would be lying back across that cold steel table there, naked, those glorious legs wrapped around my back, enjoying the pleasure that men and women have shared since the dawn of time.'

His words were deliberately calculated to both insult and excite her with their image—she couldn't quite prevent her eyes darting a swift glance at the table beside her, wondering about the chill of the hard steel against her bare back, the heat of his gaze on her naked breasts, the ache in her thighs as he stretched them wide apart…

A hot blush sprang to her cheeks, but she shook herself free of him, tilting up her head and regarding him with a look of frosty disdain. 'I don't think so,' she countered coldly. 'Oh, you have a certain expertise, but a lot of men can kiss just as capably. It certainly doesn't mean I sleep with all of them.'

He let that darkened gaze flicker down over her, noting the ripened peaks of her tender nipples still taut beneath her T-shirt, the slender curve of her hips in the close-fitting jeans. 'So—you just like to tease, then?' he queried grimly. 'What is it, some kind of power game you play? Seeing how far you can let a man go before you give him the big freeze?'

Yes—let him believe that, she prayed silently. Let him believe anything, so long as he didn't guess the truth— that her heart was aching to have him take her in his arms again, to let it all be real. Calling on every ounce of willpower she possessed, she met his eyes with cold indifference, her smile as mocking as his had ever been. 'That's something I'm afraid you're never going to find out.' And, pulling open the kitchen door, she held it ajar as she pointedly waited for him to leave. '*Goodnight*, Mr Garratt.'

He hesitated just for a brief moment, as if wondering whether to use brute force to batter down the stone walls of her defences. She felt an odd little flutter in the pit of her stomach, almost excited by the thought of being subdued by the superior strength in that hard male body...

But almost before she had time to be horrified by the drift of her own imagination, she knew that he had rejected the idea. With a wry smile he stepped past her into the night. 'Goodnight, Miss Cole,' he responded on a inflection of sardonic humour. 'Pleasant dreams.'

Pleasant dreams? She'd never had worse. When she did manage to sleep, it was only to return each time to the same disturbing dream. She was running through a thick, grey mist, desperately trying to catch at something that was slipping away from her, stumbling and crying out helplessly as she fell further and further behind. Three times she woke to find her pillow wet with tears.

A bad night's sleep, and a morning spent dealing with a spot-check by two agents from the Gambling Commission, who wanted to examine all the staff records and all the cheque clearances for the past six months, did little to raise her spirits. After lunch, feeling restless, she decided that a long walk might do her good.

The gardens were lush and exotic—emerald-green lawns dotted with beds of vivid wild orchids and spiky blue-green aloe, shaded by tall, graceful palm trees and waving casuarinas. Without really thinking about which way she was going, she found her footsteps taking the path that led past the beach cottages.

Hugh had been booked into one of them. If he hadn't left yet, maybe she might just casually bump into him as she strolled past... But as she came near to the one he had rented she saw that the door was wide open, and one of the maids was inside with a big laundry basket, vigorously stripping the bed.

She paused in the doorway, her hand on the frame, feeling her heart deflating as she was forced to acknowledge the evidence before her. He had gone.

The maid glanced up from her task, smiling a little uncertainly. 'Afternoon, Miss Natasha,' she greeted her, shyly polite.

'Good afternoon, Sandie.' At least she was able to keep her voice steady. 'Um...what time did Mr Garratt leave?'

'He checked out first thing this morning, miss. Left me a real good tip, too. Did you want to see him, miss?' There was a hint of curiosity in the girl's voice, warning Natasha that she had noticed her own reaction.

'No,' she responded quickly. 'No—it was just... Someone was asking about renting one of the cottages—I'll let them know this one has been vacated. Thank you, Sandie—you're a good worker. You deserved your tip.'

'Thank you, Miss Natasha.'

She managed what she hoped was a cool smile, and carried on along the path, away from the gardens and up through the trees that cloaked the steep volcanic hillside. It wasn't an easy walk—the path was rough and climbed in places almost straight up—and beneath the forest canopy the air was hot and still, loud with the buzz of insects and the chatter of birds.

But she knew that the view was worth it. A brisk twenty minutes brought her out above the tree-line, to a high vantage point where she could see virtually the whole island spread below her like a rich green cloak, set in the shimmering sapphire circle of the Caribbean Sea. From here, Spaniard's Cove looked like a whale-bite out of the verdant coastline, edged by its perfect crescent of sand. Further along, shimmering in the heat haze, she could see the larger bay of St Paul, with its old harbour, now a haven for millionaires' yachts. And away to the north was the new airport…

As she watched, a glint of silver told her that a plane was taking off. She watched it rise at what seemed like an impossible angle, a huge lumbering 747 that really didn't look as if it should be able to fly at all. But it banked smoothly, turning in a sweeping curve, and headed off towards the wide, empty Atlantic ocean.

Maybe it was going to England, she mused wistfully to herself—maybe Hugh was on it. Perched on a jagged outcrop of rock, she watched it go, willing it a safe flight, until the blue of the sky swallowed it up and she couldn't see it any more.

He had gone. Of course she shouldn't let it hurt her. He was an arrogant, sly, devious, underhand…bastard! And she certainly wasn't going to let herself cry, she vowed, brushing the tears impatiently from her cheeks—that would be a stupid thing to do. So she had been falling in love with him. It had only been a little bit—she'd get over it.

Without warning, a shower of warm rain burst from a single small cloud drifting across the high blue sky, setting off a cacophony of shrieks and chirrups from the forest below. The huge drops hissed as they struck the sun-baked rock of the path and were turned instantly to steam. In seconds Natasha was soaked to the skin, but she didn't care—she knew that she would be dry again almost as quickly. Turning up her face to the rain, she let it mingle with the tears she couldn't hold back, crying out the ache in her heart.

It rained for about fifteen minutes, stopping as abruptly

as it had started. A hot, damp silence followed, the only sound the soft rustling of the rainwater as it trickled down through the tree canopy. A silvery mist drifted in each hollow of the steep tree-clad slopes, swiftly evaporating in the golden sunlight that sparkled like a million diamonds on the wet leaves. Across the bay, the bright arc of a rainbow dipped into the sea.

Natasha breathed in deeply the rich, sweet perfume of jasmine and hibiscus drifting up to her on the warm, damp air. The beauty of the scene was a soothing balm to her wounded heart. She sat for a long while, just feeling herself part of the sunshine and the soft breeze that drifted in from the sea. And then at last with a small sigh she rose to her feet, and turned her footsteps back down the hill.

At this time of the afternoon, the casino was nearly always quiet—most people were dozing in the slumberous heat. She saw Lester sitting at the bar, but she walked straight on. She didn't want to talk to him—she wasn't sure that she would be able to keep the secret that she knew of his extracurricular activities.

Instead she decided to go down to the cellar to check the inventory for the stock order—it was usually the job of the bar manager, but he was away on his annual three weeks' holiday. Besides, it was cool in the cellar—she always found it a pleasant retreat.

She didn't hurry over the task. They would need several crates of champagne, she noted—they always needed a good stock of that. And the Chambertin was running a bit low. She moved on to look at the whites. The house wine was a reliable Australian Chardonnay, but they always kept some quality Burgundies for the restaurant.

Intent on counting bottles on one of the lower racks,

she was startled by a sudden noise behind her. 'Lester…! You made me jump,' she protested, straightening quickly.

'I'm so-o sorry,' he drawled with a sneer. He was slightly drunk, she realised with a certain amount of surprise—surely it was a little early, even for him? 'I didn't mean to interrupt you when you're working so hard.'

'I'm just checking the wines,' she responded coolly.

'Huh. That should be an interesting job.' He was swaying slightly on his feet. 'This isn't a wine cellar—it's a damned take-away store. As fast as the bottles come in from the delivery truck, they walk right out of the back door.'

She frowned. 'You're surely not accusing Ricardo of stealing?' she queried sharply. 'He's been with us for more than ten years.'

Lester shrugged. 'All I'm saying is that he's the only other person apart from you and me who has the cellar key. I was looking for that '78 Chambertin last night— there should still be at least three bottles left.'

''As it happens, there are four,' she informed him with grim satisfaction. 'I've just checked them.'

His expression was one of petulant annoyance. 'Where?' he demanded.

'Down at the bottom end.' She led the way to show him, indicating the rack with a gesture of her hand. 'See for yourself.'

'Ah, yes—so there are…' But he didn't really seem interested. 'So, did you enjoy your little date last night, then?' he queried with oily curiosity. 'Did you have a good time?'

Natasha slanted him a cautious glance. She had half expected some kind of inquisition—she would just have to be very careful how much she said. 'Yes, I did, thank you,' she conceded warily.

'Must have been pretty late when you got home,' he went on.

'As a matter of fact I was home well before you were,' she responded. 'I heard you come in.'

'Ah, yes.' He nodded, several times. 'You weren't asleep, then?'

'You woke me up,' she countered—but her heart had given a thump of alarm. Where was this leading?

'Did I? You're sure it wasn't something else keeping you awake?' His voice was edged with sarcasm. 'Or some*one* else?'

'I've...no idea what you're talking about,' she rapped back defensively.

He laughed, hard and mocking. 'Little Miss Goody-Two-Shoes...! You didn't know lover-boy was spotted leaving, did you? Having stayed half the damned night. What's he got that none of the others have had, eh? I always thought it'd take a blowtorch to blast through those frosty knickers of yours.'

She took a step back from that leering face.

'Not that I give a damn who you screw around with, of course. You can have the entire Miami Dolphins football team if you like—including the goddamn coaches.' He pursued her with his insults as she retreated another few paces. 'What I don't want is you thinking you've fallen in love with some sharp-eyed operator with plans to get his hands on this place by marrying you. Oh, no—there's no way I'd ever allow that.'

'If I wanted to get married, you couldn't stop me,' she threw back at him, her voice laced with contempt. 'I don't need your permission. The trust would be wound up and there wouldn't be a thing you could do about it.'

'Only if you marry with my consent,' he persisted, something nasty in his tone making her shiver. Suddenly

Hugh's words came back to her, warning her not to underestimate her stepfather.

'I know the terms of my mother's will,' she snapped, gripping the fraying edges of her confidence. 'You can't withhold your consent without good reason. Besides, the trust winds up in two years anyway, when I'm twenty-five.'

'So it does,' he conceded, a thread of menace in his voice. 'And then what, eh? "Thank you very much, Lester, and goodbye"? Oh, no, I deserve a little bit more than that, after all I've done for this place. Turned it from a little shack into a nice little money-spinner.' His face was reddening, except for the taut whiteness around his mouth. 'I deserve a little bit more than that.'

Natasha took another step back—and realised suddenly that she had retreated into the doorway of small disused storeroom in a corner of the cellar. She glanced around, and with stab of alarm noticed that it had been furnished with an old mattress and some bedding from the linen store.

One look into Lester's eyes confirmed her instant suspicion. She tried to dodge past him, but he was ready for her. Roughly he pushed her back into the dark cell.

'So—I'm going to make sure I get my share. And I'm going to get it now—before you can cheat me out of it.' His voice was coldly mocking. 'I've got the papers right here for you to sign. You're going to sell the place to a good friend of mine. And don't worry—you'll get a fair price. Minus my cut, of course. That is if you sign up without a fuss. Every day you refuse, the price goes down.'

'No way!' she insisted forcefully. 'You can't make me.'

'Oh, yes, I can. I can keep you down here for as long as it takes. With that damned bar manager away, I have the only other key to the cellar. So you can shout all you like—no one's going to hear you. And no one's going to be asking where you've gone, neither, now lover-boy's gone. A fax arrived for you a while ago, from an old schoolfriend, inviting you for a little holiday. You left this afternoon—I drove you to the airport myself.'

Natasha stared at him in blank horror. 'You're crazy,' she breathed. 'You know you'll never get away with it— the minute I get out of here I'll go straight to the police.'

'By which time I'll be safely in some nice warm South American country that doesn't have an extradition treaty,' he retorted smugly. 'And no one's going to investigate Tony too closely—I told you before; he's got connections.'

'Tony de Santo. I might have known he'd be mixed up in this somehow,' Natasha remarked, letting a sardonic note infuse her voice—she wouldn't give him the satisfaction of showing even an ounce of fear. 'It was his money you lost to Hugh the other night, wasn't it? That's what this is all about. You've been doing some kind of business with him, and now you can't pay him back.'

He laughed, chillingly assured. 'So you worked that out? It doesn't make any difference. Tony doesn't mind how he gets his money back—in fact he's been interested in taking this place over for a while. So tomorrow he's coming over to help persuade you to sign the papers.' He shoved her shoulder, pushing her back until she was touching the wall. 'That's something for you to look forward to while you're down here in the dark with no food. And the rats. I reckon by morning you'll be singing a different tune.'

With his last push she stumbled, and sat down hard on the mattress.

'Actually, it's not only the business Tony's interested

in,' he added with an unpleasant leer. 'The last time he was here, he told me he was pretty interested in you. Maybe this time you'd better try being nice to him.'

And with those parting words he slammed the door, and she heard the key turn in the lock with a metallic clunk that chilled her bones.

CHAPTER SEVEN

NATASHA sat on the makeshift bed, hugging her knees, frowning as she tried to make her eyes accustomed to the darkness. Was Lester crazy, or just drunker than she had thought? Did he really believe he could bully her into signing away her inheritance to that oily lounge-lizard Tony de Santo?

Ugh… Just the thought of the man made her flesh crawl. What sort of 'persuasion' would he use? It didn't take much imagination, she reflected with a small shudder, remembering the way he had looked at her, the way his hands had been all over her, until she had trodden deliberately on his foot as a warning to leave her alone.

The trouble was, she acknowledged, feeling suddenly very cold, Lester was quite right—no one would question her absence. They had a transient clientele, drifting through and then moving on to the next stop. No one would even ask about her—and if they did, his plausible explanation would satisfy them. Only Hugh might have had some reason to be suspicious, and he had gone.

A small sound in the far corner of the floor made her draw her feet up closer on the mattress. Lester hadn't needed to remind her about the rats. Usually they stayed out of the way when anyone was around, not liking the light—but she didn't even have a candle. She shivered again, but not from the cold. She could have only been in here for a short time, and already it seemed like hours.

Would he really keep her here until she signed those papers? In spite of everything, she still found it difficult to believe that he would. But then, if he was desperate enough… And she was quite sure that the planning behind her imprisonment wasn't his—it was much too careful. She didn't know much about Tony de Santo and the Miami crowd, but she doubted they were the sort to leave loose ends untied.

That thought led her inevitably to another, even more unpleasant. Uncle Timothy. He would be certain to raise objections to any kind of improper dealings. But he was an old man, not in the best of health. It wouldn't be too difficult for Tony or his henchmen to intimidate him into compliance. If she gave in and signed the papers, he would be their next target. She *had* to hold onto her refusal to sign.

As her eyes grew accustomed to the darkness, she found that there was a bottle of water and a plastic cup beside the mattress. She took a few sips, but sparingly— she didn't know when, or even if, Lester might bring her some more. Impatiently she shook her head, fighting down the rising tide of panic. If she started letting herself think like that she would go crazy. By the time they let her out of here—if they ever did let her out—she would be a gibbering wreck, and no one would even listen to her story.

Closing her eyes, she struggled to find some way to distract herself. *Poems—try to recite some of the poems you learned in school.* "'The curfew tolls the knell of parting day…'" No, not that one. "''Twas brillig, and the slithy toves Did gyre and gimble in the wabe…'" But her mind kept drifting…ending up most often on thoughts of Hugh Garratt.

The memory of the way he had kissed her made her lips feel warm. If only…

But there was no point wishing that things could have

been different, she scolded herself impatiently. He too had been scheming, in his own way, to get his hands on Spaniard's Cove. She could only be grateful that she had managed to convince him that he was wasting his time. By now he would be back in England.

While she was locked in this tiny, cold cellar, with no food, and an uncertain fate awaiting her.

She was just able to see the luminous face of her watch in the darkness—was it really less than half an hour since Lester had locked her in here? She lay down on the bed, gazing up at the darkness that hid the ceiling, trying to paint in her mind's eye the scene from the hilltop as she had seen it this afternoon, with the lush green tree-canopy spread below her all down the steep slope, and beyond it the open blue Caribbean Sea.

Would she ever feel the hot tropical rain on her face again, or smell the sweet fragrance of the frangipani…? Natasha peered at her watch for the millionth time. Almost ten o'clock. She had been in here for nearly six hours, with nothing to eat. Sometimes she had been able to doze a little, only to jerk abruptly awake to a renewed terror of where she was and what was happening. Her flickering hope that Lester would come to his senses and realise that he had to let her out was draining away. And soon—possibly by tomorrow—Tony de Santo would be here…

Suddenly the sound of footsteps outside the door lifted her head. Soft footsteps, hesitant—not Lester, for sure. She rolled off the mattress and hurried over to the door, rapping on it sharply. 'Help…let me out.'

'Shh! Oh, please—be quiet…'

'*Debbie?* is that you?'

'I'm trying to find the keyhole. Ah…' There was a click, the lock turned, and the door was opened carefully.

'Natasha...? Quickly—come out of there.' The tiny blonde had a torch in her hand, but she was shaking so much that its light was bouncing wildly up and down the wall. 'Oh, my goodness, are you all right?'

'I think so,' she breathed a little unsteadily. 'What's happening? Did Lester let you have the key?'

'No—I took it out of his jacket pocket when he wasn't looking. I couldn't believe it when he told me what he'd done. I'm afraid he's gone a little bit crazy.'

'You can say that again,' Natasha concurred with feeling. 'But what about when he finds out you've let me go? He'll kill you!''

Debbie shook her head, though her voice was shaking with agitation. 'He'll have to see that it was the only thing to do—the longer he kept you down here, the worse it would be. But now it can all be as if nothing happened. Because you won't go to the police, will you?' There was a surprising determination in the set of that pretty, heart-shaped face. 'It would only create a lot of unnecessary fuss, and you've never liked fuss. And besides, I'm the only other person who knows about it—and I won't give evidence against Lester.'

Natasha opened her mouth to argue, but realised before she even spoke that it would do no good. She laughed wryly, shaking her head. 'You know, you really are much too good for him, Debs. What on earth do you see in him?'

'I don't know,' Debbie confessed with a sigh. 'I suppose it's just that I'm in love with him.'

Love, Natasha reflected with a trace of bitter humour. Why did it have the power to make a fool of even the most sensible woman? She laughed again. 'Anyway, we'd better get out of here,' she urged, closing the door of the small cellar behind her and taking the torch from Debbie's shaking hand. 'In fact, we'd better get right away from the casino—at least until Lester comes to his senses. There's no telling what he might do.'

Debbie shook her head. 'I'm not going. Lester won't hurt me.'

'That's exactly what I said,' Natasha responded, frowning. 'And look what happened.'

'I know. But it isn't the same. He panicked when he lost all that money—he's had some bad luck with his investments lately. But he was hoping to get himself out of it by buying into some project with one of his friends from Miami. Only now he's got hardly anything left. I offered to lend him some, but he won't accept it.'

'Thank goodness for that!' Natasha exclaimed, horrified. Debbie's startled look made her swallow her response swiftly. The other girl had clearly believed the story Lester had told her, and now was not the moment to try to disabuse her. 'I mean…there's nothing worse than lending someone money to damage your relationship,' she temporised. 'And that would be a shame.'

'Yes…' Debbie agreed, thinking it over. 'I expect that's why he refused. You know, I think he really *does* love me—he just finds it difficult to talk about his feelings. A lot of men are like that.'

'I dare say,' Natasha conceded dryly. 'But we can't risk standing here talking about it.' Quickly she led the way across the cellar and up the stairs to the quiet passage behind the kitchens, and then, taking Debbie's hand, skipped silently up the stairs to the apartment. 'I'm just going to pack a few clothes. I really wish you'd come with me.'

Debbie shook her head. 'I'll be all right, honestly,' she assured her. 'Don't worry.'

'Well, you'd better take the key and put it back in his

jacket before he notices it's missing,' Natasha suggested. 'Maybe he won't even guess it was you who let me out.' Though there was little chance of that, she reflected wryly.

'OK.' Debbie slipped the key into her pocket. 'But where are you going to go?'

'I don't really know,' Natasha conceded wryly. 'I haven't given it much thought yet.'

She could go to a hotel, but then she would be much too easy to find if Lester and his friend Tony came looking for her. Or she could leave the island. But she had no intention of going permanently into hiding. She was going to fight for what was hers. Somehow.

'What about Lord Neville's friend?' Debbie suggested. 'I mean, I know he was the one who won all that money from Lester, but that wasn't anything to do with you. And he certainly seemed to like you. I'm sure he'd help you.'

Natasha shook her head, managing to keep her voice level. 'You mean Hugh Garratt? No good—he's gone. He checked out this morning.'

'Only out of the beach cottage,' Debbie responded innocently. 'Lord Neville told me. He's on that sail-boat—you know that lovely blue-hulled one we watched coming in last weekend? It's moored in the marina over at St Paul's.'

The yacht was tied up against the pontoon at the western end of the quay, inside the main breakwater—sleek, fifty-odd feet of gleaming aluminum hull, sloop-rigged and promising speed. Natasha had watched her a week ago, sweeping before the wind like a bird in flight as she'd winged in towards the island. Though dozens of boats passed the horizon each day, this one had caught the eye—and not just because of the smart air-brushed paint job that graded from pure white at the bow through a dozen shades of aquamarine to the darkest indigo-blue.

The Kestrel—her name was painted on her stern. The security guard on the marina had known Natasha since she was a baby—he'd used to crew for her grandfather—and had let her through without a pass. Although it was gone eleven o'clock, a light still glowed in the saloon cabin. Carefully she stepped down the ladder to the pontoon, and crossed the gangplank onto the teak deck.

She could hear laughter, and it was several moments before there was a response to her polite tap on the cabin door. At last it was opened, by a ginger-haired lad of twenty or so, whose eyes widened at the sight of her. '*G... Guten Tag,*' he greeted her, blushing a little beneath his freckles. 'Can I help you?'

A voice from inside the cabin called out to him in German, and he responded in the same language.

Natasha shook her head. She should have known—Debbie must have made a mistake, misunderstood what Lord Neville had said. 'I'm sorry—I must have the wrong boat,' she apologised, stepping back. 'I was looking for someone called Hugh Garratt.'

'Ah—*ja*, this is the correct boat,' the young man responded in polite English. 'Please, come in.' He held the door wide open for her, glancing with only mild curiosity at the holdall she had slung over her shoulder. 'Skipper, you have a visitor.'

Natasha peered cautiously past him to see an elegantly fitted cabin lined in teak, with a smoothly curved oval table and cream-coloured hide upholstery. There were three other young men of a similar age to the one who had opened the door for her, all gazing at her with undisguised interest.

Hugh had his back to her, but he had half turned to

glance over his shoulder. As soon as he saw her he rose to his feet. 'Natasha…!' For one fleeting moment she could almost have believed there was genuine warmth in his voice. But then she saw the sardonic glint in those shark-grey eyes. 'Well, to what do I owe this pleasure?' he enquired, one dark eyebrow arched in quizzical amusement as he too noticed the holdall. 'Isn't it a little late for a social call?'

Her blue eyes flashed coldly—but then she hadn't expected this to be easy. 'I…er…need to talk to you,' she responded with stiff dignity. 'I'm sorry, I…didn't mean to interrupt if you're busy.'

'That's OK—the boys were just going off to bed. Weren't you, boys?' he added in a tone of good-natured insistence.

'Ah, yes!' A long-haired lad with a French accent chuckled as he rose to his feet. 'All off to our lovely comfortable pipe-cots. We shall sleep so soundly.' He slanted Natasha a glance of appreciation as he stepped past her through a doorway that led for'ard, grinning broadly. 'Don't stay up too late, Skipper.'

Each of them passed her with the same light-hearted banter, the last one closing the door and leaving them alone in the cabin. Hugh arched one dark eyebrow as he invited her to take a place at the table, which was still littered with the debris of a leisurely evening meal. 'Coffee?' he asked.

'Thank you.'

Deftly gathering up the mess on the table, he took it through to the galley, loading it into a dishwasher. A very well-appointed yacht, this, Natasha reflected in passing—the sort that cost a small fortune to lease even for a few weeks.

Hugh returned with a coffee pot and two mugs, which

he put down on the table, and then slid into the seat opposite her. 'So…?' he prompted, slanting her a questioning look as he poured the coffee.

She hesitated, for the first time pausing to wonder if it had been a good idea to come here. She had been in such an agitated state when Debbie had let her out of the cellar that when she had told her that Hugh hadn't yet left the island it had been…almost an instinctive reaction. She had just stuffed a few essentials into the first bag she could find, slipped out of the casino by the back way and hurried down to the beach road, where she had been lucky enough to flag down a passing jitney to drive her into St Paul's.

But now she was remembering all the reasons why she couldn't trust Hugh Garratt; 'deceitful' and 'manipulative' were among the first words which sprang to mind. Could she risk putting herself in the hands of someone who, for all she knew, could be even more of a criminal than Lester?

On the other hand, what choice did she have? With Tony de Santo arriving tomorrow—none. And at least she was sure that if Hugh agreed to protect her she would be safe. The only thing she would have to worry about was the price he might set on that protection.

She couldn't remember exactly what she had said to him last night, but she knew it had been pretty cutting— something about only having had dinner with him because she'd hoped that he might be of some use to her. And she had implied that his kisses weren't that special. She knew already that he was the kind to take a very calculated kind of revenge. What if he should decide to take advantage of her desperation to make her pay for her words, to demand what she had refused him then?

A small shiver of heat feathered down her spine. But better to be forced to go to bed with Hugh Garratt than to face what Tony de Santo might have in store for her, she reflected tautly.

She drew in a long breath, her mind made up. 'Lester turned nasty,' she informed him bluntly. 'He locked me in the cellar.'

'He *what*...?' To Natasha's satisfaction, she had managed to shock him. He put down the coffee jug, the flare of anger in his eyes boding ill for her villainous stepfather.

'Debbie let me out,' she explained 'Apparently you were spotted leaving last night, and he assumed...' She felt a faint blush of pink rise to her cheeks. 'He assumed that we'd...been to bed together.'

'So he locked you in the cellar?' He conceded a harsh laugh. 'Well, I certainly never had him pegged as a Victorian parent!'

She shook her head. 'It wasn't that...exactly. It was that... Well, I really don't invite...people up to the apartment very often. I'm afraid he rather let his suspicions run away with him. He imagined that I...that you were some kind of smooth operator who was planning to seduce me into falling in love with you, and...marrying you so that you could get your hands on the casino.'

A glint of sardonic amusement lit those shark-grey eyes. 'Really? He does underestimate you!'

She wasn't sure that he'd intended that remark as a compliment, so she decided to ignore it. 'Anyway, you were right—about the money he lost to you belonging to Tony de Santo,' she continued. 'So he'd come up with this wild scheme to force me to sign over the whole place to Tony—for a "fair price", as he put it.'

'I see.' He sat back against the banquette seat, sipping his coffee, his face grim. 'And if you hadn't agreed...?'

'The price would go down for every day I refused. He was threatening to keep me down in the cellar, without any food, until I signed.' She offered him a wry smile. 'I should have listened when you warned me he could be dangerous.'

Hugh laughed on a note of dry humour. 'So, what are you going to do now?' he queried. 'Go to the police?'

Natasha shook her head. 'I can't. Debbie's my only witness—and she won't testify against him. I just hope she'll be OK when he finds out I've gone,' she added, frowning. 'I tried to persuade her to come with me, but she wouldn't. She said he wouldn't hurt her...'

'She's probably right,' Hugh assured her. 'He'd have no reason to—it's you that's in his way.'

'I suppose so,' she conceded. 'Anyway, I'm afraid that the police wouldn't really be able to do very much—on a small island like this, they really don't have the man-power.' She was distracted by the prompting of her empty stomach. 'Excuse me, do you have anything to eat?' she pleaded a little desperately. 'It was four o'clock when he locked me in there, and I've had nothing since lunchtime.'

He laughed at that. 'Of course. What would you like?'

'Anything, so long as it's quick.'

'I can knock up a mean omelette.'

'Oh, that sounds wonderful!' she declared, her mouth already watering.

He nodded, his eyes smiling. 'Coming right up, ma'am!'

Natasha watched, fascinated as he pottered around the neat galley. It seemed somehow incongruous to see such a big, raw-muscled man messing around in such a small kitchen, but he worked with a surprising finesse as he deftly cracked a couple of eggs into a mixing bowl and whipped them up with a light hand, and then tipped them neatly into a pan, flipping the edges with a spatula like the most expert chef.

'What would you like in it?' he queried over his shoulder. 'I can grate some cheese for you, or chop some mushrooms.'

'Oh…um…cheese will be fine, thank you.'

Her mouth had gone strangely dry. Watching him there, those wide shoulders filling out a faded blue T-shirt that looked ready to be torn up for dusters, his legs bare beneath a pair of long, loose cotton shorts… Whoever had said men's legs were ugly? she mused abstractedly. His were sun-bronzed and muscular, lightly scattered with rough male hair.

Oh, dammit! She had spent the past twenty-four hours trying to convince herself that she wasn't falling in love with him, but the moment she had seen him again she had known that she'd been lying to herself. That gnawing ache had started up again, chewing her up inside—all she wanted was to feel those strong arms around her again, feel the warmth of his mouth on hers…

But she couldn't afford to let herself slip into that kind of fantasy, she chided herself forcefully. She had to keep all her wits about her.

'So, I take it Lester hasn't guessed that we opened his safe?' Hugh enquired, busy with grating the cheese.

'Um… no.' It was a struggle to keep her voice steady. 'Did you manage to find out anything more?'

He shook his head grimly. 'I'm afraid not—at least, not yet. But it seems to me that if he's been using the casino as a front to launder for these guys in Miami, he must have been using a chain of bank accounts—probably all the way across the Caribbean. I've a friend who may be able to help locate some of them.' He put the cheese back in the fridge, closing the door with his knee. 'Unfortunately some countries have pretty strict rules on banking secrecy that might make it difficult to track the whole thing from him to de Santo.'

Natasha nodded. It was difficult, sitting here listening to him, to hold onto her suspicions about him. She so much *wanted* to believe he was telling the truth. But that was her heart speaking—and the heart was hardly an organ of good judgement. Just look at poor Debbie!

'So—there you are!' With a flourish Hugh tipped the omelette out onto a plate and brought it over to the table. 'More coffee?'

'Um... Yes, please,' she mumbled, hoping he would believe it was merely the sight of that omelette, light and fluffy and oozing a mouthwateringly tempting aroma, that had reduced her temporarily to a state of limp incoherence. The last thing she needed at the moment was for him to guess the kind of things that had been going through her mind.

He slid again into the seat opposite her and refilled her coffee cup for her. She nodded her thanks between mouthfuls of melting cheese, watching him covertly from beneath her lashes. What was going through *his* mind? He only ever let you read what he wanted you to read—and sometimes you couldn't be sure if it was a bluff or a double bluff, she reminded herself, recalling the clever tactics he had employed at the poker table.

And, of course, that proposal of marriage. She still hadn't worked out what he had intended. Merely a marriage of convenience? But the way he had kissed her, the way he had so nearly made love to her, belied that idea. Or had it been something even more cold-blooded? A real marriage in every sense except for one small detail.

Commitment. Not 'till death us do part' but 'till the trust is wound up, and then perhaps a little longer if we're both still enjoying the sex'.

Unless... Just how close to the edge could she go? Could she enter into a marriage of convenience with him, but on *her* terms? It was perhaps the most risky strategy of all. And if she was going to succeed, she was going to have to be careful she didn't make the mistake of letting herself succumb to the spell of those smoke-grey eyes, she reminded herself sternly. She was going to have to be very careful indeed...

But it wasn't easy, not with him sitting there so close to her, watching her with that disconcertingly level gaze. And looking out of the window didn't help; for one thing she could still see him, reflected against the darkness— and for another it was just too damned romantic out there, with the silver moon shimmering on the inky water.

'This is a nice boat,' she remarked, struggling to find a topic of conversation. 'She looks like a racer, from the shape of the hull.'

'She is,' he confirmed, lounging back against the banquette seat with his coffee mug in his hand. 'She's in cruising fit at the moment, but she's designed to do both. All this stuff strips out in a weekend.' He laughed, glancing around the elegant cabin. 'You should have seen her in May, when we were finishing the Whitbread Challenge.'

'You did the Round the World Race?' she queried in some surprise.

He nodded. 'A couple of the boys who are still on the crew came with me. We did pretty well in the early stages—we even picked up a couple of trophies for the fastest twenty-four-hour runs. But then we had a problem with a damaged mast on leg five into Brazil, and we never really got back into contention. Never mind.' He shrugged those wide shoulders in a gesture of easy unconcern. 'There'll be a next time.'

'They...the boys called you Skipper?'

'That's right.'

'You captained the boat for the race?'

'Uh-huh.'

He said it as if it was nothing much, but Natasha knew a lot of people in the yachting set, and she knew that the 32,000 mile race was about as tough as it got. One hundred and thirty-odd days of the most extreme conditions on the planet... Playing poker for half a million dollars must have seemed like child's play by comparison.

She finished her omelette, scraping up the last crumbs with her fork, and slid the plate away. Replete, she found herself growing sleepy—she had had little sleep last night, and today had been a long and exceedingly unpleasant day. The gentle movement of the boat on her moorings and the soft splish-splash of water against the hull were soothing and peaceful...

'You look as if you could do with going to bed,' Hugh remarked.

She shook her head, suppressing a yawn. 'I...have to get things sorted out first,' she insisted. 'I have to decide what I'm going to do.' Her head felt as if it was stuffed with cotton wool, but she had to focus—she had to try and think sensibly...

'How long do you think it will be before Lester realises you've gone?' he asked her.

She pulled a wry face. 'Not long. He might already have found out.'

'And then...?'

'I don't know. As Debbie said, he might come to his senses once he sobers up, and realise it would be better not to try anything else.'

'I doubt that,' Hugh mused grimly. 'There's a heck of a lot of money involved, and if he owes money to some kind of organised crime set-up he'll be pretty desperate. I warned you before not to underestimate him.'

She flashed him a look of frosty indignation. 'So I suppose you're going to say I told you so?'

He laughed, holding up his hand as if to deflect her anger. 'No. But it seems to me that the sooner you can get full control of your own property the better.'

'I know.' From across the table she watched him. Was he going to repeat his proposal, or would she have to somehow hint him into it? 'I don't really know much about the legal technicalities, but I assume that in order to remove him as my trustee I'd have to prove he was mismanaging things in some way, and I don't know if I could find any evidence of that,' she mused, a wry note in her voice. 'Besides, it would probably take a long-drawn-out court case, which would cost the earth. And heaven only knows what sort of trouble he could cause me in the meantime.'

'Unless...' The spark of mocking amusement in those shark-grey eyes gave her no information about whether he had guessed what she was leading up to.

She arched one finely-drawn eyebrow, trying to give as little away. 'Unless...?'

'Unless we get married.'

Natasha drew in a long, deep, steadying breath. He had said what she wanted him to say—but though she had planned it this way, suddenly her heart was in a flutter of confusion. Did she say yes? It was like playing poker—trying to read your opponent, trying to stay all the time one step ahead. 'I suppose it *is* one possible solution,' she conceded, her voice carefully controlled.

'It's the only one I can think of, if you want to wind up the trust quickly.'

She nodded slowly. 'That's true. But…I wouldn't want to put you to any inconvenience…'

A strangely enigmatic smile curved that firmly carved mouth. 'It's no particular inconvenience,' he responded lazily. 'Just a matter of a few legal formalities. And I shall enjoy putting another spoke in Lester's wheel. Of course, if you're worried about the financial side, we can draw up a prenuptial agreement to say that neither of us will make a claim on the other when the marriage ends.'

From across the table, Natasha slanted him a sharp glance. What was that manoeuvre about? He was still lounging back against the banquette, one long leg sprawled along it, his coffee still in his hand. He looked…totally relaxed. If she hadn't known how little that surface appearance could be trusted… 'Well…if you're sure…' she murmured demurely.

She was conscious of a faint blush of pink spreading up over her cheeks. To be married to him…even if it wasn't for real…

'OK.' The word was imbued only with the satisfaction of having one minor issue resolved. 'We might as well do it right away. The quicker we're married, the less chance Lester will have of causing trouble.'

'Yes, I…suppose so.' Her heart was beating much too fast. 'But…won't it take some time to make all the arrangements…?' she protested weakly.

He shrugged in lazy dismissal. 'It shouldn't be too much of a problem. Lots of people come to the Caribbean islands to get married these days—the wedding and the honeymoon all in one. I know a couple who did it last year—it was a second marriage for both of them, and they didn't want all the usual fuss. They told me a lot of the big hotels even have staff who can take care of everything for you.'

'Well, yes,' she admitted. 'It is quite a popular idea.' So, it was agreed. She was going to marry him. There seemed to be something deeply fascinating about the coffee mug she held in her hands—she studied it intently, conscious that the blush in her cheeks was deepening to scarlet. 'There…is just one other thing,' she added, struggling to keep her voice from drying up on her. 'This… prenuptial agreement. If you don't mind, I think we should include a clause that says we won't… I mean…'

He arched one dark eyebrow in polite enquiry.

'I want a clause that says we won't sleep together,' she stated, her blue eyes flashing him a blunt challenge.

There was just the faintest suggestion of mocking amusement behind the bland innocence of his smile. 'That seems reasonable enough,' he agreed pleasantly. 'So, now that that's settled, perhaps we could both do with some sleep. You'd better have my cabin tonight.' He put down his coffee mug and rose easily to his feet. 'I'll show you where everything is.'

'Your cabin?' she repeated blankly—she hadn't expected it to be so easy. 'But…where will you sleep?'

'There's a spare pipe-cot in the fore-peak.'

'A pipe-cot? That…doesn't sound very comfortable.'

He laughed, mocking that contrary part of her that was foolishly disappointed that he had accepted her stipulation without a single word of argument. 'I'm used to it.'

CHAPTER EIGHT

'So, Hugh and Natasha, I now pronounce you husband and wife. Be happy!'

Natasha blinked at the beaming face of island's assistant registrar, still slightly dazed by the events of the past twenty-four hours. She had just got married to a man she had met for the first time just a few days ago, a man she knew almost nothing about—a man she had insisted sign a written agreement that he wouldn't sleep with her.

She was wearing a dress hired from the hotel in the grounds of which the wedding was being held—a simple, off-the-shoulder number in white satin—and her hair had been twisted up into a cascade of shining curls, laced with tiny white flowers, by the hotel's hairdresser. Uncle Timothy had given her away, and Debbie, looking like a scared rabbit, was her bridesmaid.

From beneath her lashes she slanted a cautious glance up at the man by her side. He was wearing the same well-cut white dinner jacket he had worn to the casino, with a red silk bow tie and a flamboyant red orchid in his buttonhole. She would have had to be blind not to notice the envious glances that had been coming her way since they had arrived for the brief civil ceremony, tagged on after three others being held that afternoon beneath this flower-decked pergola close to the warm, whispering Caribbean Sea.

She really didn't know how he had managed to arrange it all so quickly—clearly her new husband was a man who was used to getting things done, she mused reflectively.

But then skippering a boat on the Round the World Whitbread Challenge demanded a certain degree of authority. As in 'do it' and it was done. Instantly.

And so she was married to him...

An odd little frisson of heat ran through her, but she suppressed it quickly. She mustn't let herself get lost in fantasies—this wasn't a real marriage. That piece of paper they had both signed this morning, e-mailed by some lawyer in England, spelled that out. They would stay married for just as long as it took to wind up the trust and put the estate into her name, and then he would be gone. And, in due course, the marriage would be quietly annulled.

'Go on, Skipper—kiss the bride!' urged Franco, one of the boys from the crew. They were all there, their concession to the occasion being dinner jackets borrowed from the hotel, worn over shorts and T-shirts—their *best* T-shirts, they had solemnly assured her—with more exotic wild orchids in their buttonholes and wide grins on their faces. They were thoroughly enjoying watching their skipper get married.

Lord Neville, who had been roped into the office of best man, stared hard at them. Even he didn't know the truth of this rushed marriage—at Hugh's suggestion they had told no one. That way there was less chance of Lester finding out that it was simply a marriage of convenience and using that to prevent the winding up of the trust.

Hugh smiled down at her, that lazy, mocking smile that always made her heart flip over. 'Come on—we have to make this look real,' he reminded her softly. 'We don't want anyone guessing anything we don't want them to know.'

As the boys cheered, he put his hands around her waist and drew her against him, bending his head to claim her mouth in a long, deep kiss that must have satisfied even the most suspicious of spies that this was a marriage of two people passionately, head-over-heels in love with each other. Natasha felt herself melting inside. It was so hard to remember, when he kissed her like that, that it was all just an act...

'Way to go, Skipper!'

A barrage of raucous comments surrounded them, and they were bombarded with a cascade of confetti.

'Hey, they must be breathing through their ears!'

Natasha tried to draw back, embarrassed, but Hugh held her just a little longer. When at last he let her go, those smoky grey eyes were sparking with sardonic amusement. 'Don't worry,' he assured her quietly. 'I've booked us a room here at the hotel for tonight, so you won't have to put up with that lot rampaging around.'

She felt her cheeks blush a deep shade of scarlet, and swiftly lowered her eyes. Tonight...

'Well, young man—congratulations.' Uncle Timothy came over to pump Hugh's hand with vigorous enthusiasm. 'Couldn't be more delighted! She'll be in safe hands now.' He turned to Natasha, kissing her cheek with avuncular affection. 'And you, my dear—I wish you very, very happy.'

'Thank you, Uncle Timothy,' she managed weakly. 'And you'll arrange the meeting with Lester for tomorrow?'

His old eyes twinkled with merriment. 'Worrying about business on your honeymoon? Tut-tut—I'm sure you and your new husband will have much more interesting things to think about than that.'

'We will,' Hugh responded, his arm around her waist as he held her close to his side—every inch the possessive bridegroom. 'That's why we want to get it out of the way, so we can enjoy ourselves.'

'Ah! Of course, of course.' The old man nodded, satisfied. 'Well, you just leave it all to me. I'll draw up the necessary papers for signature, and fix up with Lester for us all to get together at my office at…let's say two o'clock. How's that?'

'That will be fine. Thank you.'

Natasha wasn't looking forward to the appointment—Lester was going to be furious when he found out how she'd outmanoeuvred him. But there would be nothing he could do about it—the marriage was perfectly legal.

'Natasha, you're supposed to toss your bouquet,' Debbie reminded her, wistful-eyed.

'Oh, yes—of course.' She smiled, and, turning her back tossed the bouquet with a careful aim over her shoulder, making sure Debbie caught it cleanly. The older woman blushed with pleasure, as if the silly romantic tradition had some kind of genuine significance.

'Shall we go up to dinner?' suggested Hugh when they had finished posing for photographs—the photographer, too, had been supplied by the hotel.

They led the small wedding party up through the gardens of the hotel to a wide terrace, where a table had been reserved for them. Again the theme of bridal fantasy was carried through in an arch of white flowers over the chairs intended for the bride and groom. The table was spread with a pristine white cloth, laid out with silver and glassware that sparkled in the long, golden rays of the evening sun. And in the middle was a two-tier wedding cake, with a tiny marzipan bride and groom on the top and a cascade of dainty white sugar flowers down one side.

'Did you fix up all this?' she whispered to Hugh.

'It came with package,' he responded with a shrug of casual unconcern.

'You must let me pay you back once the estate is set-

tled,' she whispered, feeling a little guilty at all the trouble
and expense he must have gone to on her behalf. OK, so
he would have the satisfaction of seeing Lester defeated,
but she was the main beneficiary.

'We'll deal with all that later,' he promised. 'For now
we have speeches to make, photos to smile for, and a cake
to cut. Enjoy yourself—it's a party.'

He seemed to be having no difficulty at all in carrying
off his role with considerable style, Natasha reflected as
she watched him easing the cork from a magnum of the
hotel's best champagne and spilling the foaming golden
liquid out into the glasses that everyone eagerly held out
for him to fill.

'To Natasha and Hugh,' Lord Neville proposed, raising
his glass in a toast. 'May all your troubles be little ones.'

'Natasha and Hugh!'

Hugh turned to her, smiling that bland smile, the glint
of wicked amusement in those shark-grey eyes just for
her. 'To us,' he murmured teasingly, chinking his glass to
hers.

Somehow she managed to summon a smile in response,
though a deep ache had lodged itself in her heart. Why
on earth had she agreed to go through with this? Couldn't
she have thought of some other way to deal with Lester?
But it had all happened so quickly—it had been a crazy
day, all rush from the minute she had woken this morning,
confused at finding herself in *The Kestrel*'s luxurious
for'ard cabin. There had been no time to stop and listen
to the voices of caution whispering inside her head.

But then had she really had any other option? This way
the trust would be wound up within just a few days;
Spaniard's Cove would be hers. Lester might try to kick
up a fuss, but there would be nothing he could do. And
as for Hugh... She had had a clause inserted into their

prenuptial agreement that she would pay him a share of the estate provided he kept to the other terms. It seemed only fair that he should have some recompense for his time and trouble.

There were two other wedding parties on the terrace, but theirs was by far the noisiest—thanks to the exuberant young lads from the boat, who were soon having a rollicking good time, laughing and getting merrily drunk on the champagne as the sun set, its last golden rays painting the sky with vivid streaks of tangerine and magenta, followed swiftly by the misty blue of the gathering night.

Candles appeared on the tables and a pianist came out onto the small raised stage in the corner of the dance floor. As the first few couples took to the floor, Hugh held out his hand to Natasha. 'How about a dance with your new husband?'

She found herself hesitating, gazing at his hand, remembering much too vividly the last time she had danced in his arms. Was it just forty-eight hours ago? At Desmond's exclusive restaurant above St Paul's Bay. Remembering the subtle, musky scent of his skin, the hardness of his body against hers...the way he had kissed her...

'Go on,' urged Uncle Timothy, mistaking the blush of pink that had sprung to her cheeks for maidenly shyness. 'You're married now.'

'Yes,' Hugh taunted softly as he drew her unresisting to her feet and out into the middle of the small space between the tables. 'You're married now.'

A quiver ran through her, and she knew he must have sensed it. He knew how vulnerable she was—and he knew exactly how to take advantage of that vulnerability. He had only to touch her...

'Relax,' he murmured as he drew her into his arms. 'The bride is supposed to be radiantly happy on her wedding day, not looking as if she's about to walk to her own execution.'

'This isn't exactly a normal wedding,' she responded tautly. 'Remember?'

'Oh, I hadn't forgotten,' he countered, a deliberately sensual huskiness in his voice, his head bent so close to hers that his warm breath stirred her hair. 'Separate beds. Don't worry—I've booked a suite, so we can even have separate rooms. You'll be quite safe.'

Natasha swallowed hard, refusing to lift her eyes to his face. The trouble was, she really wasn't sure she wanted to be safe.

After that first dance with Hugh, she danced with Uncle Timothy and Lord Neville, and finally with each of the lads in turn—even poor, blushing Jurgens, the freckle-faced one who had opened the door for her last night, who was ribbed horribly by his friends for having two left feet and stepping on her toes.

As the hour grew late, Uncle Timothy excused himself on the grounds that at his age a good night's sleep was essential, then Lord Neville gallantly offered to escort Debbie back to Spaniard's Cove. The boys went off in search of a disco they had heard about, leaving Natasha and Hugh finally alone.

'So—shall we have another dance?' he suggested, holding out his hand to her again.

She nodded dumbly, letting him lead her out onto the small dance floor and wrap his arms around her, drawing her so close that she could feel the steady beating of his heart against the hard wall of his chest, and with every breath the subtly musky, male scent of his skin was drugging her senses.

It would have taken far more will-power than she possessed to resist the temptation to let her head rest lightly against his wide shoulder. An aching need was gnawing at her heart. Need, want...love. She closed her eyes, secretly squeezing back the tears that were stinging at them. She was dancing in her wedding dress as the candles guttered in the soft evening breeze blowing it from the warm Caribbean Sea, but she was only a make-believe bride.

She didn't even know how long Hugh would be staying—she had no idea of his future plans. She really didn't know him at all. The only thing she knew was that right now she would give the whole world for this to be real...

The stars revolved slowly in the dark velvet sky as they danced. The evening was slipping into night—her wedding night. Natasha tried not to let her mind drift into imagining the next few hours. She had made him sign that agreement, and he had promised to keep to it. But was that what she really wanted?

At last the moment could be put off no longer—most of the other diners had gone, and the waiters were moving around quietly snuffing out the candles and clearing the tables. As Natasha drew back out of his arms, Hugh slanted her a look of quizzical amusement.

'Looks like it's time for bed,' he remarked.

She risked one swift glance at him, and as swiftly looked away again, afraid to let herself gaze for too long into those smoky grey eyes, afraid of the spells they could weave. 'Yes, of course.' The only place she had to retreat was into her familiar icy defences. 'Shall we go?'

The white satin of her dress rustled as she walked, drawing a certain amount of unwelcome attention as they crossed the foyer. Why did everyone feel free to stare at a bride? An elderly couple stepped into the lift with them, and the woman smiled at her, her eyes misty with romantic dreams.

'Oh, you *do* look lovely, my dear. I hope you'll both

be as happy as we've been.' She squeezed her husband's hand, and they exchanged a look that held a lifetime of memories. 'We're here to celebrate our Golden Wedding, you know.'

Natasha felt her heart crease. That was what she wanted…a lifetime. But she couldn't have it. A couple of weeks…a month at most. She managed some kind of weak smile as the lift doors opened and the other couple went their separate way along the passage.

Hugh put his hand lightly on her arm and steered her towards a door at the far end. As he inserted the key-card into the lock he slanted her a look of mocking amusement. He knew she was tense—and he knew why. Opening the door, he stood aside to let her precede him into room.

On the threshold she hesitated, startled. It was the bridal suite, all rococo gilt and pink love-seats, soft lighting and romantic paintings of lovers touchingly holding hands. On the far side of the room a pair of double doors stood open to reveal a glimpse of a large four-poster bed, swathed in yards of white tulle. And in the middle of the room, on a large, low coffee table, was a huge bouquet of red roses, their petals a deep, velvety crimson, their heady fragrance filling the room.

'Compliments of the house,' Hugh explained succinctly. 'Along with the champagne. He strolled across and lifted the bottle from the ice-bucket. 'We might as well drink it,' he suggested blandly. 'Shame to let it go to waste.'

Natasha nodded agreement, not quite trusting herself to speak. It was all so perfect—the wedding on the edge of the beach, with the blue Caribbean whispering softly in the background, the lovely white satin dress, the roses… There was only one thing wrong…

He eased the cork from the bottle of champagne, and

handed her a tulip glass brimming with golden bubbles. 'What shall we drink to?' he asked.

'I…don't know…' She was thinking of that couple in the lift, celebrating their Golden Wedding together. Fifty years married, and still holding hands…

'How about the success of our little scheme?'

'Oh…yes, of course.'

But those smoke-grey eyes seemed to be giving her another message—a message that made her heart beat faster, made her a little too conscious of the way her ragged breathing made her breasts rise and fall beneath the low, off-the-shoulder neckline of her wedding dress.

He smiled slowly, chinking his glass against hers, and took a sip of his champagne. She sipped cautiously from her own glass, lowering her lashes to defend herself from that sardonic gaze. If he knew how easy it would be for him to take her in his arms right now, kiss her into helpless submission…

'Well, I…think I'll go straight to bed,' she announced, her voice a little over-bright. 'I'm dead tired. I didn't get a lot of sleep last night.'

'Nor did I,' he responded easily. 'Pipe-cots aren't the most comfortable of beds. And Jurgens snores.'

'Well, then. I… Will you be comfortable on the settee?' What was the matter with her, for goodness' sake? Surely she didn't want to risk letting him read some kind of invitation into her words, when she had gone to so much trouble to insist that she *wasn't* going to sleep with him?

'I'll manage.'

'Fine.' She felt that stupid blush of pink creeping into her cheeks. Damn him, why did he have to accept her rebuff with such cool equanimity? Wasn't he even going to *try* to kiss her, to persuade her to change her mind?

'Well…um…goodnight, then,' she stammered awkwardly.

'Goodnight.'

Drawing on every ounce of composure she could muster, she put the barely touched glass of champagne down on the table beside the roses and somehow managed to make it across the room to the bedroom, closing the doors behind her and leaning back against them with a small sigh, closing her eyes. Separate beds… That was what she had wanted.

A polite tap on the panels made her heart kick sharply against her ribs. So he had been bluffing—he *was* going to try and persuade her not to make him sleep on the settee!

Well, he needn't think it was going to be that easy, she vowed darkly as she wrenched open the door—they had signed an agreement and she intended to see that he kept to it. Her head was tilted at a haughty angle, her eyes flashing frosty dignity—but he merely stood there, smiling that infuriatingly bland smile.

'I'm sorry to bother you,' he said, formally polite. 'Could you just spare me a pillow?'

She drew in a sharp breath, struggling to maintain her equilibrium. 'Oh—yes… Yes, of course.'

'Thank you.'

He sidestepped past her, careful not to brush again her at all, and took a pillow from the bed, retreating to the other room with a last wicked smile.

Natasha sat down weakly on the edge of the bed and closed her eyes. What had she *done*? She must have been mad to think it was a good idea to marry Hugh Garratt. Mad—or in love—it seemed to amount to pretty much the same thing.

Had she really even tried to think of any other way of

dealing with the situation? If she was absolutely honest, no—she hadn't. She had let herself be lured by a fantasy—of being married to Hugh Garratt, of finding that some miracle had occurred and he was truly in love with her…

But there wasn't going to be a miracle. With a small sigh she rose to her feet and kicked off her white satin bridal slippers. Then, sliding down the side zipper, she carefully peeled off the dress and hung it on a hanger, and stood gazing at it with a twinge of regret. It was such a beautiful dress—but tomorrow she would have to hand it back to the hotel's wedding shop. It didn't belong to her.

Stepping back from it, she caught a sudden glimpse of herself in the long mirror on the wardrobe door and smiled wryly. She hadn't planned to splash out on luxury silk underwear, but to refuse when the hotel's wedding co-ordinator had been pressing it on her so eagerly wouldn't have fitted her role as a blushing bride, swept off her feet.

Besides, she had told herself, she'd needed something to go under the dress, with its low, off-the-shoulder neckline. The virginal white lace basque was sinfully sexy, catching in her small waist and cupping her small breasts provocatively. With white suspenders and sheer white stockings with lace tops, it was just the thing to drive a red-blooded bridegroom wild.

The fevered images swirling in her brain were so vivid that they almost took her breath away. What if…?

But her new husband was apparently quite happy at being relegated to the settee, she reflected bitterly. Which was for the best. She had to remember that this was merely a marriage of convenience, to last only as long as was necessary to satisfy the legal niceties, and to be followed by a nice, amicable annulment.

And then…maybe she would have an affair with him. Once there was no longer any danger of her letting herself believe it might be something more… *Oh, you fool!* she scolded herself impatiently, shaking her head. What would it take to make her let go of all those foolish dreams?

Maybe a shower could help—a nice cold one, to douse the fires that were smouldering dangerously inside her. Carefully she unwound the tiny flowers from her hair and brushed out the curls, and then, with a small sigh of regret, stripped off the scraps of lace, folding them carefully and putting them on a chair. Tucking her hair up beneath a dainty plastic cap, she stepped into the well-appointed bathroom and turned on the shower.

It wasn't much help—she was much too aware of Hugh, just in the next room. As the warm needles of water trickled down over her body she smoothed a creamy shower-wash into her soft skin, circling with slow, caressing movements of her hands over the ripe, firm swell of her naked breasts, the slim curve of her hips, her slender thighs…

Closing her eyes, she let herself drift into the fantasy that he was there with her, that it was his hands that caressed her nakedness, that his body, naked and male, was crushing hers into the corner of the shower. Her breathing was ragged as she conjured the image, so vivid that she could feel his presence, could have reached out her hand and touched that hard-muscled chest, lightly scattered with whorls of rough, sun-bleached male hair…

But there was nothing there. She was alone in the shower, feeling stupid and disappointed and achingly needy. Impatiently she turned the water off and stepped out, wrapping herself up in a thick towelling sheet. Pulling off the shower cap, she shook out her hair, avoiding even so much as a glance at her own reflection in the large mirror above the vanity unit. She knew that her eyes would be wide and glittering with heat, her mouth soft with the hunger for his kisses. She had to get a grip on herself—she still had tomorrow to get through.

Wandering back into the bedroom, she had just sat down at the dressing table and picked up a brush to work the tangles from her hair when there was another knock on the door. She drew in a sharp gasp of breath, her stomach clenching in knots as she called, 'Come in.'

Hugh had taken off his jacket and bow tie, and his shirt was loose and unfastened down the front, showing a tempting glimpse of that hard-muscled body she had been fantasising about just moments ago. He smiled at her, a glint of mocking amusement in those smoke-grey eyes.

'Excuse me,' he murmured as he stepped into the room. He slanted a sardonic glance down at the neat pile of white lace lingerie on the chair. 'I thought so. That won't give quite the right impression, will it? If Lester starts snooping around, we don't the hotel staff gossiping that we were so restrained that you had time to fold your underwear.' He picked up the basque and regarded it with critical interest. 'Mmm. I think...yes.'

With slow deliberation, he tugged off a couple of the tiny pearl buttons that ran down the front, and then, holding it from his finger, let it drop to the floor beside the bed, where it pooled into lacy drift that spoke of heated frenzy. One silk stocking he draped carefully across the mirror on the dressing table, the other across the foot of the four-poster bed.

'There.' He surveyed his own handiwork with satisfaction. 'That has more the look of a proper wedding night, don't you think?' He smiled down at her, lazily mocking. 'Goodnight, then.'

'G...Goodnight,' she stammered.

He closed the bedroom door, leaving her sitting there alone, staring at the scene he had created—a scene of wild, passionate lovemaking, of a man so hungry for her body that he had ripped off her expensive lace underwear, had tossed her stockings carelessly around the room.

But it was a lie—everything was lies—and she didn't know what was left for her to cling to any more. Picking up one of the tiny white flowers that had been woven into her hair, she twisted it in her fingers, tears sliding slowly down her cheeks.

The telephone was ringing urgently, but Natasha didn't want to answer it. Her dreams were much too pleasant— she didn't want to wake up just yet. Anyway, someone in the next room had answered it. Someone...

Memory came rushing back, pushing aside the veils of sleep. She sat up quickly, staring around wide-eyed at the extravagantly romantic bedroom, the discarded under-wear, the white satin dress hanging from the wardrobe door. That part of it, at least, hadn't been a dream.

The door opened and she turned as Hugh, looking slightly rumpled from sleep, appeared. Just a second too late she snatched up the quilt, clutching it defensively to her throat, self-conscious in the delicate scrap of silk and lace nightgown she had bought for her fake wedding night. 'Don't you believe in knocking?' she demanding frostily.

'On my wife's bedroom door?' he countered, those shark-grey eyes taunting her. 'It's for you.' With a nod of his head he indicated the telephone beside the bed.

She frowned in sudden concern. If someone was calling her at this hour, on what they believed to be the morning after her wedding night, it had to be serious. 'Who is it?' she asked with a touch of trepidation.

'Debbie.'

'*Debbie*...?' She picked up the phone quickly. 'Debbie? Hi, what's the matter?'

'Natasha?' Debbie's voice was ragged with agitation. 'I'm so sorry to bother you like this, but something dreadful's happened. There's been a burglary—they broke into your apartment, into the safe. Lester's been hurt—they've taken him to hospital.'

Natasha felt herself grow pale. Hugh was standing in the doorway, watching her, and she flickered the briefest glance up at him from beneath her lashes, looking away again swiftly, careful not to let him catch her eye. An image as vivid as a photograph had sprung into her mind, of him kneeling beside the open safe...

'Lester's hurt?' she queried, her voice a little unsteady. 'How?'

'They tied him to a chair and hit him on the head,' Debbie told her, sounding on the edge of tears. 'I don't think it's too bad—he didn't want to go to the hospital, but I insisted.'

'Yes, of course,' Natasha agreed automatically. 'Did they take much?'

'No—Lester seems to have disturbed them before they'd finished. But they made a terrible mess,' Debbie added wryly. 'It'll take ages to clear up.'

'I'll be right over.'

'I'm so sorry. It's such a terrible shame for something like this to happen while you're on your honeymoon.'

'Don't worry about that,' Natasha returned grimly, slanting another swift, hard glance in Hugh's direction. A burglary—and didn't he have the most perfect alibi? 'I'll see you in half an hour.'

Hugh was regarding her with one eyebrow arched in query as she put the receiver back on the cradle.

'There's been a burglary at the casino,' she informed him, her voice taut. 'They attacked Lester—he's in hospital. I have to go over there—if you wouldn't mind leaving while I get dressed?'

'A burglary?'

'That's what I said.'

'I'll come with you.' He started to fasten his shirt. 'I'll have Room Service send us up some breakfast.'

She returned him a stony glare. 'You can have breakfast,' she ground out. 'It isn't necessary for you to come over—I can manage perfectly well on my own.'

That questioning eyebrow arched again. 'What's the problem?' he enquired.

'Nothing.'

He laughed, that slow, lazy, mocking laugh, and came over to sit on the edge of the bed, one finger beneath her chin to tilt her face to his as she tried to turn away. 'It seems a pretty serious sort of nothing, the way you're snapping my head off,' he remarked with dry humour. 'Or are you always this grouchy first thing in the morning?'

She gazed up into those smoke-grey eyes, resolutely resisting their spell. 'It just seems like…rather an odd coincidence,' she countered, a jagged edge of suspicion in her voice. 'There's never been a robbery before, but now… You knew where the safe was. And you knew the combination.'

'I also knew there was nothing in it worth stealing,' he pointed out, on a coldly sardonic inflection.

Natasha hesitated. That much was true…

'But you don't trust me so I'm the first person you're going to suspect—isn't that right?'

'I don't have much reason to trust you,' she retorted.

'How do I really know that a single word of what you told me is true? About your nephew, and Lester scamming that money off him? How do I even know that you'll keep to our agreement—that you're not planning some way of getting the casino off me after all?' Her voice was rising as all her doubts and insecurities came bubbling to the surface. 'How do I know you're not a bigger liar than Lester? I don't know anything about you!'

Those smoky grey eyes glinted with some kind of secret laughter, as if he found her outburst somehow amusing. 'And yet you were willing to marry me,' he taunted softly. 'That seems like quite a big risk to take with someone you know nothing about.'

CHAPTER NINE

THE room was certainly a mess. The desk was tipped on its side, the lamp smashed, and the books from the bookcase which had concealed the safe had been scattered all over the floor. The chair that Lester had been tied to was on its side, a length of rope still hanging loosely around it. The local police inspector welcomed Natasha with wry smile.

'Ah—Miss Cole… Oh, I beg your pardon—it's Mrs Garratt now, isn't it? In spite of these somewhat unfortunate circumstances…' his glance encompassed the scene of devastation '…may I offer my congratulations?'

Thank you, Inspector,' she responded, her voice taut. 'This is my…husband.' The word seemed to stick in her throat as she watched Hugh politely exchange greetings with the policeman.

'Have you found anything to indicate who was responsible?' Hugh enquired, glancing at the forensics officer, who was on his knees beside the safe, delicately brushing white powder around the lock.

The inspector shook his head. 'No fingerprints, if that's what you mean. At least, not on the safe. There are a number of other sets elsewhere—including, presumably, Mr Jackson's own.'

'So the burglars were wearing gloves?' Natasha put in, slanting an instinctive glance at Hugh's hands, remembering the way he had flexed those strong, clever fingers in the surgical gloves…

'No, Miss…Mrs Garratt. The door of the safe has been

wiped clean. Tell me, when does your housekeeper come in?'

'The maid would have been in yesterday morning,' she supplied, frowning slightly.

'Would it have been likely that she would have polished the door of the safe?'

'Well…no.' She shook her head, puzzled. 'I don't suppose she even knows it's there.'

The inspector nodded his head slowly. 'That's rather what I thought.'

'Seems a little odd,' Hugh remarked, a note of interest in his voice. 'Why would they take the trouble to wipe the safe if they were wearing gloves? And if they weren't wearing gloves…'

'We would have expected to find their fingerprints elsewhere,' the inspector confirmed. 'The desk, for instance, or the lamp.'

Hugh had gone over to the chair and was looking at the rope. 'May I?' he asked the inspector.

'Certainly.'

Hugh picked up the rope and examined it with mild curiosity. 'Nylon. I dare say it was tied pretty tightly?'

'Not tightly enough, apparently,' the inspector responded evenly. 'Mr Jackson was able to free himself and ring Miss Lowe.'

'He rang Debbie first?' Natasha put in, puzzled by what seemed like a silent exchange between the two men.

'Yes.' The inspector's face was an enigma. 'It was she who called the police.'

'Really?' Hugh arched a quizzical eyebrow. 'I wonder why he chose to do that?'

'He was probably confused,' Natasha suggested, feeling the shifting sands of doubt beneath her feet. 'He had been hit on the head.'

'Apparently,' the inspector conceded.

Natasha shot him a sharp glance. 'What do you mean?' she demanded.

'It wasn't a serious blow,' the inspector explained carefully. 'Really quite…minor.'

The implication was clear. 'You mean…he could have done it himself?' she queried, bewildered.

The inspector cleared his throat, as if reluctant to voice precisely what he was thinking. 'It's…a possibility,' was as far as he was prepared to go.

'Fingerprints wiped from the safe, but nowhere else,' Hugh enumerated. 'Lester tied up, but with knots loose enough to escape from. And a minor but interesting blow on the head—interesting enough to throw Debbie into a distracting panic, anyway.'

'But…why?' Natasha protested, floundering in confusion. 'Why would he go to the trouble of faking a burglary and hitting himself on the head? It doesn't make sense.'

'Because he wanted you to suspect me,' Hugh responded, the glint of mockery in his eyes reminding her that he was exactly who she *had* suspected. 'Hoping to split us up so that he would have a chance of preventing you from having the trust wound up.'

Natasha frowned, forced to acknowledge the logic of his argument. 'I suppose…it's possible…' She lifted her eyes to his, searching in their depths for the truth. She wanted to believe him—but could she trust the instincts of her own heart? She nodded slowly. 'It's…possible. Perhaps we'd better go to the hospital.'

Natasha was silent as they drove to the hospital. So far, none of her suspicions about Hugh had proved accurate. He had told her the truth about Lester being involved in something less than legal with Tony de Santo, he hadn't been responsible for the burglary, he had even offered her a prenuptial agreement which prevented him from making an excessive claim on her when their marriage ended.

When their marriage ended... But she didn't want it to end.

From beneath her lashes she slanted a covert glance up at the man by her side in the back of the air-conditioned taxi. She had fallen in love with him, deeply and for ever. But, having married him as some kind of business arrangement, she could hardly now tell him that she wanted to change the terms. It would seem as though she had trapped him.

The island's cottage hospital was on the outskirts of St Paul's. They had arranged with Uncle Timothy to meet him there, instead of his office. A nurse in the corridor directed them to Lester's room, and they found the elderly solicitor already there. Lester was sitting up in bed, a dressing across his forehead just above his temple. As Natasha and Hugh walked in he was complaining petulantly to one of the nurses that the mattress was uncomfortable.

'Oh, but the doctor says you'll probably be able to go home tomorrow,' Debbie reminded him, patting his hand soothingly.

'Huh! I've had a serious head injury,' he grumbled impatiently. 'I had concussion. That can be dangerous, you know.' He glanced up, fixing Natasha with a hostile glare. 'Ah—so, you're here, are you? About time. I don't suppose I'm going to get any thanks for preventing a burglary, even though I could have been killed.'

Natasha sat down calmly on the chair Hugh brought out for her, folding her hands in her lap. 'You do seem to have had a remarkably lucky escape,' she commented in a dry tone.

'I did—no thanks to you. If you'd been there it wouldn't have happened in the first place.'

'Oh?' She arched one delicate eyebrow in polite question. 'Why?'

He shot a meaningful glance towards Hugh. 'I don't think I need to explain,' he countered gruffly. 'If you've got any sense you can work it out for yourself.'

'Oh, I think I can work out what happened,' she responded with a touch of sweet sarcasm. 'Besides, if I had been there, I would probably still have been in the cellar.'

He scowled, avoiding that line by fussing irritably with his bedclothes. Meanwhile Uncle Timothy had produced a sheaf of legal-looking papers from his briefcase and was laying them out on the table beside the bed.

'So you've gone and married him,' Lester sneered, regarding these preparations with disfavour. 'You little fool. I warned you not to let some fancy operator take advantage of you. You should have listened to me. Well, you needn't think I'll consent to winding up the trust.'

'I'm afraid you can't prevent it, old chap,' Uncle Timothy put in with a comfortable smile of satisfaction. 'There are no valid grounds for withholding your consent.'

'No grounds?' Lester demanded, rounding on him in cold fury. 'I'll give you grounds, you doddering old fool. He's nothing but a damned fortune-hunter, that's my grounds!'

'Oh?' Timothy was still smiling. 'You've looked into his background, then?'

'No, I damned well haven't,' Lester barked. 'He made damned sure there'd be no time for that, rushing her into it.'

'Oh, it wouldn't have taken you long,' Timothy responded calmly. 'You could simply have looked him up in the *Fortune 500* list.'

He took a magazine from his briefcase and handed it to Lester, folded open at a place he indicated. Intrigued, Natasha craned her head to look. There was a small photograph of Hugh, with a paragraph of biography. Beside it was his name, and an estimate of his fortune. Her eyes widened and she turned to stare at him, stunned.

'Why didn't you tell me?' she demanded.

He shrugged those wide shoulders in a gesture of casual unconcern, a glint of wicked amusement in his smoky-grey eyes. 'I was afraid you'd only be marrying me for my money,' he responded, tongue in cheek.

'Oh…!' She felt a hot blush of pink colour her cheeks. 'You…you've been laughing at me—all this time.'

He caught her fist, lifting it to his lips and placing a kiss on her obstinately clenched fingers, those eyes conveying a message that made her heart flip over. 'Not quite *all* the time,' he murmured, huskily soft.

The night air was as soft as velvet, stirred by just the faintest breeze. *The Kestrel* swayed gently on her anchor chain—Hugh had decided it would be safer to move her from St Paul's Bay, and so in the early evening they had sailed her round to this small, quiet bay further along the coast.

The boys had gone ashore for their evening meal—Natasha could see the glow of their camp-fire on the beach. One of them had a guitar, and from time to time the sound of their singing or laughter drifted out across the water. The only other sound was the occasional creaking of the masts, and the steady slip-slap of water against the hull.

She and Hugh had eaten their dinner on deck, and now

they were lounging on the boat cushions in the shallow for'ard cockpit, watching the stars. Natasha slid her hand along the smooth teak banding that edged the deck. 'She really is a lovely boat,' she remarked. 'Even with just that light breeze she seems as if she's going to take off and fly.'

Hugh smiled with a proprietorial pride, lounging back to cast his eyes along the sleek curve of the gunwale. 'She's certainly a beauty. The summit of a lifetime's ambition!'

'You really own her yourself?' she queried a little awkwardly.

'Uh-huh. Helped design her, too. Well, I interfered a lot, anyway. But they couldn't chuck me out—I'd bought the boatyard.'

'You told me you were in the building trade.'

'Oh, my brother runs that side of the business for me now.' He grinned lazily. 'Right from when I was kid, growing up on the wrong stretch of the waterfront, I wanted to do nothing but mess about in boats. I gave myself twenty years to make enough money, and I worked damned hard, but it was worth it.'

Natasha appeared fascinated by the veining in the wooden decking, tracing it with her fingertip. 'I...wish I'd known,' she mused. 'Lester's suspicions almost had me convinced that you *were* some kind of fortune-hunter. But you wouldn't need to be, would you? I mean...it would be pretty much small change to you—even the whole plantation.'

'Pretty much,' he acknowledged, the lilt of amusement in his voice holding no trace of mockery.

'Why didn't you tell me?' she asked, turning her eyes to his. 'When I...offered to pay you a share of the estate for marrying me...'

'Maybe because that would have been too easy,' he responded softly. 'Maybe I wanted you to trust me because your heart told you to.'

'Wh…why was that so important?' she stammered, tension constricting her throat.

'Because without trust,' he asserted, his voice and smoky grey eyes spinning their beguiling spells around her, 'love doesn't stand a chance.'

She laughed a little unsteadily—for some reason it was becoming difficult to breathe. 'Who mentioned love?' she protested.

'I did.'

'Don't be silly.' She turned her head sharply away from him to stare blankly out at the dark horizon, her heart thumping against her ribs. 'It's just…sexual attraction—nothing more than that. We…we've only known each other for less than a week.'

He laughed, and she sensed him moving closer to her. 'You trusted me enough to marry me,' he pointed out, his voice now inches away.

'Yes, but…that was different. It was…just a matter of convenience.'

'So it was.' The brush of his fingertips down her bare arm made her shiver with heat. 'It was a convenient way of persuading you to marry me. Now let's see if you can trust me enough to let me make love to you.'

He drew her back into the crook of his arm, tilting her head against his shoulder, feathering warm, soft kisses across her eyelids and around the corners of her lips. She could feel herself sinking into his sensuous spell, the musky scent of his skin drugging her mind…

'But…what about the prenuptial agreement?' she protested weakly, struggling to sit up.

He laughed, a glint of lazy mockery in his eyes. 'I

thought you'd done a degree in Business Studies?' he taunted.

She frowned, puzzled. 'What's that got to do with it?'

'You know it wasn't a valid contract. The signatures weren't witnessed.'

'Oh...!' A hot blush of scarlet flooded up over her cheeks. She *had* known—but she had conveniently tucked the thought out of her mind, probably because subconsciously she hadn't wanted any reason not to go ahead and marry him. 'Aren't you worried that I might take you for half your fortune?' she taunted, trying to cover her confusion.

'Not at all,' he responded with absolute confidence as his mouth came down to claim hers. 'I'm not planning on us getting divorced. Ever.'

His kisses were tracing a scalding path across her temple, around the delicate shell of her ear, and on down to the slender column of her throat, tipped back in a vulnerable arch across his arm to expose the hollows behind her collarbone which were so sensitive to the heat of his mouth, while his hand had moved up to curve over the ripe, aching swell of her breast.

It would be so easy to surrender—all she had to do was let go... But some part of her was still holding her back. The habits of suspicion, long-ingrained, died hard. Doubts still nagged at the fringes of her mind. All this talk of love was all very well, but could it really be for ever...? She was risking so much, leaving behind her beloved Spaniard's Cove and everything she had planned for it, for a pocketful of promises...

'I...do *want* to trust you,' she whispered, her breathing ragged, closing her eyes on a brief moment of blissful pleasure as his thumb brushed across the taut bud of her nipple, hardening against the constraining lacy cup of her bra. 'But I keep thinking...'

'Don't think,' he advised huskily. 'Listen to your heart.'

His mouth claimed hers again, kissing her with a deep tenderness, coaxing her lips apart with a languorous sweep of his tongue as he sought the soft sweetness within, stirring the embers of her responses, plundering all the most secret recesses with a ruthless possessiveness against which she had no defence.

She was barely even aware that he had been deftly unfastening the buttons down the front of her loose cotton shirt until she felt his hand smooth across her bare midriff, brushing the soft fabric aside. A low moan, almost of agony, escaped her throat. Her breasts ached for release from the taut scrap of lace that held them, the tender peaks rawly sensitised by the slight abrasion of the dainty cups.

With one tantalising fingertip he traced the outline of the delicate lace, right down into the soft shadow between her breasts. 'You see?' he murmured, low and husky. 'It's easy when you stop trying to reason it all out and just do what your heart tells you to do.'

She stared up at him, her eyes misted. 'But is it my heart telling me?' she protested, bewildered by the wanton creature she seemed to have become, 'Or is it my body?'

'You're thinking again,' he chided, shaking his head in mocking reproof. And then, scooping her up in his arms as if she weighed no more than a feather, he carried her back along the deck towards the door of the cabin, his stride not faltering with the gentle movement of the boat. 'I'm going to have to stop you thinking.'

Natasha didn't protest. Sometimes even when the stakes seemed recklessly high you still had to take a chance—to be too afraid of losing meant that you would never win the prize.

It proved awkward to manoeuvre her down the steps and through the cabin door, so Hugh was forced to put her down. She laughed a little nervously, not resisting as he pulled her after him into the cabin and into his arms. With an urgency that woke an answering excitement inside her he dragged apart the last buttons of her shirt and pushed it back off her shoulders, dropping it to the floor, his hands sliding around her bare waist, his mouth descending to the sensitive hollows at the base of her throat.

'So, Mrs Garratt,' he growled, kicking the door shut behind her. 'At last...'

Cupping her face in his hands, he dusted scorching kisses across her trembling eyelids, over her cheekbones, finding the racing pulse beneath her temple. Her head felt dizzy, and she put up her hands against him to steady herself, encountering the hard wall of his chest. Fuelled by her own urgent need, she began to unfasten his shirt, impatient with the buttons.

He laughed, teasing her eagerness, helping her as she fumbled over the last few buttons, shrugging the shirt back off his wide shoulders with an easy movement that made all the hard muscles across his chest move fluidly beneath his sun-bronzed skin. Drawing in a sharp gasp of breath, she wrapped her arms around his waist, drawing herself in close, feeling the raw power of his body against hers, tasting the salt tang of his skin with her lips and tongue as she trailed her hot mouth along the line of his collarbone and down across the smooth, sculpted shape of his pectoral muscles, rough with male hair.

Heat was flaring inside her, melting away any last shreds of doubt. Something that felt this good just had to be right.

His hand had tangled in her hair, dragging her head back, and his mouth crushed hers, bruising her lips. But she didn't care—something inside her was thrilled by the knowledge of how much he wanted her. Deftly he unfastened the catch of her bra, tossing it aside—it draped itself across the back of the helmsman's seat, a froth of delicate white lace. The saloon was beginning to resemble the scene of erotic frenzy he had created in the bridal suite last night, she reflected fleetingly—only this time it was for real.

His strong arm was curving her against him, crushing her tender breasts against his chest, that smattering of male hair deliciously rough against her nipples as her head tipped back beneath the plundering invasion of his kiss. And then he lifted her to perch on the edge of the high helmsman's table, and she wrapped her legs around his waist, resting back on her hands to balance herself as he brushed his fingertips up over her body, making her shiver with heat.

His hungry gaze lingered on the ripe, naked swell of her breasts, daintily tipped with rosy pink buds. 'Beautiful,' he murmured, huskily soft. 'Just beautiful…' He cupped them in his hands, moulding their firm roundness, smiling wickedly into her eyes as he teased the tender nipples, pinching them teasingly between his fingers, making her gasp at the almost unbearable pleasure. 'And so incredibly responsive…'

Her spine arched luxuriantly, offering him her body in wanton invitation, to taste and savour at his will. He bent his head, dusting the smooth, creamy flesh with hot kisses, his sensuous tongue scalding a lazily circling path that traced the curving contours, torturing her with a simmering anticipation as he edged slowly, tantalisingly towards the taut, puckered peaks.

A shudder ran through her as she felt him lap over first one, then the other, swirling around each as if it was a ripe red fruit, rich with juice. His strong white teeth nipped at them teasingly, tormenting her with sweet sensations—and then finally he took one deep into his mouth and began to suckle with a hard, hungry rhythm that pulsed through her like some primitive drumbeat, heating her blood like a fever.

Her fingers curled into the crisp hair at the nape of his neck as she gazed down in a kind of bemused wonder at his dark head, at his mouth locked around her aching breast. Had he meant what he had said out there on the deck? He had used the word 'love'... Though in truth he hadn't actually said that he loved her, not in so many words. It was too soon. How could she be sure that his feelings went any deeper than this searing desire for her body? That they would last any longer than it took for that desire to be sated, burning itself out in heated lust until there was nothing left?

But she didn't care. She loved him with a love that ached fiercely inside her—she would have walked through fire for him if he had asked her.

His hands had slipped down the length of her spine, easing her closer against him, and she felt him unfasten the belt of her trousers; the zip swished softly as he pulled it down. She kicked off her sandals, wrapping her arms around his neck, and as he lifted her down from the table she felt the cotton fabric slither down her thighs and fall to the floor, where it lay ignored, along with the rest of their clothes.

Now only the tiny white scrap of her lace briefs shielded her modesty—pretty ineffectually, she realised, as his hands smoothed over the slender curve of her hips, savouring her near-nakedness with a predatory satisfaction that sent a quiver of apprehension through her.

But she smiled up at him with a shy boldness, reaching up to put her hands on his shoulders, feeling the warm resilience of his hard muscles, warning of a raw male power barely restrained by the force of his will. His fingers trailed across and down over his wide chest, through the rough curls of hair, circling with fascination around the dark, flat nipples. And then on, down over the ridged pack of muscles around his midriff...down to the heavy silver buckle that fastened the thick leather belt of his jeans. There she hesitated, a little unsure.

'Go on,' he urged her, his voice a low growl.

Her fingers felt awkward as she struggled to unfasten the belt. Then she had to concentrate on the snap of his jeans. She was conscious of a hot blush of pink in her cheeks as she bent her head over her task—there was no mistaking the hard bulge beneath the thick denim. It was...just a little intimidating.

He waited, patient, as she managed the first couple of snaps. Her mouth felt dry, and unconsciously she moistened it with the tip of her tongue. The next one was going to be more difficult—she fumbled over it, trying not to actually touch him. But by the fourth snap she knew it was going to be unavoidable. She moved her hands towards it, but drew back instinctively, her heart thumping in alarm.

He caught her fingers, imprisoning them against him as she tried to pull away, and a tiny cry of panic escaped her throat.

'Hey...' He put his hand beneath her chin to tilt up her face, but she kept her lashes lowered, unable to bring herself to look at him. 'What the hell's wrong now?' he demanded roughly.

'I'm sorry. I...' One tiny tear escaped from the corner of her eye. 'I...'

Suddenly he gentled, his fingers brushing back over her cheek, stroking away the tear. 'Have you ever done this before?' he queried in soft amazement.

She shook her head dumbly.

He drew her close into his arms, stroking a soothing hand down over her hair. 'Why didn't you tell me sooner? I had no idea... You know I won't hurt you, won't frighten you. I love you.'

She drew her head back, gazing up mistily into his eyes. 'You...do?'

He nodded, smiling down at her. 'Isn't that what I told you before? I love you—that's why I wanted to marry you. All that other business was just incidental. And I want you to love me—if you can learn to trust me enough to let you do that.'

She gulped back the foolish tears that were stinging her eyes. Whatever the future might hold—next week, next month—she was sure that for the moment he really meant what he was saying. That was enough.

'So we'll take it slowly,' he promised, lifting her into his arms. 'Very, very slowly.'

In spite of the restricted space, his cabin in the stern of the boat was deeply luxurious. Concealed lighting glowed softly on the polished teak that lined the walls and ceiling, and the bed was wide and comfortable, covered in a fitted quilt the colour of a rich red Burgundy wine.

Hugh laid her down on the bed, swiftly disposing of his own jeans and sandals before coming to join her, drawing her up into his arms so that she lay along his body, stroking her hair back from her face. 'Just let me know how you're feeling,' he whispered gently. 'I'll try my very best to hold back—though it's not going to be easy.'

She nodded, believing him.

His hand slid down the length of her spine as some powerful magnetic force drew her mouth down to his. And she quickly discovered that it was interesting to be on top—she felt more in control. She let her tongue sweep slowly along just inside his lips, probing playfully into their corners, delighted when he groaned in tortured pleasure. She took his sensuous lower lip between her hard white teeth, nibbling along it with tiny, gentle nips, until his arms tightened fiercely around her.

'Careful,' he warned. 'Too much teasing could prove dangerous.'

She laughed, knowing that she had no reason to be afraid of him. Bending her head again, she let her hair fall like a silken curtain against his cheek, this time kissing him properly, exploring with delicious excitement all the secret recesses of his mouth as he had explored hers.

His hands stroked slowly up over her back, around to caress her naked breasts, and she lifted herself slightly to allow him room, overwhelmingly aware of her bare thigh sliding over his, of the thick hardness of his arousal lying between them, a vivid reminder that no matter how gentle and patient he was now, sooner or later she was going to have to yield to that ultimate demand.

He was kissing her deeply, tipping her over onto her back beside him and holding her close in the crook of his arm, giving himself the freedom to gaze down at her firm, ripe breasts as he caressed them, his eyes smouldering with pleasure at the sight of their inviting nakedness, pertly tipped with puckered nipples as pink and dainty as fresh raspberries.

She watched in a kind of fascination as his strong, clever hands stroked over her peach-smooth skin, one long finger trailing a lazy path around the taut, hardened peak. But then, as he tweaked it teasingly, pinching it lightly between his fingers, her eyes fell shut and her back arched, the exquisite pleasure slicing through her and piercing her brain.

An odd little cry escaped her throat. She wanted to feel the heat of his mouth there again, and she moved supplicatingly beneath him, offering the invitation. His soft laughter told her that he had understood. She felt his tongue, hot and moist, lapping over one rawly tender nipple, and now it was a moan of sheer rapture she uttered, turning to a sobbing intake of breath as she felt his firm lips close around that delicate crest of pink, felt the deep, pulsing tug as he suckled it with a hard, hungry rhythm, driving her into a zone of pleasure she had never known existed.

She knew when his hand slid slowly down over her slim midriff to the edge of her tiny lace briefs, but she didn't care. She felt his unfamiliar touch as he stroked down over her thighs and back up, brushing lightly over the lacy triangle, coaxing her to let him slip his hand down towards the secret core of her femininity.

She tried to relax, but she was trembling as he hooked his fingers into the filmy lace and began to ease it slowly down. Inch by inch she felt it slip over the curve of her hips and down her slim thighs, until with one swift flick of his wrist they were free of her ankles and tossed aside, leaving her naked in his arms, quivering with mingled vulnerability and anticipation.

And then his eyes slid down over her, slowly, possessively, lingering on every naked curve. Her skin felt the scalding heat of his gaze, as if he was branding her as his personal property.

'I've seen you like this in my dreams,' he murmured smokily. 'Naked and beautiful... I can't believe how much I've wanted to make love to you. Sometimes I thought I'd go crazy.'

Somehow she managed a tremulous smile. 'Me too,' she whispered. 'I wanted you too...'

His mouth came down to kiss her again, deep and tender, and she felt his hand move down over her thighs, now with not even that flimsy scrap of lace to protect her. In spite of herself she tensed, shy of the strange sensation of his fingers coiling into the soft crown of hair. 'It's all right,' he coaxed softly. 'Just let it happen. Part your legs for me—just a little. That's right…'

Drawing in a long, quivering breath, she obeyed, accepting his touch with just the slightest tremor of vulnerability. His fingers slipped into the delicate crease of velvet, exploring with a cherishing gentleness that soothed her apprehension; each new sensation was a revelation of pleasure she hadn't expected, the caressing strokes making her sigh, her thighs parting wider in unconscious invitation, licensing his access to her most intimate secrets.

A tiny gasp escaped her lips as one long finger dipped deep inside her, but at the same moment the pad of his thumb found the tiny nub that was the focus of all her shimmering nerve-fibres, arousing it with a masterful expertise, and as the pleasure rippled through her in wave upon wave of intensity, piercingly sweet, her spine curled in pure ecstasy.

He was holding her in the crook of his arm, watching her flushed face as the shadows of pleasure flickered across, smiling at her unguarded responsiveness. And then he laid her back against the pillows as his hot mouth began an interesting exploration southwards, taking in every diversion along the way, until she felt its scalding touch against the silken inner curve of her thighs.

Now they were way beyond anything she could ever have imagined, and she could only follow where he led, letting him spread her thighs wide apart as his head dipped between them, his hot, sinuous tongue taking the place of his thumb, swirling over that hidden pearl with a flagrant sensuality, and she caught her breath on a ragged sob as heat pooled in the pit of her stomach like liquid gold.

She had wanted this, dreamed about it as she had watched him strolling around the casino even that very first night, so casually self-assured, those predatory grey eyes glinting so wickedly. But she could never have imagined that it would be like this. She was lost in a world of erotic sensuality, totally focused on their two bodies. Nothing else existed in time or space—the whole universe could have exploded and she wouldn't even have noticed.

And when he moved back up the bed to fold her in his arms again, she felt only the quivering tension of anticipation. Arching beneath him, she surrendered willingly to the first hard thrust as he took her, even welcoming the brief, sharp stab of pain as proof that now she belonged totally to him, her body as well as her heart, mind and soul.

With a gentle hand he stroked her hair back from her face, dusting it with kisses. 'All right?' he queried softly.

'Yes,' she whispered, moving beneath him in an instinctive supplication as old as Eve. 'Oh, yes...'

As the boat swayed gently on the quiet waters of the secluded bay, their bodies moved to their own elemental rhythm, slow and easy at first, as he allowed her time to become accustomed to the feel of him, thick and hard inside her—then faster, thrusting deep, then slow again, circling and stretching her deliciously, rocking together in a perfect unison as if this were some kind of ancient dance.

Their skin glistened with sweat as they rode the waves of pleasure, reaching ever higher and higher, spinning in a wild vortex like the eye of a storm. Hugh had warned her that it wouldn't be easy for him to hold back, but it didn't matter—her arms were wrapped around him as she surrendered to every demand, aching with the hot, sweet pleasure that flooded through her until finally it seemed to spill over, drowning her in its molten tide, ebbing away at last to leave her dazed and exhausted, tangled up in his arms, as with one final, fierce thrust he let out a shuddering groan, his weight crushing her beneath him on the tumbled bed.

CHAPTER TEN

'BREAKFAST, sleepy-head. Or maybe that should be lunch.'

Natasha opened her eyes to a patch of sunny blue sky filtering through the bronzed glass window panel above her head. Hugh, wearing only those disreputable loose shorts, the waistband riding low around his hips, his chest bare, was standing beside the bed with a tray in his hands. At the sight of him her mouth felt suddenly dry, a hunger that had nothing to do with breakfast kicking her in the pit of her stomach.

'Ah…!' Laughing, he recognised the look in her eyes, and put the tray down carefully on the shelf beside the bed. With a swift movement he flicked back the covers from her naked body, one hand stroking down over her slender curves in a gesture of lazy possessiveness. 'I was thinking pretty much the same thing myself.'

She tried to protest, but it lacked conviction. She had lost count of the times they had made love through the night, sleeping at last only when the birds had begun tuning up to welcome the dawn. But it had only made her want him more, and now the still-smouldering embers kindled instantly into flame as she responded again to his touch, her body melting beneath his caresses, yielding to the sweet pleasure as he took her with a deep, thrusting demand, lost in the mindless rapture of loving him.

At last, sated, he helped her to sit up against the pillows. 'Lustful woman. Now your cornflakes have gone cold,' he teased, reaching across to get the bowl for her, nestling her into the crook of his arm to eat them. 'Eat them up—I have news.'

'News?' she demanded between eager spoonfuls. 'What news?'

'Eat your cornflakes and then I'll tell you.'

'I'm eating them!' she squawked in protest. 'Tell me now.'

'OK, OK. I think we may have tracked down at least a couple of links in the chain of Lester's activities. Remember that cop I met in Miami? He called an hour ago. He's managed to turn up some very interesting information.'

'Wow! That's brilliant!'

'Hey… Careful with those cornflakes!' he protested as she bounced on the bed, spilling milk. 'Anyway, I've arranged to fly over this afternoon and meet with him.'

'This afternoon…?'

He nodded, his eyes serious. 'We need to get at this information before Lester has a chance to cover his tracks. I'll try to get back this evening—but if we do turn up any more promising leads it may be worth my staying over for a day or two to follow them up. You'll be safe here with the boys.'

She nodded, trying to smile. 'Yes…of course…' She wanted to ask if she could go with him, but she didn't want to seem clingy.

He laughed, that low, husky, sensual laugh, and plucked the empty cereal bowl from her hands, reaching across her to put it on the shelf beside the bed. 'But I don't have to leave for half an hour,' he growled, bear-like, rolling on top of her. 'There's a lot you can do in half an hour…'

With Hugh gone, the day seemed awfully flat. Natasha, lounging on the sun cushions on the for'ard deck, tried to tell herself that it was only natural to feel a sense of anticlimax after the excitement of the past few days, but she couldn't help feeling bored. And lonely. She missed Hugh. She knew it was stupid—he had been gone for only a couple of hours. But she couldn't help it.

Left alone, she was prey to a thousand anxieties. Marry in haste... And they could hardly have been more hasty. OK, at the moment Hugh seemed to be in love with her— but was it based on anything more substantial than the wild flames of sexual desire that ignited between them whenever they came close to each other? Would it burn itself out as quickly as it had begun?

It was hard to believe that just a week ago she hadn't even known he existed, she reflected with a small sigh. She had been independent and happy—well, reasonably happy, anyway. Now she felt as if she was on a roller-coaster of emotion, out of control and terrified that she was heading for a serious fall.

At least the boys were good fun to have around. They had been a little shy of her at first, but they had soon warmed up, amusing her with their tales of the Whitbread race, making her laugh with the way they constantly abused and insulted each other—although it was clear that they were all the best of friends, ready to rely on each other in life-or-death situations out on the world's most dangerous seas.

Jurgens had appointed himself her loyal servant, bringing her iced drinks and constantly asking if there was anything she wanted. He cooked her a delicious crab curry for dinner, but her appetite really couldn't do justice to his culinary efforts.

Finally, in an attempt to distract herself from her blue mood, she asked him for the mobile phone and tapped out the casino's number—she had been too busy yesterday to check what was happening in her absence. Until the trust was wound up there was still the nagging worry about what Lester might do.

She held the phone cautiously as she listened to the ringing tone, ready to disconnect immediately if Lester answered it—though he was rarely in the office this early. But, to her surprise, instead of the assistant manager's it was Debbie's voice she heard. 'Debbie?' Her voice was sharp with anxiety. 'What are you doing there? Is everything OK?'

'Oh… Natasha. Hi—how are you? Everything's fine. I'm not in the office—I'm upstairs. I'm just fetching a few things from the apartment for Lester. I thought it might be him ringing from the hospital; that's why I picked up the phone. They're keeping him in for another night—his blood pressure's a bit high.'

'I'm not surprised,' Natasha responded dryly. 'I've always said he'd blow a gasket if he wasn't careful.'

'He's still in a foul mood,' Debbie confided. 'I suppose it's understandable, having had that nasty bang on the head, poor love. The silly thing is, they wouldn't have got away with anything worth stealing from that safe anyway—he only uses it for papers and things. Anything important's in the other safe.'

Natasha frowned sharply. 'What other safe?'

'You know—the one he had installed in his room.'

'He's got a safe in there as well?' Natasha demanded, feeling a sudden surge of excitement.

'Yes. I…assumed you knew about it.' Debbie's voice faded into uncertainty. 'Oh, dear—you won't tell him I told you, will you? Even I'm not really supposed to know about it, only I saw him closing it one day when he thought I was having a bath.'

Natasha's mind was flipping into overdrive. If there was

any evidence to be found at the casino, it would be in that safe. And now was the best time to look for it—while Lester was safely in hospital, before he had a chance to dispose of it.

'Listen, Debbie, this is important. I need to know what's in that safe. I'm coming over. Don't tell Lester anything.'

'But...'

'Please. I'll be over as soon as I can and I'll explain it all to you then. Wait for me.'

'Well...all right,' Debbie conceded doubtfully. 'But I promised to go back to the hospital this evening, with his things. He's sick of wearing hospital pyjamas and wants his own.'

'I'll be there in half an hour.'

She clicked the 'disconnect' button and closed the phone, her brow shadowed with thought. 'Jurgens, I have to go over to the casino,' she announced urgently. 'Do you think you could find a taxi or something to get me there?'

Jurgens' earnest face took on a troubled look. 'To the casino? But the Skipper said I was to look after you,' he insisted.

'All right—you can come with me if you like.' She didn't have time to waste arguing with him. 'Just see if you can find us some kind of transport.'

Half an hour later she was clinging to his back as they bounced along the rutted island roads on the ancient moped he had somehow managed to borrow. By the time they reached the casino Natasha felt bruised all the way down her spine. In spite of his determination to obey his orders to 'look after' her, she was inclined to think she'd send him back on the darned thing while she got a taxi.

They slipped into the casino by the back entrance, exchanging brief hellos with the kitchen staff who, under-standably, were startled to see her. With Jurgens as her conscientious shadow, she hurried straight upstairs to the apartment. Debbie was still waiting, agitated, her face pale as she paced the floor.

Natasha had spent most of the journey—when not dis-tracted by the discomfort of her rear end—trying to work out how best to explain it all to the older woman. In the end she had decided that she should simply tell her the whole story. 'Sit down, Debs,' she advised wryly. 'This is going to upset you.'

She hadn't overstated. Debbie's innocent blue eyes widened at each new revelation, beginning to fill up with tears. 'Oh, the poor boy!' she whispered when Natasha described what had happened to Hugh's nephew. 'But Tony de Santo? Why would he owe money to him? Ugh—he makes my flesh crawl.'

'Mine too,' Natasha acknowledged with a touch of as-perity. 'The thing is, if Lester's mixed up with those kind of people he could be in big trouble—either from them or from the law, whoever catches up with him first.'

'And you think there's something in the safe that could have something to do with it?'

'I don't know, but I think so.' She watched anxiously as Debbie chewed over the information she had just im-parted, her clear brow creased into a troubled frown.

'I don't want him to go to prison,' she argued, still unwilling to accept the unpleasant truth.

'It might not have to come to that,' Natasha urged, feeling a little guilty at what she was fairly sure was a lie. 'He could get immunity by giving evidence against them.'

'But that could be dangerous,' Debbie protested.

'He's in a pretty dangerous situation anyway,' Natasha

pointed out. 'These are not nice people to be involved with.'

'No…' Debbie shook her head, twisting her hands in her lap. 'Oh, how could he be such a *fool*?'

'Look,' Natasha prompted gently, 'I know this is difficult for you, but will you show me where the safe is?'

Debbie hesitated, and then nodded reluctantly. 'I… suppose it's for the best.' She rose to her feet and led the way into Lester's room. 'It's…at the back of the cupboard, behind the drawers,' she indicated, pointing. 'But I don't know the combination.'

It was a built-in wardrobe that ran right along one wall, fitted inside with shelves and several sets of drawers. Natasha opened the door that Debbie had pointed to, and knelt on the floor to carefully slide out the drawers and stack them beside her. Behind them was an innocent-looking back panel.

'Are you sure this is the one?' she queried.

Debbie nodded dumbly. 'He had some kind of key— not a proper key, just a bit of bent metal.'

Jurgens came over to look, stooping to peer into the space. 'It's an Allen key,' he announced, putting his hand into his pocket and pulling out an impressively large penknife. Sorting swiftly through its various appendages, he found something that looked just like a bit of bent metal, and reached into the cavity. After a few moments' fiddling, he grinned in triumph and sat back on his heels, bringing the back panel with him. 'There…!'

'Jurgens, you're a wonder!' Natasha declared.

The young man blushed deeply. 'Ah, well, you know…'

Natasha peered into the cupboard again. There was a safe there—not very large, but certainly big enough to hold papers of some kind. She nodded, and sat back on the edge of the bed, frowning in deep concentration. Lester wouldn't have used the same combination as the one in the sitting room. So what other numbers would be significant?

As she gazed blankly around the room, as if seeking inspiration, her eye fell on the telephone beside the bed. It was the type with letters as well as numerals on the dial-pad. Now why would Lester go to the trouble of getting one like that? Unless... Quickly she knelt by the safe again. 'Debbie, what's the number for the letter L?' she asked excitedly.

Puzzled, Debbie peered at the telephone. 'It's the four.'

Natasha turned the combination wheel to four. 'And for E?'

Taking all the remaining numbers that spelt out Lester's name, Natasha tried the handle—and with a satisfying click the safe door swung open. Inside there was a metal box, which she drew out—the safe was actually quite deep, able to hold more than she had expected.

She put the box down on the floor and lifted the lid. 'What's in it?' Debbie asked, coming to kneel beside her as Jurgens peered over their shoulders.

'There's a couple of smaller boxes—this one looks like it could have held diamonds,' Natasha mused, not wanting to disturb the contents too much. 'And.. Ah, now this looks interesting.' She reached in and took out a small notebook, and flicked open the pages. 'Except it looks like it's in some kind of code...'

'Natasha...?'

They all turned, startled, at the sound of Hugh's voice. The door banged open and he crossed the room in two strides, hauling her to her feet. 'You damned fool!' he raged, his eyes blazing with anger. 'What are you doing here? Couldn't you stay safely on the boat for one afternoon?'

She barely had time for a single gasp before he was kissing her with a ferocity that took her breath away. And with a surge of pure joy she realised that he was angry because he was worrying about her. And you didn't worry about someone unless you really cared about them...

When at last he let her go he hugged her close, glaring furiously at Jurgens. 'I thought I told you to look after her?' he demanded.

'Don't blame poor Jurgens,' Natasha pleaded. 'I insisted on him bringing me over. If I'd known you'd be back tonight I'd have waited for you.'

'I decided that even catching Lester out wasn't worth missing a night with you,' he murmured smokily, his eyes glinting with unmistakable promise. 'What was so damned urgent that it couldn't wait until tomorrow?'

'We've found Lester's secret safe,' she informed him, concealing her delight behind an affectation of dignity. 'Debbie told me about it, and I thought it might be important. Lester's still in hospital, so it seemed like the best possible opportunity to see if I could open it. And I did—look.' She handed him the book with a triumphant flourish.

He took it from her, studying some of the pages with careful attention.

'Can you work out what it means?' she queried excitedly.

He nodded. 'Putting it together with the information I got this afternoon, it all fits,' he confirmed. 'It's exactly what we were looking for—the proof in his own writing...'

'Very clever,' came a sneering voice behind them.

Debbie let out gasp of shock. 'Lester! You're supposed to be still in the hospital.'

'I discharged myself,' he responded coldly. 'And it looks as though it's a good job I did. I thought I could at least depend on *your* loyalty, but I see that behind my back you've all been conspiring together.'

'Oh, Lester—I did it for you,' she protested tearfully, reaching for his arm. 'You could get into terrible trouble...'

'Oh, you stupid bitch,' he snarled, shaking her off roughly. 'I'm already in far more trouble than you could ever imagine. Thanks to you.' He turned his baleful glare on Hugh. 'You were so clever, weren't you? You really set me up.'

'Just as you set up Peter Seymour.'

Lester returned him a blank look. 'Peter who?'

'You don't even remember him, do you? He's my nephew. He's just twenty-one years old—and you very nearly ruined his life.'

'I can't remember every kid,' Lester countered dismissively. 'Anyway, I could have got myself straight—I had it all nicely worked out—if you hadn't damned well interfered again.'

'You're crazy,' Natasha put in. 'I would never have agreed to sign over Spaniard's Cove to Tony de Santo.'

Lester laughed, an unnervingly crazy sound. 'Oh, yes, you would—once Tony had got here. He's got ways of making people do what he wants. But it's me he's going to be after now, so I've got nothing to lose—I've got to make a run for it anyway. I've got everything all set—I just came back here to pick up a couple of things. And here you all are—handing me the perfect opportunity to settle up before I go.'

Natasha felt herself tense. At this moment he was mad enough to do anything...

'I've thought a lot about killing you, Garratt.' There was a glint of wild hatred in his eyes as he lifted a gun and pointed it at Hugh. 'You took everything I'd worked for all these years—my little nest-egg—in one night. But killing you would be much too quick—I want you to suffer. So I'm going to take the thing that you want the most.'

Abruptly he turned the gun on Natasha, and with a sudden shock of horror she realised that he was really going to pull trigger.

'No!' With a lightning reaction Hugh pushed her out of the way.

'No...!' Natasha felt herself falling backwards, her cry not for herself but for Hugh, who was now in the line of the bullet that Lester had meant for her.

'No...!'

The gunshot exploded at the same second as Debbie's wild shriek as she launched herself at Lester, trying to knock the gun away.

There was a silence that lasted as long as a heartbeat, and then Debbie began to scream.

Pinned to the floor beneath Hugh's weight, Natasha saw a pool of blood spreading scarlet from the shoulder of the other girl's pink blouse. Lester was swearing violently, struggling to get out from beneath her and a toppled chair, as Jurgens, his face white behind his freckles, but set with grim determination, stepped in swiftly and grabbed the gun from his hand. And from downstairs came the sound of shouts and footsteps as the casino staff, hearing the sound of the gunshot, raced up to see what was happening.

Hugh was on his feet almost at once, quickly pulling Natasha up from the floor. 'Are you all right?' he asked, cupping her faced in his hands, his eyes shadowed with concern.

'Yes.' She reached up and wrapped her arms tightly around his neck, pressing her eyelids shut and breathing in deeply the warm, live, musky scent of his skin. 'I thought he was going to kill you.

'I thought he was going to kill *you*,' he returned thickly, hugging her convulsively close for just one brief moment before letting her go, their eyes exchanging the swift message that any more could wait until later.

Natasha turned her attention to poor Debbie and hurried to her side, relieved to find that, although she was bleeding badly from the wound in her shoulder, it could have been a great deal worse. 'You fool!' she chided her gently, reaching for one of Lester's shirts that had been on the chair and using it to stem the blood. 'That was a crazy thing to do.'

'I didn't want him to go to prison,' Debbie whispered, leaning weakly against her. 'If he'd killed one of you, he would have got life. I know he's done some terrible things, but...I still love him.'

Lester—hauled to a sitting position by Hugh, who had relieved Jurgens of the responsibility of the gun and now looked as if he would be prepared to use if it necessary— was staring at Debbie, looking almost as shocked as she was. 'Debbie...? I'm...I'm sorry...' he stammered, reaching out an unsteady hand to touch her arm.

'Oh, Lester...! You *fool*.' And she burst into tears.

'Jurgens, you'd better call for an ambulance—and the police,' Hugh instructed grimly. 'And tell them to hurry.'

Their 'later' proved to be several hours later, after they'd seen Debbie off in the ambulance and Lester in the police car, given their statements and soothed the agitated casino staff. The moon, only just a little past the full, was sailing high in the sky as they climbed from the taxi that had brought them back from the casino to the secluded cove where *The Kestrel* lay quietly at anchor.

Natasha paused for a moment, gazing up at that slightly narrowed silver disc while Hugh paid off the taxi. He came up behind her, slipping his arm around her waist and smiling down at her. 'What are you thinking?' he queried softly.

'Oh…just that the first night you came to Spaniard's Cove the moon looked like that, except the other way round—just coming up to the full. Eight days ago. It's hard to believe—everything seems to have happened so quickly.'

'True,' he conceded. 'But now we have a little time to catch our breath.'

'Yes.' She turned into his arms, folding her own arms around his neck and curving her body against his. 'We nearly didn't. I thought…when you pushed me out of the way…you'd been…' A shudder ran through her, and she hugged herself close against him, breathing again that subtle, musky scent—so male, so alive. 'If he'd killed you…'

He stroked a kiss along her trembling eyelids, brushing away the tears that were wetting her lashes. 'Shh… It's all right, it's over now. And we have each other, and the rest of our lives.'

'Yes…' Blinking back the tears, she opened her eyes to gaze up into his. 'We do, don't we?'

'You believe that now?' he asked, his voice softly serious.

'Yes.' She reached up on tiptoe, her lips parting hungrily to welcome his kiss.

All her doubts had vanished, blasted away by the sound

of that gunshot. The rest of their lives… Yes, she knew now that he had meant it. The truth of it was in his kiss, a kiss of such deep tenderness, promising to cherish her for the next fifty years, to their own Golden Wedding and more.

And she gave him the same promise back, curving her supple body into the hard length of his…until the flames of a hotter fire rekindled, and their breathing became ragged, urgent—and the soft moonlight shadows beneath the whispering palms that fringed the white sandy beach became too beguiling an invitation to resist…

An hour or so later they were strolling hand-in-hand along the water's edge, bare feet dabbling in the warm, rippling wavelets. The moon sparkled silver on the dark Caribbean Sea, reflecting like the million stars in the velvet cloak of the midnight sky.

'I have to admit it wasn't quite the response I might have expected to a proposal of marriage,' Hugh was saying, soft laughter in his voice. '"I wouldn't want to put you to any inconvenience!"'

Natasha laughed too, glancing up at him in shy happiness. 'I just never thought…not for a minute…that you might *really* want to marry me.'

'I know. I suppose with that devious stepfather as your principal example of male integrity it really wasn't surprising that you found it difficult to trust me.'

Natasha smiled wryly, shaking her head. 'I *was* afraid to trust—I didn't think it could last. I've seen it all so many times around the casino—men who fall for a pretty face, and then within a year or so they're bored, and looking for a change. It always seemed kind of like borrowing a book from the library and then taking it back two weeks later. I thought that love had to take much longer.'

He laughed, soft and husky, lifting the hand he was holding in his and laying a kiss on the band of gold around her third finger. 'Well, it really doesn't matter now. Apart from poor Debbie, it's finally worked out right.'

'Yes. And even Debbie didn't seem to mind getting a bullet in her shoulder, now that Lester's finally decided he really does love her. And at least with him in prison she'll know exactly what he's getting up to!' she added on a lilt of amusement.

The water rippled around their feet, the sand tickling their toes as it ebbed away. 'And in a few days the trust will be wound up and you can close down the casino,' Hugh remarked.

She nodded, one small shadow falling across her happiness. She would miss Spaniard's Cove. 'I expect I'll be able to sell it for quite a good price now, with the tourist industry booming. When we go back to England, I...'

He shook his head firmly, and she slanted him a look of puzzled enquiry.

'Who said anything about going back to England? You don't really want to leave Spaniard's Cove, do you? We'll stay here and turn it into a holiday resort, just as you planned.'

She stared up at him, her heart spilling over. 'You're sure...? You really want to stay here?'

'Of course.' He laughed, a rich, glorious sound, lifting her off the ground and spinning her around. 'Why would I want to go back to cold, wet, rainy old England when I can stay here in paradise?' He set her back on her feet, still holding her close, those smoky grey eyes telling her everything her heart needed to know. 'A paradise complete with my very own angel.'

THE CHILDREN'S DOCTOR

by

Joanna Neil

When **Joanna Neil** discovered Mills & Boon her life-long addiction to reading crystallised into an exciting new career, writing for Medical Romance™. Her characters are probably the outcome of her varied lifestyle, which includes working as a clerk, typist, nurse and infant school teacher. She enjoys dressmaking and cooking at her Leicestershire home. Her family includes a husband, son and daughter, an exuberant yellow Labrador and two slightly crazed cockatiels. She currently works with a team of tutors at her local education centre to provide creative writing workshops for people interested in exploring their own writing ambitions.

Joanna Neil has a brand-new Mills & Boon Medical Romance® available next month. Look for *The London Doctor*.

CHAPTER ONE

THE sound of a steel band drifted across the deserted cove, a relaxed and dreamily heady tempo that seemed to invite the tapping of feet and the rhythmic swaying of hips. Listening to it, Anna smiled. Wasn't this what the Caribbean was all about?

She breathed in deeply, soaking up the sights and sounds, absorbing the atmosphere all around her. A tropical heat haze shimmered over the golden sand, and there was only the faintest breeze to stir the fronds of the palm trees fringing the beach. It made her thankful that she had chosen to wear just a skimpy cotton top and a skirt that swathed her hips and left a good deal of her legs bare.

The music must be coming from the other side of the headland, she decided, scanning the horizon. At the far end of the cove, a limestone bluff thrust its way into the sea, and she could see numerous small inlets which had been formed there by the weathering of the crags over time. The ground below was strewn with rocks, adding a touch of grandeur to the landscape.

As she looked around, she suddenly became aware of snatches of a different sound being carried on the air, one that mingled with the lively throb of steel drums and made her pause for a moment to listen more intently. What was it?

She frowned. It wasn't the sound of the sea...that was too calm, surely, with waves lapping at the shore in desultory fashion, breaking up into lacy ribbons of white foam that melted away almost as soon as they had formed. No, it was something else that she had heard.

Then, with a faint sense of shock, she made out a muffled sobbing, like that of a child in pain. The sound squeezed at her heart and spurred her into action, driving her to anxiously search amongst the boulders to find out where it was coming from.

After a while, hidden behind a large rock, she came across the huddled form of a small boy. He looked as though he had hurt himself, and instantly compassion washed through her like a tide, making her want to hug him to her.

'Oh, you poor little thing,' she murmured softly, bending down beside the child. 'What's wrong, sweetheart? Have you hurt yourself?'

He couldn't have been much more than three years old, about the same age as her nephew, and she felt an overwhelming rush of sympathy for him. Concern, too. What on earth was he doing out here, alone?

'Shall I have a look at you and see if I can do anything to help?'

The little boy stopped crying for a moment, staring at Anna with wide brown eyes that seemed to grow larger with every second, but he didn't say a word.

She smiled encouragingly. His reaction to her didn't surprise her very much...he was only little and he was right to be wary of strangers.

This little boy had warm golden skin tones and

JOANNA NEIL 7

black hair that hugged his head in a mass of tiny springy curls. He was very much like Daniel in his colouring, and the knowledge tugged at her heart all over again.

'Is it your arm?' she asked, seeing the way that he was holding it, stiffly, as though moving it would have caused him more pain.

He nodded slowly, crying quietly again in soft little hiccups, but she was relieved to find that he understood what she was saying. She said carefully, 'What happened, can you tell me?'

'I felled over...' His lip began to tremble at the memory, and Anna put an arm around him in a comforting gesture, taking care not to put pressure on his shoulder. The collarbone looked slightly distorted, and her professional training told her that the long slender bone might have been broken. The collarbone was easily fractured in a fall onto the shoulder or an outstretched arm, and as a paediatrician she had come across the injury many times.

'I think you're being very brave,' she told him. 'Perhaps I can do something to help you. I'm Anna. What's your name?'

'Sebastian,' he lisped, choking down a convulsive sob. 'I want my mama... My arm hurts...'

'I know it does. We'll try to find her in a minute, I promise.' She soothed him quietly, holding him against her and lightly stroking his head until he was calmer. 'I think you might have snapped the bone in your shoulder,' she explained gently. 'That's why it's so painful, but it will mend, given time. A bandage might take the weight off it and help to make you feel a bit better. I'll see if I can find something in my bag that will do the trick, shall I?'

He didn't look too sure about that, but when she delved in her canvas bag and brought out one of the toy cars she had brought with her in case she managed to find Daniel, he looked at it curiously.

'Well, I never,' she said, looking at the shiny red sports car and feigning surprise. 'I wonder how that got in there? Here, would you like to play with it?'

She passed it to him while she searched for her silk scarf, and when she had retrieved the filmy square from the depths of the bag she quickly fashioned it into a figure-of-eight bandage, looping it carefully around his forearm and fastening the ends securely around his neck.

'There. Does that feel any better?'

He nodded slowly, still uncertain, but said politely, 'Yes...fank you.'

'Good. I'm glad.' As long as he was careful to keep the arm still, he shouldn't suffer too badly, but he ought to have some medication to relieve the pain, and that meant he would need to see his own doctor.

There was also a bump on his head and a slight graze, which needed checking out, and she would feel far happier if his parents were around to take care of him.

'Which way did you come, Sebastian? Do you remember?'

'From the party...over there.' With his free arm he pointed to a narrow inlet which cut into the headland and which Anna thought must lead to the next bay, the place where the music was coming from. The tide was out, and the passage through the rocks looked dry for the moment.

She frowned, turning back to the child. How could anyone be so selfish as to carry on partying and forget all about the boy? He was hardly more than a babe.

'I was going that way myself,' she told him. 'I'll take you back over there, and we'll see if we can find your mummy and daddy, shall we?' With any luck, they would already be out searching for him.

Sebastian's halting voice cut into her thoughts. 'Dada Carlos...' he said tremulously.

Anna guessed he still needed reassurance, and as she began to gently wipe his tear-stained face with a tissue from her bag, she repeated softly, 'Carlos... Is that your daddy?'

His eyes widened, shimmering still. 'Dada Carlos...' he said again, but happily this time. 'He's coming to fetch me...' And when she turned to follow the direction of his excited gaze, she was startled to see that a man was emerging onto the beach through an arch in the rock.

He stood for a moment, a tall, dark-haired man, silhouetted against the headland, his body lean and honed to physical perfection. Then he turned, his glance carefully searching the area until finally it came to rest on Anna and the boy. He started towards them.

He was long-limbed and lithe, Anna noticed, his movements supple and well co-ordinated as he stepped sure-footedly from rock to rock. He was wearing casual clothes—a T-shirt that spanned broad

shoulders and hugged a flat stomach, and light coloured trousers that faithfully moulded lean hips.

He came closer and Anna was able to see him more
clearly. His face was strong boned, firm jawed, his
features distinctively carved. She couldn't be sure and
he looked to be of European descent, but she guessed
there might be a Latin American streak. Like the
boy's, his skin was golden toned, but his hair was
different, crisply black, straight, short and attractively
styled.

Anna frowned. He was a man with responsibilities,
the father of a three-year-old child who should have
been kept under firm supervision. What was either
parent thinking of, leaving their son to his own devices, at the mercy of the rocks and the sea?

The man was within a few feet of them now, and
as he approached he cast a swift but thorough glance
over Anna before turning to the boy.

'So, here you are, Seb,' he said, his voice deep and
huskily accented. 'I've been looking for you. You
shouldn't have wandered off,' he added in a reproving
tone. 'We were very worried about you.'

Sebastian lowered his head, but said nothing until
Carlos, looking at the makeshift bandage, asked on a
concerned note, '*Qué pasa?* What happened to you?
Are you hurt?'

The boy's lip began to quiver all over again. 'I
wanted to look at the rock pools,' he managed, looking up at Carlos with tear filled eyes, 'but I
slipped...and I hurt my arm.' His little face crum-
pled.

The man bent to look at the shoulder, and then said,

'Poor lad, you are in a bad way, aren't you? But I can see that someone has bound it up for you. Was it your new friend who did this?'

Sebastian nodded solemnly. 'Anna maked it better…a bit… It's very hurting.'

He nodded. 'I can see that it still hurts.'

Carlos had been concentrating his attention on the boy so far, but now his glance shifted Anna's way, his gold-flecked eyes surveying her thoughtfully.

'It seems as though we're in your debt, Anna. It was good of you to take the time and trouble to stay with Sebastian and I'm very grateful to you for what you have done. You seemed to know exactly how to make him more comfortable, and we're both thankful for that.'

He sounded sincere enough, but Anna was still riled about his role in the affair and she wasn't going to allow herself to be sidetracked by his smooth manner. The man had neglected the infant and she wasn't about to let that pass without comment.

'There's no need to thank me. I would hardly stand by and do nothing, and I was glad to do what I could to help. It was upsetting, seeing him in such a state.' She paused, then added tautly, 'Perhaps if he hadn't been left to wander here on his own in the first place there would have been no need for me to step in.'

The tawny eyes flared and she wondered if her rebuke had scored a hit, but, instead of answering her, he looked down at the child once more, assessing him keenly.

Anna decided to press her point home. 'I think he has most likely broken his collarbone. The poor child is in a good deal of pain, you know, and he really ought to see a doctor as soon as possible.'

Carlos frowned as he brought his attention back to Anna. 'You're right. I'll see to it.'

'Good. I'm glad about that.' Sebastian was making little hiccuping sobs, and she guessed he was frightened, as much as anything, by what had happened to him. She cuddled him. 'I expect he'll need an X-ray, so that you can be sure of the extent of the damage,' she murmured.

He nodded. 'We'll go now.'

Anna gently stroked Seb's arm. Now that his father had arrived to take over from her, there was probably little more she could do for the boy, but she was very conscious of the child's trembling and she was feeling terribly reluctant to let go of him.

Seb looked up at her. 'You said you was coming with me,' he said haltingly, between his sobs, 'and we find my mama. I want you come with me.'

Carlos's glance shifted over both of them. 'Would you be able to come with us?' he asked. 'I think it would make Seb feel a lot better if you stayed. He's feeling hurt and probably he's frightened, too, and a little insecure just now.'

'I know,' she murmured. 'I guessed as much. Yes, I can come along with you.' She wanted to be sure that the child would be looked after properly. His father had shown little responsibility for the boy's welfare until now, and if she went with them she would feel as though she had done the right thing, and she would be certain that everything possible had been done to make him more comfortable.

She glanced towards the headland. 'I was going in that direction anyway. I was on my way to the harbour when I came across Seb.'

'*Bueno.* That's good. Thank you. It'll be much more reassuring for Seb if you're with us.'

The little boy managed a watery smile, and reached up to slip his free hand into hers. He looked up at her and whispered, 'Can I keep the car?'

Anna blinked in surprise. She had forgotten about the little red car. 'Of course you can keep it,' she said, and a tiny glimmer of relief came into the child's eyes.

Carlos's well-shaped mouth twitched into a wry smile. 'Three-year-olds obviously have very different priorities to us.' He reached down to lift the boy up, and she released him carefully into his arms. 'I'll carry you,' he told Seb quietly. 'We don't want to risk you taking another tumble, do we?'

He held him gently, taking care not to put pressure on the injured limb, and all three of them started to make their way across the beach to the bay on the other side of the promontory.

As they approached the archway in the rocks, the sound of music and laughter became louder.

Anna sent Carlos an oblique glance. 'Do you live close by?' she asked. 'I suppose you must, if Seb was right in saying that he had come from the party over there.'

'He was right,' he answered. 'Perhaps I should have introduced myself before this. I am Carlos Barrantes...my house overlooks the harbour.'

'I'm Anna Somerville,' she told him in return.

The rocks here were becoming precarious, and as she struggled to keep her balance he put out a hand to steady her, clasping her arm easily with his strong fingers. Her nerves sparked in response to his touch, and she forced herself to be calm. He was simply helping her out after all, and there was no need for her defences to go shooting to red alert.

'Were you celebrating a special occasion?'

'In a way. My friends and I are enjoying a small get-together this afternoon on the beach to celebrate a successful year... The harvests have been good, and business plans have gone well for the most part.' He sent her a sideways glance. 'And you? Were you planning on exploring the harbour, or are you headed for somewhere specific?'

'I was hoping to meet up with someone who lives near there,' she told him. She wasn't exactly sure where Nick's house was, but she could make enquiries some other time when she saw the lie of the land.

'Have we made you late?'

She shook her head. 'It doesn't matter. It wasn't a precise arrangement.'

In fact, Nick didn't even know that she was here. She was just hoping that her brother-in-law would be at home, and that she would be able to talk to him about her nephew, Daniel. She wasn't particularly looking forward to the meeting—he had never been the easiest of men to deal with, and this was no ordinary situation that she had to handle, was it? Was she up to it? She grimaced. The truth was, she had to make it work for her sister's sake.

By now they had reached the headland, and they

made their way through the narrow opening and onto the next beach. Here, as the vista opened up in front of her, Anna could see a party in full swing in the sheltered sweep of the beach, just a short distance away from the small harbour where a few boats bobbed idly on the water.

Close by, at the foot of steps leading to a verdant, terraced hillside, a barbecue had been lit, and the appetising smell of food wafted on the air, teasing her nostrils.

A couple of dozen people were dancing to the rippling sound of steel drums on the wide sweep of sand. Others were simply talking to each other as they helped themselves to drinks from a selection of punch bowls that were set up on a table in the shade of palm trees. More tables were laden with a tempting array of food—rice dishes, chicken, fish and salad, along with every kind of fruit imaginable.

'My car's parked over by the quay,' Carlos murmured, leading the way and nodding to people he recognised as he passed by them. 'It's just a short drive to the clinic.'

'Aren't you going to take him to the hospital in the town?'

He shook his head. 'The Mount View Clinic is nearer, and he'll be diagnosed more quickly there.'

'Oh, I see.' She frowned. She had heard of the clinic. It was a private enterprise, where cardiac patients were treated mostly, but presumably there was a range of other facilities, too. Carlos must be a man of means, to be able to drop in there at a moment's notice and still rely on getting immediate service.

They walked swiftly to the quay and found his car. It was impressive-looking, a large executive, midnight blue car. He settled Seb carefully into a child seat at the back, and the boy asked tentatively, 'My mama?'

Carlos bent down to him. 'Your mama was feeling a little poorly, Seb... Nothing bad, just that there was too much heat and it made her feel a bit faint. She has gone to lie down for a while. I'll make sure that you see her as soon as we get back from the clinic. Will that be all right?'

The boy hesitated a moment, then nodded. 'I fink so.'

'Good. That's settled, then.' Carlos came around the car and held the door open for Anna. She slid into the passenger seat and immediately felt the luxury of the car cloak her. Then Carlos climbed in beside her and started the engine, and they were on their way. They took the mountain road, following a circular route and climbing higher all the while.

They had been travelling for little more than five minutes when, as they swung around the next bend, the landscape suddenly opened up.

Anna caught her breath as she took in the sight of the wide sweep of a bay, with blue, crystal-clear waters reflecting the golden glitter of the evening sunlight. Above the bay, set back against the verdant mountain slopes, was a large, sand-coloured building surrounded by trees and exotic tropical plants.

That surely must be Mount View. It was the only building around and it was majestic, with wide windows and flower-filled balconies overlooking the sea.

It looked like a massive five-star hotel, Anna

thought as they approached it and finally drew to a halt on the wide driveway in front of the main doors.

'Here we are, Seb. Let's get you inside and take a picture of that shoulder. Then we'll be able to see just what's happened.'

Seb looked anxious, and Anna said gently, 'No one's going to do anything to hurt you, Seb. There's nothing at all to be worried about. I expect the doctor will give you something to take away the pain.'

Once again, Carlos picked up the child and took him into the building. Anna followed, her eyes growing large as she looked around the foyer. It was opulent in here, with deep-pile carpeting and smooth marbled pillars and overhead fans that hummed gently and made her think she was in another world. This was just a sample, and she could only imagine that the rest of the clinic was equally grand.

She daren't think how much it would cost someone to stay in a place like this. If the truth were known, she had never been comfortable with the fact that some people had to pay for treatment when they were unfortunate enough to be ill.

'We'll take him along to X-Ray first of all,' Carlos murmured. 'I'll have a word with the radiologist and explain the situation.'

'It's only a picture, Seb,' Anna explained. 'Just like having your photo taken, only the photo shows a little bit of what's inside you.'

Within minutes Seb had been X-rayed by a young woman who gently coaxed him into sitting for her. The boy looked wide-eyed and uncertain, and Anna smiled at him reassuringly.

Just a short time later the radiologist brought the films to Carlos.

'Look, you can see it quite clearly,' she murmured. 'They show a clean break.'

He looked at them carefully, then nodded. 'He'll need to keep the figure-of-eight bandage on for a while, until it heals.'

Anna was surprised at his confident statement. Did he know about medicine?

He hunkered down beside Seb and showed him the films. 'Can you see where the bone is broken, Seb?' He drew a long finger along the X-ray film. 'There it is, see? You'll have to take care not to knock it again. If you keep the bandage in place, it will mend and in a few weeks it will be stronger than ever.'

He smiled at the boy. 'Let's go and get you something to take the pain away. You've been a very brave boy. I'm proud of you.'

Seb managed a small smile, and held onto Anna's hand as they walked along a wide corridor.

It occurred to Anna that Carlos seemed to know his way around the place very well. He was leading them to the treatment room now, and his stride didn't falter once.

'That wasn't so bad, was it, Seb?' she asked as they walked along. 'We'll go and see the nurse now, and we'll ask her to put a dressing on the cut on your head as well as give you medicine.'

The child hadn't shown any signs of drowsiness or nausea so far, and she felt fairly confident that there was no concussion. She was glad of that. He had suffered enough and she didn't want to see him go through any more than he had already.

As a doctor, she ought to be able to keep a sense of perspective...a certain amount of distance between herself and the patient, she knew that...but it was much easier said than done. Somehow, each child she came across in her line of work managed to wind his or her way into her heart and steal a little bit of her...and Seb did remind her so much of her small nephew.

'Hello, Mr Barrantes.' A young, fair-haired nurse came to greet them and usher them inside the room. She looked down at Sebastian. 'What's happened here? Poor Seb, you look as if you've been having a bad time of it.'

Clearly, she knew Seb as well, and Anna found herself getting more and more puzzled as time went by.

'I felled over, and I broked my bone,' Seb told her. 'It hurts.'

'I bet it does, and you've banged your head, too. You poor little thing. Let me have a look at you and see if I can make you feel a bit better.'

Carlos lifted him up onto the treatment couch, and stood back a little as she gently dealt with the cut on the child's forehead.

As the nurse set to work, Anna said quietly to Carlos, 'People seem to know you around here. Seb, too. Are you frequent customers?' If they were, it didn't sound too good, did it? Were they always having accidents like this?

He made a wry face. 'They know me because I

own the clinic,' he told her. 'I'm a doctor, a surgeon. I work here.'

'Good heavens.' Anna was astonished. She blinked up at him, and tried to take it in. 'Now I see how you managed to find your way about the place so easily.'

Even so, she frowned. Just because he was a doctor and owned the clinic, it didn't alter the fact that the little boy had been allowed to wander off and get into that situation in the first place.

Surely someone in his position should have known better? He hadn't responded to her comments before, though, had he? Now, more than ever, she wanted to know what had happened.

CHAPTER TWO

KEEPING her voice low so that Seb and the nurse
wouldn't hear, Anna said carefully, 'You still haven't
explained to me how Seb managed to wander off on
his own. As far as I understand it, his mother wasn't
feeling well and he was left to his own devices, and
that could have led to something very serious happening. He could have ended up being much more
hurt than he was. I'd like to know what happened.'

Carlos studied her thoughtfully. 'His mother was
taken ill quite suddenly…nothing serious, but she is
pregnant and the heat made her feel faint. When she
collapsed, we all rushed to help her, and I think Seb
may have slipped away while we were making sure
that she was all right.'

He glanced at the little boy, who was sitting up
straight on the couch and beginning to appreciate being the centre of attention as the nurse fixed a dressing
in place on his forehead.

'Perhaps he was frightened and wanted to get away
from all the fuss. When I turned around to reassure
him that his mother was going to be all right, I realised that he had gone and I went after him. I don't
suppose he was out of our sight for more than a few
minutes.'

'Oh, I see…' At last he had given her some kind
of explanation. 'I suppose that's understandable, up

21

to a point,' she conceded doubtfully. 'Children are
like quicksilver, aren't they? They can be lost in a
flash.'

'Unfortunately, you're right.'

The nurse said with a smile, 'All finished. Just a
spoonful of medicine now.' She popped the spoon in
Seb's mouth and he swallowed carefully. 'There.
Good boy. We're all done.'

She smiled up at Carlos and handed him the bottle
of painkilling medicine. 'You can take him home
now.'

Carlos helped the child down from the couch and
held his hand as they went back towards the car. Seb
was walking proudly now, Anna noticed with a smile,
showing off the sticker that the nurse had placed on
his shirt.

On the drive back to the quay she said, 'Have you
had the clinic for a long time?' Carlos looked too
young to have achieved so much. He was probably
only in his mid-thirties, and she couldn't imagine how
he could have established something like that in just
a short time.

'I had it built about four years ago. Mostly we treat
cardiac patients there, although we sometimes carry
out other treatments as well. For a long time I thought
there was a need for a clinic out here. A lot of people
want to be able to have cardiac surgery fairly quickly
after they've been diagnosed as needing it. They don't
want to run the risk of their condition deteriorating
before an operation is available. Unfortunately, there
was nowhere locally where they could go. The hospital waiting lists can be very long.'

'So you believe that you're fulfilling a need.'

'I'm sure that I am.'

'It must have taken a small fortune to establish something like that,' she murmured, 'let alone to keep it running.'

He didn't appear to be taken aback by the directness of her comments. 'That's true enough. I was fortunate. I inherited a certain amount from my grandparents, who used to be landowners, and, of course, there are sponsors who take an interest.'

It wasn't long before they arrived back at the harbour, and Carlos slotted the car smoothly into a parking place by the quay. Anna glanced at Seb and saw that he was falling into a slumber, his eyelids flickering faintly as he tried to keep them open.

She said softly, 'Look at him. He's tired out. It must be all the stress of the afternoon catching up with him.'

'I'll take him back to his mother so that he can rest,' he murmured, going around to lift him out of the car. Seb leaned his head on Carlos's shoulder and he looked so cosy that Anna guessed he would soon be fast asleep. 'Come and join the party on the beach for a while, and I'll come back to you in a moment.'

'There's no need for you to do that,' she said quickly, as they walked towards the shore. 'Stay with him. His mother might still be feeling ill and not able to look after him.'

'Someone's with her. I made a point of making sure that she wouldn't be left on her own. I have to come back here anyway and organise a few things. Stay a while and enjoy the food and have something to drink. You must be thirsty by now, and it's the least we can do to thank you for looking after Seb. I'm really very grateful to you for everything that you've done this afternoon.' A smile tugged at his mouth. 'Please, wait for me. I'll only be a minute or so.'

'Well, maybe just for a little while,' she told him. She *was* thirsty after the heat of the afternoon, and for the moment the sights and sounds of the Caribbean were all around her, helping her to relax. The food smelt delicious, and the gentle lilt of the music began to gradually work its way into her soul.

'I'll get José to look after you while I'm gone. If there's anything you want, just ask him and he'll get it for you.'

It was all done so smoothly. Carlos made a simple, quiet request, and his wishes were obeyed without hesitation.

José came over to her right away. He was a young man in his late twenties or thereabouts, lean and dark-haired, and he didn't seem to mind at all being asked to take care of her.

'Let me get you a selection from the table,' he said, disappearing for a few minutes and then coming back to hand her a plate that was piled high with delicious titbits to tempt her palate. 'I've brought you a glass of fruit punch, too. I think you'll like it,' he added with a wry grin.

Anna accepted the glass from him and took a careful sip of the drink, rolling it lightly over her tongue and feeling the instant kick in her throat as she swallowed.

'Rum?' she asked, her eyes watering, and he nodded, smiling.

He was right—it did taste very good. She tried to relax and enjoy what was left of the afternoon, sampling the food he had brought her with appreciation and occasionally taking a slow sip of her drink. After a few minutes she went to sit in the shade of the palm trees and watch the festivities going on all around her.

The people were friendly and quite a few stopped to chat, curious to know about the English girl in their midst. For the most part she answered amiably enough, saying that she was here to work and expected to stay for several months, but she carefully evaded any searching questions about her background.

Carlos Barrantes's friends, especially one or two of the younger men, wanted to know if she had any romantic attachments back home, but she wasn't about to give them any details of her love life. One young man, perhaps encouraged by a little too much alcohol, became slightly more amorous in his attentions than the others, but just as she was beginning to feel uncomfortable José appeared, and the man melted into the distance.

'Thanks,' she murmured gratefully, guessing that he had been keeping watch, and he nodded.

'Are you OK?'

'I'm fine, thanks.'

She wasn't sure she was ready to handle romantic overtures right now. Over the last year or two, she had come to the conclusion that romance simply didn't seem to be working out for her. Perhaps her ideals were set too high, but she felt a strong need to be cautious around men. She certainly didn't want to repeat the mistakes that Sarah, her sister, had made. Sarah's marriage had gone badly wrong, and now her husband, Nick, had taken their child.

At least now that Anna was out here she might be able to talk to Nick and persuade him to see Sarah's side of things. He couldn't just go off halfway across the world with their child and expect to get away with not taking him back home, could he? With all the miles that separated them, it was difficult for Sarah to sort things out herself.

Thinking back to that phone conversation with her sister just a few hours ago, she gave a shaky sigh.

'I'm sorry to put all this on to you, Anna,' Sarah had said huskily. 'I just don't know what else to do. I don't want to involve the authorities just yet, not while there's still a chance we can sort things out between us.'

'I think that's probably the best way to handle it for now,' Anna had told her. 'And you mustn't worry about me. I want to help any way I can, and it looks as though I'm going to be close enough to where Nick lives to be able to keep an eye on things. I'll let you know as soon as I find out anything at all, I promise.'

'It's so unfair,' Sarah had said. 'He was supposed to have brought Daniel back to me after four weeks, and there's been no explanation at all as to what's happened. I had a feeling he would do something like this. I hate being stuck here with this wretched broken leg and having to leave everything to you.'

'I know it's hard, but you must try not to worry,

Sarah. It will only wear you down. Anyway, it's not as if he's disappeared into thin air, is it? We'll find him soon enough, and I'll talk to Nick and have a go at making him see sense. I'll do whatever I can from this end, I promise.'

Anna took another sip of her drink, and mulled over the conversation. She rubbed her bare arms as a breeze stirred the trees around her and she felt suddenly chilled. Lost in thought, she wondered what had happened to the heat of the sun that had warmed her up until now. Clouds were beginning to build up across the blue of the sky, and it looked as though rain was threatening in the next hour or so.

A shadow loomed beside her, and Carlos Barrantes said, 'You're looking very solemn, Anna. *Lo siento.* I'm sorry...I hope I haven't kept you waiting for too long.'

She blinked, adjusting her gaze to take in his tall, powerfully muscled figure. 'No, it doesn't matter. You weren't gone for very long at all.' Absently she chafed her bare arms once more.

'Are you cold?' His gaze slanted over her slender curves, and she quickly shook her head.

'No, I'm fine.' His eyes narrowed as she made the denial, and to fend off any further enquiry she asked, 'Is Seb all right?'

'He's fast asleep.'

'I thought he might be.' She smiled. 'I suppose the medicine will have started to work.'

'I should imagine so, by now.' He glanced around, nodding to José, who appeared to be mouthing a question to him, and Anna watched the interchange, wondering what it was all about.

He turned back to her a moment later. 'I'm sorry about that... I didn't mean to be inattentive, but José needed to borrow my car.'

The music had stopped while they'd been talking, and it gradually began to dawn on Anna that something odd was going on all around them. There was a good deal of movement taking place as tables were cleared and the musical instruments were being packed away and carried off in some haste. It was plain to see that the party was breaking up, and people were beginning to leave.

She was puzzled. Why had the leisurely atmosphere suddenly disintegrated ever since Carlos had returned? True, the air was cooler now but, even so, it didn't seem reason enough to abandon the festivities so abruptly.

'Everyone appears to be leaving,' she murmured. 'I think maybe I had better go, too.' Perhaps she would head for the harbour and try to find Nick's house.

He frowned. 'It's not a good time to think of leaving just now, with the wind getting up. It happens here sometimes...not often, but the weather can change and it can become blustery very quickly.'

'I expect I'll manage,' she said. She looked around, and realised that the crowd of people was rapidly dwindling. It all seemed so strange. Why was everything happening so quickly? Was something going on that she didn't know about?

'Where did José have to go?' she asked uneasily.

'He's going to drive some of my friends home. It will be quicker for them by car.'

'You put a lot of trust in him, don't you?'

'Yes, I do. He works for me at the clinic, and I've always found him to be reliable.' He searched her face keenly. 'Didn't he look after you properly?'

'He looked after me very well.'

'Good,' he said. 'That's what I had expected.' He cast a careful glance up at the sky where dark rain-clouds were beginning to gather and murmured, 'We should talk later. Just now it's more important to think about your safety. I'm afraid we're in for a storm, and we should take shelter.'

'But the weather was beautiful just an hour or so ago,' she said in surprise. 'Surely it will pass?'

'I'm afraid it won't. Things can get out of hand quite quickly out here in the Caribbean, and I think we should be taking cover before it gets too bad. Let me take you up to my house where we can be comfortable.'

'Oh, no, you don't need to do that. I'm not afraid of a summer storm.'

His brows met in a dark line. 'I don't think you understand,' he said, his voice threaded with seriousness. 'This is no summer squall. There has been a hurricane warning on the radio, and we have just a short time to prepare ourselves for what is to come. It is important that we find shelter as soon as we can.'

'A hurricane?' she echoed, the breath leaving her lungs in a sudden rush. 'I wasn't expecting anything like that so soon after arriving in the Caribbean.'

'There is no doubt, and this is the hurricane sea-son.' His gaze flicked over her. 'What matters now is that we get away from here as soon as possible.'

She shook her head, unable to take in what he was saying. If it was true, it really was bad news...but surely it wasn't very likely after a lovely day today? As to going along with him, she really wasn't in any hurry to shut herself away with a man she had only just met, no matter how respectable he appeared to be. Anyway, surely his priorities should be his wife and his child?

'I can look after myself,' she said, crossing her fingers mentally that she would be able to get back across the bay before the wind took hold. 'It will only take me a few minutes to get home. I only live across Blue Water Bay—'

'No, that's too far. I really can't let you take that risk.' His expression was darkly autocratic now, his mouth held in a firm, unyielding line. 'I must insist that you come with me.'

'No...that's all right, I can manage.' She didn't know an awful lot about hurricanes, but from what she had heard there was usually time enough to get to safety and batten down the hatches.

She started to turn away, but he caught hold of her arm and brought her back to him.

'Since you're with me,' he remarked crisply, 'you're my responsibility. We'll stay together.'

'I can take care of myself,' she protested.

His mouth made a derisive twist. 'I don't think so. You have no idea what you are up against. You're obviously very new to this area, or you would understand what I am saying.'

He started to draw her away from the beach to-wards a flight of steps that led to higher ground.

She said quickly, 'Look, I have to get to the harbour. I need to meet up with someone.'

'I'm afraid your meeting will have to wait. Right now you have to come with me, and this is no time to argue.'

Carlos held her firmly, and his touch had such a potent effect on her nervous system that heat surged through her veins, pulsing like an electric current until her ears throbbed with sensation. She tried again to pull away from him, and he looked down at her in exasperation.

'We don't have time for this,' he said grittily. 'If you don't stop behaving like a foolhardy juvenile, I shall be forced to throw you over my shoulder and carry you up to the house. Believe me, that will not improve my temper.'

His features were determined, and Anna had no doubt he meant every word of it. Dry-mouthed, she shivered as an unexpected gust of wind swirled around her and buffeted her with such force that it threatened to topple her over.

Carlos reacted instinctively, his arm closing around her and pulling her into the shelter of his hard body, so that her soft curves were crushed against him. The breath caught in her throat as she registered taut male sinews and powerful muscles.

Around them, the once smooth beach was being stirred up into a mini-sandstorm, and pieces of drift-wood that had lain on the beach just a moment ago were lifted as though by some invisible force to be held aloft on a wild current of air. Seconds later they were hurled in a willful paroxysm of violence against the harbour wall.

She watched it all happen with a sense of shock. It came to her then, in a heart-stopping moment, that perhaps what he had been saying about the storm was the truth after all, and the hurricane must be more imminent than she had imagined.

The awful reality was that she was stranded here, and totally dependent on him.

CHAPTER THREE

A TURBULENT blast of air eddied around Anna, whipping at her legs, so that she had to struggle to keep her filmy skirt in place. Holding onto it as best she could, she finally asked in a small voice, 'How long is the hurricane likely to last, do you know?'

He looked up at the brooding sky, then threw her a sideways glance. 'It's hard to say. It could be over by morning, I suppose.'

Anna's jaw dropped. *By morning?* There was no way she was prepared for that.

He must have seen her look of horror, because he said dryly, 'I see you've recognised the seriousness of the situation at last. Perhaps now we can hurry up and find shelter before we both become yesterday's news.'

A pulse started to hammer in her throat. She pulled in a shaky breath and tried to calm herself, desperately hoping that he couldn't hear or feel the sudden frantic thudding of her heartbeat. Around her the wind swirled and tormented, lifting her hair and tossing it about with reckless abandon.

Carlos wasn't about to wait for her to get herself together. 'This way,' he said, tugging on her arm and pressuring her towards the steps that led away from the beach. 'We've wasted enough time already.'

He moved so fast that she might have stumbled if

it hadn't been for him practically lifting her off her feet and hauling her along with him. They went swiftly towards the quay, then bypassed the harbour front and started to turn away from it towards higher ground. Here there were steps built into the hillside, and he took her up them, keeping hold of her as he balanced himself against the force of the wind with a hand firmly gripping the rail.

Anna began to tremble violently as the cold air assaulted her bare arms and legs, and she put up a hand to protect her face from the lash of the biting wind.

'Lean into me,' he said, drawing her up against his hard, masculine frame. 'Let my body shield you from the gale.'

He had her in a firm grip, crushing her to him so that their bodies meshed, and there was no room for her to manoeuvre. Her legs tangled with strong thighs and she could feel the vitality pulsing through every part of his body.

How could this be happening to her? She had only met this man just a few short hours ago and now here she was pressed up against him in a way that did nothing whatever to spare her blushes.

Her only consolation was that he was generating a good amount of heat to counteract the chill of her bare limbs, and that wasn't altogether surprising, given the amount of energy he was expending, battling with the elements. She relished the warmth that closed around her like a blanket, and tried not to think about the enforced intimacy.

'It's not far now,' he said, and she marvelled at his

stamina. Her own breath was coming in short bursts after all the exertion, yet his voice was as deep and firm as ever. 'My house is just a bit further up here.'

She was wholeheartedly glad that it wasn't far away. Around her she could hear the creaking of trees and the rattling of loose weatherboards on the houses, the slam of wood as it hit stone, and it was scary to think that all this chaos had erupted in such a short time. She was almost thankful that Carlos was so close, and that his male strength was something she could rely on.

They climbed for a few minutes more, then he led the way along a narrow, winding route until they came to a private road leading to a high stone wall. Halfway along the length of the wall there was a gated entrance, marked by pillars on either side.

'Here we are,' he said, aiming a remote-control device at the wrought-iron gates so that they swung slowly open. 'This is my home.'

By now the force of the wind was making breathing painful and the only way to avoid the brunt of it was to keep her head down. After they had hurried some way along the drive, though, Anna looked up, and then gasped as she saw in front of her a magnificent, white-painted plantation-style house.

It was two storeys high with a covered veranda all around, as far as she could see, and a corresponding upper balcony. Pale blue shutters sealed off the windows from the storm, and she wondered who had taken care of that task. His wife, probably. It must mean that she had recovered from her earlier bout of illness.

It would also mean that Sebastian was here and that she would most likely see him again. It would be good to see him when he was more like his normal self, after the initial pain of his injury had worn off.

Carlos let them into the house through the screen door, and as soon as they were inside the wide entrance hall, and the inner door was shut behind them, Anna became aware of the total contrast between this and the outside world.

While Carlos made a quick check of the alarm system she took the time to push her fingers through her long, wind-tousled hair, and then she looked around. The hall was as large as a room in itself, the floor laid with palely gleaming golden oak, and in all reflected a pleasing atmosphere of peace and serenity.

Her gaze was drawn to the finely textured wall coverings all around, which had a delicate, silk-like quality, soft hued to reflect the light. The high ceiling added to the impression of openness, and the flower arrangements that adorned little alcoves here and there added vibrancy and colour. The whole effect was welcoming and inviting, and she couldn't help feeling that in here they might be well and truly secure from the havoc being created outside.

She stood for a moment, simply absorbing the quiet of the place. Then it slowly began to dawn on her that perhaps there was another explanation for the apparent tranquillity. Could it be that the wind outside had dropped as suddenly as it had begun?

Carlos came to stand beside her and she asked tentatively, 'Is it my imagination, or have things suddenly quietened down?'

'They may have calmed for the moment,' he agreed. 'Though we'll feel it less in here anyway because of the high walls surrounding the place.' He threw her a cynical, narrowed glance. 'You weren't, by any chance, thinking that the storm might suddenly be over, and that you could actually leave, were you?'

She felt the betraying heat race along her cheekbones. Why did the man have to see right into her thoughts like that? She tried a nonchalant shrug. 'I just thought there was the possibility it might have blown itself out, that's all.'

'You don't know much about hurricanes, do you?' he said pithily.

Her shoulders stiffened at his tone. 'Not an awful lot, no.' She resented his sarcasm, and she tacked on succinctly, 'But, then, I haven't spent most of my life in this region of the world.'

'That's been fairly obvious from the outset,' he commented. 'Just to be absolutely clear about what's going on—this one may be in its infancy just now, and we may be experiencing a bit of a lull, but generally a hurricane will grow and become more powerful, and when the storm returns the wind will be back in full force. Believe me, you wouldn't like to be out there when that happens.'

She pulled in a quick breath at his clipped summary. 'I suppose I'll have to take your word for that, won't I?' This whole situation was making her edgy with frustration and she looked at him with doubt clouding her eyes. 'I'm new to all this,' she said raggedly. 'It isn't something I was prepared for.'

His eyes glinted. 'Is that a concession? Can I take it that you're resigned to sitting it out now?'

She winced. 'I don't appear to have any other options, do I?'

He raised his eyes heavenward. 'At last, she begins to see sense.' Moving closer, he placed a hand at her elbow and nudged her forward. 'Come on through to the living room, *por favor*. You'll be more comfortable in there.'

He drew her across the hall to another set of doors that opened out into a large room, bordered completely on two sides by full-length glass windows. These were blanked off right now by louvred shutters, which somehow cleverly managed to let in a degree of natural light.

Someone had lit the lamps that sat on tables or in little nooks, and golden light spilled out to enhance the warmth of pastel-toned walls. Had his wife done that, too? Had she gone to settle their little boy and soothe him while the storm lasted?

That thought gave her some degree of comfort as she stood for a moment, trying to take it all in.

'This is beautiful,' she said at last, softly, her glance travelling slowly around the room. She really hadn't expected to be so overwhelmed by the sheer elegance of this house, but it truly was beautiful, and there was a feeling of light and spaciousness in everything she had seen so far.

In here, all was simplicity, each item in the room flawless, from the delicately figured silk screen that stood to one side and the graceful simplicity of a Grecian statuette to the stylishly upholstered sofas that faced each other across the smooth lines of a low, glass-topped table.

He indicated the sofa nearest to her. 'Sit down, and I'll get you something to drink,' he suggested. She settled herself on one of the softly cushioned seats. 'Would you like coffee, or something stronger?'

'Coffee will be fine, thanks.'

He left her then, and she sat back and looked around once more, feeling the ravages of the last hour slowly ebb away. She wondered about Carlos, and about how much of the character of the man was revealed in this house. Everything in the room had been carefully chosen, she guessed, to reflect an exquisite taste, a desire for those fine touches that would add to the perfection of the architectural design.

When he came back a few minutes later with a tray of coffee, Anna said quietly, 'Have you lived here long? It looks as though you've put a lot of time and effort into making this house special.'

'This was my parents' home at one time,' he said. 'It's built on the edge of a coffee estate they owned for many years before they moved on to other projects. My father is more interested in the manufacturing side of things nowadays, food processing and so on. He's American, and he has a lot of interests in the United States, as well as here.'

He placed the tray on the table and she saw that he had laid it with coffee-pot, cups and a plate of freshly made triangular-shaped sandwiches, along with a selection of nibbles that looked enormously tempting.

'What about your mother? Does she have a career of her own?'

'She writes for magazines, mostly. Articles on the places that they visit or special cookery features. She's Spanish, so she tends to enjoy writing about dishes with a European flavour.'

'It sounds like interesting work,' Anna commented with a smile. 'So, what has happened to the coffee estate? Has it been sold?'

'No, I took it over from them.'

She frowned. 'Isn't that an awful lot of work for you with all your other commitments? The clinic, I mean.'

'It could be, but this estate is in partnership with several others, and I have managers to oversee it. My work as a surgeon takes up the bulk of my time.'

She was puzzled. 'What made you take up medicine when you had all this? You can't have needed to go in for all that training, all the hard work, when you could have simply carried on in your father's footsteps.'

'*Es verdad.* That's true enough...but I had a young friend who had a heart problem,' he said quietly. 'His family had travelled a lot, and he developed rheumatic fever when they were in a country where medicines were hard to come by. The fever damaged a valve in his heart.'

He frowned, thinking about it. 'I watched him struggle day by day. He couldn't even walk a short distance to the shops without becoming short of breath, and he was often in pain. More and more I found myself wishing that something could be done to help him. In the end, a surgeon replaced the valve in his heart, and after that his health was much better.'

She could imagine how he would feel. 'That must have had a profound effect on you.'

'It did. It made me think a lot about medicine, and when I went through school I became determined to study hard. Later on I decided that I wanted to take up surgery. Luckily I had the dexterity to manage it.'

'And then you set up your own clinic.' She smiled up at him. 'Do you still see your friend? He must be very proud of you.'

He nodded. 'You've met him already.'

'Have I?' She was puzzled, thinking back to all the people that she had met this afternoon.

'José looked after you, didn't he? He's been a friend of mine for a long time.'

She was startled. 'I didn't realise...he looks so well.' She frowned. 'What does he do at the clinic? Did he take up medicine as well? I wouldn't have thought he would be strong enough to face up to the rigours of training and all the hours on the wards. It's a very demanding job.'

'You're right. He chose to work in administration instead. He's very good at what he does.'

He pushed a plate towards her. 'Help yourself to a sandwich. It's getting close to supper time, and you must be hungry again by now.'

She glanced down at the slim gold watch on her wrist. 'Heavens...' she said with a faint sense of shock. 'I hadn't realised how fast the time had slipped by.'

'Does that matter?' he asked with a wry twist to his mouth. 'There isn't much you can do if you're caught up in the middle of a hurricane except to sit it out.'

She grimaced. 'I suppose you're right. I'm sorry that I didn't take on board what you were saying straight away. It just hadn't occurred to me that I might be caught up in one almost as soon as I landed here. It's really good of you to take care of me like this.'

'You're very welcome. It's the least I could do, to make sure that you're safe.' He made a face. 'These storms happen on and off at this time of the year. Mostly we're prepared for them, and on average they're not on a grand scale so they don't wreak the havoc you might expect. It's only every few years or so that one comes along and is so fierce that it's given a name of its own.'

'You're used to them, then?' She helped herself to a sandwich and bit into it with appreciation, surprised to discover that she was actually very hungry.

'You could say that.' He took a swallow of his coffee and put his cup down. 'Why don't you tell me about yourself? You said you had only just arrived here. Does that mean you're here for a holiday?'

She shook her head. 'No, I'm not on holiday. I'm here to work.'

'Really?' His tawny eyes flashed with interest. 'Tell me about it. What kind of work will you be doing?'

'I'm a doctor, too,' she explained. 'I'll be working at the public hospital, on the children's ward mainly.'

His dark brow lifted. 'That explains things,' he said thoughtfully. 'I wondered how it was that you were able to help Sebastian so well. At the time I thought perhaps you had learned first aid.' He smiled at her. 'So, are you a specialist…a paediatrician?'

'That's right. I've always wanted to work with children, as far back as I can remember, but I came to a point where I wanted to widen my experience.'

'Is that what you're going to be doing here?'

She nodded. 'I want to learn something more about tropical medicine, so when this job came up I thought it would be ideal. I've travelled quite a bit with my parents in the past—my father's a TV journalist and he reports from various parts of the world—but I've never visited the Caribbean until now. I thought this would be a great chance to get the best of both worlds.'

'Do you know anyone out here?'

'Only my brother-in-law. He lives by the harbour, and I was hoping to see him while I'm over here.'

'Perhaps I know him. What's his name?'

Was it likely that Carlos would know Nick? Then again, her brother-in-law was a wealthy man, too, and maybe his path had crossed Carlos's at some point. She said quietly, 'Nick Armand. He has a house close to the Harbour Lights Hotel.'

'Nick Armand, the hotelier?'

'That's right.' She gave him a searching look. 'Do you know him?'

He nodded. 'I do. He's a good friend of mine, as it happens. But you won't find him at home.'

Anna frowned. 'How can you be sure of that?'

'He's gone away for a few weeks with his young

son…your nephew, presumably. He had it in his mind to go on a tour of the islands.'

Anna gasped. 'Are you sure?'

'Don't you believe me?' Once more the brow lifted.

Anna winced.

'What I meant was that I just didn't expect him to have taken off like that with Daniel…not without saying anything to anybody…to Sarah, I mean…to his wife.'

'His wife is in the UK,' he said laconically. 'It was her choice to stay there, from what I've heard. Nick is simply giving his son the kind of childhood he believes he deserves, a chance to have fun and see something of the world.'

'He doesn't have the right to just decide things like that on a whim, though, does he? Daniel should be with his mother.'

'Should he? Has that been settled in the courts? As I understand it, there has been no divorce as yet.'

Anna drew in a deep breath. 'I'm not going to discuss my sister's marital affairs with you. Daniel was supposed to be returned to his mother weeks ago! They had an agreement.'

His mouth made a cynical twist. 'It doesn't look to me as though that agreement stands any longer.'

Her green eyes sparked. 'You don't see anything wrong in what he's doing, do you?' Carlos was very much like Nick in a way, a wealthy man with all the authority and self-assurance that affluence brought. She guessed he would be used to having his own way in most things, and he would more than likely take Nick's side.

He shrugged eloquently. 'Who is to say that a mother is always the best parent for a child? Men can have an equal capacity to love their offspring. It isn't written in stone that a child should always be with his mother.'

'I've always believed that the bond was unbreakable,' she said in a strained voice.

'I'm not saying that it isn't. I'm merely pointing out that there are two sides to be considered.' His glance skimmed her taut features. 'When he gets back in a couple of weeks' time you'll have your chance to talk to him, and perhaps then you will have a more open mind on the situation.'

She shook her head. 'I shan't change my mind.' This wasn't good news, and it was difficult for her to accept that she would simply have to sit back and wait for Nick to return. Added to that, some time in the next few hours she would have to phone Sarah and break the news to her. It wasn't a conversation she was looking forward to.

'Let's not argue about it, anyway,' he said with a faint smile. 'You were telling me about your new job. I'm sure it must have been an opportunity too good to miss. How long will you be here for?'

'Several months. I'm here in place of someone who has taken maternity leave.'

She was distracted momentarily by the sound of the wind howling through trees outside, whipping at the branches until she heard ominous cracking sounds. So Carlos had been right, and the gale was back. Fearfully, she wondered what kind of devastation was going on all around them. It was almost too frightening to contemplate.

'Don't think about the storm,' he told her, and she looked up with a start to see that he had been watching her. 'You're safe enough from it in here. The walls are strong and the shutters are all in place to protect the glass. Believe me, this place has stood the test of time, and there's nothing that can be damaged in even the severest gale.'

She chewed at her lip. 'Yes, I can see that must be right. It's just that it takes some getting used to.'

'Try to forget about it. You were telling me that you're here for a few months,' he prompted her, and she wondered if he was trying to take her mind off things. 'What happens after that?'

With an effort Anna dragged her attention back to what she had been saying. 'I suppose after that I'll have to take some time to think about what I want to do. There was some talk of a job in London being made available for me. At least I'll have gained greater knowledge of tropical medicine and, the way I see it, the more experienced I am in all forms of medicine, the more choices I'll have in the long run.'

He helped himself to a sandwich. 'That sounds sensible enough.'

She nodded. 'And in the meantime, I thought I would make the most of being here in the Caribbean. There's no point in coming somewhere like this and not seeing as much of it as you can. I've been reading up on some of the best places to visit. If I get the chance, I'll try to fit some of them in whenever I have time off.'

'You don't want to stick to the tourists' favourite haunts,' he said wryly. 'There are other beauty spots—quiet, secluded places that are less well known to the cruise-ship passengers.'

'I expect you have to be a local to find them.'

'True enough.' His glance flicked over her. 'I could show you, if you like.'

The offer had come out of the blue, and now she eyed him cautiously. Perhaps he thought she had been hinting.

'Thanks…' she murmured. 'That's very kind of you, but I expect you'll be too busy with other things to do that.' She needed to tread warily here, didn't she? After all, why would he want to spend time with her, when he had a wife and child who were relying on him to take care of them?

'Other things?' he queried lightly.

'Well…your family, for a start,' she answered on an even note. 'I'm sure they must expect you to spend your free time with them.' How uncaring could he be, that he needed her to spell it out for him? 'Especially your son. After all, he's not much more than a baby, and he needs you.'

He threw her an odd glance, but recovered his composure soon enough, looking at her in a strangely detached way so that for a second or two she thought she might have struck home. Then, bemusedly, he repeated, 'My son?'

'Sebastian. Don't you think he depends on you?'

He blinked, clearly needing a moment to take this

in. Then he said softly, 'Ah…now I think I see what's going on in your mind.' He paused before adding, 'There is one thing I should perhaps tell you…'

'What's that?'

His gold-flecked gaze rested on her upturned face, his mouth shaping a faint smile. 'I am not Sebastian's father.'

She let out a small gasp. 'But…but he called you Dada Carlos…'

He seemed to be amused by that. 'He has called me that ever since he has been able to talk. His father is away on business quite a lot, you see, and his mother—my sister—has relied on me to act as a father figure in many ways.' He gave a rueful grimace. 'Unfortunately, I think the name has stuck.'

'Oh…' Anna didn't know what to say.

'Oh, indeed.' His tawny eyes sparkled as he registered the pink flush of her cheeks.

Dazedly, she tried to take it all in. How could she have got things so wrong? Everything that had happened this afternoon and evening seemed to have conspired to confuse her, leaving her uneasy and uncertain.

She sent him a troubled glance. 'Then…you're not married,' she managed weakly, still trying to adjust to everything he had said.

'I'm not married.' His lean, sculpted features seemed to darken a fraction, a muscle flicking along the line of his jaw.

She said weakly, 'And you don't have a child?'

His brows drew together. 'That goes without saying.'

It also explained how the house could stay looking so perfect, didn't it? Everything she had seen so far was immaculate, not a thing out of place, and it simply didn't look like the sort of home where a child could rampage about.

She drew in a deep breath. 'I had expected that Seb and his mother would be here. I thought, when I saw that the lamps were lit and the shutters were drawn, that someone must have prepared the place. I assumed it must have been your wife...'

He shook his head. 'Martha, my housekeeper, would have done that before she went to her own home. She's very good, and the truth is I rely on her far more than I should. She has never let me down.'

'Oh, I see.' She was floundering now. 'Somehow, I had taken it for granted that I would see Sebastian again. I was sort of hoping that I would see him when he was fully recovered.'

His mouth made a crooked shape. 'Somewhere along the way you've developed a soft spot for him, haven't you?' His glance shifted lightly over her guarded expression, then he said wryly, 'You're much too sensitive to make a good doctor, Anna. How on earth will you cope with the children on your ward if you worry over each one with such intensity? You'll end up as a shadow, with all the substance drained out of you.'

'I'd sooner that than not to care at all,' she retorted stiffly.

His sceptical glance spoke volumes. As though to underline her difficulties, she heard the shutters begin to rattle, as though the elements of nature were building up to a crescendo of rage once more and were making a determined effort to shake them loose. She hoped Carlos had been right when he'd said they wouldn't succeed.

'Why don't you try to relax?' he suggested, reading her strained expression.

Anna wasn't too sure that was possible. After all, she was alone in the house with a man she had met only that afternoon, and from the furious sound of the storm outside she was likely to be with him for some time to come. Added to that, she had discovered that there was no wife and no child to act as a protective barrier.

He was watching her, waiting for a response, and she said carefully, 'Maybe I'll feel happier when the storm is over.'

'Possibly.'

She wasn't fooling him for a moment, and she found herself wondering if it was possible that he could actually read her mind.

He reached for the coffee-pot. 'Would you like more coffee?'

She shook her head. 'No, thanks. I've had plenty.' She stretched, trying to ease limbs that were beginning to ache after the climb up from the harbour. 'Actually, I'm feeling quite tired now. Perhaps I ought to go and freshen up. That might make me feel a bit better.'

'I'll show you where the bathroom is.' He got to his feet and said lightly, 'If you want to call it a night now, that's fine by me. The storm isn't going to let up for a few hours yet, so you may as well settle yourself to the idea of staying over. You can have my sister's room, if you like. She uses it when she comes to stay, so there are clothes of hers in there that you can borrow.'

'Won't she mind?'

'It's highly unlikely. Saskia's very laid back and, anyway, at the moment she wouldn't fit into any of them.' A gleam lurked in the depths of his eyes. 'She's about seven months pregnant and showing every bit of it.'

'Will she be all right? You said she was feeling faint earlier, didn't you?'

'We have to keep an eye on her. She was anaemic, so her obstetrician prescribed iron tablets, but until they take effect she's tired a lot of the time. Then her blood sugar varies, so that's another thing that needs watching.' He grimaced. 'The biggest problem is that the baby's lying in an oblique position. It will mean that we have to take special care during the delivery, because if it doesn't turn before then she'll need a Caesarean section.'

'Presumably the decision to go ahead with that will be taken in good time. It's not something her doctor would want to leave to the last minute.'

'Try telling my sister that. She hates the thought of an operation.'

He waited while Anna stood up, then led the way out of the lounge and up a flight of stairs. At the far end of the landing he pushed open a door and said, 'Here we are. This is Saskia's room.'

Like the rest of the house, it was furnished in exquisite taste. The divan bed looked soft and inviting to Anna's weary eyes, and she fell in love with the sun-drenched colour scheme, reflected in the warm apricot bedcovers and the filmy voile curtains that were draped across floor-to-ceiling windows.

Carlos crossed the room and drew back a sliding glass door. 'Your bathroom's through here. Help yourself to whatever you need, and if you can't find what you want, just ask.'

She followed him, her gaze travelling over the ivory-coloured suite and gleaming gold fittings, and the glass shelving that housed all manner of toiletries. She would be spoiled for choice. There were ornaments, too, dainty porcelain swans and little dishes filled with an assortment of bath pearls and perfumed soaps, which added a delightful touch to what was already a beautifully feminine room.

'Oh, it's lovely. Thank you. I shall be fine in here.'

Anna turned to him, a smile curving her mouth, and then she caught sight of a mirrored wall to one side of the room. Lifting her glance, she let out a little cry of dismay as her reflection stared back at her.

'Oh, no…oh, how did that happen? I look an absolute fright…'

The woman in the mirror looked like a total stranger to her, an untamed, wanton creature with a mass of honey gold curls tumbling about her face and shoulders in wild disarray, her green eyes wide and startled. As to her clothes…she daren't even think about the state they were in. The fabric of her skirt had moulded itself to her thighs, leaving even more of her legs bare than before. As to the top, it must surely have shrunk.

'Oh, lord,' she muttered. 'I didn't realise…'

Carlos looked on with lazy interest, his glance moving warmly over her from head to toe as he leaned negligently against the wall.

'You look absolutely fine to me,' he murmured, an odd huskiness coming into his voice. 'Slightly tousled maybe, a touch abandoned…but very definitely sexy.'

His gaze lingered momentarily on her softly feminine curves, a smile touching his mouth. 'And a body that would turn hearts to flame,' he added thickly. 'But it's the eyes that add the finishing touch, I think… Pure emerald…beautiful.' His mouth tilted. *'Madre de Dios*…if I were a saint, I'd relinquish my vows of chastity here and now.'

He moved away from the wall, coming closer, and Anna flashed him a warning glance. 'Don't even think about it,' she muttered.

He laughed softly, making a wall with his hands in self-defence. 'It's OK,' he murmured. 'I got the message.'

'Good,' she said huskily. 'I'm glad about that.' She looked at him warily, her emotions totally confused.

With a rueful twist to his mouth, Carlos started to ease back from her. 'I'm going,' he said.

Anna watched him walk away, but he paused at the door, turning to say softly, 'Of course, if you should change your mind at any time…' A half-smile played over his lips. 'If the storm should bother you, for instance…'

'I won't change my mind,' she told him cautiously, and waited for him to go.

Obligingly, he stepped out of the room, closing the door behind him, but the unmistakable rumble of his husky laughter stayed with her, drifting mockingly on the air.

CHAPTER FOUR

ANNA blinked as sunlight streamed in through the windows and made a feathery dance on her eyelids. Still dazed from sleep, she stared around her, taking in every angle of the unfamiliar room until at last she remembered where she was. Carlos's house.

She sat up in bed and looked quickly around. Someone must have come in and pulled back the shutters while she slept, because there was sunshine and warmth in every part of the room, the start of a beautiful new day.

There was no sign of Carlos, but there was a tray with a pot of freshly made tea on the table beside the bed and a silk robe had been carefully laid on a chair by the dresser.

She frowned. How long had she slept? Was it very late? One thing was for sure, she had better get a move on and get herself washed and dressed before he had the chance to walk back in and throw her into confusion all over again. A flush of heat suffused her whole body as she thought back to last night and the way he had looked at her.

The clothes she had worn yesterday had mysteriously disappeared, so she had little option but to search the wardrobe and borrow something of Saskia's as he had suggested. A cool-looking pale yellow shift dress looked about the right size, and she slipped it on, thankful that it fitted her as though it had been made for her, except for the length which was a little shorter than she would normally have worn. She would tell Saskia how grateful she was if ever she had the chance to meet up with her.

Hurrying downstairs a few minutes later, she went looking for Carlos, and heard noises coming from a room somewhere to her left. It was probably the kitchen, judging from the clatter of pans, and she headed in that direction.

A buxom woman was standing by the hob, skilfully tossing eggs in a pan, but she turned when she heard Anna come into the room.

'Hello, there.' The woman greeted her with a smile. 'I'm Martha. Sit yourself down at the table, girl. I've cooked you some eggs.' She scooped the mixture from the pan and slid it on to a plate.

Anna returned the smile. 'That's how I like them. Thank you.'

'Good. You go on, then, and get started.' She nodded towards the oval table. 'Best you eat 'em while they're hot.'

Anna sat down at the table, and did as she was told. The food was delicious, and there was a jug of hot coffee to wake her up to the day. She helped herself and wondered where Carlos was, but when she asked the housekeeper, she simply shrugged and said, 'He had to go out. He's always busy, busy.' She rolled her eyes heavenward. 'He works too hard. Even on Sunday, he has to go out. He says you must wait for him to come back, please.'

Anna wasn't too sure about that. Who could tell

how long he might be? She still had a lot to do in preparation for work tomorrow. 'Was it you who brought me the tea and opened the shutters in my room?' she asked.

The woman nodded. 'It's good to see the sun in the morning. My old bones don't like the cold.' She gave a mock shiver. 'Last night was no good at all.'

Anna finished breakfast a few minutes later, and when Carlos still hadn't come home she decided that she couldn't wait around for him. Perhaps the hurricane had affected the plantation in some way and he would be delayed for some time.

'Thanks for breakfast,' she told Martha. 'I'd better be on my way now. I'll see to it that Saskia's clothes are washed and sent back just as soon as I can.'

'But you are going to wait, aren't you, girl? Lord, what will Mr Carlos say when he gets back, if you've gone already?'

'I'm sure he won't mind at all, Martha. I'll leave him a note to thank him for letting me stay, and I'll explain that there are things I must do. I really can't stay any longer.'

Her first day at the hospital started bright and early.

'So you're Dr Somerville?' Tom Raynor, the registrar, greeted her with a smile and clasped her hand warmly in his. He was tall and slim, young for a registrar, Anna guessed, perhaps in his early thirties, with fair hair that was tidily cropped. 'I'm glad to meet you, Anna. I've heard a lot about you, and I'm happy to have you on board. From what I've heard, your qualifications are quite impressive.'

'Well, thank you,' Anna murmured. 'I'm looking forward to working here.'

'You might not be so keen after you've been here a while,' he said with a laugh. He drew her towards the office. 'Have you had a chance to look around yet?'

She shook her head. 'Not yet. I had to come in on the bus this morning, and it didn't leave me much time.' With all that had gone on over the weekend, she hadn't managed to sort out a car for herself yet. The bus had dropped her off outside the gates, and that was the first sight she'd had of the hospital.

It was a modern building, large by any standards, with separate blocks for Outpatients, Pathology and Clinical Sciences. The wards were housed in wings that looked out onto paved and attractively landscaped areas.

'Well, not to worry. Come and have a coffee, and then I'll show you around before the morning rush starts. We've been really busy here just lately, so your input will be more than welcome. You'll be covering all the main paediatric wards along with me—surgical, medical and infectious diseases—but we'll start you off on admissions this morning.'

The morning rush came before they were ready. There were two admissions in the first hour, both patients with fractures, and Anna hardly had time to take a breath before a third child was brought in.

She hurried forward, ready to assess the child's condition, then came to a sudden halt when she realised with a shock that the man carrying the infant was Carlos. He was dressed in formal clothes this morning, and she had a swift impression of an expensively tailored grey business suit and a beautifully laundered linen shirt. Even his shoes looked impeccable.

'*Buenos dias*, Anna,' he murmured, slanting her a quick glance. 'I have a small patient for you. Her name is Jessie. Will you attend to her, *por favor*?'

Anna's mouth had dropped open in surprise at the way he had appeared out of the blue, and now, as he quietly voiced his request, she clamped it shut and tried to pull herself together.

'Of course.' The nursing team quickly found a trolley bed and Carlos gently laid the infant down on it.

The dark-skinned little girl was just a baby, really, Anna judged, about eighteen months old, and she looked very poorly. She was listless, and there was a bluish tinge about her mouth. Then she coughed and squirmed in distress, breathing raggedly.

Anna bent over the child. 'Hello, chick,' she said softly. 'Poor little one…you're not very happy today, are you? Let's have a look at you and see what's wrong.'

Very gently, she examined the child, soothing her as she listened to her chest through her stethoscope. There were bubbling noises coming from the tiny lungs, and she was wheezing. Anna checked her temperature. When she had finished, she looked up and saw a young woman hovering anxiously nearby.

'Are you Jessie's mother?' she asked.

The woman nodded. She, too, was dark-skinned, probably in her early twenties, tall and slender, and she was beautiful, with well-defined cheekbones and a full, wide mouth.

Carlos intervened smoothly. 'Anna, this is Grace, Martha's daughter.'

Anna was startled. 'Really? Hello, Grace.' She smiled at her. 'I've met your mother. She was very kind to me.' She paused for a moment, then asked, 'Can you tell me how long Jessie has been ill?'

The child coughed again and began to cry miserably, and Grace looked at her distractedly, biting her lip.

'She's been snuffling these last few days,' she said. 'I thought she just had a cold, but this morning she was hot, and she doesn't look right.' She was shaking her head, clearly fretting about the little girl. 'I asked Mr Carlos if he would have a look at her. I don't like asking but I don't know what to do.'

Carlos shook his head. 'That's all right, Grace. You did the right thing.'

Anna said quietly, 'I think it was a good thing that you brought her here. I believe that Jessie has a virus infection which has affected her lungs and made her feverish. She's finding it quite hard to breathe just now, and I think she needs a little bit of help to make her more comfortable.'

Grace looked anxious. 'What will you have to do?'

'We can give her oxygen and humidify the air for her so that she won't have to struggle so much. We'll arrange for her to have physiotherapy as well to help clear the mucus from her chest.'

Grace's eyes widened. 'She needs to stay here?'

'Yes, I think so, Grace. She'll be better off in hospital for a few days at least, until her chest is clear.'

The mother said shakily, 'It's bad, then? Is she very

poorly?' The child coughed again and started to cry, and Grace reached down to stroke the infant's hair with a trembling hand.

'She is poorly, but this is a virus that can sometimes affect children of Jessie's age,' Anna said gently. 'It isn't unusual. She'll be better off in hospital, you know…we can keep an eye on her here.'

Grace was looking deeply unhappy, and Carlos intervened softly, 'You could stay with her. I'm sure we can find you a place to sleep. It won't be anything grand, but at least you'll be close by. Would you like to do that?'

Grace nodded, and he gave her a slight smile. 'We'll arrange things for you.'

Anna said quietly, 'It will be reassuring for Jessie to have you close by. We'll move her onto the ward now, and we can start the treatment straight away. I'll prescribe a course of antibiotics to prevent any secondary bacterial infection. Try not to worry. You can rely on us…we'll take very good care of her.'

The nurse on duty came to take them both up to the ward, and Anna wrote out the treatment chart, then said, 'Maria will look after you both. If there's anything at all that you're bothered about, just ask away.'

Carlos reached out and touched Grace's arm. 'I'll come and find you and see how you're doing. If there's anything you need, just let me know.'

'Thank you. Thank you for seeing Jessie and for bringing us here.'

'That's all right. You're welcome.'

The nurse took Grace and the child away, and in

the quiet that followed their departure Anna looked around and realised that she was now alone in the examination room with Carlos.

She glanced up at him. 'We'll look after her.'

'I know you will.'

She said hesitantly, 'I'm sorry that I couldn't stay yesterday to say goodbye to you. There was so much I had to do back at the apartment.'

'That's all right. I understand. Did Martha look after you all right?'

'Yes, she did, thanks. I didn't know how much longer you were likely to be. I wondered if perhaps your crops had been affected by the storm and that might be the reason you were delayed.'

'No, it wasn't that. My crops were fine. The beans had already been harvested and sent for processing. I was called out to the clinic, and things took longer than I expected.' He grimaced. 'It came at a bad time... I'd hoped to drive you home, and make sure you were all right.'

'It didn't matter. Anyway, your patients come first.' She shrugged lightly. 'I'm all right, as you can see.'

Perhaps the shrug was a mistake. His glance followed the movement, slanting over the skirt and top that clung to her like a second skin. Then his gaze lifted to dwell on her shining, freshly washed hair, and she saw a faint glint of amusement come into his eyes.

'I certainly can.'

A flush of heat ran through her cheeks. She didn't need three guesses to know what he was thinking, did she? The memory of that night would haunt her for ever, and no matter how conservatively she dressed from now on, that wanton image would always be with her. As to her hair, it still refused to be tamed, but at least today she could be confident that it was clean and lustrous with health.

She said cautiously, 'I imagine Martha must be worried about her little grandchild. It must have seemed as though Jessie's illness came out of the blue.'

'She was concerned about her,' he said, and there was compassion in his voice. 'That's how I found out about it—she told me that she thought the baby was feverish, and there was something about all this that didn't sound quite right. I didn't think it was just a cold, so I decided I'd better go over to Grace's house and see for myself.'

'It's just as well that you did.' She looked at him with warmth in her eyes. 'She could have been very ill if she'd been left much longer.'

'I know. Just as I know you'll look after her now that she's here.'

'You can depend on it.'

He smiled at her, then glanced down at the watch on his wrist. 'I should go or I'll be late for my ward round. It's supposed to start in five minutes and I don't want to keep my patients waiting any longer than I have to. I'll see you later, Anna.'

He turned and moved swiftly away, and for the second time that morning Anna felt her jaw drop.

'Ward round?' she echoed, but he was already striding out of the room and within moments he was moving briskly along the corridor. She swallowed hard and started to go after him, but instead she had a breathless collision with Tom Raynor at the door. He had been carrying some books and files, and now they all dropped to the floor.

'Whoah,' he said, laughing. 'Slow down. What's the rush?'

She stared at him blankly, her mind still fogged by what Carlos had said. Then she looked at the books scattered all over the floor and bent to help him pick them up. 'I'm sorry, I wasn't looking where I was going.'

Absently, she glanced down at the files that littered the floor. 'What is all this?' she asked. 'Have I messed up anything important?'

'I'm studying for more exams,' he explained. 'I want to make consultant some day, so I'm working hard in my spare time.'

Fleetingly she scanned the covers of the textbooks as she handed them back to him. 'I'm impressed,' she said. 'You must have been busy raiding the library shelves for all these.'

'Only in part. Mr Barrantes lent me some.' He winced as he looked over the creased pages. 'With strict instructions to get them back to him in good condition.'

'Oh, dear.' She grimaced, then moistened her lips with the tip of her tongue. 'Tell me about him,' she said in a strained voice. 'Does he work here?'

'Didn't you know?' Tom got to his feet and raked a hand through his hair. 'He's the visiting cardiac consultant. He's a brilliant man, one of the best surgeons in the field. He divides his time between several

of the hospitals in the Caribbean, and we're lucky to
have him around.' He looked at her closely. 'Why do
you ask? Is something wrong?'

'Oh, no,' she said weakly, her head going into a
spin. 'Nothing at all.' She straightened up. She had
told the hospital's best cardiac consultant that he
shouldn't have allowed a three-year-old to wander off
on his own, and she had argued with him over paren-
tal rights. How would she ever live it down if that
ended up on the hospital grapevine?

'He looked as though he was in a hurry when he
swept out of here just now,' Tom remarked. 'Was
everything all right?

She was beginning to recover a little from the
shock, and she answered carefully, 'Yes, I think so.
He was worried about being late for a ward round.'
She paused, then said hesitantly, 'You obviously get
along well with him, if he's lending you books.
What's he like to work with?'

Tom looked thoughtful. 'He's OK, on the whole.
Fair-minded, but he likes things done a certain way
and he doesn't tolerate mistakes lightly. He can be a
bit volatile occasionally, I suppose, but not usually
without cause. Actually, he's been a bit preoccupied
these last few months.'

'Why is that? Has something happened? A family
problem?'

He shrugged. 'I'm not too sure. He's a very private
man...but rumour has it that he was thinking of getting married to a girl he'd known since childhood,
and then something went wrong. No one really knows
what happened, except that she went away for a time.

It isn't something he talks about, and no one is going to volunteer to get their head bitten off by asking.'

Anna slowly absorbed that snippet of information. 'This happened recently, did it?'

He shook his head. 'No, all that happened a long time ago…but I do know that the woman came back recently, and they seem to be fairly close again. Her family has something to do with the Friends of the Hospital charity. The Marchants are very well-to-do, and Francesca's been around quite a lot lately to organise events.'

'Oh, I see,' Anna said flatly, then frowned. Why did she feel so deflated by what he had told her? She wasn't becoming attracted to Carlos, was she?

Tom interrupted her errant thoughts. 'You said you came on the bus this morning. Whereabouts are you staying? Maybe I could give you a lift home later?'

'That's a nice thought.' She smiled up at him. 'I'm leasing an apartment on Blue Water Bay. Is that on your way?'

'It certainly is. I'll come and pick you up at the end of the shift.'

'Thanks, Tom.'

He left a few minutes later, and Anna was called away to the examination room to assess a new patient. He was a boy in his early teens who had been brought into hospital by his parents.

The boy looked seriously debilitated, she thought, as well as thoroughly fatigued and sickly.

'We're on holiday,' the father told her. 'We came down here from Florida and we've been doing a tour of the islands. Jack hasn't been himself for about three or four weeks now, but we didn't think it was anything too bad to begin with. Then he seemed to go downhill pretty fast.'

Anna looked at her young patient. 'Perhaps I could examine you, Jack. Just lie back and relax while I check you over. Can you tell me how it started?'

'I was sick…vomiting,' he said, 'and then I started to ache all over.'

'A bit like flu?'

'Yeah, that's right.'

'We thought it was just something he'd eaten,' his mother put in, 'and we expected that he would be all right in a few days. He's been tired, and he hasn't wanted to eat, but we thought that was normal.'

Anna quickly completed her examination and noted that the whites of the boy's eyes had turned yellow, and that there was a similar tinge to his skin.

'I'll need to do a blood test to confirm it,' she told them, 'but I think what's happened is that Jack has a form of hepatitis. He's jaundiced, which means that his liver's not working properly, and that's why he feels so sick. It's not too serious, but it will make him feel ill for a few weeks.'

She wrote out the blood-test form and waited until the nurse, Maria, had finished settling the boy back against his pillows before handing it to her.

'We'll keep him here for a few days, just to keep an eye on him and assess him for treatment, but after that it's really a question of bed rest and special attention to his diet.'

'But he's hardly eating anything as it is,' his mother said anxiously.

Anna nodded. 'That's understandable. He won't be able to tolerate fatty foods while his liver function is disturbed, so we have to make sure that he avoids those for the time being. It's best if he has small portions of whatever he does eat in the meantime. When the time comes, we'll make sure that you have a diet sheet to take home with you.'

'Thank you, Doctor.' Jack's father looked doubtful. 'Will you be giving him some medication to help him over this?'

'Depending on the results of the tests, we'll probably give him steroids to help improve the liver function and analgesics to relieve his pain. Basically, though, this is a viral infection, and his system has to try to overcome the virus. The best way to help him to do that is to make sure he has plenty of bed rest and small but regular meals. I'm hopeful that in a few weeks' time he'll be feeling much better.'

It wasn't encouraging news to give them, but so far Western medicine hadn't come up with anything better. Hepatitis was a nasty illness.

Towards the end of her shift, Anna went to check on her smaller charges, making her way up to the ward where little Jessie had been admitted. She came across Carlos heading in the same direction, and they took the lift together.

'I thought I might find you on your way up here,' he murmured, glancing at her. 'Have you finished for the day?'

She nodded. 'I wanted to see how Jessie was before I go home.'

'How have things gone for you on your first day?'

'It's been hectic,' she said with a faint smile. 'To be honest, I haven't had time to think about how it was going…it just went. The time seems to have flown by.'

'Do you think you're going to be happy here?'

She nodded. 'I think so. So far, everyone has been really friendly and helpful. They see me looking lost and point me in the right direction.'

'They're a good bunch of people.' He flicked her a sideways glance as they stepped out of the lift. 'How are you getting home this evening? Do you need a lift?'

'I've got one, thanks. Tom's taking me…he said it's on his way.'

She didn't hear his murmured comment. He pushed open the door to the ward, letting her go through first, and she quickly scanned the room, looking for Grace.

They found her sitting by her daughter's bed. She looked up as they approached and made an attempt at a smile.

'How is she doing?' Anna asked quietly, picking up the infant's chart and checking her progress. 'Her temperature seems to have dropped a little. Is she breathing any better?'

'She's still restless,' Grace said, 'but I think she's sleeping.'

Carlos looked at the child, who was lying in a cot. 'Did the physiotherapist come and work on her chest?'

'Yes. She came a couple of hours ago.'

'It'll take time to clear her lungs,' Anna said, drawing up a chair, and trying to reassure Grace. 'Her colour has improved a little, I think.'

She sat down and scanned the woman's drawn features, noting the fatigue around her eyes. 'Are you all right here? Have they found you somewhere to sleep for the night?'

'There's a room I can use, just down the corridor. But I shall stay here for now. I want to be here if she wakes up.'

'As long as you don't tire yourself out. Have you managed to get yourself something to eat and drink? There's a cafeteria down on the next floor.'

'Yes, thank you. The nurse showed me where to go. I'll be fine.'

'That's good. Try not to worry.'

'These are early days yet,' Carlos said, then glanced obliquely at Tom, who had come onto the ward and was approaching the bed.

Tom nodded to both of them, then turned to Anna. 'Maria told me you were up here,' he murmured. 'I came to see if you were about ready to sign off for the day.'

'Yes, I'm all done for now.' Turning to Grace, she said, 'I'll be back on duty in the morning, but if there's anything you're not sure about in the meantime, the nurses will help you out.'

'OK. Thanks.'

Anna got to her feet and took a last look at Jessie before she started to leave the ward. She glanced at Carlos. 'Are you heading home now?'

He shook his head. 'I'll stay and talk to Grace for a while.'

She nodded and turned to walk away with Tom.

'I'll have you home in no time at all,' he murmured. He pushed open the swing door to the corridor and laid a hand lightly on her shoulder to usher her through.

'That's great. Thanks.' She looked up at him in appreciation, then glanced back towards Grace to give her a final wave, but it was Carlos's unreadable gaze that held her attention. He stirred up all kinds of odd feelings inside her, and she had absolutely no idea how to deal with them.

CHAPTER FIVE

SEVERAL days had passed, and Anna was at last beginning to relax a little. She was gradually becoming much more used to the general routine of the hospital, and at the same time she was quickly getting to know and like her young patients.

Jack, the boy with hepatitis, was still looking tired and drained, but she was pleased with his progress so far.

'You haven't vomited in the last two days, have you, Jack?' she asked now.

'No, I haven't. I hate being sick.' He opened his mouth and pointed a finger down his throat in a parody. 'Yeuk.'

'Yeuk's the word.' She chuckled. 'How are you feeling, apart from that?'

'Fed up,' he said, wrinkling his nose. 'I was supposed to be going to see the coral reefs and snorkelling, and instead of that I've been stuck in here, feeling rotten. It's not fair.'

'It isn't fair, that's true, but maybe you'll be able to do those things soon enough. The reefs aren't going anywhere.'

'Nor am I, by the looks of it,' he said in disgust. He started to scratch at his arm as he spoke, and Anna frowned, watching him.

'Is that giving you a problem?'

'It's an itch,' he said, rubbing even more vigorously. 'It's driving me round the twist.'

Anna took a closer look at the arm. 'It's part of the illness,' she told him. 'Sometimes your skin can get over-dry and that can be a bit of a nuisance. It might help to take a cool bath, but I can give you a lotion to relieve it.' She smiled at him. 'In the meantime, if you're nice to Maria she might find you a different computer game or something else to cheer you up and take your mind off things.'

His eyes brightened. 'A football game?'

'I expect we've got one somewhere. Don't play it for too long, mind. We don't want you tiring yourself out.'

She made a note on his treatment chart and handed it to Maria, leaving the pair of them to chat as her pager started to bleep. At least the boy was feeling well enough to complain. Checking the pager, she went over to the surgical ward, where the staff nurse met her at the door.

'Would you come and have a look at Joseph for me?' Suzy Monterey was a conscientious girl, slim and dark-haired and looking a little anxious at the moment. 'His blood pressure's rising and I'm concerned about him.'

'He's one of Mr Barrantes patients, isn't he?' Anna asked.

'Yes. Mr Barrantes operated on him yesterday morning. He'll be in to see him later today, and I don't want to call him before time if I can avoid it.'

'I don't suppose he would mind if you were worried about one of his patients. Even just a phone call would be enough perhaps, then he could decide for himself whether he needed to come in.'

'Oh, I did phone him, about an hour ago. A woman answered, though—Marchant, I think she said her name was—and she said he'd had a very late night and had only just gone into the shower, so it wasn't a good time to call him out unless it was an emergency. I wasn't sure I could class this as an emergency.'

'I see.' Anna swallowed hard. Was this the same woman that Tom had told her about, the one Carlos had been planning to marry at one time? It had to be, didn't it? And from the sound of things…if she had stayed there the night…she was definitely back in his life. Why else would she be there when he had only just got out of bed?

Anna's mind closed down, a cloak moving in on her imagination. For some reason she didn't want to think about why he'd had a late night.

'Have I done the wrong thing in asking you to come and look at him? I waited a while, but I was beginning to get more concerned about the boy.'

The girl's anxious question brought Anna abruptly back to the problem at hand. 'No, of course not,' she said quickly. 'You did absolutely the right thing. Call me at any time if you're concerned. I don't mind at all.' She made an effort to focus. 'Mr Barrantes operated, you said. Did the surgery go all right?'

'Oh, yes, there were no problems at all. Mr Barrantes is very good, everyone says so. It's just that I'm fairly new around here, and I don't want to make any mistakes, especially where Mr Barrantes is concerned.' She added nervously, 'He's very particular about his patients. Everything has to be done just right.'

Anna could understand her wariness if she was new to the hospital, though her caution was probably misplaced. 'OK, don't worry. I'll go and have a look at him and try to find out what's happening. Are his parents around?'

'They've gone down to the cafeteria to get something to drink. Joseph was dozing, so they thought they would go together.'

Anna went over to the boy's bedside and looked down at him. He was just seven years old, she noted from his chart, a dark-haired, frail-looking boy who had a heart condition that had been present from birth. He stirred as she approached, and blinked up at her.

'Hello, Joseph,' she said with a smile. 'How are you feeling today?' His complexion, which she guessed would normally be olive, was pale, and there were dark shadows around his eyes. 'Are you in any pain?'

'No,' he mumbled, turning his head into the pillow. 'The nurse gave me something to take away the pain.'

'That's good.' Joseph didn't volunteer any more information, and Anna guessed that he was still weak from the surgery he had undergone.

She glanced down at his notes. He had been born with a defect that caused an obstruction to the flow of blood through the aorta, the main artery of the heart. Throughout his young life the pressure within the heart would have been high and its workload would have been too great to handle for any sustained length of time. The condition was quite rare, but if it was discovered, the optimum time for surgery was around his age.

'Is there a problem?' The deep voice intruded on her thoughts, and she looked up in surprise to see Carlos standing by her side. Her glance tracked the length of his tall, powerfully masculine figure, and her pulse began a chaotic thump-thump before she quickly brought herself under control.

'His blood pressure is raised,' she explained. 'We weren't expecting you in until later, so Suzy asked me to check him out.'

'I decided to come in early so that I could take a look at him.' He nodded to Suzy, and said quietly, 'You did the right thing in getting an opinion. Better to check up than leave anything to chance this soon after an operation.'

Had Francesca passed on the message after all? Anna's mind swerved away from that tricky area, and she tried to concentrate on the job in hand. She was familiar with the surgery that Carlos had carried out. He would have removed the section of the aorta that was obstructed, and then he would have carefully rejoined the two ends so that the blood could flow without restriction. Even so, there could often still be a problem with high blood pressure after surgery.

He went over to the bedside and looked down at the child. 'Are you feeling sleepy?' he asked the boy softly, and Joseph nodded. 'That's OK,' Carlos murmured. 'I won't disturb you for long. I just want to have a quick look at your chest to make sure that everything's all right.'

The child was too lethargic to make any comment so Carlos gently went ahead and examined the site of the incision. Anna could see that it was perfectly clean and that there was no sign of inflammation.

'That's looking fine,' he told the boy, tucking the sheet carefully back in place when he had finished. 'Try to get some rest now. I'll come and see you again a bit later on.' He went to join Suzy at the nurses' table in the middle of the ward.

Anna glanced at Joseph's bedside table and saw that there was an action figure toy lying on its side. 'Is this your soldier friend?' she asked, and the boy nodded soberly.

'He's been fighting,' he whispered.

'I thought he had. He's wearing a bandage, isn't he? Do you know, I think he might feel better if he lies down next to you. Would you like that?'

The boy nodded, and Anna put the figure carefully into his hand. She was rewarded with the glimmer of a smile.

As she walked back to the others, she was conscious of Carlos's gaze resting steadily on her. By the time she reached them, though, he was saying quietly to Suzy, 'I think for the time being we'll increase the dosage of the blood-pressure tablets. That should bring it down a little. Once the wound settles down internally, we may be able to lower it again. The diuretics should help with that.'

'I'll see to it,' Suzy said.

He looked at her directly. 'You did the right thing in calling me this morning. It doesn't matter if I'm not due in. I always want to be kept informed.'

Suzy was smiling with relief as she went to see to the medication, leaving Anna alone with Carlos.

'Are you going to be free for lunch today?' he asked, and she was so startled that she found herself nodding.

'I think so, unless something crops up in the meantime. I was going to the cafeteria at about one o'clock. Why?'

'Something I wanted to ask you…it'll wait till then. Good. I'll see you later. I need to go and check up on another of my patients now.' He gave her a brief smile and went off in a bit of a hurry, leaving her to wonder what on earth he could want to ask her. Still thinking about it, Anna returned to her own work.

She spent the rest of the morning in Casualty, dealing with a crop of accidents mostly involving tourists. One was a teenager who had been brought into hospital by his parents.

'This is Toby,' the young nurse said, drawing back a curtain in the treatment room. 'He thinks he might have been bitten by something.'

Toby barely looked up as Anna went into the examination cubicle. He looked to be around thirteen years old. He was sitting morosely on the couch, staring at the floor as though he resented being dragged in here when he could have been doing more interesting things.

'I'd better have a look at you, Toby,' Anna said cheerfully. 'What do you think might have bitten you?'

He managed a brief glance in her direction and pulled a face. 'Dunno.'

Thankfully his father had a little more to say on the subject, and with a look of exasperation he told Anna, 'He was swimming in the lake by our campsite a few days ago. I told him it didn't look too clean and to keep away from it, but you know what kids are. Anyway, now he's got a rash on his leg. Maybe something had a nip at him when he was in the water. Or maybe it was a mosquito. I don't want him going down with malaria or anything like that.'

Anna picked up a magnifying glass and examined the inflamed area carefully, before saying, 'He won't suffer from malaria, you'll be glad to know…but, judging from what you've told me and from the rash, he might have been attacked by a little worm.' She put down the magnifying glass and looked at father and son.

'A worm?' They both echoed the word, and father and son were staring at her with horrified expressions.

'That's right. The larvae burrow into the skin and cause what we call "swimmer's itch" before it goes on to lay eggs inside the body. So what we have to do is give Toby a drug that will kill the parasite.'

'Ugh!' Toby bent double, looking as though he was about to throw up, and Anna smiled.

'It's not that bad, Toby. I believe we've caught it in time. If you'd delayed, you might have developed a very nasty illness called schistosomiasis, but you're lucky that your father brought you here right away. If I were you, I'd listen to him next time he tells you not to swim in infected water.'

'Oh, yipes…that's gross.'

Toby was still exclaiming some minutes later as his father led him away to the pharmacy.

'He thinks that's bad news,' a familiar, gravelly voice said, and Anna turned around, still smiling, to come face to face with Carlos. There was a gleam of amusement in his golden eyes.

She managed to say lightly, 'He wasn't too happy, was he?'

He lifted a dark brow. 'It's a good thing you didn't tell him the local story about how the little worm can battle his way upstream against the strongest current...and what might happen if he were to urinate in the water just as the little worm was swimming by...'

'Ouch! That doesn't bear thinking about.' She laughed, and Carlos's mouth crooked attractively. She found herself mesmerised by the slightest of movements of his face, watching the angle of his jaw, the way the corners of his eyes crinkled when he smiled.

'Are you about ready to go for lunch?' he asked. His gaze steadied on her, and she made a hasty effort to get a grip on reality. He was a consultant, he lived in another world from her, and it would be madness to let herself get carried away by daydreams, wouldn't it?

'Just about,' she murmured. 'Just give me a minute to sort my notes.' She signed a batch of treatment charts and handed them to the nurse, then added, 'I don't suppose there's any change in Joseph's condition? I was concerned about him earlier on. He didn't look too good, did he?' She couldn't help thinking about the little boy with the dark eyes who had been too weak to care much about what was going on around him.

'His system is still adjusting to the shock of the operation. He's never been a strong boy, but these are early days yet, and we'll do what we can to encourage his recovery.'

They walked together towards the cafeteria, and Carlos's gaze flicked over her. 'It was good of you to take the time to come and help out. You seem to have settled in here well. Is everything going all right?'

'Well enough, I think. At least I'm managing to find my way about the place now. I'm having to divide my time between several areas, but I think I'm getting to grips with it.'

'From what I've seen, you're coping brilliantly. You were very good with little Jessie, and Grace tells me you've made a point of going to see her every day. Last time I looked in on her, she was looking much better. I wouldn't have known she was the same child if I hadn't seen for myself how poorly she was to begin with.'

'Jessie improved by leaps and bounds once her lungs were clear. I'm thinking I might be able to discharge her soon.'

He nodded. 'I guessed you might. Grace was out of her mind with worry just a few days ago, but she's a lot more relaxed now. You helped both of them. Martha's happier, too. She was very concerned about her little granddaughter.'

'I'm not surprised. She was so tiny, and she looked helpless.'

'You look after all of your small patients very well.

Are you coping with the tropical medicine side of things? You said you wanted to gain more experience on that score—is it working out?' He pushed open the door of the cafeteria, and they went over to the buffet bar to make a selection from the food set out there.

'So far. At least, I haven't come across anything I can't handle yet…and Tom has been a great help.'

Carlos frowned, his brows drawing together in a dark line. 'He may not always be on duty at the same time as you. You shouldn't rely solely on Tom Raynor.'

'I won't, of course.' She wondered why he had reacted so sharply to that, but she guessed he was a stickler for having everything done properly. 'I have done my homework,' she murmured. 'I've been working towards this specialisation for some time, and I've been reading up on all the latest developments.'

He looked at her quizzically. 'That won't necessarily mean you won't come across something that has you flummoxed.'

She was thoughtful for a moment as she tipped pizza and peppers on to her plate. 'Actually,' she conceded, 'there was one incident that threw me. A woman brought a child in with a gaping wound, and when I took off the temporary dressing she had put on it, I was staggered to find that she had draped slices of pawpaw over the cut.' She had been startled to see the melon-like fruit used that way.

His eyes crinkled. 'That's not unusual hereabouts. People often bandage pawpaw in place and leave it for a couple of days. They believe it keeps the wound clean and helps the healing process.'

There was an empty table by the window, and they took their trays over to it.

'Does it work?'

'A lot of folk medicine works. Sometimes people cook pawpaw and eat one or two slices to lower a high blood pressure. They use coconut oil for scalp problems, and that seems to do the trick. They say it can be rubbed into the head as a cold remedy, too, but I can't say I'm too sure about that one.'

She grimaced. 'I've heard that honey is supposed to be a pretty good antiseptic, but I don't think I'd be too keen to spread it on a wound.'

His mouth twitched. 'You're obviously a modern-day woman. It wouldn't do for you to be stranded on a desert island and left to your own devices, would it?'

'Not unless someone was there to provide me with a fully packed medical kit and emergency supplies.'

His tawny eyes flashed, his glance travelling over her and searing her where it touched. 'In that case, I've no doubt you would have any number of men queuing up to help out,' he observed dryly.

His comment left her floundering. 'I don't know about that,' she muttered, her skin heating at his mockery.

He chuckled, then went on to say calmly, 'I want to ask something of you, *por favor*, to do with my small patient, Joseph.'

Immediately she sobered. 'Anything... Is something wrong?'

'Nothing's wrong, but his parents want him to be moved to the Mount View clinic so that he can convalesce there and receive more dedicated attention. He'll need to be supervised on his journey, and I wondered if you would agree to go along with him? I saw how you were with him today, and I'm sure he would be happier if you were there to keep him company. He's been asking for the golden-haired doctor who looked after his soldier friend.'

A smile touched her lips. 'Has he? I'd be glad to help any way I can. When is he going?'

'His parents want him to go there tomorrow evening.'

Anna frowned. 'Isn't that too soon?'

'Not if we take great care to see that his journey is smooth, and if you're there with him to watch his progress.' He looked at her thoughtfully. 'Did you have other plans for the evening?'

'Not exactly.' She hesitated, then went on, 'I had thought about going back down to the harbour to see if I can find Nick at home, but I suppose I could go today instead. I have to stay a little later at the hospital tonight, that's all, so I won't have as much time with them as I'd like. You did say that Nick should be back by now, didn't you?'

'That's right. That's one of the things I wanted to see you about. I heard from your brother-in-law this morning. They arrived home yesterday.'

'Did they?' Anna sat up, alert all at once. 'Did he mention my little nephew?'

'He said that Daniel had a great time on their trip.'

'It would be lovely to see him soon,' she murmured

wistfully. She thought about Sarah back home, counting the days.

'You're very fond of him, aren't you?'

'Oh, yes. He's my one and only nephew and I think the world of him.'

'Well, you'll probably be able to see him now.'

'I hope so. I'd like to be able to tell his mother that he's all right, and it would be good if he could just talk to her on the phone. Up to now, Nick has been awkward about keeping in contact, and I really want to persuade him that it's in Daniel's interests to be able to talk to his mother.'

He looked at her thoughtfully. 'Perhaps I should wish you luck?'

'Even though you don't see my side of the argument?' She pulled a face. 'To be honest, I think Sarah could do with a little luck.'

'If your sister is so concerned about her son, why hasn't she come over to see him? She must know where Nick lives.'

'It isn't as simple as that. She would have come, but she was knocked over by a joy-rider, and now she has a leg in plaster. Even so, she would have followed him, but her doctor wants to keep an eye on the injury. It wasn't healing as fast as it should.'

Carlos grimaced. 'I've always thought that joy-riding was a dreadful way to describe what actual happens.'

He paused, his glance narrowing on her. 'Does this mean that you'll be free go with Joseph?'

'Yes, I'll be glad to.'

'Thanks. I'll arrange for an ambulance to make the

journey to Mount View, and I'll bring you back here afterwards so that you can collect your car.'

She shook her head. 'You don't need to do that. I haven't managed to get one yet. With the hours I've been working here, there hasn't been time for me to sort anything out.'

'That must be tiresome for you. How have you been managing—do you get the bus?'

'No. It hasn't been too bad so far. Tom has been picking me up and dropping me off at home each night.'

'Has he?' His glance flicked over her. 'That's very good of him. I didn't think his shifts would always coincide with yours.'

'He said it wasn't any trouble, and that it was on his way.'

'Are you still looking to buy a car?'

'Eventually, yes, when I can get to a garage.'

He felt in his jacket pocket and brought out his wallet. 'I've a friend who is a car dealer,' he said, fetching out a card and handing it to her. 'Give him a ring and tell him that I recommended him to you, and he'll have a car delivered to your door. Just tell him the sort of thing that you want, and he'll arrange it. He won't overcharge you, and you can be sure that the vehicle will be sound. If you're not happy with what he brings, he'll take it back again at a later date.'

It sounded like the answer to her prayers. 'Thanks,' she murmured. 'Perhaps I'll do that.'

That evening, Anna went over to the harbour, hoping that she would be able to see Nick and little Daniel.

It would be good to be able to phone Sarah and tell her that she had made some headway.

As far as she could tell from the address Sarah had given her, Nick's home was close to the hotel that he owned, set back in its own grounds a short distance from the quay. She followed the path through the lush tropical gardens that bordered the hotel, breathing in the scent of exotic blooms, and came upon the white-painted colonial-style house just a few minutes later.

She went up to the pillared porch and rang the bell. Then she stood back and waited, trying to calm her breathing. She didn't want to be flustered, but so much depended on her getting this right.

Nick answered the door a minute or so later. 'Anna...' He frowned, then stepped back to allow her inside. 'Sarah told me that you would be coming out here. She said something about a job.'

'I'm working at the hospital,' she told him. 'I'm not living too far away from you either. I've an apartment in Blue Water Bay.' She looked around as he led her through the house, but there was no sign of Daniel.

'If you were hoping to see Daniel, he's already in bed and fast asleep,' Nick commented. 'I'd sooner not wake him.'

Anna tried not to be dismayed by his cool tone. She had only just made contact with him, and things were almost bound to be difficult at first.

'I can understand that,' she said softly. 'Do you think I could go up and have a look at him, though? It's been a while since I saw him.'

He looked as though he would have liked to have

refused, but he said grudgingly, 'Maybe just a peek, then. I don't want him disturbed. He's been a bit feverish lately, and he needs to rest.'

'Is he ill?' Anna was concerned. 'Is it anything serious?'

'No, he'll be fine. He just needs his sleep.'

She nodded. 'I'll be quiet. I won't wake him.'

He led her to Daniel's room, and she crept in and stood by the bed, looking down at the sleeping child. He had his thumb in his mouth and he was mumbling incoherently, little snatches of words that Anna strained to hear. He looked so small and defenceless that she wished she could pick him up and cuddle him and kiss his soft cheek.

Nick touched her arm, though, and signalled to her to go with him back down the stairs, and she realised with aching clarity that he didn't trust her. He was too guarded around his son, and she would need to tread very carefully.

As Carlos had said it would be, the ambulance was waiting when she finished her shift at the end of the following day. Seven-year-old Joseph had been transferred into it. He was still weak, but he managed a tentative smile when she went to sit beside him and she saw that he had not one but two action figures with him this time.

'Are they fighting each other?' she asked, but he shook his head.

'They're friends. Samson's helping Tank to get better.'

'He's looking better already,' Anna said thoughtfully. 'I expect he'll be able to have his bandage off before long.'

Joseph's parents were following behind in their car, since there wasn't much room in the ambulance, and Carlos had gone on ahead of all of them so as to be ready to shepherd his patient into the clinic.

Anna talked quietly to the boy as they drove smoothly along, but after a while he appeared tired so she let him rest and gazed out of the window instead, following their route along the winding mountain road.

'We're nearly there,' she told Joseph quietly a few minutes later. 'It's a beautiful place. I think you're going to like it there.'

The ambulance turned into a side road that led towards the building, and finally came to a halt in the parking bay.

Porters came to ferry the boy carefully inside, and his parents were already at the main doors, waiting anxiously to see that he had come to no harm.

Carlos gestured to Anna to come over, and she went to stand by the boy's trolley as his parents moved to one side.

'We'll take him up to his room and see that he's comfortable for the evening,' he murmured.

'OK.'

He led the way to the lift, and together they went up to the second floor. Here they disembarked onto a wide corridor, where paintings of Caribbean landscapes, orange groves and busy market scenes added bright touches of colour to the walls.

'Through here,' Carlos said, and the porters manoeuvred the trolley into a large room where glass doors opened out onto a balcony.

'Oh, this is lovely,' Joseph's mother said. 'It's so clean and fresh, and you have your own television and music centre. See?' A slight woman, with dark curls framing her face, she smiled at Joseph and went around the room, pointing out everything that would brighten his stay. 'Your father and I have a room next to this one, and there's a day room where you can go to be with other children. This will be good, Joseph…yes?'

Joseph smiled, but leaned back against his pillows, and Anna said quietly, 'It's a lot for him to take in just now. Perhaps we should take a few moments to examine him and see that he's settled in properly.' She glanced at Carlos, and he nodded, gesturing for her to go ahead.

She took the boy's pulse and checked his blood pressure, and found that both were slightly elevated. 'We should let him rest for now,' she murmured. 'The move has been rather too much excitement for one day, and he needs to sleep now. Perhaps later, when he's more up to it, he'll want to look around.'

'You're right,' his mother said. 'We'll go and un-pack our things next door, and look in on him later.' She went to her son and kissed him tenderly. 'Close your eyes and try to sleep and get well, Joseph. If you need us at all, just press the buzzer, here, see?' She handed him the intercom that linked his room with theirs. 'We'll be back in a little while to see you.'

'A nurse will stay with you, Joseph,' Carlos said gently. 'Her name is Freya, and she's going to look after you while you're here. When you feel up to it, later on, she'll find you some toys to play with.'

He spoke quietly, aware that Joseph's eyes were already closing, and as Freya came forward to check his chart, Carlos went with Anna to the door.

'He's very frail,' Anna said softly as they walked back to the lift. 'What are his chances of a full recovery?'

'Only time will tell us that. With any luck, now that he has had the operation, we can start to build up his strength. At the moment he isn't eating very much, and that is one of the first obstacles we have to overcome.'

They took the lift back down to the foyer, and Carlos ushered her through wide double doors into a spacious room.

'I'll get you a coffee,' he said, 'and something to eat. Wait here, while I go and organise something.'

'Are you sure you have time for that? I know you have things to do with Joseph, and his parents will want to talk to you. I don't want to get in the way. I'm happy enough to sit and wait for you while you do that.'

He looked down at her, a smile tugging at his mouth, and he reached for her, his hands circling her arms. 'It's the least I can do to thank you for your help, Anna. It'll be more comfortable for you in here…it's more private, and you'll be able to relax while you're waiting for me.'

His touch was warm and gentle, and it made her feel incredibly secure and wanted. 'Thanks,' she said lightly. 'I hadn't expected you to take care of me like this.'

'*De nada*,' he murmured, dropping a swift and unexpected kiss onto her startled mouth. 'You're very welcome.'

The kiss stayed with her long after he had left the room. Her lips tingled in response to the feather-like brush of his mouth on hers, and she was bemused and bewildered by the whole experience. Why had he done that?

Anna touched her mouth with her fingers, savouring the sweetness of the memory that lingered there, until she heard sounds of movement in the corridor outside. How could she explain her dream-like state to anyone who might happen to come in here?

She looked around dazedly. The room she was in was furnished as a lounge, with inviting armchairs and low tables, and two walls were taken up with sliding glass doors. Confused, and needing to sort out her chaotic emotions, Anna went and opened the doors and stepped out onto the paved terrace, breathing in the scent of the sea air and the fragrant blossoms all around.

Carlos had kissed her, and now the blood was fizzing through her veins. She would never be the same again.

CHAPTER SIX

ANNA stared out over the terrace, looking at the beautifully landscaped gardens. In the distance, surrounded by shrubbery and a raised rock garden, there was a pond with a fountain, each droplet of water glittering in the evening sunlight.

'Hello…' A woman's voice sounded huskily behind her just a moment or two later. 'You must be Anna. Carlos told me that I'd find you in here.'

She turned to see that a young woman had come into the room. Her resemblance to Carlos was striking in the angular lines of her face, the straight nose and the beautifully shaped mouth. Her eyes were hazel, gleaming and alert, and her long, dark hair was cut in a feathery shape that enhanced her features. She was also very pregnant.

'You must be Saskia,' Anna said in surprise.

'I am. I am so very pleased to meet you, Anna. I've been wanting to thank you for the way you looked after Sebastian when I was taken ill.'

'I was glad to help. Are you feeling all right now?'

'Yes, thank you. I'm under strict instructions to put my feet up every afternoon, but you know how it is…' She laughed. 'There is always so much to do.'

'I can imagine. You must have your work cut out, looking after Sebastian.'

'That's true. For the moment, at least, he is with

Carlos, trying to cadge chocolate biscuits from him.' Her smile lit up her face. 'Carlos is very good with him but, then, he likes children. He has always got on well with young people.'

'Was he expecting you to come here today?' Anna couldn't get her head round the fact that Saskia was actually here, at the clinic. Was that a coincidence, or what?

Saskia nodded. 'Yes. He told me he would be here this evening, so it would be a good time for me to come over, and it fitted in with my plans. He took a blood sample from me just a moment ago to check my iron levels. He sometimes checks my glucose levels, too—they've been raised since I've been pregnant. It's easier for him to do it here, than it is for me to go to see my obstetrician.'

'I can imagine it would be.' Saskia was seven months pregnant, and right now she was looking slightly out of breath. Anna said gently, 'Shall we go in and sit down? I don't know how long Carlos will be, but you look as though you could do with getting the weight off your feet.'

Saskia chuckled. 'You're right. I'm totally worn out with chasing after Sebastian all day.'

Carlos came into the lounge just then, pushing a heavily laden tea-trolley. 'I keep telling her to rest more,' he said, sliding the trolley into position against the wall. 'She could take time out when Seb's at pre-school classes, but she never does. She's always busy doing something. I might as well talk to myself for all the notice she takes of me.'

Sebastian came from behind Carlos just then to

sneak one of the biscuits from a plate. Anna watched him, a smile touching her lips. He looked bubbly and full of fun, and it was a delight to see him like that.

'H'llo, Anna,' the little boy said through a mouthful of crumbs. 'See, my arm is much better now.'

'So I can see.' The arm was still in a sling, but he moved it almost freely and Anna said happily, 'I'm very pleased about that, Seb. I wondered how you were doing.'

Carlos came over to her and offered her a plate piled high with delicacies—spicy-looking patties, creamy hors d'oeuvres and cheesy nibbles. She selected a patty, taking a bite and savouring the taste on her tongue.

'Can I see the pond?' Seb asked, rushing over to the glass doors.

Saskia sighed. 'See what I mean? He's never still, this one.'

'I'll take him to look at it,' Carlos said. 'You two relax and get to know each other for a while.'

'Are there fish?' Sebastian wanted to know, and Carlos nodded.

'Yes. Lots of them. Come on, I'll show you.'

He took the boy out onto the terrace, and they walked out into the landscaped grounds, leaving the two women to help themselves from the trolley and chat.

When he came back a while later, Seb was full of what he had seen, and raced to tell Saskia. 'I nearly felled in,' he confided. 'I wanted to poke the fish with my finger, but Dada Carlos said, no, they wouldn't like that.'

Saskia raised her eyes heavenwards and Carlos chuckled. 'I held onto him,' he said. 'I know this little one. He's such a bundle of energy that you need eyes in the back of your head.'

Turning to Anna, he added, 'If you're ready, perhaps we should make a final check on Joseph, and then I'll see you back to your apartment.'

'Yes, I'm ready.'

'*Bueno.*' He glanced at Saskia. 'Who is driving you home? Do you want me to ask José to take you?'

'He has already offered. I just need to go and find him.'

Anna intervened. 'Why don't you both go and sort out your arrangements with José while I go and check on Joseph?' She smiled at Saskia. 'It was really good meeting you, Saskia.'

'Me, too. I expect I shall see you at your hospital barbecue in a couple of weeks, shan't I?'

'Barbecue?' Anna was puzzled. 'What barbecue?'

'Didn't you know?' Saskia's brow rose. 'Oh, you must go to it…everybody does. The Friends of the Hospital organise it…my brother is on the committee, so it will be very good…they try to raise funds. You will be there, won't you? It'll be fun. I shall really look forward to it if I know you'll be there.'

'Well…yes, if I'm not working, I expect I shall.' Now she came to think of it, over the last few days there had been murmurs about an event coming up, but she had been too busy to dwell on them at the time. 'I'd like to see you again, and Seb, too.' She bent down to Sebastian and ruffled his hair lightly. 'It was lovely, you being here. You take care of that arm, young man.'

'I will.'

When she had said all her goodbyes, she left them to go and sort out Saskia's lift home, and made her way up to Joseph's room.

The child was fast asleep. He looked peaceful enough now, though the shadows were still there around his eyes and his skin had an almost translucent quality about it.

Freya had been taking regular observations on his condition, and Anna was pleased to discover that his blood pressure had come down a little. Carefully, so as not to disturb him, she started to check his various tubes and drips for herself, and she had just about finished when Carlos came into the room.

'He's doing all right so far,' she murmured. 'I don't think the journey has upset him too much.'

He nodded, then looked at the sleeping boy and said in a low voice, 'Dr Sanchez will take care of him while we are off duty. He'll be in good hands. Come on, I'll take you home.'

The car ate up the miles with incredible ease. Carlos drove fast but with expertise, his hands in firm control of the wheel along the winding mountain road. They didn't talk much on the journey back, and Carlos switched on the CD player so that soft music filtered through the speakers. Anna leaned back against the richly upholstered seats and tried to relax.

It was difficult, though, with Carlos being so close. She only had to turn her head a fraction and she could see his long legs. The slightest movement strained the material of his trousers, accentuating the line of his powerful thighs.

She didn't want to be so aware of him, but just lately it had been getting to be more and more of a problem whenever he was near. He had his own very special kind of magnetism, but she had to work with him on an almost daily basis, and the last thing she needed was to have the blood rushing to her head whenever she set eyes on him. She averted her gaze, and concentrated on the view from the window instead.

It wasn't long before they had turned off the road that hugged the mountain terraces and turned instead onto the main route, which led into town.

'We're almost at the turning for Blue Water Bay,' he murmured. 'You'll have to show me which apartment block is yours.'

Now that they were getting closer to her home, Anna wasn't sure she wanted him to see where she lived. There were too many differences in their lifestyles, and this was just one more that showed how great the divide was between them. He was a wealthy consultant, the owner of a luxurious private clinic, and she was just a lowly junior paediatrician, living in a run-down apartment. The chasm that lay between them would be even more apparent when he dropped her off there.

'You could let me out here if it's easier for you,' she said when they reached the turn-off on the harbour road that led to his estate. 'I can walk the rest of the way.'

Cool eyes surveyed her briefly. 'I'll take you to your door.'

There was nothing for it but to go along with him. She just hoped he wouldn't be too taken aback by the place she called home for the time being. It wasn't situated in the best part of town, and in her building as many apartments as possible had been crammed into a small space. The corridors were poky, and the walls were so thin that you could sometimes hear what was going on next door.

Its saving grace was that her living room looked out over Blue Water Bay, and every time she sat at the window and took in the beautiful view, she felt at peace with herself. She didn't think Carlos would be impressed, though. It wasn't at all what he was used to.

'This is it,' she said at last, reluctantly. 'This is where I live.'

He parked on the road outside the main entrance, and came around to the passenger side of the car to help her out and walk her to the front of the apartment building.

It was quiet at this time of the evening. Most of the families who lived here would be indoors, having supper. She thought of the little boy, Leroy, whose family lived in the apartment next to hers. He would often come and say hello and tug her into his kitchen so that she could share her evening meal with his family.

'Aren't you going to invite me in?' Carlos asked when she hesitated at the main door. 'I'd like to see where you live.'

'I would,' she said diffidently, 'but, to be honest, it's very cramped in my apartment, and the windows will have been closed up all day. The air-conditioning has broken down, and I'm not sure you'd be very comfortable.'

'Why don't you let me be the judge of that?' he said smoothly. He pushed open the large wooden door and ushered her into the hallway, a hand cupping her elbow.

'We'll have to take the stairs,' she told him. 'The lift isn't working either.' He had made up his mind to come with her, and there wasn't much she could do about that. It would have been plain bad manners to turn him away.

'Hi, Anna.' Eight-year-old Leroy popped his head round a corner of the stairwell and beamed at her, the whites of his eyes shining brightly in his chocolate brown face. 'You coming in for supper with us tonight?'

'Not tonight, Leroy,' she said with a smile. 'Thanks all the same, but I've a friend with me. I'll be round tomorrow perhaps, if your mother is happy about that.'

He nodded, grinning. 'She says you can come round any time…she's always got a stew pot on the stove. Plenty for everyone.' He looked at Carlos. 'Are you looking after Anna?' he asked pointedly. 'She needs someone. She's all on her own, except for that man who comes here sometimes. My mom reckons—'

'I'll talk to your mother later,' Anna cut in swiftly,

unlocking her door. 'Just tell her thanks for the screw-driver she lent me. I fixed the lock and it's fine now.'

'OK. See you later.' Still smiling, Leroy disap-peared into his own apartment.

'Sounds as though he has your welfare at heart,' Carlos murmured.

'They're nice people,' she said, pushing open the door. 'They've been really good to me since I arrived here.'

He followed her into the living room, and stood for a moment looking around at the plain walls, which she had enlivened with pretty water-colour paintings she had bought from one of the shops by the harbour.

Anna went over to the windows and pushed them open to let in the warm evening air. The scent of flowers drifted up from the window-boxes that some of the tenants had planted to add a touch of colour, and she breathed it in, trying to calm herself.

'Something's on your mind.' Carlos had followed her to the window, and now he stood close behind her, his dark head just a fraction away from hers. 'Tell me about it.'

'There's nothing to tell.'

'Isn't there?' He was sceptical. 'Why didn't you want me to come here?'

'I was afraid you wouldn't like it,' she said hon-estly. Her green glance was troubled. 'You and I are from such different backgrounds, and I've seen the way you live. We're worlds apart.'

He frowned. 'Does that matter?'

'I don't know. I suppose I'm uncomfortable about it.'

'Why should you be?'

With a soft sigh, she turned to face him properly. 'Perhaps you're not conscious of how much you have, compared with others. You have a beautiful house and your lifestyle probably echoes that. There's nothing wrong in that. You're very fortunate, and hard-working, too, but I worry about people who don't have the advantages you have, the people who can't afford to use your clinic…the Leroys of this world who simply get by the best way they can. His father catches fish for a living. They have very little, but they don't think twice about sharing what they have with me.'

'They may not have access to the clinic, but they can still get treatment at the hospital. They aren't losing out in any way. I do what I can for the hospital by working there and trying to raise funds for it through the Friends of the Hospital. I don't see how you can blame me for being privileged.'

'I don't blame you. You asked me why I felt uncomfortable bringing you here, and I'm trying to explain, that's all.'

His gaze narrowed on her. 'This doesn't have anything to do with wealth at all, does it? It's more to do with how you feel about me as an individual, as a man—isn't that the truth of it? Are you afraid you might be getting too close to me, is that it? Is that why you're putting up barriers?'

Her voice broke in a ragged laugh. 'You're wrong about that. Believe me, I have no interest in you at all. You're the last man I'd even look at. I have more in common with Tom than I do with you.'

For a moment his head went back and he looked as though she had slapped him, his expression one of stunned disbelief. Then, as he slowly recovered, his jaw moved in a way that could only spell trouble.

He said softly, 'Is that so?'

His gaze moved over her, a slow, totally masculine appraisal that took in every detail of her appearance, from the gleaming golden cascade of her hair right down to the smooth shapeliness of her long legs.

'Perhaps I should persuade you otherwise,' he growled. Then he was reaching for her, his hand possessively circling her slender waist and drawing her to him. His tawny glance travelled slowly upwards to the soft fullness of her mouth and lingered there.

She really should have seen it coming and tried to stop it, but in those few breathless moments her own gaze was transfixed, mesmerised by the heated promise in his glittering eyes as he pulled her closer still, crushing her feminine curves against the hard contours of his body.

And then it was too late, because his head bent closer and his mouth claimed hers in a kiss that was earth-shatteringly fierce. His lips moved possessively on hers, demanding, plundering the softness of her mouth as though he would take everything she had to offer. Unguarded, Anna's senses went haywire, her heartbeat thundering so loudly that she felt sure he must hear it. His arms closed around her, and the warm intimacy of his embrace was like a drug, swirling through her veins and going straight to her head.

She hadn't expected to feel such hectic confusion, or to find that her treacherous body would betray her in such a way, making her legs weak and insubstantial and her body melt against his in delicious, fluid response.

Then he dragged his mouth from hers and for a devastating second or two she felt the loss almost like a pain.

'Is this what you were afraid of?' he said raggedly, his breath warmly fanning her cheek. Then his mouth brushed hers once more, seductively enticing a quivering response, his tongue lightly tracing the soft contours of her lips, leaving a trail of fire and playing havoc with her emotions.

She had never known a kiss could be like this, stirring up everything that was primitive in her soul, making her eager for more. His body was hard and urgent against hers, searing in the intensity of its demand.

She felt him groan huskily, and as his kiss softened, gentled, she was lost to everything except the sweet invitation to respond. Her common sense, all her instincts, told her that this was wrong, but she paid them no attention. Instead, her body was pliant, supple, meshing with the hardness of his so that she could feel his strong thighs pressuring her, feel the urgent demand of his hands as they stroked and caressed her.

He made her feel wild and reckless, his kisses compelling her to respond with a fiery passion that she had never experienced before.

'You see how wrong you can be, *querida*?' His voice was thickened, rough around the edges. 'You say you feel nothing for me, yet your body clings to mine as though we were made for each other.'

She looked up at him in dismay, her green eyes wide and troubled. What was he saying? How could she have let him batter down her defences and leave her helpless like this? Oh, she was a fool, a crazy idiot, to let him get away with it.

She recognised the glimmer of mockery in his eyes, and it was like a knife, lancing her body. He had used her ruthlessly, and now he was taunting her, making her know just how reckless she had been.

'This was a mistake,' she said huskily. 'It should never have happened.' Sick with herself, she pushed him away. It was enough that she had to battle with her emotions, without having him stand there and watch her do it. 'I want you to go.'

He stared at her, a nerve flicking along the line of his jaw. 'Perhaps you're right,' he muttered thickly. 'Things got out of hand. They should never have gone this far.'

He turned away from her, and strode briskly to the door. She heard it close behind him and only then did she take a shuddery breath and acknowledge how hurt she felt.

Wretchedly, she realised just how big a mistake she had made. He would never want someone like her, would he? She had challenged his masculinity and he had set out to make her see the error of her ways, that was all.

She pulled in a shaky breath. She had learned a lesson, hadn't she? She wouldn't make the same mistake again.

CHAPTER SEVEN

ANNA didn't see much of Carlos over the next couple of weeks, and life was hectic at the hospital so that when she went home in the evening she was too tired to do much more than fall into bed. More often than not she would be asleep almost as soon as her head touched the pillow.

On Friday, two little girls were brought in with symptoms of vomiting and diarrhoea, and both of them were looking really poorly. Anna quickly ordered tests so that she could find out what causing their illness.

'These infants look in a bad way.' Carlos appeared as she was checking on the children. He frowned, looking down at the huddled little figures in the cots and scanning their sweat dampened features. 'Was it something they've eaten?'

'Probably,' she answered, wondering what had brought him on to the ward. 'I'll know more about what's happening when I get the results of the blood tests. In the meantime, I'm rehydrating them by giving them glucose electrolyte solution and intravenous fluids.'

'Analgesics, too?'

'Yes. They've been given something for the pain. They've been complaining that their joints and muscles are hurting, according to the mother. Both of them are very weak.'

'Blood tests could take some time. Sometimes the earlier treatment is started, the better chance we have of dealing with it.'

'I know.' She grimaced. Toxin induced diarrhoea could be a major cause of infantile death in some parts of the world, and she desperately wanted to find a quick solution. 'It isn't something I've come across before, so I want to be sure of my facts before I start any other treatment.'

'Are there any other symptoms?'

'Numbness and tingling around the mouth—I think their hands and feet have been affected, too.'

'Hmm…was their last meal fish?'

She nodded. 'Yes. I can't be certain what fish in particular, because there were several different types in the same dish.'

'It's a pity they are too young to answer questions with any degree of accuracy. There is one toxin that causes a reversal of sensation…something hot feels cold, and vice versa. It would simplify the diagnosis if we knew what their sensations were.'

Anna felt a ray of hope. 'Trina told her mother that she had burnt herself on the cold water tap. At the time I thought she was confused because she was such a small child, still learning how to talk, and she might not really understand the difference between the words ''hot'' and ''cold''. Children do muddle them sometimes, don't they?'

He smiled. 'They do, but in this case it could be that she had it right. I think we may be dealing with ciguatera. There's a medication that's effective if given in the early stages. Shall we give it a try?'

'Yes, of course. The sooner the better.'

Following his advice, she wrote out the medication chart and handed it to Maria. 'Start the dosage straight away, Maria, and we'll do observations every fifteen minutes. Let me know if there's any change.'

'Leave it to me.' Maria hurried to get the antidote, her shining bob of dark hair swinging lightly as she turned away, and Anna walked back to the office with Carlos.

She was feeling uneasy about having to rely on him to come up with the diagnosis, and maybe he realised that because he said softly, 'Don't blame yourself for not getting to know the cause of the illness straight away. The blood tests will confirm it, but I've dealt with this form of poisoning far more often than you.'

'I didn't think it was that prevalent these days,' she murmured.

'That's true, in a way, but sometimes micro-organisms are thrown up from the ocean floor after a storm, and go on to cause toxins in fish like snapper, or grouper and barracuda. Most fishermen know to avoid areas where the toxin is to be found, but they're not infallible.'

'I suppose I'll know better next time.'

'That's true.' He sent her an oblique glance. 'I wanted to thank you again for helping out with Joseph at the clinic.'

'How is he? I wanted to go over to the clinic to see him, but most evenings I've been working late and there just hasn't been the opportunity.'

'He's not very strong, but he's been asking about you. He wants to know why you don't work at the clinic.'

She smiled at that. 'I suppose he's used to seeing you appear at both the hospital and the clinic, and he thinks we might all do the same. Tell him I'm thinking about him, will you? I'll go and see him when things are less frantic here.'

'I'll do that. Have you remembered the barbecue tomorrow?'

She nodded. 'Yes, I have thought about it. I'll be working for some of the time, but I'll try to come along and show my face.'

On Saturday afternoon, Anna went to see Nick again. It was the first opportunity she'd had to visit since that last evening when Daniel had been asleep because Nick had been too busy to arrange a time that suited him.

Now, though, he let her into the house, and showed her through to the living room, saying cautiously, 'I wasn't sure whether you would come today. It's the Friends of the Hospital barbecue this afternoon, isn't it?'

'Oh, it'll be going on until late this evening,' she murmured. 'I won't be missed for a while. Besides, I had to work this morning, and I wanted to come here before I did anything else.' She glanced at his taut features. 'How are you?'

'Still busy,' he said laconically. 'I'm having the hotel restaurant extended, and I'm having to supervise a lot of the work.'

'I heard about that,' she said. 'From what people say, it's going to look really good when the work's finished.'

'That's the general idea.'

Even though they had arranged this meeting, she sensed that he was in no mood for small talk and she said thoughtfully, 'Where's Daniel? Is he playing outside?'

'No.' He paused, and regarded her steadily. 'He isn't here.'

She stared at him, not quite taking in what he was saying and feeling as though she had been winded. 'But when I phoned, you said that I would be able to see him. I was really looking forward to it—it's been such a long time since I was able to talk to him. What happened?' A sudden thought struck her. 'He isn't ill, is he? I know he was feverish last time I was here, but I thought he had got over that...you didn't say anything had happened.'

'He's gone to a friend's house. I didn't think it was a good idea for you to see him. It will only upset him and make him unsettled. He's getting used to being here with me, and I don't want him disturbed right now.'

Anna felt as though he had punched her. She felt the blood drain from her face, and after she had taken a moment or two to recover from the shock, she said huskily, 'How could you do that? Do you understand how cruel you're being? Not just to Daniel and Sarah, but to the rest of his family. Don't you realise that I care about him as well, and so do his grandparents? Don't we matter to you at all?'

His eyes darkened. 'You think I'm being selfish, don't you? Well, maybe I am. But while you're all so concerned about your own feelings, who is going to listen to my rights, my needs as a father?'

'No one has said that you don't have any rights, or that we don't want to listen. We all want to work things out for the best. Can't you see that—can't you at least try to meet us halfway?'

His mouth firmed. 'I want my son with me, Anna. Like it or not, I've made up my mind and that's how it's going to be. There's nothing more to be said.'

He wasn't giving any ground, no matter what she said to try to persuade him to see reason, and she left the house just a short time later, feeling more upset than she had been in a long time. Worse still, what on earth was she going to say to Sarah? How could she tell her that he wasn't even prepared to listen?

She didn't feel at all like going along to the barbecue now. The last thing she wanted was to have to mix with people and make light-hearted conversation, but how could she get out of it? The whole thing had been arranged in order to gather in funds for the hospital, and it would look bad if she wasn't there. Perhaps she could put in an appearance for just a short time, and then slip quietly away.

The barbecue was in full swing when she finally arrived there at the end of the afternoon. The area that had been marked out for the event was set back a little from the beach on a partially terraced area, shaded to one side from the fierce heat of the day by a latticed wooden sun screen, around which foliage sprawled, adding a touch of tropical greenery.

The smell of cooked steaks and spiced chicken floated on the air. The thought of food made her feel ill, and she wondered if she could stay on the sidelines for a while, looking on, and not have to talk to anyone for a while. Her optimism was short-lived.

'Hello,' Tom said, coming across to her. 'You look hot and bothered. Shall I fetch you a glass of fruit juice?'

'Thanks. That would be good.'

He brought it to her and they went and stood under the cover of an awning, where a fan had been set up to cool the air.

Anna looked around. To one side, against a background of tilting palms and banana trees, she could see stalls offering goods for sale—items of clothing, jewellery or bric-à-brac—and people were browsing, or stopping to buy something that caught their fancy.

There was entertainment, too. A trio of musicians had set up on a section of raised decking, pouring out songs with a lively salsa rhythm. Under normal circumstances she might have enjoyed listening to the sounds and perhaps joining in, but right now she felt numb inside after her meeting with Nick.

Her glance moved to the side of the bandstand, and she suddenly felt as though her heart had slammed against her chest wall when she saw that Carlos was standing there.

He wasn't alone, though. He had his arm around the waist of a young woman, and his head was bent close to hers as she smiled up at him. She was wearing a beautifully cut linen suit, tailored to emphasise a perfect figure. Her dark, shining hair was woven into an attractive pleat at the back, and as she lifted a hand to run her fingers lightly down his shirt front, Anna saw that her nails were smoothly manicured and painted with a gloss that matched the vivid coral lipstick she wore.

Anna watched their absorption in each other with a rapidly sinking heart and felt drab in comparison. Her mouth suddenly felt unusually dry, and she took a careful sip of her drink, letting the cool liquid moisten her parched throat.

'That's our consultant's girlfriend,' Tom said, following her glance. 'Francesca. She's quite something, isn't she?'

'She's beautiful,' Anna agreed, a horrible sick feeling starting in the pit of her stomach. 'What makes you think they're back together again?'

'He's been seeing a lot of her lately. You know what the hospital grapevine's like. No one can keep anything quiet for long.'

That was true enough, and she was already wishing that she hadn't asked. She didn't want to think about Carlos's love life.

Her glance strayed back to him and the woman, and she saw that there was a small boy with them. He suddenly appeared from behind Francesca and tugged on her jacket, claiming her attention. He was around two years old, small and thin-looking, with black hair and golden skin tones. He looked tired, and she watched as Carlos lifted the boy up into his arms.

'I didn't realise that she had a child,' she said, puzzled. 'I thought you said she was going to marry Carlos?'

'She was, as far as I know. I don't know all the details but, from what I've heard, he and Francesca have been linked for as far back as they can remember. They come from two of the oldest established families around here. I know he thinks the world of her.'

It wasn't surprising that Carlos was drawn to her. Apart from being attractive and beautifully groomed, she would fit in very well with his social scene. They were two of a kind, from the looks of things, and for some strange reason the knowledge stuck in Anna's throat.

'So what happened? Did she marry someone else?'

'I'm not sure about that. I know she met someone and went away for a time, and Carlos seemed to be completely thrown by that. Just a few months ago, though, she came back, and to everyone's surprise she had a child with her. There was no sign of the man, so the word is that it all fell through. I suppose that's why Carlos has taken up with her again.'

Tom was probably right. If he had loved her from the beginning, why would that have changed if she had been the one to break it off? Anna struggled to push all thoughts of the two…three…of them to the back of her mind. It knotted her stomach to think of them together.

Tom shifted restlessly. 'Let's go and sit down at one of the tables, shall we? I haven't eaten since lunchtime, and I'm getting hungry now, aren't you?'

She wasn't. Between her session with Nick and now seeing Carlos in intimate conversation with another woman she was beginning to feel pretty wretched. She wished the evening would end.

Tom filled plates with a selection of food for both of them, adding fresh mango and pineapple to her tray for dessert, and took them over to a table where they could sit on the terrace and watch the sea roll in over the smooth sand.

They sat there for some time, and Anna tried her very best to relax. She sipped her chilled fruit juice and looked out over the tranquil water and wished that life could be simple and easier to handle.

Then Carlos's deep voice broke in on her thoughts, smoothing over her senses like dark chocolate, and she blinked, looking up at him. He was with Saskia, and Anna wondered where his woman friend had gone. 'You looked as though you were miles away,' he murmured.

'Did I?' Why did he have to be so incredibly male and set all her senses humming? He was dressed casually, in an open necked blue shirt and perfectly cut cream trousers that emphasised his powerful, long legs.

She quickly dragged her gaze away from him and looked at his sister instead. 'Hello, Saskia. Why don't you come and sit down? You look hot.'

Carlos pulled out a chair for her, and Saskia sat down, easing her bump into a comfortable position. 'I'm whacked,' she said. 'I don't know why I ever got myself in this state in this climate.'

Carlos's brow quirked. 'Don't you?' he murmured, and she grinned, slapping him light-heartedly with the back of her hand.

He sat down beside Anna, and said, 'I wondered if you would get here at all today. I know you were working this morning, but I wasn't sure what time you were finishing. I was called away, otherwise I'd have given you a lift.'

'There was no need and, anyway, I had to go to see Nick before I came here. Besides, I have my own car now. I followed your advice and rang the garage. They were very good, and they found me a decent little runabout that suits me really well. It gives me a bit more independence and saves me a lot of time, not having to get the bus when Tom's shifts don't coincide with mine.'

His eyes darkened. 'I'm glad that's all sorted.'

Tom said lightly, 'We saw you with your friend by the bandstand earlier. Do you want to bring her over to sit with us? We can soon find some more chairs.'

Carlos shook his head. 'I took Fran home a few minutes ago. Ben was getting fractious with the heat, and she wanted to get him to bed. She's been here for most of the afternoon, so she doesn't feel she'll be missing out.'

Saskia murmured, 'Carlos had to come back here to call the raffle. It was a bit of a rush.'

She and Tom started to chat quietly, and Anna let her attention wander. The little boy had looked tired, as though he'd been ready for bed, and it had probably been natural for Carlos to offer to take them home. Would he have stayed with Francesca if he hadn't been obliged to come back here? But she wasn't going to dwell on that…it provoked too many dismaying possibilities.

Her thoughts swerved to Sarah. How was she going to tell her sister about this afternoon's visit to Nick? Sarah would relish the opportunity to be able to take her child home and put him to bed. It was far too upsetting to have to let her know that the day when she might have her son back was even more distant than they had imagined.

Perhaps she wouldn't mention the visit to her. She would wait until she had better news.

'So what's on your mind?' She jerked her gaze upwards to find Carlos studying her with narrowed eyes. 'From the first moment I saw you this afternoon, I had the feeling that something's wrong. You look as though you wish you were anywhere but here.'

'Do I?' She winced. 'I'm fine. Just a little tired, probably. I've just worked a seven-day stretch, and I'm ready for a couple of days off.'

'Are you having problems at work?'

'No, not really. It's been hectic, but so far it seems to be going well. I discharged little Jessie, and last week I let Jack go home. He was coping better with the hepatitis but, of course, he'll need to take things slowly for some weeks to come.'

He nodded. 'Grace was over the moon when she had Jessie back home.' He studied her keenly. 'You were fond of Jessie, weren't you? I could see it in your eyes when you looked at her in her cot. I was worried that you might be getting too involved again.'

Anna tried a shrug. 'It's hard not to get attached to them. It tears me apart when I see them looking so helpless and ill, but when they start to recover they

can be bright and lively and chirpy as ever within a
very short time. That's the best part about this job.'

Saskia sighed heavily, and Anna glanced in her direction. She was gazing wistfully at the people who
were dancing on a small circle of wooden flooring in
front of the bandstand. 'How do they find the energy?' she muttered woefully. 'I can't wait to get myself back in trim again and join the real world. All I
want to do just lately is sit and vegetate.'

Carlos leaned over and squeezed her shoulder
gently. 'You've only a couple of weeks to go,' he
said cheerfully. 'You'll be back on form in no time
at all.'

'Promises, promises.' She looked from one to the
other of them. 'Why don't you two go and dance? I
need to sit here and rest my bones, but you don't have
to.'

Carlos quirked a brow at Anna. 'Would you like to
dance?'

'Oh…' She was taken aback by the suggestion. 'I
thought I might just sit here and keep Tom and Saskia
company.'

Saskia shook her head. 'We're perfectly happy as
we are and, anyway, Tom's going to fetch some more
drinks. It's not often I get the chance to relax without
Sebastian, and it's a huge relief just to sit here and
do nothing. He's gone to a party of his own today.'
She flapped a hand at them. 'Go on, both of you.'
She reached into her bag and drew out a fan to waft
a cooling breeze over her hot face.

Carlos held out his hand, and Anna found herself
being drawn to her feet and fluidly manoeuvred in
place beside him. His other hand went around her

waist, and she felt as though her skin were on fire, his touch provoking warm and tingling sensations that rampaged through every part of her.

The music changed, softened to a slow, lazily sensual rhythm, and he held her close so that they moved as one on the tiny dance floor. The gentle pressure of his hard thighs nudging hers made her feel dizzy and out of control, and her limbs felt light and insubstantial. It was just as well that he wasn't letting go of her. He swung her gently round in time with the music, their bodies merged in delicious intimacy.

'I know something's on your mind,' he said softly. 'Tell me what it is. I want to know. I want to help.'

'I already told you, there's nothing.'

He shook his head. 'I know you, Anna. I can sense when something's troubling you. If it isn't work, what is it? Is it Nick? You said you went to see him this afternoon—how did it go?'

'He was busy…he didn't really have any time to spare,' she said quietly. 'It wasn't a good time to see him.'

Carlos frowned. 'Wasn't he expecting you?'

'Yes, but…' She took a deep breath and said shakily, 'I think he had changed his mind. He didn't really want me there.'

'Because of your nephew?'

She said huskily, 'I think so. He's afraid that Daniel will be confused and upset if he sees me. I wouldn't want that…but I think Nick's wrong. I think Daniel would be happy to know that I care about him, that his mother cares about him. I just… Somehow I just don't seem to be able to get through to Nick…' She broke off, biting her lip. 'I don't expect you to understand. You're his friend, you know how he feels. You sympathise with him, don't you?'

'That doesn't mean I can't see your point of view. You're his sister-in-law, part of his family now, and he owes you a hearing at least. I'll talk to him for you.'

'No, don't do that. I...I can handle this myself. I don't need you to intervene on my behalf. I can manage.'

The music came to an end, and when she would have moved away from him he reached for her, his hands gripping her arms. 'Why won't you let me do this for you, Anna? I can help, I know I can.'

She shook her head. How could she let him risk losing a friendship that went back over several years? 'This is my problem,' she said thickly. 'I'll sort it out.'

She twisted away from him. 'Look, I've had a difficult day, and I think I'll go home now. I need to get away, to think things through on my own.'

'Anna, wait...' He would have come after her, but someone stopped him, wanting a word, and she took her chance and hurried away.

She said a swift goodbye to Tom and Saskia, who looked surprised but accepted her excuse that it had been a long day and she needed to go home and take a cool shower.

Within minutes she was in her car and heading back along the road towards Blue Water Bay.

Back at her apartment, Leroy's mother, Bea, met her at the door, looking agitated, and Anna wondered what on earth could have happened.

'Oh, my, oh, my...it's chaos everywhere,' Bea

said, throwing up her hands. 'Old Roback left his tap running upstairs, and went away for a few days!' She shook her head. 'I think there's a big, big problem. You come and see.'

Not knowing what to expect, Anna cautiously opened her door and they trooped inside. The damage was plain to see as soon as she went into her living room. Water had seeped through the ceiling and it must have been going on for a great length of time because the plasterboard had given way and most of what had once been a ceiling had crashed down onto Anna's floor.

She stared at the mess in stunned silence. That was all she needed to end the day.

'I thought he'd made a big problem,' Bea put in. 'What are you going to do, Anna?'

Bemused, Anna said in a thickened voice, 'I'm not sure right now, Bea. I think I need time to take it in.'

'I bet you've got no electricity either,' Bea muttered, looking up at the shattered central light fitting. 'I'll cook for you tonight and tomorrow.' She shook her head at the sight of it all. 'Leroy's going to be mad that he's not here... He's gone away to visit with his friends. He went on the boat yesterday.'

She paused, then added on a worried note, 'I heard rumours there was dengue starting up in the north. I sure hope he keeps away from the mosquitoes.'

Anna frowned. The virus was spread by a species of mosquito that usually bred in small containers that collected rainwater, like discarded plastic boxes or earthenware jars or even used tyres. Most towns had a policy of encouraging people to be careful about leaving such things lying about, so that the habitats for the mosquitoes would die out. Insecticides were used, too, to try to eradicate them.

With any luck, Leroy wasn't anywhere near the area where the outbreak had occurred and, anyway, he would be back home in a day or so.

All the same, she said quietly, 'I expect he'll be fine. Just keep an eye on him when he gets back, and if there's any sign of vomiting and diarrhoea, or fever, get him straight to a doctor.'

They heard footsteps on the stairs, and then there was a sharp knock on the apartment door. Anna went to open it and found Carlos standing there, his hand resting impatiently on the doorframe. Dazedly, she looked at him, not able to take in the fact that he was actually here at the apartment.

'You left in such a hurry,' he said, 'but I couldn't let you go off like that without finding out if there was something I could do. We need to talk.'

Slowly, her mind began to clear, and she pulled the door open wider. 'You'd better come in.'

Bea came into the hallway and nodded to Carlos, before saying, 'I got to go and see to something on the stove. You let me know what you're going to do.'

'I will. Thanks, Bea.'

Carlos stepped aside to let Bea go out, then looked searchingly at Anna. 'You're still in a state, aren't you? I can see it in your eyes.'

'I've just had a bit of a shock,' she murmured, 'that's why.' He frowned, and she added resignedly, 'Come and see for yourself.'

She took him through to the living room and he stood and looked around, his eyes widening.

'Well, this is certainly a mess, isn't it?' he said

finally. 'You can't stay here, not with things in this state.'

'I don't know what to do yet. Bea's just offered to cook for me, but if it's going to be like this for some time… Presumably the landlord has insurance to cover this kind of event, but putting it right could take a while.' She frowned, thinking things through. 'I suppose I could always take Tom up on his offer.'

Carlos's gaze narrowed on her. 'What offer was that?'

She said slowly, 'When the air-conditioning broke down here, he said I could stay at his place.'

'That wouldn't be a very wise thing to do. I know you and he seem to be getting on very well, but it could be a bad time for you to decide to move in with him. He's supposed to be studying for specialist exams that are coming up soon. He needs to concentrate his mind, not give himself up to distractions.'

She had forgotten about Tom's forthcoming exams. Even so, she wasn't sure how to take Carlos's warning. His words had an edge to them and she wasn't too happy at being told she would be in the way.

'You're assuming that me being there would be a problem, but I don't see myself as being a difficult house guest, and Tom obviously doesn't. He must have thought about it before he made the suggestion.'

His mouth twisted derisively. 'I think it's highly unlikely that Tom has thought it through at all beyond the fact that he'd be more than glad to have you around. He's hardly to blame for that. He's young, and still inclined to be hot headed, and you're a stunningly attractive young woman. It's no wonder he can't think straight these days.'

She was taken aback by his words. Stunningly attractive? She blinked and said, 'I hadn't noticed him having any problems.'

'You wouldn't have. You walk on through the hospital, getting on with your job, without seeing the trail of broken hearts you leave behind.'

Her eyes widened. 'I haven't a clue what you're talking about. You're making this up, aren't you?'

His tawny eyes flashed. 'I'm not making anything up. I wish I was. I see it every day when I go on my ward rounds.' A hint of impatience came into his voice. 'If it isn't the adult patients who are bemoaning the fact that you aren't their doctor, it's the junior doctors who can't keep their minds on what they're supposed to be doing. It's almost reached a point where I feel like banning you from walking through my wards. I'd hate my patients to have heart attacks before I've had the chance to operate on them.'

Her mouth had dropped open in astonishment, and he reached out and tilted her jaw with his forefinger, before brushing his thumb gently over the fullness of her lower lip. His touch was feather-light, but it created ripples of sensation that flowed right through her down to her toes and made them curl.

'This, too,' he murmured, 'is just an example of what I mean. You have a very pretty mouth, Anna, and it is far too much of a temptation around here.'

Abruptly she clamped it shut again in sheer surprise, and he laughed softly. 'So, I'm getting through to you at last, am I? That's good.'

Carlos ran a gleaming glance over her. 'Now, what's to be done about your accommodation? We can't have you falling over plaster debris and work-men when you have an important job of work to do.'

'I could look into finding myself a room at the hospital, I suppose.' She would have to remind Tom about his exams, and explain that she didn't want to get in the way of his studying. 'There's probably a place where I can at least sleep, and then I could get my meals at the hospital.'

He shook his head. 'That won't do at all, Anna. Those rooms are poky and miserable, and you don't need to put up with having to live in one of them. You can stay at my house. There's plenty of room there, and Martha will be glad to have someone else to appreciate her cooking.'

He gently turned her towards the living-room door. 'Go and pack a few things and I'll take you home with me.'

She looked at him in a bewildered fashion. 'You want me to go home with you?'

'That's what I said.' His eyes glinted. 'It's a big house and there's plenty of room in it for both of us. I hope you weren't planning on giving me an argument about that?'

She wasn't even able to think straight right now, let alone give him an argument. Somehow, though, she did have the feeling that she was being steam-rollered all over again.

CHAPTER EIGHT

CARLOS was clearly waiting for an answer, and Anna said hurriedly, 'I wouldn't want to put you out at all. I know how busy you are and, besides, it might not look too good, with you being the consultant here. People might talk…'

She was conscious that she was babbling, but the thought of staying with him for any length of time, of being so close to him for any time at all, was making her uncommonly nervous.

His brow rose. 'People can say whatever they want…but preferably they'll say it to me and then I shall put them right. That shouldn't worry you.'

'That's easy for you to say.'

'If it bothers you, you can be comfortable with the fact that Martha will be around to act as a chaperone. People will have no cause to comment. It's all completely open and above board, as they say.'

Anna thought about that. In part it was true. Martha would be there most of the time, though she had her own home to go to when she had finished work.

Still uncertain, she said quietly, 'Perhaps you're right. I don't know how long it will be before the apartment will be straight again, and the hospital rooms aren't meant for more than an overnight stay. I'll have to think it through.'

'There's nothing more to think about.'

'Isn't there?'

'Nothing at all.'

He made it sound as though only a mad person would refuse. 'Well…I suppose, if it won't be any trouble to you, then…yes, I will. Thank you.'

'*De nada.* You're welcome.'

He had it all worked out, didn't he? She only hoped she was doing the right thing in letting him talk her into it.

He waited while she hurriedly packed the things that she thought she might need.

'It's going to take some clearing up in here,' he said, casting a glance over the gaping hole in the ceiling and the damage that the water had done to the furniture and flooring.

'It looks as if this has been ruined,' she muttered, holding up the radio that had been on a table and had now been rendered useless. 'Funnily enough, I think I'll miss that as much as anything. I like to listen to the music while I'm getting ready for work in the morning. I wander round in my robe and get breakfast and so on, and the music helps me to relax and makes me feel good.'

'I can imagine,' he murmured, and she thought she caught a glimmer of something in his eyes, but it was gone a second later. Perhaps she had been mistaken.

'Are you ready now?' he said a few minutes later, when she took a final glance around.

Anna nodded. 'I think so. I can't think of anything I might have forgotten.'

'You should find whatever you need at my house,' he said evenly. 'If not, just let me know.'

'You've been good enough to me already. Thank you. I'll just go and say goodbye to Bea.'

While she did that, Carlos carried the cases out to his car and locked them in the boot, then came to help her into the passenger seat.

'I thought I would follow in my car,' she said, but he lifted a dark brow at that.

'I can give you a lift to and from work every day. It seems a waste to use both cars when we will be heading in the same direction.'

Perhaps there was some sense in what he was saying… Anyway, it would only be for a few days, with a bit of luck.

They took the road to the harbour, and Carlos said lightly, 'Martha will be pleased to see you. She's been full of admiration for you since you looked after little Jessie.'

He gave his attention to the road then, and it wasn't long before they arrived at his house. He parked the car on the wide drive, and ushered her inside.

True enough, Martha was in her element when Anna walked into the kitchen a minute or so later.

'Well, look at you,' the older woman exclaimed. 'Aren't you as skinny as ever? We've got to feed you up now you're here.'

She came over and gave Anna a huge hug that very nearly squeezed the breath out of her. Out of the corner of her eye, Anna caught Carlos's gleam of amusement, and her own mouth twitched.

'That's for lookin' after my Jessie. She was so poorly we didn't know what to do. But she beautiful

now, thanks to you. She's my little angel, you know.
I don't know what I would do without her.'

'I'm really glad she's well again, Martha,' Anna
said with a smile, when she could breathe again after
Martha had released her from the hug. 'But, you
know, it was Carlos who brought her to me. He knew
that she needed to be in hospital, and he was the one
who made sure she was looked after properly.'

'Maybe...but he knows you are a good doctor. He
knew you would take care of her.'

There was no telling Martha that she had only done
what any competent doctor would have done. She was
determined to give Anna the de luxe treatment.

There was so much food on offer for supper that
she had to refuse seconds, saying laughingly, 'I
couldn't manage another thing, Martha, honestly.'

'We'll take our coffee out onto the balcony,' Carlos
suggested when they had cleared away. 'Come and
sit awhile and get some air.'

They went through to the lounge, and this time the
glass doors were wide open, leading onto polished
wooden decking. There was a hammock seat out
there, and Anna settled herself on it, looking out in
wonder over the magnificent view of the harbour below them. Huddled around the harbour were rolling
hills, covered in lush tropical growth, eventually giving way to the steeper slopes of mountains in the
background.

'It's beautiful,' she murmured, breathing in the fragrant air and feeling the warmth of the evening sun
on her bare arms. 'It must make you feel so liberated

to be able to come and sit out here whenever you want, and just take in the view.'

'It does,' he answered, and there was an odd huskiness about his voice that drew her attention. She glanced up and caught his steady, enigmatic gaze, and wondered what he was thinking. He certainly wasn't taking in the landscape. But then he came to sit beside her and her mind fizzed into overdrive, thrown by his nearness.

As he settled himself, he stretched taut muscles, and she was instantly and heart-stoppingly aware of his long legs and of the warmth that emanated from his body, just a fraction away from hers.

To distract herself, she gazed out over the mountains. If she looked carefully, she could just make out a sand coloured building in the distance. 'Is that the clinic?' she asked.

'It is,' he murmured, stretching an arm out casually along the back of the hammock.

Awareness prickled along the back of Anna's neck. She felt his closeness as though he had actually touched her, and her heart began to thud in erratic response. He was totally relaxed, though, and she wondered if he had any idea at all what this intimacy was doing to her.

'How is Joseph?' she asked, dragging her mind away from such dangerous ground. 'You said yesterday that he wasn't very strong. Isn't he recovering as he should?'

'He has a chest infection,' Carlos answered carefully. 'He's been worrying us a bit over these last couple of days.'

'Oh, no…' Her pulse quickened. 'That's the last thing he needs right now.'

'I've been concerned from the outset that he would succumb to something like this. We gave him antibiotics, but his lungs still filled with fluid. We're giving him a more powerful drug now, to deal with the infection more aggressively. I'm hoping that he's beginning to respond to the treatment at last. He doesn't have a lot of energy, of course, being so thin and small for his age, and he tires very easily. He needs building up carefully, so that he'll be able to fight these things.'

She frowned. He was such a lovely little boy, and she would dearly love to see him smile again. 'I must go and see him soon. Would that be all right?'

'Of course. I'm sure Joseph would like that, too.' He looked down at her, a faint smile hovering around his well-shaped mouth. 'You haven't changed at all, have you, in these last few weeks? You still care too much.' His glance trailed over her features, taking in the clear green of her eyes, and drifting down to rest lazily on her mouth.

'It is a very endearing quality, Anna. Even though it may lead you into heartache, your compassion shines through. No wonder your small patients love you.'

Somehow, without her knowing how it had happened, he seemed to have moved closer, much closer, to her, and then his head bent towards hers, blotting out the evening sunlight, and her gaze meshed with his.

His mouth brushed hers, gently, coaxingly, exploring the soft contours of her lips with a tender expertise that made her senses whirl. It was as though she had drunk too much of a fine wine and it had seeped into her bloodstream and was intent on causing havoc throughout her entire body.

He deepened the kiss, sliding an arm around her, his hand coming to rest lightly on the small span of her waist. She moved into the embrace, curling up against him in restless invitation, and his hand slid along the curve of her hip, shaping the line of her thighs and resting with sweet possessiveness in the hollow behind her knee.

She heard him mutter hoarsely, 'This has to be madness.' He lifted her closer, kissing her with a deepening passion that took her breath away.

It didn't seem like madness to her. It all seemed so right, so perfect, being with him like this, she thought hazily as his warm body pressed her into the soft cushions of the hammock. His kisses were urgent now, his lips tasting her mouth, her cheek, trailing over the sensitive column of her throat. His hand moved to cup the soft mound of her breast, and her body trembled, aching for more.

She felt him groan, a shuddery, thickened sound against the curve of her neck. She wanted this to go on for ever, but just as her body was melting into his, he shifted away from her.

'I'm sorry, Anna. This is all wrong. I didn't mean this to happen. I brought you here to help you, not for this.' He raked a hand through his hair and stared down at her, lines of strain beginning to show around his mouth.

Anna felt unutterably lost, defenceless against his sudden change of heart. When her mind began to clear at last, though, she thought she knew why he had drawn back.

'Are you still in love with Francesca?'

He stared at her in disbelief. 'Fran has nothing to do with this.'

'Doesn't she?' Anna looked into his eyes and saw the pain written there, and felt afraid, but still she persisted. 'You loved her once, didn't you?'

His mouth twisted. 'I suppose this is the grapevine at work, isn't it? Everybody talks, everyone thinks he knows everything there is to know.'

'Then tell me. Did you love her? Weren't you going to marry her? Can you tell me that isn't true?'

He grimaced. 'Fran and I have known each other since we were very small. I suppose I've always loved her in a way, and at one time there was talk of us perhaps getting married. It didn't work out that way and, anyway, she met someone else. End of story.'

'Is it? She's back in your life again, isn't she?' How could she ever hope to take the place of the woman who had been part of his life since childhood? The link was too strong to be broken.

'She came back here a few months ago, and she naturally comes to me for help and support. That doesn't mean that we've taken up where we left off, no matter what the grapevine says.'

But that might only be because Fran hadn't made up her mind what she wanted. The image of the two of them close together, his arm around her waist, came back to haunt her. 'You must have thought about how the two of you would go on when she came back.'

'Maybe I did,' he said in a roughened voice. 'Does it matter?'

'Yes, I think it does,' she said huskily. 'It means you haven't made up your mind yet about what it is that you want.'

'Look, Anna. I don't think this is something we can talk about now. It's late. You've had a difficult day, and I have work I must do before morning. We'll talk about this some other time, when perhaps we'll both make more sense of it. I'll see you at breakfast.'

She stared at him dazedly as he turned away from her. He hadn't denied thinking about starting over again with Francesca, had he? And he wasn't telling her that he had no feelings for her.

Breakfast? It would taste like ashes in her mouth. She had never felt so completely and utterly wretched in her life before. Was she making the biggest mistake of her life? Was she falling in love with him?

She made up her mind she wasn't going to question him about it again. Carlos would have to tell her whatever there was to know of his own accord.

Instead, the next morning at breakfast, she told him, 'I want to stop by the apartment and pick up my car.'

It wasn't a good time to mention it, because he was scowling and terse, and clearly running late for his appointments.

He said curtly, 'I hope you aren't thinking of going back to stay at the apartment.'

'No, it wasn't that.' Neither of them had mentioned

the previous evening, but it was there between them like a granite block. 'I want to go and visit Nick again some time, as well as Joseph, and I don't want to have to rely on you all the time for lifts.'

'As you please. You should be able to come and go whenever you like, of course.' He hesitated, as though he was about to say something else but then thought better of it. Instead, he added softly, 'By the way, don't wait supper for me tonight…I have to go out.'

He dropped her off on the way to work, and for the rest of the day she didn't see anything more of him. She went to bed before he returned home late that night, and she heard his car coming along the drive in the early hours of the morning. It was only then that she fell into an uneasy slumber.

'He's been to visit with that Francesca and her boy,' Martha told her in the morning, and Anna winced inwardly and wished she hadn't known that. It didn't help, to know that she had been right all along. Her mind worked overtime enough already, imagining them together.

'Is he sleeping in late today?' she asked, when Carlos didn't come down to the kitchen, but Martha shook her head.

'He had to make an early start. He's working at another of his hospitals today.'

'Oh, I see.' How on earth did he keep up the pace?

The evening followed a similar pattern. He took a phone call from José, and Anna realised from the tone of his conversation that he wasn't likely to be back until very late.

There was an uneasy pact between them in the days that followed, and Anna tried to keep herself busy whenever he was at home, finding things to do that would take her mind off him being around. It wasn't a problem that occurred too often. She was fast beginning to realise how hard he worked, dividing his time between the clinic and his various hospital consultancies...and Francesca, of course.

She went to see Nick again, taking a chance that he wouldn't turn her away. This time little Daniel, three years old and full of bubbly mischief, came running to the door to meet her as Nick opened it.

'Anna...' Daniel gazed at her, wide eyed, a big smile on his face, then said, 'Come and look. Come and see what I've got.' He grasped her hand and tugged her into the hallway, his hazel eyes shining.

'I will,' she said, giving him a smile in return. After all this time it was good to feast her eyes on her lively little nephew. 'Just give me a minute, livewire.' Above the child's head, Anna's gaze met Nick's. His eyes were dark, filled with restless impatience.

'I wondered how long it would be before you came back.' He grimaced. 'He'll show you everything we've gathered from every island we've visited,' he said. 'It will take for ever.'

He closed the front door behind her and she took the opportunity to study him afresh. Daniel took his features from his father—black hair, straight nose, the skin tone a pale bronze.

She gave an unsteady little laugh. 'It sounds as though he had a great time.'

'We both did. I like having my son with me. I'm

spending time with him, getting to know him all over again.' He looked at her steadily. 'I know why you're here, Anna, but I'm not ready to give him up without a fight.'

'I'm not suggesting that you give him up,' Anna said hurriedly. 'Only that you talk to Sarah and try to sort things out between you.'

His mouth twisted in an expression of scorn. 'Since when could Sarah and I talk without it finishing up in an argument?'

Anna sighed inwardly. This was going to be tougher than she could ever have imagined. He wasn't giving an inch, was he?

She tried a smile. 'I'm not asking a lot, am I? I thought that perhaps I could just see you and Daniel for a while. I'm living close by, I'm working at the hospital, and I just thought it would be good if I could see Daniel every now and again. Would that be all right?'

His features relaxed a fraction. 'If that's all you want—of course. Somehow, though, I doubt it.'

He ushered her along the wide hall towards a door at the end. 'Come on through to the study. You'll have to start off in there, anyway. Daniel wants to show you his collection.'

'We went to the coral reefs,' Daniel chimed in. 'And we went in a...' He looked at his father for clarification.

'A glass-bottomed boat,' Nick supplied. 'It was good fun, wasn't it?'

'Yes...and then we went to the beach and we found some shells...' Again he looked at Nick.

'Conch shells. Go and fetch them, then you can show Anna properly.'

Anna stayed with them for an hour, and she was relieved that at least she had been able to see Daniel and she would be able to phone Sarah and tell her that he was looking well.

She hadn't got anywhere at all with Nick. There was no softening in his attitude at all. He wouldn't even consider phoning Sarah and talking over the situation with her. As to letting Daniel talk to his mother, he was dismissive, saying curtly, 'That would only cause more problems. Daniel is happy as he is. Talking to Sarah would only make him upset.'

She couldn't reason with him, and she made a tactical withdrawal, satisfied for the moment that at least he had agreed to let her come back and visit on a regular basis.

'We've a patient coming in by ambulance,' Maria said on Wednesday morning. 'Suspected dengue fever, according to his doctor, with haemorrhagic complications. You know there was an outbreak in one of the northern islands?'

Alarm bells went off in Anna's head. 'Yes, I'd heard. Who is it?'

'His name's Leroy,' Maria said, her blue eyes frowning. 'Eight years old. Apparently he went to the island for a visit friends, and he returned home a couple of days ago.'

'Leroy?' Anna repeated in a whisper. She felt for the chair behind her and put a hand on it for support.

'That's right.' Maria looked up from the notes she

had been reading. 'You look shocked—why? Do you know him?'

'Does he live on Blue Water Bay?'

Maria nodded, and Anna felt a pain as though she had been kicked in the stomach. 'Yes. I know him,' she said hoarsely. She turned quickly, heading for the office, her stomach suddenly beginning to churn. 'I'll go and make the arrangements for his admission right away. He'll need to be nursed in isolation if the doctor is right about the complications. We'll need to use infection-control measures.'

Carlos walked into the office as she finished making the arrangements. He took one look at her face and said, 'What's wrong? What's happened?' She must have looked deathly pale, because he pulled out a seat and lightly pushed her down into it. 'Whatever it is, you'd better sit down and take a few moments.'

'I haven't time. The ambulance is on its way...' She looked up at him, anxiety clouding her green eyes. 'The little boy who lives in the apartment next to mine is coming in with suspected dengue haemorrhagic fever. I need to be ready to care for him. He's a lovely boy,' she added in a whisper. 'Always full of fun.'

She hesitated, then said, 'I've never dealt with this illness before, and the consultant in charge isn't answering his phone. I have to get this right, Carlos, but I'm too close to him, and all at once I'm feeling scared that I won't be able to do it.'

He put a hand on her shoulder and squeezed gently in a comforting gesture. 'You will. You're a good doctor, Anna. Have faith in yourself. You'll know what to do.' His brows met in a dark line. 'Is the boy in shock?'

'I don't know.' They both knew that the illness caused bleeding which could result in fatal shock if the child's systems shut down. The best chance for his survival was if they managed to recognise the signs of impending shock early and took measures to prevent it.

She took a deep breath. 'So far, all we have to go on is the report that the doctor phoned in. Leroy was complaining of an intense headache, and pains in his muscles and joints. He has a very high fever.'

'I'll come with you to the ambulance,' he said. 'We'll do this together.'

'Thanks, Carlos.' She was shaky, in shock herself, and she knew she had to prepare herself adequately for what was to come. 'I'm glad you're here with me,' she said unevenly, getting to her feet. With him by her side, she would be stronger.

He nodded, putting an arm around her shoulders, and together they went out to the main doors of the hospital to meet the ambulance.

The paramedics wheeled the boy out on a trolley and trundled him towards the building. Anna looked at Leroy quickly, assessing him visually.

Beads of sweat were breaking out on his face, and there was a discharge from his eyes, the result of conjunctivitis, another feature of the illness. He was mumbling something, though Anna couldn't tell what he was saying.

'Are you hurting?' she asked him, leaning closer, and he nodded.

She stroked his head lightly. 'I'll give you something to take the pain away,' she told him sympathetically. 'Don't worry, Leroy. We'll look after you.'

His young face looked drawn, and she could understand why. The local people sometimes called the illness breakbone fever.

'This is Mr Barrantes,' she told him. 'We're going to take you up to a room now, where we can make you more comfortable.'

Leroy's mother climbed down from the ambulance, and Anna gave her a quick hug.

'Is he going to be all right?' Bea asked anxiously. 'He's been vomiting and he had bad diarrhoea. I took him to the doctor straight away, like you said, but this happened very quickly.'

Anna's face was strained as she looked at Bea. 'I promise you, we'll do our very best for him, Bea. Let's get him up to his room as quickly as we can, and I'll examine him.'

As soon as they had transferred him to the bed in his room, she made a swift, gentle examination. 'His liver's enlarged,' she told Carlos quietly, 'and there's congestion on his lungs. His skin's bruised from the bleeding inside.'

'That's what we would have expected,' he acknowledged. 'Let's get him onto intravenous fluids right away to replace the fluid he's lost.'

She nodded, and turned to Maria, who was busy taking the boy's temperature and pulse. 'We'll give him oxygen as well to help with his breathing, and medication to relieve the congestion in his lungs. Put your best nurse onto thirty-minute observations, will you? What's his temperature now?'

'Forty-one degrees,' Maria said, wincing. 'Shall we do sponge baths to bring it down?'

'Yes, please…and we'll give him paracetamol. That should lower it a bit.'

Quickly, Anna prepared the site on Leroy's arm and put in the IV line, carefully checking the fluids she was administering before going on to deal with his oxygen supply.

After a few minutes more, she stepped back and pulled in a deep breath. For the moment she had done all that she could for the boy, but she stroked his head once more and murmured gently to him before she left, 'Try to get some rest, Leroy. The nurse will stay close by, so that you can let her know if you need anything. I'll come and see you in a while.'

Bea came to stand by his bed, and said, 'Bless you, Leroy, my baby. Your mama's going to stay with you as well. I won't be far away from you while you're in here.'

Anna moved quietly away from the bedside, and Carlos went with her.

'You did just fine,' he said approvingly. 'I knew you would.'

Now that the initial spurt of activity was over, Anna was surprised at the way she had been able to push her fears and anxieties to one side. When she had been with the boy, it seemed as though all her professional training had come to the fore, enabling her to deal with the situation.

Now, though, she was beginning to feel shaky all

over again. 'All we can do now is wait,' she said unhappily. 'I wish that this wretched disease could be eradicated once and for all.'

'They're working on a vaccine,' Carlos murmured. 'It should be ready for general use soon. Anyway, there's one consolation…if he comes through this all right, he should have immunity to it for life.'

'Let's hope so.' She gave him a tremulous smile. 'Thanks for staying with me. You made me feel a lot more confident than I might have done otherwise.'

'Any time.' He gave her a quick hug. 'You only have to ask, and I'll be there whenever you need me.'

She absorbed that slowly as they walked back to the office. If only he meant that in all its senses. Somehow she was coming to realise that she would dearly like to have him around as part of her life, come rain, come shine, but that was the last thing on his mind, wasn't it? Had he already pledged himself to Francesca?

She said thoughtfully, 'What did bring you here today? I didn't think to ask you earlier.'

'I thought you might want to hear the news about Joseph. He's improved a lot just these last few days. His chest infection's cleared up, for one thing. I wondered if you would like to go and see him later today.'

'Could I? Oh, yes, that would be wonderful…except that…' She frowned. 'What am I going to do about Leroy?' She was torn both ways.

'It could be days yet before there's any real change. Besides, I can give Maria my phone number, and she'll let us know as soon as anything happens.' His glance flicked over her. 'You won't be able to do any more by staying here, and you'll only make yourself more upset.'

She sighed heavily. 'I suppose that's true enough.' She nodded. 'All right, then. I'd love to go with you.'

'Good. We'll call in at the market on the way and pick up something to cheer him up.'

They set off as soon as Anna's shift finished. Still uneasy about leaving Leroy behind, Anna stared out of the car window and watched the scenery go by without seeing any of it.

Carlos must have sensed her distraction, because he said quietly, 'You're still thinking about him, aren't you? That's the problem with working in a general hospital. You come across difficult situations almost every day of your working life. Have you ever thought of going in for something other than this?'

She was startled enough to come out of her reverie and stare at him. 'And do what?'

He shrugged lightly. 'There must be other work that would give equal satisfaction but without taking such a toll. Have you thought about going in for preventative medicine…working in children's health clinics, maybe?'

'As part of a general practice, you mean?'

'Something like that.'

She shook her head. 'I'm used to hospital work, to dealing with patients who are ill. I think perhaps I need to make more of a difference, to feel that I'm doing something positive to turn the tables.'

He sent her a thoughtful glance. 'You could always come and work at the clinic. You might not find it quite so traumatic. The outcomes are usually better there for patients, partly because we mostly see them before the illness has reached a difficult stage or because they're there to convalesce.'

'Do you need someone at the clinic?'

'I need someone who specialises in paediatrics.'

She was quiet for a moment, then said honestly, 'I'm not sure that I could work in a place where people have to pay for treatment. I've always thought it was wrong that people who are ill shouldn't be able to get the care they need without having to use up their savings or scrimp and scrape to get the best care available.'

He looked at her thoughtfully. 'Some people can afford it,' he murmured. 'They don't want to wait for the health services to work through their waiting lists, especially when it comes to cardiac surgery. It's their choice to jump the queue. They can afford to come to the Caribbean, and then they want to convalesce in beautiful, restful surroundings.'

He smiled at her. 'If you had to choose between staying in an austere ward, where the norm was a quick turnover in patients and harassed nurses and doctors with too little time to deal with you or spending time in a peaceful, luxurious environment, which would you choose?'

She made a wry face. 'I think that's my point. I shouldn't have to choose. If I was ill, I would like to be able to expect the best treatment available without having to pay for it.'

'But that's a dream world, not reality. Health services are overstretched.'

'Maybe.'

They had reached their destination by this time, and Anna could see the village ahead of them, with its neat, colour-washed houses, nestling on the terraced hill slopes.

Carlos parked the car in a dusty lay-by and they set out to explore the various stalls of merchandise that had been set up along the side of the main road.

There was an abundance of bananas, pineapples and guavas, as well as all kinds of fresh vegetables, and at intervals along the way there were kiosks selling hot food, which were attracting quite a crowd.

Anna bought a bag of spiced cakes and a toy boat which she thought Joseph might like to sail in the wash-basin in his room, and Carlos found a carved wooden monkey that climbed a ladder and flipped over when you squeezed the bottom rung.

'He'll love it,' she said with a smile, then asked more seriously, 'When do you think he'll be ready to go home?'

'A couple of weeks, perhaps. I'd like to see him put on a bit more weight first, and I'll be happier when his blood pressure's settled down. He's doing well, though.'

Joseph looked very different from the weak little boy she had seen just a few weeks ago. He gave her a cheeky grin when she walked into his room at the clinic, and went to fetch his action figure.

'Look, Anna. He doesn't have his bandage on any more.'

'Well, that's good news,' she said, giving him a hug. 'And aren't you looking better?'

He nodded gleefully. 'My head doesn't hurt any more now, and I haven't had a nosebleed for ages.'

They were both symptoms that would have been caused by the high blood pressure he had experienced throughout the course of his illness. It was a good sign if he wasn't getting them now.

'Mr Barrantes says if I keep getting stronger, I might be able to go home in a couple of weeks.'

'That's wonderful. That's something to look forward to, isn't it?'

'I'm very pleased with the way you're doing, Joseph,' Carlos put in quietly.

Joseph's smile grew even wider.

They stayed with him for about half an hour, but by then it was clear that he was becoming tired so they left him alone with his parents, who were going to supervise his bedtime. His mother was reading aloud to him as they waved goodbye.

It was getting late when they arrived back at Carlos's house, and Martha had left supper for them in the kitchen before she'd gone off to her own home.

They helped themselves to rice and chicken with freshly sliced red and yellow peppers, and home-made bread spread with golden butter. Afterwards, they sipped coffee and relaxed properly for the first time that day.

'Why don't you go out onto the balcony for a while?' Carlos murmured when they had finished. 'I'll clear this lot away.'

She did as he suggested, going to stand by the parapet and breathe in the warm night air, watching the moon rise in the darkening sky. It was a beautiful night, and the stars were out in full, glittering brightly as though all were well in the world. She sighed softly.

'Are you still worrying about Leroy?' Carlos asked, coming to stand beside her.

'I can't help it,' she muttered huskily, looking out over the harbour, where the lights of the waterfront properties were strung out like a golden necklace. 'I used to see him every day at the apartment, and he would tell me silly jokes and make me laugh, and bring me pictures that he had drawn. I just couldn't bear it if he doesn't pull through.'

He reached for her and turned her around to face him. 'We're doing everything we can. There's nothing more anyone can do.'

'I know that,' she whispered. 'I know you think I shouldn't get involved, but I can't help it.' It wasn't just Leroy that was on her mind. There was Daniel, too, and Sarah back home in England, waiting for better news.

He put his arms around her and drew her close, kissing her lightly on her forehead. 'We all feel like that at times. Sometimes we care so much that it hurts.'

Anna looked at him uncertainly, trying to contain her distress. 'You feel it, too?' But of course he did. He was just better at keeping his feelings hidden than she was.

'You know I do. I wouldn't be human if I didn't feel wrecked if I lose a patient. It happens…you do everything you possibly can, and more, and still sometimes it happens. The key is to keep hope inside you, to feel positive about what you're doing and do your best to transfer that intensity of feeling to your patient.'

'I'll try,' she said in a low voice, and his arms tightened around her.

'I'm here for you,' he said thickly. 'Remember that.' He drew her head down on to his chest, and ruffled her hair lightly, soothing her with slow, gentle movements of his hand across her back.

Carlos's gentleness was her undoing. She loved the feel of him, the warmth, the understanding that flowed from him and smoothed over her senses like honey.

She lifted her head and gazed up at him, and there was a moment of stillness, of some unspoken message winging between them, and somehow their lips met and clung, and the world started spinning on its axis. The kiss went on for a long time, endlessly sweet, filling every part of her with trembling need.

Her hands trailed restlessly over his chest, her fingertips registering the warmth of his skin through his shirt and the heavy thud of his heartbeat.

'Anna, *querida*,' he said raggedly, reluctantly dragging his lips from hers, 'I want to hold you and kiss you, and take away all the pain and heartache, so that you know nothing but me, nothing but what is here and now.'

His lips tracked across her mouth, her cheek, and left a searing trail of fire wherever they touched her sensitive flesh. She moaned softly, wanting him, needing to feel his hands on her, stroking, soothing, making her think of nothing but him.

'I need to touch you,' he muttered huskily. 'You're

so beautiful, so desirable.' His hands were coaxing now, shaping every curve of her body, lingering with exquisite delicacy on the soft swell of her breast, sliding down to stray beneath the thin top she wore. She felt the heat of his long fingers on her bare skin and the sensual glide of his hands as he found her breasts again and traced each burgeoning nub with such tenderness that her head began to swim and she ached for more.

'Let me see you,' he muttered thickly, pushing at the thin material of her top. 'I want to see you, to taste you.'

There was a buzzing in her ears, a ringing sensation as though the blood had rushed to her head and was making her dizzy. She heard his shuddering groan as his head bent lower and his mouth tenderly claimed the taut peak of her breast.

Her breath caught as sensation raced through her entire body and melted her limbs, and then, incredibly, with a muttered curse he was moving away from her, leaving her alone once more, bewildered. Her body was stunned by the shock of rejection, her head was still ringing with the incessant sound of the blood soaring through her veins.

Except that the sound was real. The ringing wasn't just in her head, it was coming from here on the balcony. As she gazed around in bemused dismay, she realised that it was the phone that was making such an unwelcome intrusion.

'*Dios.*' Carlos sucked in air through his teeth. 'I wish I could simply ignore it.'

'You can't,' she said unevenly. 'It might be a patient…it might be news about Leroy.'

Stricken with dismay, she watched him stride over to the table and pick up the phone. His voice was calm and steady as he spoke into the receiver.

Anna looked around, feeling the night air lightly touch her bare skin. Slowly, she started to come to her senses and began to straighten her clothes with fingers that trembled.

She didn't hear much of Carlos's conversation, but when he'd finished the call he said quietly, 'Saskia has gone into labour. The obstetrician wants to do a Caesarean, and she's giving them trouble. I shall have to go and talk to her.'

'Oh, I see… Yes…yes, of course you must.' Anna pulled in a deep breath. 'Is the maternity unit far away?'

He shook his head. 'A couple of miles, that's all. I'll go now.' His eyes were dark and unreadable as he looked at her. 'I don't know how long I'll be. Don't wait up.'

He left within minutes and Anna didn't know whether she ought to be glad or sorry that she had been saved from herself. Would she have regretted what might have happened between them if he'd stayed?

CHAPTER NINE

BY MORNING, Anna had decided that it was probably just as well that they had been interrupted the previous night. It would have been too humiliating if things had gone too far, and then later Carlos had told her it had all been a bad mistake.

After all, he had meant to comfort her, that had been how it had started, and no one could have known that things would get out of hand so quickly.

'*Buenos dias*, Anna.' He came down for breakfast and leaned against the fridge in a lazily masculine way that made her senses leap and immediately turned all her good intentions to ashes. He was wearing dark trousers and a crisp blue shirt that rested flatly against his rib cage and drew her gaze to the tight line of his abdomen.

He had a perfectly muscled body. Just seeing him standing there made her feel hot all over, and hastily she looked away and tried to get her thoughts back together again.

'Good morning.' She returned the greeting and hoped he hadn't noticed the tremor in her voice. 'How is Saskia? I didn't hear you come in last night, or I would have asked you then.'

'I crept in, so as not to wake you,' he murmured. 'She's had a little girl. Both of them are doing well.'

'Oh, I'm glad,' Anna smiled, relieved. 'What happened?'

'It was much as we had expected. The baby still hadn't turned when she went into labour, and was lying in an oblique position. It would have been nigh on impossible to deliver it safely without risking a haemorrhage and putting Saskia's safety on the line as well as that of the baby.'

He winced. 'I did my best to try to persuade her that she ought to do as the doctors were asking and have a Caesarean. I thought I was beginning to make some headway, and then her husband turned up and added his arguments to mine. His flight had come in on time and he had a mad dash to the hospital, but it was a relief all round to see him walk through the door. He managed to talk some sense into her.'

'Why was she so set against the idea of a Caesarean?'

'Some crazy notion that she wouldn't be able to have any more children because of the operation. I don't know how many she's planning, but obviously two aren't going to be enough for her.'

'Even so, to be so adamant when everyone was advising her to go ahead seems odd.'

'That's true, but I don't think she realised that she was putting the baby at risk. We had to explain to her that the baby was tiring and there would be problems if she didn't let them get on with it. That's when she changed her mind.' He chuckled. 'The operation was so easy and so quick that now, of course, she thinks a Caesarean might be the best possible way to have a delivery.'

Anna lifted a cynical brow. 'She might not think that when it takes her a month or so to get over it.'

'She's a strong woman. She'll manage just fine. Besides, my parents have gone to stay with her for a while, so that my mother will be able to help her out a lot in the next few weeks.'

'Has Seb seen his baby sister yet?'

'He saw her first thing this morning, apparently. I phoned to see how Saskia and the baby were doing, and she said they were both feeling fine but tired. Seb told her he thought they ought to have provided him with a baby brother instead of a girl.'

Anna laughed. 'That sounds like Seb. Still, I expect he'll get to like being the man of the house.'

'More than likely.'

Martha came and gave Carlos a nudge. 'Are you going to stay in front of my fridge all morning? I need to get to things, you know.'

'Sorry, Martha.' He moved out of the way, coming to sit opposite Anna at the table. 'Is there any coffee left? I could do with a wake up brew this morning.'

'Plenty. It's freshly made.'

He didn't look as though he needed it. He looked as alert and vital as ever, as though he had just come out of the shower and was invigorated. His hair was still damp and faintly spiky, giving him a sexy, dangerously male appeal.

Just then Anna's phone rang, and she picked it up and heard Sarah's voice.

'Sarah…it's good to hear from you. Are you OK?'

'I'm fine, Anna. I just wanted to let you know that

I'm coming over to see you in a day or so. I'm not sure of my flight details yet.'

'Are you? That's wonderful. I thought you might at some point, but I wasn't expecting it to be quite so soon. I thought you were still having to go to the hospital for check-ups?'

'I am, but this is more important. I can't go on feeling helpless like this any longer. I wondered if you could find me somewhere to stay? Anywhere will do, as long as it's fairly close to Nick's place.'

'I can do that, of course, but how's your leg? Are you up to travelling yet?'

'It's as good as it needs to be. I just have to get over there and see Daniel. I can't bear being stuck here, not able to talk to him or give him a cuddle. I'm missing him so much.'

'I'll find you somewhere, Sarah,' Anna promised. 'I'll let you know the details when you get here.'

'Thanks.'

Sarah cut the call a few minutes later, and Anna started to mull over possibilities in her mind.

'That was your sister?' Carlos asked. 'Is she coming over here?'

She nodded. 'I'm not sure she's up to the journey yet, but she's made up her mind anyway. I'll have to search for somewhere for her to stay. My apartment's still not fixed up, so I might go down to the tourist agency and see what's available.'

'There's no need for you to go to so much trouble. She can stay here.'

Anna looked at him in surprise. 'Are you sure about that?'

'I'm very sure. I'd like to make your sister feel welcome here. There's plenty of room, so she ought to be comfortable enough.'

Anna felt a surge of relief come over her. Even so, she said warily, 'I don't know how long she's planning on staying. You've already done more than we could expect by having me here.'

Amusement flickered in his golden eyes. 'You mean two of you are going to be double trouble? I think I can take the risk.'

'It's just that she's desperate to see Daniel.'

'That's understandable. She must be missing him.'

'She is. She's desperate to have him back with her.' She frowned, and added with a grimace, 'I don't think I could bear it if something like that happened to me. I don't know how she copes. Sarah's brought up Daniel for three years, from when he was a baby, and for a good deal of that time she did it on her own because Nick was away, building up his hotel business in various parts of the world. Now he expects to simply step in and take his son from her.'

It was a heartbreaking situation to be caught up in, and she didn't see how either parent could emerge from it unscathed.

Still toying with the problem, she got to her feet and started to clear away the dishes, until Martha batted her away. 'You go and get yourself off to work, girl. I can clear away the breakfast things.'

Anna retreated to the living room and collected her bag.

Carlos followed, his searching glance travelling over her preoccupied features. 'Have you ever thought about having children of your own? You work with them every day, so you must care about them a lot, and yet you've never spoken about there being any man in your life in the past. Do think about being married at some point, with a family of your own?'

'I've thought about it,' she admitted. 'I don't know if I'm ready for all that, though. I've watched my sister's marriage fall apart, and I don't know if I'm strong enough to go through something like that. Being emotionally involved with someone leaves you terribly vulnerable, doesn't it?'

His eyes darkened. 'That's very true.'

He said it in a sober, heartfelt manner, and she asked quietly, 'Is that how you felt with Fran?'

'I'm not sure how I felt. But I suppose it's never easy to break up with someone you've been deeply involved with, is it?'

'Are you glad that she's back?'

'Oh, yes. She was troubled, and she went through a difficult time, but now she's here where she belongs and back on course again, and I can give her all the help and support she needs.'

Where did that leave her? He was being open and honest with her, and she ought to be thankful for that, but it left her in a quandary. She was beginning to realise that her feelings for Carlos went deeper than she could ever have imagined. No one else could ever make her feel the way he did, she was sure of it, and yet there was no future for her with him, was there? There couldn't be, while he was obviously still seeing another woman. She would only ever be second best, wouldn't she?

'What do you think Sarah will do about Daniel?' he asked, and she blinked and had to drag her attention back to what he was saying. 'Will she apply to the courts for custody?'

'Probably, if she doesn't make any headway with Nick. I think she would be happier if it didn't come to that, though.'

Carlos nodded. 'She's right. It would be far better if they could settle this between themselves.' He glanced at his watch. 'It's getting late,' he murmured. 'We had better leave for work.'

'Are you at the hospital with me this morning?'

'Yes. I've a ward round to do, and I need to check my operating schedule. I have to fit in an extra surgical procedure next week, and I want to make sure that my timetable is running smoothly.'

'Is it something that has cropped up out of the blue?'

He shook his head. 'No. I'm operating on Fran's little boy.'

She was stunned by what he had told her. She said huskily, 'Fran's child?'

'Ben, yes. He was born with a heart defect. The ductus arteriosus failed to close at birth. He was born prematurely, and his doctor treated him initially with indomethacin, which sometimes helps to close the duct, but it wasn't successful in this case.'

Anna was shocked. 'She must have been desperate to get the right treatment for him. Any mother would be.'

He nodded. 'I said from the first that I would do the operation if she wanted me to. Fran's been through a lot, and when she turned to me for help I wanted to do whatever I could.'

No wonder they were so close to each other. She said unevenly, 'Has he taken a turn for the worse—is that why you're operating now?'

She had come across this type of defect before. The channel between the pulmonary artery and the aorta, two of the large vessels which emerge from the heart, normally closed at birth and allowed blood to be pumped around the body. If the channel didn't close properly, some blood would be directed to the lungs, making the heart work harder to pump sufficient blood to the rest of the body.

'No. He's been ill on and off for the last year with chest infections and there hasn't been a good time to do the operation. We think he's ready now, though, so we're setting it up for next week. If we leave it any longer, we run the risk of him becoming more debilitated than he is already.'

'Is he being admitted to our hospital?'

'No. I'll do the surgery at the clinic. Fran thinks he'll be happier there. She's been bringing him over for visits for the last few weeks to get him used to the place.'

'He isn't very old, is he? It's a lot for any young child to go through.'

'He's two and a half. It's best that he has the surgery now, or his development will be stunted and he runs a high risk of heart failure. Already he's thinner and shorter than he ought to be and he gets short of breath easily, but if the operation's successful, he should start to thrive.'

Anna swallowed hard. 'You're very fond of him, aren't you? I saw the way you were with him that day at the barbecue, and it was fairly obvious then that you think the world of him.'

'I do. After all, he's Fran's child, and he could have been my own, if circumstances had been different. As with Sebastian, I've had a lot of involvement in his upbringing.'

His own child. Anna paled at the thought. Just how deeply did he still care for Fran if he was thinking along those lines?

Even so, she felt a peculiar surge of pity for the woman who had such a sick child. 'It must have been difficult for her,' she said huskily, 'bringing up a child with problems like that, especially if she has had to do it all on her own. The father isn't around, is he? What happened?'

Carlos's eyes darkened, became unreadable. 'Out of the blue, she met someone and fell head over heels in love with him. She knew her family wouldn't approve. He was from the wrong side of the tracks, so to speak, so she went away with him. She hadn't intended to get pregnant, but she was troubled, a little wild, back then, and she made a mistake.'

Anna could only guess how hurt Carlos would have been when all this had happened. She asked huskily, 'Where is the father now?'

'He died in a car accident. He was coming back from a party, late one night, and took a bend too fast. He'd been drinking.'

'I'm sorry.' She moistened her lips with the tip of her tongue. 'That must have been awful for her.'

'It was at the time.' He frowned. 'She tried to go on alone, to make the best of things, but it was hard. Eventually, she came to realise that her family didn't blame her for what she had done, and she came home. She needed their help to look after the child. He was never strong, and she was desperate for their support.'

'And she turned to you. That could have been more of a problem for her...if you had been hurt by what she had done.'

'I've known Fran since she was a child. How could I stop caring about her and wanting to help her just because she had made a mistake?'

Anna felt as though all the breath was seeping out of her. Carlos must love her very much.

That was why he had been seeing so much of Fran lately, staying with her into the early hours of the morning. It wasn't just her son he cared about, it was her, too.

But maybe Fran was still thinking about Ben's father?

That would explain why Carlos had turned to Anna for a few brief moments, wouldn't it? Deep down he still hankered after his first love, but he had to wait for her to get over the other man who still had a place in her heart.

Anna felt ill, thinking about it. She said quietly, 'It must be difficult for you, doing the surgery on a child you know and love.'

'More than you could imagine,' he said tautly.

He moved to the door, ready to set off for work.

They drove separately to the hospital, where he left her to start on her own daily routine while he went off to deal with his own patients.

Anna made a conscious effort to push her troubled thoughts to the back of her mind and went straight to the room where Leroy was being nursed.

'Has there been any change?' she asked Maria.

'Not yet. He's still very ill. His temperature's still too high, and there's been no sign of any real improvement.'

It wasn't the news she wanted to hear. She sat with Bea for a while, trying to offer what encouragement she could, but they both knew they were involved in a waiting game. The boy's recovery would depend very much on how his body responded to the supportive care he was being given. If he couldn't cope and he went into shock, the outcome could be something neither of them wanted to contemplate.

'Keep fighting, Leroy,' Anna whispered, standing by his bed and watching the perspiration filming his brow. He wasn't aware of her being there, and she wondered if her words had reached him at whatever level of consciousness he had fallen to.

He had to get well. She wasn't going to let him die. She checked the volume of fluids they were administering, and took careful note of the urinary output. 'That all looks OK,' she said quietly to Maria. 'Let's make the sponge baths more frequent and see if we can get his temperature down that way.'

At least the two young girls who were being treated for ciguatera poisoning were looking healthier. The diarrhoea was under control now in both children, and the vomiting had stopped.

'I'm pleased with the way they're coming along,' she told the anxious parents. 'If they keep this up, we might be looking at letting them go home in a day or so. We just need to make sure that their temperatures stabilise over a twenty-four-hour period.'

It was a long day. The end of Anna's shift came at last, and she started the drive home, feeling wearier than she had for some time. It was probably her wretched emotions that were to blame for that, rather than any lack of sleep.

With Leroy still making no visible progress, and Carlos wrapped up in his feelings for someone else, she felt like burying her head in her pillow and drowning in self-pity.

She wouldn't do that, though. She was made of stronger stuff, wasn't she? And Sarah was on her way over here and she needed to put on a positive front for her. Sarah had enough problems of her own, without having to listen to Anna's woes.

Anna met her at the airport the following day. She put her arms around her and held her tight, and told her, 'I'm glad you're here. I missed you.'

She scanned Sarah's slim figure. Her sister looked thinner than she remembered. The leg was still in plaster, but at least it was a smaller, more manageable cast.

'Look at you,' she murmured softly. 'You must be tired out after all that travelling. Let's get you back to the house.'

Carlos met them at the door. '*Cómo estas*, Sarah?'

he asked, looking her over and coming forward to give her a helping hand into the living room. 'This leg is taking a long while to heal, isn't it?'

'I'm fine, thanks,' Sarah told him with a smile. 'Yes, I suppose it is taking a while to mend, but that was probably on the cards from the beginning. It was broken in three places.'

'Three places?'

She pulled a face. 'I was knocked down by a car, and I fell awkwardly, which added to the problems, but at least I'm starting to make some progress now. This smaller cast is a relief anyway. It's lighter, for one thing.'

He frowned. 'But it must have been a struggle for you, coming all this way with your leg still not properly healed. How have you managed?'

'I managed well enough. I took taxis mostly to get around, and people have been very kind. Anyway, I'd have coped whatever problems there were. I've waited long enough to get here, and I wasn't going to wait any longer.' Her blue eyes were clear and determined, and anyone could see that she wasn't going to be stopped now. 'Thank you very much for letting me stay here. It's really good of you.'

'*De nada.*' He returned the smile. 'You're welcome. I know how much your problem has been weighing on Anna's mind, and this way I can at least do something to help matters. Feel free to use my house as yours for as long as you're here in the Caribbean. If you want to bring your son here, that's all right by me.'

All at once, Sarah's eyes looked misty, and Anna

guessed she was feeling overwhelmed. 'You're being very kind to me.' Her voice broke. 'I don't know what to say.'

'Then don't say anything. Go and rest your leg and talk to Anna. I shall be out for the rest of the afternoon. I have to go to the clinic and check up on my patients, so you'll have the place more or less to yourselves. I'm sure Anna and Martha will be only too glad to look after you.'

He went out a few minutes later, and left them alone in the house. Anna did what she could to make Sarah feel at home, but after a while she sensed that there was only one thing she could really do to help. She left Sarah alone with the phone so that she could call Nick in private.

At the hospital a few days later, Carlos asked, 'How are things going with Sarah and her son? Has she made any headway?'

Anna shook her head. 'None so far. Nick isn't letting her near him. He hasn't even let her talk to him on the phone.' She grimaced. 'The way he's going, he's not leaving her much alternative but to go ahead and pursue things through the courts, is he? I suppose he's not too bothered about that either. Presumably he thinks that because he has money, he'll win hands down.'

'Possibly,' Carlos murmured, 'though it isn't necessarily the case that he would win. After all, if they divorce, he'll have to make her a fair settlement, and the courts may decide that she has the greater claim.'

She looked at him quizzically. 'I thought you were

on Nick's side in this. Does this mean you're changing your mind about who should have custody?'

'Not at all. I've said all along that there are no rights or wrongs about this, just heartache if they don't get it sorted out.'

Anna sighed. 'Nick's been letting me visit Daniel recently, but now I feel as though I can't go and see him. It wouldn't be fair on Sarah. This whole thing's a terrible mess.'

'You shouldn't be taking any of this on yourself,' he said with a frown. 'You have enough to deal with at work.' He gave her a searching glance. 'Is there any news on Leroy?'

'Nothing,' she said in a small voice. 'We just keep on waiting and hoping.' She pulled in a deep breath. 'This is the danger time, when shock could develop, so I've asked Maria to increase the observations and let me know as soon as there's any change.'

He nodded. 'A decreasing platelet count and a rising haematocrit would indicate an increased possibility of impending shock. Let's hope it doesn't come to that.'

He scanned her face briefly. 'If you feel up to it, Joseph was asking if you would be coming to see him before he goes home. I said I would ask you. I'm thinking of releasing him in a couple of days.'

'I'll come over tomorrow, after work, if that's all right.'

He nodded. 'That should be fine. I'll tell him that you'll try to make it, barring emergencies.'

'When will you be operating on Ben?'

'Later today. I'll be at the clinic for some time

because I want to keep a careful eye on him for a while afterwards.'

She could understand that. She watched him walk away, and knew that if Ben had been her child there would have been no one she would have trusted more to see him through this.

'He's looking as though he has plenty on his mind,' Tom said, catching up with her as she went to chase up the results of some blood tests.

'He's going over to the clinic to operate on Francesca's little boy,' Anna told him. 'I think he cares an awful lot about what happens to him.'

'It won't be the first child he's taken a special interest in. There have been quite a number over the short time I've known him. I don't think he can help himself, especially if the parents are in a desperate situation. He often operates free of charge, you know, and arranges to have all their after-care done for nothing at all if it means the child can have a new lease of life.'

'Does he?' Anna was stunned. 'I didn't know that. He didn't give as much as a hint.'

'He wouldn't. It's not something he talks about. It's not his way. I only found out because some of the patients told me. He's a very private man when it comes down to it, and I don't suppose any of us really knows him all that well.'

She was quiet for a moment, taking it all in. And to think Carlos had actually told her that she was too involved with her patients to make a good doctor...when all the time he was every bit as sensitive as she was. Just thinking about it brought a lump to her throat.

Tom was watching her, a faint frown tugging at his brow, and she braced herself and asked him carefully, 'How are you getting on with your studying? Are you taking the exams soon?'

He made a face. 'Next week. I think I'm not doing too badly. I'll be glad when it's all over, though, and life can get back to normal.'

Anna gave a shaky laugh. 'Don't we all think that?' She didn't think her life would ever get back to normal now that she had come to know Carlos. He filled her thoughts every waking moment, and even her dreams, too.

Carlos didn't come home that night, and she guessed he had stayed over at the clinic. Had things not gone as he had planned? Anna fretted a little, wanting to know, wanting to be there with him, but she couldn't do that, could she? She was an outsider in that trio, and she would simply be in the way.

All the same, she had said that she would go and see Joseph, and she meant to keep her word. She made quick preparations the next evening after work, worrying a little about whether Sarah was going to be all right while she was away.

'I'll be fine,' Sarah told her. 'I'll watch a video, or perhaps I'll read a book.' Anything to take her mind off her fruitless attempts to see her son, Anna guessed, and she could have wept for her.

Just as she was about to leave the house, though, there was a knock at the door, and when she went to open it, her mouth dropped open in astonishment. Nick stood there with Daniel at his side.

'I came to see Sarah,' he said, and Anna stood back, wide eyed, and let him in. She gave Daniel a hug.

'Your mummy is going to be so happy to see you,' she told him. 'She's in the living room over there. She's been waiting for such a long time to give you a cuddle.'

'Over there?' Daniel echoed, then with a whoop of glee he ran off towards the double doors and disappeared into the room.

Nick and Anna exchanged glances. 'Have you had a change of heart?' she asked.

He gave an awkward shrug. 'I suppose, in the end, I had no choice but to come,' he said. 'Daniel has been asking for her. I ran out of things to tell him.'

Anna put her arms around him and squeezed him tightly, a blur of tears masking her eyes. 'You did the right thing,' she muttered huskily. 'I'm really glad you came.'

He looked uncomfortable at being hugged, and at first he was stiff in her embrace. After a moment, though, he relaxed and said with a wry face, 'I expect we'll sort something out. You and your sister are two of a kind. You don't give up easily, do you?'

'Not easily, no,' she murmured.

'Carlos told me that neither of you would let it go. He told me I was a fool to try to keep Daniel from his mother.'

'He said that?' Anna looked at him, surprised, and stepped back a fraction.

'More than that, in fact,' Nick said, looking chastened. 'Most of it not repeatable in present company.' He grimaced. 'I suppose he had a point. I don't want this dragged through the courts when maybe we could come to some kind of agreement.'

'I think you're being very wise,' she murmured unsteadily, still fazed by the knowledge that Carlos had intervened. 'Try to keep calm and talk things through with Sarah. I'm sure that somehow you'll be able to work it out for the best for both of you.'

A muscle flexed in his jaw. 'We have to try.' He gave an almost imperceptible nod in her direction, then straightened his shoulders and started to walk towards the living room.

Anna crossed her fingers that they would manage to keep from arguing for the next hour or so. She wasn't going to be here to act as referee.

Joseph was waiting for her in the patients' day room when she arrived at the clinic a short time later. He was playing a computer game, and when he looked up at her his face was glowing with health.

'Look at you,' she said with a smile. 'There's colour in your cheeks, and I'm certain you've put weight on. You look so much better.'

'I am. I'm going home tomorrow. Mr Barrantes says I'm as fit as a fiddle and he can't think of any reason to keep me here any longer.' He grinned at her. 'That's good news, isn't it?'

'It's brilliant news. The very best.'

'I've made him a card to say thank you for looking after me.' He reached into his dressing-gown pocket and pulled it out. 'Look, here it is. Do you think he'll like it? It's a picture of him, with a big smile on his face, and I'm there in my bed, saying, "I'm better now."'

Anna looked down at the picture, drawn with a seven-year-old's innocent hand, an interpretation of two figures who were clearly colourful and impressive. 'He'll love it,' she told him.

He smiled broadly. 'Good.'

She stayed with him for a while longer, then left when his mother came to fetch him for his bedtime drink.

Joseph's nurse, Freya, met her as she was leaving the room.

'Mr Barrantes said that you might be coming here this evening,' she greeted Anna. 'You've seen Joseph? He's doing very well, isn't he?'

'Very well,' Anna murmured. 'He looked so different from the way he was at the hospital a few weeks ago.'

'Yes, that's true. Mr Barrantes has taken very good care of him. He's a wonderful surgeon, you know. Are you going to have a word with him before you go? He's in the office, I think. Just along the corridor.' She pointed towards a set of fire doors. 'Through there, and it's the second room on the right.'

'If he's not too busy?' She would dearly like to know how Ben's surgery had gone.

She wondered how Francesca would be coping. The child was very young, and any mother would be traumatised by something like this.

The defect was a fairly common one—eight per cent of congenital heart defects involved the duct.

Usually, with the kind of operation Carlos would have performed, there was little risk, but it seemed odd that he hadn't come back to the house last night, and she hadn't seen him at all today.

'He had a hefty operating schedule yesterday and today, and he wanted to stay and check on the post-operative procedures. I think he might be free now, though.'

'The little boy, Ben, who had his operation yester-day afternoon—is he all right?'

'He's in Intensive Care. As far as I know, every-thing went well. I'm afraid I can't tell you any more...unless you're a relative?'

Anna shook her head. 'No. I'm just a friend of Mr Barrantes, that's all.'

A friend. Was she anything more to him than that? She walked along the corridor and through the fire doors, slowing down when she came to the office. The door was partly open and she would have gone in there, except that she could see that Carlos wasn't alone.

She stood very still, frozen to the spot. Francesca was with him, and they had their arms around each other in an intimate embrace. Carlos was bending his head to hers and all of a sudden Anna couldn't bear to see any more. She didn't want to see him kissing her. It was too much to take in.

Her heart was hammering like a wild thing in her chest and she wanted to run down the corridor and get out of this place as fast as she could. She felt sick, the nausea rising up in her like an unwelcome tide.

What had she expected? That Carlos would simply forget his former love and turn to her?

That was just a dream, a figment of her imagination, conjured up in a moment of moonlight madness. He had always loved Francesca, he had made no secret of it.

Now that her son was ill he was there for her, ready to take care of him, and to support her. They were probably closer to each other now than they had ever been.

Anna turned silently away and stumbled back the way she had come. She had to get out of this place quickly, before she broke down completely and humiliated herself.

CHAPTER TEN

'How is Leroy this morning?' Anna asked Maria. She looked at the boy, still lying in bed in a debilitated condition, and guessed the answer before Maria spoke.

'There's been very little change, except that his breathing seems a fraction easier with the medication to relieve the congestion on his lungs.'

'That's something, at least.' Anna frowned. 'You're doing a great job. Keep up the sponge baths and keep an eye on his skin condition. We don't want him suffering from bedsores as well as everything else.'

She finished off her ward rounds and with lunchtime looming she thought about going to find a coffee in the cafeteria, more for the chance to retreat from the world for a while than for any thought of food. She needed time to think, to get over what she had seen last night.

Carlos had left the house early that morning, before she had come down for breakfast, and Sarah had been full of her evening with Daniel. It was good to see her sister looking so animated and happy. It helped to numb some of her own pain.

One of the nurses from Casualty came to find her just as she was heading for the lift.

'We've a young girl who's just been brought in,

showing signs of shock after a jellyfish sting. Would you come and have a look at her?'

'Yes, I'll do that.' Anna mentally said goodbye to a few moments of peace and followed the nurse to the examination cubicle. Jellyfish stings could be nasty. Some jellyfish were really large and dangerous, and could bring about very unpleasant reactions.

Her patient, a young girl of around eleven, had been vomiting, and now she had collapsed back onto the bed, sweating and obviously in a good deal of pain.

'Hello, Caitlin,' Anna greeted her. 'I'm Dr Somerville. Would you like to tell me what happened?'

'I went for a swim at the beach,' Caitlin answered jerkily. 'Then, when I was coming back to the shore, I stood up and I must have trodden on something.' She paused to pull in a shaky breath. 'Will you get it out for me? Please, get it out…it really hurts.'

'Of course. I'll just have a look at your foot, and then we'll see what we can do to make you feel more comfortable. It's your right foot, is that the one?'

'Yes.'

The sole of the foot was badly swollen and inflamed, and the tentacles of the jellyfish were still in place. Looking at them, Anna could see that they were from a particularly vicious type of creature.

'Better not touch them with our bare hands,' she muttered to the nurse who hovered nearby. 'The stinging capsules discharge their venom when they're touched, and we don't want to risk any more damage. We'll inactivate them first, and then try to remove them. We'll need a half-and-half solution of baking soda and water.'

The nurse went off to get the solution, and Anna told her patient, 'It looks as though you've been attacked by a sea nettle jellyfish, Caitlin. We're going to put your foot into a solution that should stop the stingers from doing any more damage, and then we'll be able to remove the tentacles.'

'Just make it quick,' Caitlin said through her teeth.

'I'll give you something for the pain,' Anna murmured, and dealt with that while she was waiting for the nurse to come back. She used an analgesic, and also gave the girl an antivenom medication.

As soon as the nurse arrived with the solution, Anna helped the girl to put her foot into the bath and made sure that she kept it there until it had done its job.

Then she carefully set about removing the tentacles one by one with tweezers. When she had finished at last she said, 'There, that's done. You should start to feel better soon, but I think we'll keep you here for an hour or so, Caitlin, just to make sure that everything's settled down.'

Turning to the nurse, she drew her to one side and added quietly, 'I think she'll probably be all right now, but we need to put her on the side ward and watch for any signs of worsening shock. Look out for any breathing difficulties, convulsions or collapse. The parents can stay with her.'

'Will do.'

Anna went off in search of coffee.

The cafeteria was emptying now, as the lunch hour

faded. Helping herself to a cappuccino, Anna went to find a table by the window where she could be quiet and solitary.

Her peace was short-lived.

'Anna…I wondered if I would find you here. I've been looking for you.'

She looked up to see Carlos standing by her table. He put his tray down and slid into the seat opposite her.

'Freya told me that you had been to visit Joseph yesterday. I meant to come and join you, but I was tied up for most of the evening with other things.'

She almost winced. She knew very well what those things were, and she didn't want to dwell on them, even for a minute. She said, 'He was looking well. You must be pleased.'

'I am. It's always good to see patients on the mend.'

'How is little Ben?' she asked in spite of herself. 'Did everything go well with him?'

'It was straightforward enough. Being so young, it always looks worse afterwards than it perhaps is, with tubes and monitoring equipment and so on. He's making a good recovery now, though.'

'I'm glad.' She stirred the coffee, making swirls in the frothy topping. Carlos looked in good form today, and why wouldn't he? Wasn't everything going his way?

'Are you all right?' he asked. 'You look preoccupied. Is anything wrong? Is it Leroy?'

'No, there's been very little change in his condition. I wish there was more I could do for him but, apart from supportive care and keeping alert for any major changes, there's nothing I can do. It's frustrating.' She wasn't going to tell him what else was going on in her mind. It would be too painful and she couldn't bear to see pity in his eyes.

'Sometimes it's as well to do nothing. Let nature do the work.'

'Maybe.' She glanced up at him. 'I didn't know that you were going to talk to Nick. Whatever you said to him seemed to have a profound effect...he came over last night with Daniel, and it looks as though he and Sarah have talked properly for the first time in months. Sarah was really happy this morning.'

'Was she?' He smiled. 'I'm glad about that. It seemed such a terrible situation to have the two of them at loggerheads and the child caught up in the middle of it. Have they come to any agreement?'

'I don't think they've got quite that far just yet. Just an acceptance that they'll both spend some time with Daniel.'

'Do you think she'll eventually go back to England with the child?'

'I expect so. Our family are over there most of the time, and Sarah will probably want to go back to work there at some stage.'

'What about you? What will you do when the work at the hospital comes to an end?'

'I don't know. I haven't made up my mind yet.' She had been putting off making a decision about that. Perhaps in the back of her mind she had been hoping that she might be able to stay, but now she wasn't sure she could do that. How could she live here and work with Carlos, knowing that he was in love with someone else? 'I'll probably go back to England with Sarah, and find myself a job in a hospital close to where she lives.'

She glanced down at her watch. 'I ought to be getting back. I want to check on Leroy.'

'I'll come with you.'

They walked back to the ward together, and went to stand by the boy's bed.

'His breathing was a little easier this morning,' Anna said quietly, 'and some of the swelling has gone down. I don't think his liver is as enlarged as it was. Those are all good signs. I just wish we could be sure that this is a turning point.'

Carlos frowned, looking at the temperature chart. 'Perhaps we can,' he murmured. 'Look, there's been a drop here of one degree.' He looked at her, his eyes creasing in a smile. 'It doesn't sound a lot, but I think we could be making some headway at last.'

She came to look at the chart with him, and he put an arm around her and hugged her close. 'It's a first sign, nothing more, but it's a good sign, Anna.'

She closed her eyes and absorbed the news, conscious of his closeness, of the warmth of his body next to hers, the reassuringly steady thud of his heartbeat.

'We've waited such a long time,' she whispered. 'It has to be the start of something good.'

Carlos's pager sounded just then, and he groaned, checking it. 'I'll have to answer that,' he said quietly. 'I'll come back and see you later on.'

She nodded. 'I'll be here.' Now that she had seen

this first breakthrough, she was going to watch Leroy until there was stronger improvement. She wanted to be here when that happened.

Carlos returned, as he had promised, though it was much later on in the afternoon when he came to find Anna in the patients' lounge. She had stayed on long after her shift should have ended.

'Maria said you were in here,' he murmured.

Bea was restlessly moving about the room, alternately sitting down and getting to her feet, not knowing what to do with herself.

'Go and get yourself something to eat,' Anna said firmly after a while. 'If there's going to be any change in him, he'll need you to be strong and on top of things. You won't be able to help him at all if you're feeling agitated and weak.'

After a few more circuits of the room, Bea gave in. 'I'll be back in ten minutes,' she said. 'You tell him.'

'I'll tell him. Off you go.'

Carlos watched Bea walk away, and came to put an arm around Anna's shoulders. 'Let's go and have a look at him, shall we?'

Leroy was sleeping peacefully when they went into his room and Anna could see the change in him straight away. 'His temperature's dropped again,' she said with a smile. Her gaze meshed with Carlos's. 'He's going to be all right, Carlos. He's going to get well.'

Leroy stirred and mumbled something, and Anna leaned closer, trying to catch what he was saying.

'I can't make it out properly,' she told Carlos, shaking her head, 'but I think he said something about ice cream.'

'Then he's definitely on the mend,' he said with a grin. 'When his appetite's back and his temperature stays down for twenty-four hours without antipyretics, we'll know he's well on his way to full recovery.'

They stayed to tell Bea the good news, and once Leroy had begun to wake up properly and had managed to sit up a little in bed, Maria went off to the hospital kitchen to find a supply of ice cream.

It was about an hour after that when they finally thought about going home.

'I don't think I want to go back yet,' Anna said softly. 'I'm too restless to want to do normal, routine things.'

'Shall we go to the beach?' Carlos murmured. 'We could take a walk along the bay.'

He took her to a nearby cove, where they wandered aimlessly across the smooth sand and listened to the waves lapping on the shore. The sun was setting and casting a golden glow over the palm-fringed beach, and when Anna looked out over the crystal-clear waters of the warm Caribbean Sea, she saw the rays reflected in the shimmering water. Further out, yachts lazed at anchor, their sails wafting lightly in the faint breeze.

'It's so restful here,' she murmured. 'It's beautiful.'

'And yet you're thinking of leaving all this behind you.' He drew her down onto the warm sand, and they sat, side by side, looking out over the blue waters of the peaceful lagoon. 'Can't I persuade you to stay? You're a good doctor, Anna. We need people like you out here. I could find you a place at the clinic if you'd only think about it.'

'I—'

She frowned and started to speak, but he cut in, saying quickly, 'I know you said that you don't like working in a place where people have to pay for treatment, but we can work around that. I'm going to set up a wing especially for free patients, a children's unit, and I need someone to be in overall charge of it. With your paediatric experience, you'd be ideal.' He searched her face for her reaction. 'Will you at least consider it?'

'It sounds perfect,' she said softly, 'but I'm not sure that I could stay here.' It would hurt too much to see Carlos every day and know that he wanted someone else. She wasn't strong enough to cope with that, was she?

'Because of Sarah and Daniel? Would you still feel the same if I found them a place where they could stay? A little house…somewhere for Sarah to call home whenever she's here. She could stay in it permanently, or she could come and go between here and England and it would always be hers.'

Anna's green eyes widened. 'Why would you do something like that?'

'Why not? I can afford it, and it would help to resolve part of her problem. She and Nick would be able to see Daniel whenever they wanted—I could even find her a job if that's what she wants.'

'I meant, why would you want to do this? I know you're generous—Tom told me about the work you do already for people at the clinic for nothing—and I know how much you care for people, but why is it so important to you that Sarah has a home here?'

His gaze was steady. 'I want you to stay here, and I'll do anything I can to persuade you not to leave, and that includes persuading your sister to accept my offer. I want you here with me. Is that too difficult to understand?'

His offer was breathtakingly tempting, but she was totally confused by it. 'There are lots of doctors… paediatricians…who would do just as good a job as me. Any one of them might want to work at the clinic.'

He looked pained. 'Are you turning me down?'

'I'm trying to understand.'

'Why is it so hard for you to accept that I care about you, that I want you to stay here with me? I need you, Anna. I can't begin to think about what life will be like if you leave me.'

He put his arm around her and held her close. 'Don't say no to me, Anna…please, don't do that. Won't you say that at least you'll think about it?'

Anna watched the sun sink lower in the sky, mesmerised by the gentle motion of the palm trees swaying lightly in the warm breeze. None of this was real, was it? He wasn't really saying what she had thought he was saying.

'But you'll have Fran with you—she'll be here for you. She needs you. Why should it matter so much if I go away? You love her, you said you loved her.'

'Yes, it's true, I've always loved Fran. We practically grew up together. But she's not you. It's not the same at all. At first I might have wondered what my true feelings were for Fran, but a long while ago I realised that they were more protective than anything else…brotherly, if you like. She's like a sister to me.'

Anna stared at him, her eyes large with surprise. 'You never once said that she was like a sister to you. You said that you were going to be married.'

'Did I?' Carlos frowned. 'I might have said that we were talking about getting married, or that it was expected that we would marry. That's something else altogether.' He shook his head. 'Believe me, I've never seriously wanted to marry Fran.'

He paused, studying her face. 'Our parents, now, they had other ideas. They're very traditional, and it seemed to them that we would be a good match, that our marriage would bring the two estates together in a partnership that could only be good all round.'

His mouth twisted. 'Unfortunately for them, we had other ideas.'

'Did Francesca feel the same? She never wanted you?'

'Not as a husband, but she couldn't tell her parents that there was no hope. They were making so many plans. They had it all worked out, and even though I told them that I wasn't son-in-law material, they didn't believe it, or they didn't want to believe it. They thought they could persuade us to change our minds. Perhaps to a certain extent we even considered it at one time…a marriage of convenience that would suit everyone. But it wouldn't have been right. We both knew that. Anyway, Fran met someone else, and decided to run away.'

His gaze searched her face, reading the doubt in her eyes. 'Don't you know that it's you I love?'

'But I saw you together,' she said unhappily. 'That evening when I came to the clinic to see Joseph, you were holding her in your arms.' Even now, it hurt her to think about it.

'Why didn't you come and talk to me?' He frowned. 'I would have told you that there was nothing going on between us.'

Anna wasn't convinced. 'It looked to me as though there was.'

'Fran was upset. She'd been to see Ben after the operation, and he had tubes coming out of him and drips in place, and she was afraid that he was very ill, that he might not get better. She was very emotional. Ben's only two years old, and very tiny. He looked helpless and she couldn't cope with that.'

Anna's brow furrowed. 'I suppose I can understand that. I don't think I could cope if it was my child lying there, even though I see sick children all the time. It's bad enough when they're your patients, but if they're your own flesh and blood... Poor Fran. Is she going to be all right? You said Ben was recovering well, didn't you?'

'He'll be fine, and so will Fran. She's stronger now, and she'll get her life back together.' Carlos drew her into his arms. 'It's you I'm concerned about. I want to know that you're going to be here with me. I love you, Anna. I want you to stay with me, live with me, be my wife.'

'You do?'

'More than anything.' He looked at her anxiously,

and said in a roughened voice, 'You do care for me, don't you? You must, or why else would it bother you if I was with Fran?' He gently brushed her cheek with his fingers, and murmured thickly, 'I'll make you happy, Anna. I'll do whatever I can to make sure that you never regret staying here. That's a promise. Just say that you'll stay, and that you'll marry me.'

'But how can I? What will your parents say? After they pinned all their hopes on Francesca, they might not like me at all...'

'They'll love you, just as Saskia loves you. Anyway, it was Fran's parents who were most keen.'

'But we're worlds apart...'

'You *are* my world,' he said huskily. 'Without you I'm nothing, I have nothing—don't you understand that? Say that you'll marry me.'

Anna's mouth curved in a smile. 'I will, I—'

She didn't get to say any more, though, because Carlos kissed her then with a passionate intensity that took her breath away. He eased her down onto the soft, cushioning sand and she cradled his face in her hands, her fingers exploring the craggy contours with love and need.

'I love you,' she whispered, and she felt his shuddery sigh against her breast as he held her tightly as though he would never let her go. He rained kisses over her nose, her cheeks, her throat, then looked down at her with warmth and tenderness in his eyes.

'You and I will have such a good life together,' he murmured against her cheek. 'I'll always love you, Anna...that's my promise.'

As the moon silvered the sky and cast its powerful magic over them, Anna smiled up at him and knew that his promise would last for all time.

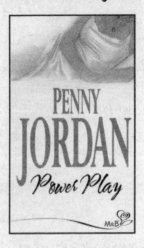